Above the Clouds

The Back Story

To the memory of my parents, Harvey Booker Whitfield and Josie Pearl Whitfield. The lessons I learned from them carry me through to this day. Special recognition goes to my mother for insisting I take typing in high school. I pushed back on this and did everything I could to unenroll myself in typing. Things went a little better when I was the only boy in typing class.

A shout out to Ms. Theressa Hudson. She was my typing teacher. I want to thank you for helping me understand it was not girlish for a young man to know how to type.

A special shout out to my wife, Patricia. She put up with the late nights and discussions as I banged this series out. I will not disclose what she said about Carl Allen's character after I described him to her.

#OneLove

V. KARL WHITFIELD

PAGE PUBLISHING, INC.
Conneaut Lake, PA

First originally published by Page Publishing 2021

ISBN 978-1-6624-3744-1 (pbk)
ISBN 978-1-6624-3745-8 (digital)

Printed in the United States of America

CHAPTER 1

The Beginning
#AWorldOfTurmoil

It was Labor Day 1957, another of those hot and sultry summer days that steamed East Texans limp and lethargic. Rachel Hampton, a seventeen-year-old Black girl, was in labor with her first child. The child was born at 11:00 a.m. with a big red spot in the middle of his forehead. Rachel was scared; she was a seventeen-year-old who had just become a mother, and her eighteen-year-old husband had enlisted in the US Air Force. Rachel had married her husband, Bradley, the previous May, and he'd enlisted in the Air Force shortly after that.

The new baby, whom they named Carl Allen, was born into a world full of turmoil. *Brown v. Board of Education* had been handed down by the Supreme Court in 1954, and the country struggled as it tried to end segregation in the Southern USA and across the country. The climate in the country was tense and drama filled as Orval Faubus, the Arkansas governor, called the Arkansas National Guard to Little Rock. Governor Faubus's goal was to prevent nine Black students from enrolling in Little Rock Central High School. The civil rights movement was ramping up, and Little Rock, Arkansas, was a front line for this battle.

The governor of Arkansas decided to defy the Supreme Court order and issued his proclamation in response to President Eisenhower deploying federal troops to enforce the decree handed down by the Supreme Court three years earlier.

> My fellow citizens, we are now an occu-
> pied territory. In the name of God, whom we all
> revere, in the name of liberty we hold so dear, in
> the name of decency, which we all cherish, what
> is happening in America?
>
> —Orval Faubus

The child's life started as President Eisenhower dispatched the National Guard to Little Rock, Arkansas, to enforce the desegregation order. Amid the extreme turmoil and drama in the country and the blazing, white-hot heat of the Texas summer, Rachel brought Carl Allen home. The newborn baby shared a home with his mother and her parents, Riley and Janice James. The home was a shotgun house situated on a red clay dirt road in a section of the city called Harlem North. Sixteen months later, Carl, who was by then a toddler, welcomed a sister to the house and his world. Rachel and Bradley named this newborn girl Hannah Leigh. Life was good for Carl; he had no clue of the turmoil going on in the country where he lived.

At the age of three, he was taught to read and write by his maternal grandmother. Janice took time with the toddler, teaching him to write letters of the alphabet. Carl came face-to-face with his first test of wills—he wrote with his left hand, and his grandmother was superstitious, believing left-handed people were "evil." Carl was trained to write with his right hand as he learned the alphabet and numbers from 1 to 100. Life went on as the young man continued to grow, and in May 1963, the family welcomed a second baby girl, Carol Anne.

In September 1963, on the eve of his sixth birthday, Carl was taken to J. H. Moore Elementary School to be enrolled in first grade. Rachel was shocked to learn the young man needed to be six years old by August 31 to be enrolled in first grade. Carl missed the age deadline by thirty-six hours! The young man was instead enrolled in a church kindergarten program at New Bethel Baptist Church. Rachel was poor but was able to enroll Carl in the kindergarten program because her older sister, Sarah, who taught school in Los Angeles, paid Carl's tuition.

The program was great, and Carl could already read and write when he went to first grade the following September. Later that year, on a sunny and unseasonably warm late-November day, Carl was in the yard, playing, when Rachel came to the door and called him inside. He reluctantly went inside as she said President Kennedy was in a parade in Dallas. Carl had no idea he was witnessing history as he and Hannah stood on either side of Rachel's chair, watching President Kennedy's motorcade as it wound through the streets of downtown Dallas.

He and Hannah had no idea who President Kennedy was; they just knew he interrupted their playtime outside. They also knew it was important, because Rachel sat and watched the TV attentively and demanded they be quiet. They heard shots on TV, and Rachel screamed. A few seconds later, Rachel started to cry as she told Carl and Hannah President Kennedy had been shot and killed in Dallas. The TV switched to Walter Cronkite, who took off his glasses, wiped tears from his eyes, and announced President Kennedy had died; he'd been killed that day in Dallas.

Rachel was crying, saying she could not believe they killed the president! Carl didn't understand the historical significance of what he'd seen on TV, the Kennedy assassination. The mood was somber with the adults. They were all big fans of the president and his fashionable wife. Carl heard his grandfather say President Kennedy was going to move the country forward. He had no idea what his grandfather meant when he said President Kennedy was trying to move the country forward; his youth shielded him from the problems faced by the adults in his life.

The following September, Carl was enrolled at J. H. Moore and started first grade with about forty other kids. Carl was ahead of the other kids in the class and became bored. It was hard for him to wait while the other kids learned what he already knew, how to read and write on a basic level. The year went by, and Professor Davis, the J.

H. Moore principal, approached Rachel with an offer. Carl had been held back because his birthday was after the deadline of August 31, and he was essentially a year behind kids his age.

The principal suggested Carl skip the second and third grades and start the next school year as a fourth-grade student. Professor Davis believed the behavior issues Carl exhibited as a first grader were the result of his being bored. He felt Carl needed to have work that was more challenging and required him to focus. Rachel rejected this because she did not believe Carl was mature enough to be a grade ahead of people his age, and she did not want him to "flunk" if the work proved to be more of a challenge than he could handle. Professor Davis assured Rachel that if Carl flunked fourth grade, he'd still be with the class of kids he was supposed to be with.

Rachel decided to keep Carl in his assigned grade, and he was placed in the second grade. There was a major shift in the family's life. Rachel finished Wiley College and got her first job as an English teacher at Central High school in Jefferson, Texas. Carl, Rachel, and Hannah started life in Jefferson at Central. Rachel started her career as a high school English teacher. Carl was a second-grade student, and Hannah started the first grade. Carl sat in class on the first day of school and thought he did not know anybody in that room!

One thing remained the same: his work was still at a very high level for a kid his age.

Rachel settled her young family into a rent house on Ferris Street in Jefferson, and life went on. Carol had not started school and was left with Riley and Janice in Marshall. About a year later, the young family left the house on Ferris Street and moved to a rent house on Broadway Street. Life was good for the family, and Carl started to see more of the unvarnished world. Rachel was a young teacher, not much older than the students she taught.

A lot of the girls at Central High stopped by the home, and Rachel welcomed each of them. Rachel hired a young lady named Judy Allen to babysit Carl and Hannah when she was not home. This worked good for Rachel, allowing her to have a life while she knew her kids would be safe. Being very nosy, Carl would pretend to be asleep when Judy put him to bed. A few minutes later, he would hear the front door open and sneak out in the hallway through the other door in his room. He got an eyeful when he saw a young man who also attended Central High, James Alexander, come into the house.

It wasn't long before he and Judy were on the couch, kissing and hugging each other. Carl thought it strange when James got on top of Judy like they were wrestling. He thought it was really weird when James and Judy started to moan. A few minutes later, he heard the key in the door and ran back to his room; he did not want to explain to Rachel why he was not in the bed, asleep. He lay in bed, listening as Rachel explained to Judy she was not to have "company" while babysitting the kids. Judy apologized and asked for another chance, promising she would not have James at the house again.

A few months later, Judy and James got married in what Carl heard was a "shotgun" wedding. He had no idea what that was, but he could see Judy's stomach looked like she'd swallowed a watermelon! That ended babysitting by the young women, and Rachel moved one of her peers in as a roommate. Carl was in the fourth grade, and things around the house got lively when Agnes, also a teacher at Central High, moved her stereo and records in with her. They played records and danced all the time. Carl was shown how to operate the stereo and would deejay the impromptu parties.

Carl learned the art of socialization. There was always a group of young women at the home. Since Rachel and Agnes both could sew and had a sewing machine, prom time was especially busy. Carl played records while the young women sewed their outfits and cooked dinner. They showed Carl how to dance, and he learned to "swing out" and a dance called the tip. Life was good, and he was having fun. Agnes was a home economics teacher and always tried new recipes. Carl was especially happy when one of the young women sewed a shirt for him.

She told him, "When you sew from a pattern, the shirt, blouse, or dress is one of a kind." He was thrilled to have a shirt that nobody else at school had, and he wore the shirt a lot. The kids at school were not impressed. Carl realized most of them wore clothes that had been made at home from a pattern. His innocence was shattered one afternoon in the summer between his second- and third-grade year.

A group of kids was playing on the Central campus when they heard shots. He and the other kids went toward the sound of the shots and saw a crowd gathering.

The smell of gunpowder filled the air as they got closer. The older Black people pushed the kids back, but not before Carl and the other kids saw the body of a Black man lying on the ground, bleeding. As the man lay on the ground, dying, the group looked up and saw a White man standing a few yards away with a rifle in his hand. It was an eerie feeling and sight, a Black man lying on the ground, shot, on one side of the railroad tracks, while the White man who'd shot him stood a few yards away, on the other side of the railroad tracks.

Carl was snapped back to reality when he heard Rachel scream his name as she ran toward him. He saw fear on her face and tears in her eyes as she snatched him up and demanded he bring his "little nosy ass" to the house.

Carl had just seen the results of a free murder. Rumors swirled about why the White man had killed the Black man, and Carl heard most of them. He could not understand why someone would want to kill another person. Carl had questions, and Rachel answered some for him, telling him the world was full of mean and evil people.

She tried to protect Carl from the harsh realities of the world and told him there were some things he'd understand better as he got older. He later realized the man that did the shooting was never arrested for murder; it was called justifiable homicide. Carl wondered how you could kill a man and not be sent to jail. The mood in the Black community around Jefferson was somber as reality sank in: you can kill Black people with impunity and not be charged with murder. Carl knew it wasn't fair but realized there was nothing he could do.

The rumors eventually died down and the adults didn't talk much about what happened, but the kids could sense there was fear by the way their parents hovered over them. Eventually, though, life returned to normal, parents stopped hovering over the kids, and the shooting at the railroad tracks became a distant memory. But for the kids who witnessed this incident, it was one of those moments that can be filed in the loss-of-innocence category.

Then summer wound down, and Carl started the fourth grade. During the first week of school, he found himself sitting in the principal's office with Rachel.

His being mischievous and inquisitive often ended up with him in the principal's office. Mr. Jones, the elementary school principal, came out, and Carl knew whatever he'd done, it was big! He usually got his three licks from the principal and went back to class, but Rachel was there with him today. Carl was confused because he had not been given the "Go to the office" order in a stern voice by his teacher. He was scared as they walked in Mr. Jones's office. School had been in a little over a week, and he was already in a conference with the principal and his mother.

They sat down, and Carl listened as Mr. Jones explained to Rachel her son was borderline genius. Mr. Jones explained to Rachel that Carl exhibited all the traits of a high-IQ person: he finished his work in a fraction of the time the other students took, and he became bored when he did not have anything left to do. Mr. Jones told her the testing they'd done at the end of Carl's third-grade year indicated he was in the top 5 percent of kids his age in the nation. Mr. Jones explained Carl's memory was excellent and he read over four hundred words a minute.

He went on to say his curiosity and love for playing pranks on people were a result of his being bored. Mr. Jones said Carl's vocabulary and conversation were at an extremely high level. Mr. Jones told Rachel these were all indicators of a high level of intelligence, especially in kids. Rachel could not believe she was having another conversation about skipping Carl, she thought she had put that subject to rest. Rachel explained she knew Carl was smart—she lived with him daily—and assured Mr. Jones she already knew everything he told her.

Rachel said the people who wanted to skip Carl had not considered his level of maturity. She explained he was a brilliant student but she didn't believe he was emotionally ready or mature enough to be in a higher grade. Mr. Jones asked Rachel if she'd been approached about skipping Carl before, and she said she had, at the school where he attended first grade. Rachel told Mr. Jones she'd been asked to let

Carl start what would have been his second-grade year as a fourth grader. Rachel explained this didn't happen because she had just finished college and accepted the teaching position at Central High.

Mr. Jones told Rachel he did not come to her with this on a whim; he'd watched Carl two school years, and he was intellectually exceptional. She said she did not want Carl to grow up too fast; she wanted him to enjoy his childhood and felt skipping him would kill his joy. Rachel explained Carl was very laid-back and it took a lot to upset him, and she wanted to keep him that way as long as possible. She went on to tell Mr. Jones she was the first to know Carl was borderline genius—she had watched as he read the dictionary when he was in first grade, memorizing words and their definition.

Rachel stood up to leave and told Mr. Jones, "There is one thing I know about Carl that you and Professor Davis never mentioned: Carl has a near photographic memory." Then she told Carl, "I asked them to call you into this meeting so you could understand what being smart can do." Rachel explained that Carl would be staying in fourth grade; she was not going to consent to him being skipped to seventh grade.

As they walked out the door, Mr. Jones told Rachel he'd seen this before, an intellectually exceptional child left with less-than-challenging work and they become bored with school.

Rachel thanked Mr. Jones for his time as she shook his hand and they left. They walked into the hallway, and Carl peppered Rachel with questions about being skipped two grades. He ran the thought through his mind and felt he'd like to be in seventh grade. Rachel told Carl he could not talk about this to the other students, as they parted ways, him going back to class and her going to finish her conference hour.

Carl immediately told his classmates about the meeting and the possibility he might be skipped to the seventh grade. None of the kids believed him, and they laughed as they accused him of lying. Carl was now face-to-face with reality: he was dealing with classmates who were barely keeping up, and he was talking about being skipped. It was funny to them that he thought he was going to be skipped two grades.

Later that day, at recess, a fight broke out between Carl and Ronnie Simmons, one of the boys who teased him.

The teacher sent both boys to the principal's office, and this time, Carl knew why he was there. Mr. Jones was not surprised to see Carl and Ronnie in the office for fighting; he'd seen them beefing on the playground. The irony was not lost on Mr. Jones, how a couple of hours earlier he was discussing skipping Carl, and now the latter was in the principal's office for fighting. The boys got their three licks and returned to the playground to finish recess. The trip to the principal's office and ensuing three licks cured Carl of talking to his friends and classmates about being skipped.

The fight on the playground pushed Carl's talk of being skipped off the minds of his classmates. They were now talking about who won the fight. Carl decided to ignore the meddling and finish the day without another incident. Carl's attention turned to girls, and he started to notice the girls at school, carrying their books, walking them to class, and talking to them. He talked to some of the high school girls that hung out at his house, and they gave him pointers. One of the high school girls, Sybil Morris, told him he should stop wrestling with Jackie and treat her like a girl.

Jackie Hunt was Hannah's best friend who lived around the corner from them and was always with him and Hannah. Sybil explained to Carl that he needed to handle girls with care and not "tackle" them like he tackled the boys. Sybil also said he had to pay attention to the girls because they got mad if you didn't. Jackie walked to and from school each day with them and insisted he and Hannah walk her all the way home after school. There was a girl at school that caught Carl's eye, Connie Coleman, a pretty girl in the same grade as Hannah.

Carl walked her to class and carried her books at school. The next day at lunch, Carl sat at the table with Connie and talked to her about school. A few minutes later, one of the boys called to Carl from the playground; they were about to play football. He hurriedly told Connie he'd see her later, then got up from the table and ran to the playground. Connie was mad at him a lot because at lunch he wanted to play football and she wanted him to sit with her and talk.

Carl drew the line and decided he would play football after he sat with Connie and ate lunch.

After school that day, Jackie asked why he was sitting at the table with Connie. He told her they were just talking, and if she wanted, she could sit at the table with them. So the next day at lunch, Carl had a table, with Jackie Hunt and Connie Coleman sitting with him. A few days later, Ronnie Simmons sat at the table with Carl, Jackie, and Connie. Ronnie had told all his friends he didn't think it was fair Carl was sitting with two of the prettiest girls at school.

A few days later, a date was announced for the annual sock hop.

The sock hop was a big deal, and all the kids wanted to attend. Carl knew he wanted to take Connie and was excited when he asked Rachel what he should do. He wanted to ask Connie, but she was mad at him for playing football at lunch. Rachel suggested he ask Connie; she might be mad, but she'd still go to the sock hop with him, she assured him. So at lunch the next day, Carl asked Connie, and just like Rachel said, she agreed to go with him. It put her in a good mood, and she didn't get mad when he went to the playground to play football with the boys.

When they walked home that day, Jackie walked in front of him and didn't let him carry her books. Carl didn't know what he'd done, but she seemed to be mad. The next day at lunch, Ronnie Simmons sat at the table with them and asked Jackie to go to the sock hop with him. Jackie was happy and agreed to go to the sock hop with Ronnie.

The sock hop grew closer, and it was time to order the boutonnieres and corsages the girls and boys would wear. Carl was curious why the dance was called a sock hop, and Rachel explained the dance was held in the gym and everyone had socks on.

Rachel further explained you had to pull your shoes off to keep from scuffing the gym floor. Rachel was getting Carl's order for the corsage when he told her Connie's last name was Coleman. He saw the change in Rachel's expression as they finished his order for Connie's corsage. It was Friday afternoon, and they were getting ready to go to Marshall for the weekend. Riley arrived to pick them up. He loved spending time with him, for they always had a lot of things to do.

The next day, Rachel told Carl to go to his aunt Bertha's house and ask if she knew Connie Coleman.

He thought this was weird, but went down the street to his aunt Bertha's house. Bertha was the older sister of his father, Bradley, and lived about one hundred yards down the street from Riley and Janice's house. That was another reason Carl loved coming to Marshall—he had cousins, aunts, uncles, and his other grandmother right down the street. Carl made it to his aunt Bertha's but didn't make it inside the house; he was in the yard, playing with his cousins and the other neighborhood kids. A few minutes later, Carl heard his aunt Bertha call his name.

She stood in the door and motioned for him to come inside the house. Carl went inside, and she asked about Connie, the girl he wanted to take to the sock hop. He told her she was in the class with Hannah and they went to school together. Bertha asked Carl if he knew her phone number, and she was shocked he knew her phone number. Carl gave Bertha the phone number for Connie, and although it was a long-distance call, she made the call. Bertha handed the phone to Carl, and a few seconds later, a man picked up on the other end.

Carl asked to speak with Connie, and the man asked who he was. Carl told him his name, and he heard the man shout for Connie to come to the phone. A few seconds later, he heard Connie's familiar voice on the other end of the phone and started to talk. She was happy to hear from him, and they talked for a few seconds before Bertha told him to ask her what her mother's name was. Carl had no idea what was going on and gave Connie the background, telling her he was at his aunt Bertha's house and for some reason they wanted to know who her mother was.

Connie said her mother's name was Ethel, and Carl told his aunt. His aunt said, "I believe you and this girl are kinfolk." Connie called Ethel to the phone, and Bertha got the phone from Carl. He didn't know where this was going and sensed something was not right—Bertha and Ethel were talking like they were old friends! Bertha hung up the phone and said, "Connie can't go to the sock hop with you. Your grandmothers are sisters." She told him Connie's mother, Ethel, was the first cousin of his dad, Bradley!

CHAPTER 2

Sock Hop Blues
#HeShouldHaveAskedJackie

Carl was crushed as Bertha then laid it out for him: Connie's mother's mother and his father's mother were sisters! Bertha told Carl, "Nephew, find another girl to take to the sock hop." Carl left his aunt's house not really understanding what had just happened. When he went to his aunt Bertha's house, he had a sock hop date, and when he left, he did not have a sock hop date! He walked in the house and explained to Rachel that his aunt had told him Connie was kinfolk. Carl was a little bent out of shape that he could not take her to the sock hop.

He started to lament he'd already bought a corsage with Connie's name on it. Rachel said she had not ordered the corsage and suggested he ask Jackie Hunt, the girl who walked to school with him and Hannah. Carl thought about it a minute and decided to ask Jackie if she'd go to the sock hop with him. Although he was at the table, he didn't hear Ronnie Simmons ask Jackie to go to the sock hop with him. Carl remembered Jackie had given him her phone number and went through his books to find it. When he found the number and picked up the phone to call Jackie, Rachel stopped him.

She said he couldn't just call and ask her to go to the sock hop—she'd be insulted! Rachel explained she knew he asked Connie and she'd feel she was his second choice. Carl was really confused; she had told him to ask Jackie, and now she was telling him to hold on before he asked her. Rachel told Carl to wait until they went back to Jefferson and go over to her house.

The next day, Riley took them back to Jefferson. After they put their bags in the house and rested, Carl went around the corner to Jackie's house.

Rachel gave Carl instructions and told him to ease into asking her to go to the sock hop with him. She also told him to be prepared if she was already going with someone else or told him no. Carl made it to Jackie's street, and she was outside, playing with a bunch of kids. Jackie saw Carl and took a seat on the steps; she didn't want him to think she was a tomboy. He waved at her and played football with the boys, trying to build his courage to ask her to go with him to the sock hop. The boys eventually tired of playing football, and Carl noticed Jackie was still sitting on the steps.

He took a seat next to her, and they talked about school and homework. Jackie said she had done her homework and had laid out her clothes for the next day. He asked if he could carry her books the next day, and Jackie looked at him, saying he should carry Connie's books. After she flippantly said Connie was his girlfriend, she asked why he wanted to carry her books. Carl told her he found out they were kinfolk and she couldn't be his girlfriend. He told Jackie the sock hop was coming up and they had to turn in their order for corsages the next day.

He asked Jackie if he could order a corsage for her.

She looked at him again and asked why she should go to the sock hop with him. Carl thought, *This is what Rachel was talking about.* He looked at her, saying she should go to the sock hop with him because he asked. She told him Ronnie Simmons had also asked and she was going with him. Carl was hurt but remembered what Rachel had said, that she might be going with somebody else. He had seen Ronnie Simmons talking to Jackie and realized that was what he'd been doing. Carl stood up to leave, and Jackie asked if he liked her.

Carl said he did like her, then started to walk home. He wanted to tell Rachel what went down, and he really needed to talk to her. When he made it home, he told Rachel what happened, and she told him to gut it up. *That's life.*

Ultimately, he went to the sock hop by himself; he couldn't take Connie, and Jackie was going with Ronnie Simmons. When he and Hannah made it to the gym, it was packed—all the kids at school were there! He saw Connie, and they danced with each other, having a great time! Carl realized he had feelings for Jackie when he got angry because she and Ronnie were dancing.

His anger didn't have time to fester; he was busy dancing with Connie and some of the high school girls. Carl was in elementary school, but the older girls at their house had taught him the tip and swing-out, two popular dances. When the high school girls saw he could do the tip and swing-out, they wanted to dance with him. Jackie wore it well, but she was in her feelings because Carl was having a great time.

The sock hop finally ended, and Carl waited outside for Hannah to come out. Rachel said he needed to wait for Hannah after the sock hop even though she had an escort.

He was surprised to see Jackie standing outside and was more surprised when she said she was waiting for Hannah. It was an awkward silence as they stood there, waiting for Hannah to come out. After what seemed like an eternity, Hannah finally came out, and they walked the short distance across Broadway Street. There was a moment of truth when he and Hannah made it home and he left Jackie on the sidewalk, talking to Hannah. He walked toward the house, and Hannah yelled, "We have to walk Jackie home!" He stood on the porch, about to go inside when Rachel came on the porch.

She told Hannah and Jackie to hold on a few minutes; she had something she needed Carl to do right quick. When he walked in the house, Rachel closed the door and told him, "It's decision time, young man." He could sense from Rachel's tone and body language that she was serious. She went on to say he might not want to walk her home but he needed to take a deep breath and go walk her home.

She said she would not make him do it but she strongly suggested it. She told Carl to make his decision—the girls were outside, waiting.

He took a deep breath and made the decision to walk Jackie home. He'd learned to go with Rachel when she strongly suggested something. When Rachel saw he was going to walk Jackie home, she went on the porch and told them he was almost done. A few seconds later, Carl walked out and went to the sidewalk with Hannah and Jackie. He thought about something Rachel said: "You can't be salty when things are not going your way." Carl thought, at that moment, things were not going his way at all.

They were walking Jackie home when Hannah said, "Jackie likes you, Carl."

He kept walking. He did not know what to say and was glad when they made it to Jackie's house. They stood outside while Hannah and Jackie talked about the sock hop and the fun they had. He was happy when Hannah finally said she was ready to go home. Jackie walked on her porch as Carl and Hannah walked toward their house. He heard Jackie call his name and turned to see what she wanted. She asked if he still liked her, and he reluctantly said he did still like her. She told them bye and she would see them on the way to school the next day.

On the way home, Hannah said Jackie liked him and he could not be mad at her for going to the sock hop with Ronnie Simmons. Hannah reminded Carl, as soon as Jackie found out he could not take Connie, she told Ronnie she was going home with them. Hannah and Carl walked home with Hannah talking about how good a time she had at the sock hop.

The next morning, Jackie was sitting on the porch, waiting for them. Carl spoke to her and realized he wasn't mad any longer. Jackie smiled when he reached for her books and Hannah teased him, asking why he never carried her books.

Carl ignored her as they crossed Broadway Street on the way to school. He thought how Hannah was always talking about something she didn't know about. The bell had not rung when they got to school, and they stood outside, talking about the sock hop. Jackie wanted to know where he learned to do the dance called the tip—all the high school kids were doing it. Hannah chimed in and said the girls that'd be at their house used him as a dance partner and taught him the tip. Hannah said they also taught him to swing out, another popular dance.

The bell rang, and they went to class. At lunch that day, Carl was sitting at the table when Connie and Jackie came and sat with him. They were talking and having fun when Ronnie Simmons, too, sat down with them. Connie asked Ronnie if he had fun at the sock hop. Ronnie said he did have fun and hoped he could take Jackie to the next sock hop. Ronnie then sarcastically asked if she and Carl had fun at the sock hop. Connie told him she had fun at the sock hop but she and Carl found out they were second cousins. Ronnie flippantly asked what that had to do with him.

Carl listened as Ronnie talked about how much fun he and Jackie had at the sock hop. He was happy when Gary Lyons called him to come play football. He jumped up from the table and trotted to the playground, leaving Ronnie in midsentence with Jackie and Connie. Jackie was upset Carl had left them to play football, leaving her and Connie with Ronnie Simmons. When lunch was over, Carl walked to class oblivious that Jackie was upset with him. When school was out, Carl found Hannah to walk home, but Jackie was nowhere to be found.

When he and Hannah started walking home, he saw Jackie ahead of them and called to her. He followed Jackie as she ignored him and kept walking toward her house. When she ran in the house, he knocked on the door, but nobody came to the door. He finally got the message and went home, wondering what was wrong with Jackie. Later that day, he talked to Rachel about what happened between them and was shocked when Rachel said this was his fault. She laid it out for him, telling him if Connie had not been his cousin, he had dropped Jackie like a hot potato.

Rachel asked Carl to think about why Jackie walked to school with him and Hannah. She said he'd treated Jackie horribly before and after the sock hop. She reminded him that he was mad at Jackie and all she had done was like him. Rachel suggested Carl wait for Ronnie to come back to their table and tell him Jackie was his girl and see how she reacted. She then said, "The two of you are going to have to work through this together." Rachel asked Carl if he truly liked Jackie, and he said he liked her a lot. Rachel told Carl to not play with Jackie, that if he didn't like her, to leave her alone.

She could tell from his body language and the way he acted that he *did* like her.

The next morning, Carl and Hannah were sitting on Jackie's porch when she walked out the door. Jackie turned around and walked back inside the house with Hannah on her heels. Jackie said she did not want to walk to school with Carl—she was mad at him. Hannah said she understood and asked her to give Carl a chance. They both laughed when Hannah said, "My brother is real smart when it comes to books, but he is real dumb when it comes to girls."

Hannah said she didn't have to talk to him. "Just give him your books and I bet he takes them." Jackie took Hannah at her word, walked outside, and handed her books to Carl. They didn't speak, and Carl took her books when she handed them to him. He walked her to the door of her class and handed her books to her, then asked if she would sit with him at lunch. Jackie didn't answer, just walked in class and left him standing at the door. At lunch, Carl sat at a table and waited for Jackie to show up. A few minutes later, she walked to the table with her lunch tray and asked if she could sit down.

Carl nodded, and she sat down beside him. Carl and Jackie were eating lunch and talking when Ronnie came to the table and sat down. He asked Jackie how she was doing, and she said, "Good." The mood was very quiet as they ate, until Ronnie spoke again, asking Jackie if she was going to the basketball game that evening. Carl asked Ronnie why he sat at the table with them when other tables were available. Ronnie looked at him saying, "I wasn't talking to you, and I sure didn't ask you about going to the game."

Ronnie kept talking and said, "You act like she your girl!"

Carl might have been dumb about girls, but he saw the door open and said, "Jackie *is* my girl."

Ronnie laughed and told Carl, "That's what you said. I didn't hear her say anything." Ronnie asked if she was Carl's girl, and Jackie realized they had put her on the spot. She didn't answer the question, and Carl spoke up.

He turned to her and said, "I'm sorry for not asking you to go to the sock hop first. I asked Connie to go and she said yes, then we found out we were cousins."

He looked Jackie in the eyes and continued, "When I came to ask you to go with me, you had already agreed to go with Ronnie."

She looked at him, accepted his apology, then told Ronnie, "I'm Carl's girl."

Ronnie was crushed when Jackie said that, and left the table. Carl looked at Jackie and told her Rachel said they had to work through this together. Jackie asked what being his girl meant. He told her he really didn't know but thought it meant walking her to school and carrying her books. She looked at him, saying, "If that's what it means, I've been your girl a long time."

They laughed together as Carl thought about it and said, "I guess you right, you have been my girl a long time." They finished their lunch, smiling at each other when Gary Lyons called Carl to come play football. As much as he wanted to go play football, he realized he needed to stay at the table and talk to Jackie.

The bell rang, ending lunch, and Carl walked Jackie to class. When she walked in the room, the girls needled her, that she had a boyfriend. Carl had the same problem—the boys made fun of him because he had a girlfriend.

Gary Lyons chided him, saying, "Carl can't play football because he has a girlfriend!"

Things went well during the next few weeks. They spent a lot of time together. One evening, he was playing records and eating with the high school girls when they asked about his new girlfriend. When Carl said he walked his girlfriend to school and carried her books, they felt he needed pointers on how he should treat Jackie. Sybil Morris, one of the high school girls, said, "You need to hug and kiss her, be affectionate." He didn't believe what he was hearing—these girls told him to kiss Jackie!

He looked at Sybil saying, "That is disgusting!"

They laughed at Carl, and another of the high school girls, Diane Morgan, reminded them he was ten years old and in the fourth grade. They stopped mocking Carl about his girlfriend and asked him to play music for them. He danced with them, doing the tip and swing-out. When Carl played Percy Sledge's song "When a Man Loves a Woman," Diane Morgan stepped up and showed him how to slow-dance with a girl. Carl learned how to hold a girl and thought it was yucky, but he listened and learned to slow-dance.

Diane said he'd appreciate them showing him this dance when Central had the next sock hop. He was happy when Rachel came home and turned the music off so everyone could do their homework.

The next morning, Jackie was waiting for them to walk to school. As they walked to school, he asked if she liked to dance, and Jackie said she loved to dance! They compared dance moves, and Carl saw he and Jackie did not tip the same way. He liked the way Jackie did it better; it was more rhythmic and flowed with the beat.

The bell rang to start the school day, and they ran to class to keep from being late. At lunch, Carl and Jackie talked about the different dances they could do and who showed them the dances. When Gary called Carl to play football, he didn't go and instead told him he'd play the next day.

Over the next few months, Carl and Jackie became very close friends and were inseparable. As he carried Jackie's books one day, he noticed her name was different; it was not Hunt. She had written her name on her book covers as Jackie Hampton.

Carl asked her about it, and she draped her arm around his neck, kissed him on the cheek in a playful manner, and said, "I'm your wife."

Carl laughed and repeated what she said. "*My* wife."

She echoed him, saying, "Yes, *your* wife!"

He looked at her when she said, "You can kiss your wife every day."

When they finished eating lunch, Carl ran to the playground to play football, and Jackie was mad!

That afternoon, when they walked home, she didn't let him carry her books. He and Jackie had enjoyed several months of happiness, but she was now mad at Carl!

She might have been mad with him, but she didn't stop walking to and from school with them.

The next day, it was his turn to get mad. Ronnie Simmons was sitting there, talking to Jackie. He didn't say a word, just sat down with them and ate lunch. When Gary called him to come play football, he left them at the table talking. When they walked home that evening, she offered him her books and he refused, saying, "Let Ronnie Simmons carry your books, Jackie!" She smiled inside, knowing she'd made him mad. Jackie's older sisters had said, if he got mad about Ronnie Simmons, then he liked her.

Summer came, and Carl was happy to be out of school, for he got to spend a lot of time with Riley and Janice. Riley's brother, Rudolph, lived across the street, and the kids loved to go over and talk with him. Carl and Hannah realized Carol had been spoiled by Riley and Janice! She didn't want anyone to play with her toys and would cry when either Hannah or Carl tried to play with them.

One hot summer morning, Riley woke Carl up and they drove to the farm in the country. Carl was fascinated as he looked around and saw the vegetables growing in the garden.

He helped Riley load the truck with watermelons, cantaloupes, squash, and greens. Although it was a hot and humid day, Carl loved riding in the truck as he and Riley rode around Marshall, peddling watermelons and other fruits and vegetables. He was especially happy when they sold out, until Riley told him they were not going home, that they were going back to the country to load the truck again. When they went home for the day, Carl was happy Riley gave him five dollars for his labor.

After a few weeks, he grew into his role as Riley's sidekick as they rode all over town, selling watermelons.

Riley had a special horn on his truck and taught Carl a "barker" line. He would lean out the window and scream, "Hey, little girl playing in the sand, run, tell your mama here the watermelon man!"

When Carl screamed his lines, Riley followed with a blast of his horn and screamed, "Watermelons!"

When Carl and Riley were not working, they'd sit on the porch, talking. Carl would sit and listen as Riley's friends came by and talked to him.

Later that summer, Carl, Riley, and Rudolph were at the farm, and Carl saw a barrel with copper coils running out of it. Carl thought the barrel looked like one of the science experiments he had seen at School.

Carl went with Rudolph to the farm every day and learned the craft of making moonshine. He and Rudolph came home one evening, and Rachel asked where they'd been. She knew Carl had been gone all day, and she knew her uncle was a moonshiner. He told Rachel he'd been at the still with Uncle Rudolph and they had been working. Rachel ran out of the house and across the street to her uncle's house, livid with him for showing Carl how to make bootleg whiskey.

She stood in her uncle's yard, arguing with him about why she did not want Carl to learn the whiskey business. Rudolph had enough and yelled across the street to Riley, telling him to come get her. Riley stuck his head out the door and told Rachel she needed to bring her ass back across the street and leave Rudolph the hell alone.

The next morning, Riley woke Carl up and told him they needed to go for a ride. Carl dressed, knowing he was in trouble but not remembering what he'd done. As they rode around, Riley said there were some things he would not be able to tell Rachel.

His granduncle Rudolph made bootleg whiskey, which Rachel and Janice did not approve of. He told Carl, "When you go to the still, tell your mother you were working in the garden. We plant and work the fields when we go to the farm, so you will not be lying to her." Riley knew he was playing fast and loose with the truth, but the young man needed to know how to make a living in the rural South, because jobs were scarce. Riley said, if Rachel asked questions, he'd handle it and not allow her to whip him. Riley explained how Rudolph ran the whiskey operation and he ran the farm operation.

Riley told him he knew how to make whiskey but it caused a lot of problems between him and Janice. It made sense to Carl now: the men coming to Uncle Rudolph's house were buying whiskey!

As they loaded watermelons in the truck, Riley told Carl he could not tell anyone what they were doing, or they would be sent to jail. Carl was shocked but knew to keep his mouth closed; after all, he did not want to go to jail!

Carl sold watermelons almost every day and made money at the end of the day. When he and Riley got home every evening, he would walk to the store with Rachel, Hannah, and Carol. Naturally, Carl was a rock star to his mother and sisters—he had money to spend at the store every day when he finished work.

One day, as they rode around, selling watermelons, Riley stopped at the store for lunch. Carl asked for a loan against his wages later that day. Riley agreed to give him an advance, and they went into the store and bought lunch. As they sat in the truck, eating, Riley told him there was no reason for him to be broke since he got paid each day they worked. He told Carl he was going to be a man one day and he needed to make sure he always had a piece of change in his pocket.

Riley said it was good to take them to the store but he didn't need to spend all his money. He offered his grandson a suggestion: "Don't let them know how much money you have." To help Carl with this, Riley paid him while they were outside so his mother and sisters did not know how much money he made that day. But Carl kept going to the store after work and spending all his money. So Riley decided he needed to show him in a different way why he needed to save some money.

The next day at lunch, Carl asked Riley for an advance and he refused, explaining he'd been paid the day before.

Riley went into the store and bought his own lunch, leaving Carl in the truck to think. Riley sat and ate lunch with Carl watching him, and when he got through eating, he cranked the truck to leave. Carl resigned himself to the fact that he was not going to get lunch that day. They had made it to the edge of the parking lot when Riley stopped, reached in his pocket, and handed Carl three dollars. Carl took the money, went into the store, and bought a honey bun, Vienna sausages, and soda. He knew this was not the end of it, because Riley hated to eat while they were rolling.

He ate lunch listening as Riley explained why he needed to save some money when he got paid. He told Carl, "When ya'll go to the store this evening, spend half of what you made today. Instead of telling them how much you made today, tell them how much they can spend." Carl thought about it and told Riley he would try that when they went to the store.

That evening, Riley paid Carl five dollars for his work. When he went to the store that evening, he told them how much they could spend. This caused his mother and sisters to be very angry with him; they wanted to know why he would not spend more of his money.

Carl said he did make more money but needed to save some for lunch the next day. Although they were mad at him, they bought the snacks and went home.

That night, Rachel and Hannah needled Carl about being tight with his money and holding a dollar until it hollered.

The next day, he and Riley rode around, selling watermelons, and when they stopped for lunch, Carl went in the store and paid for his lunch. Riley was impressed he'd learned the lesson, and started to teach him others.

CHAPTER 3

You Can't Borrow Lunch Money Err Day
#WhyYaWorkingAndBegging

Riley wanted Carl to be an upstanding man and knew he needed guidance to help him get there. As they ate lunch, Riley explained why he needed to keep some of the money he made for times when money was not so good. Carl understood what Riley was saying; it felt good having money before he got paid! This lesson was driven home a couple of weeks later, when the rain caused them to miss a week of work. They were not able to get in the field to get watermelons and vegetables, so if he hadn't saved some of his money, he would have been broke.

Carl took the lesson to heart and started to save most of his money from the work he did with Riley. As summer went on, he and Riley kept working, and Carl saved a total of $175. Just before school started, he used some of his money to buy clothes he wanted but Rachel would not buy. The summer ended, and Rachel packed her family up for the trip to Jefferson for the upcoming school year. It was different this time when Riley dropped them off—Carol stayed with them. She was going to start kindergarten and would not be living with Riley and Janice any longer.

Riley and Janice dropped them off, and Carl took the bags in the house to put everything up. When they arrived at Jackie's, she and Hannah hugged each other as Carl stood and watched. When he hugged Jackie, there was something different about this hug. They sat on the porch, talking and catching up on the things they had done that summer.

School started a few days later, and Carol was crying because she did not want to go to kindergarten.

The first day, Rachel, Carl, and Hannah walked Carol to kindergarten, at Mrs. Lee's house. Rachel explained he'd have to walk Carol to Mrs. Lee's house every morning and go back and get her that afternoon. Carol was crying hard as Rachel walked out of Mrs. Lee's house that morning. The next morning, Rachel got Carol ready for school, then reminded Carl what he had to do. Carl, Hannah, and Carol walked out the door, and Jackie was waiting for them on the porch. This surprised them. Since they had to walk Carol to school, they thought Jackie would go on without them. Jackie laughed and told them she was going to walk Carol to Mrs. Lee's house with them.

When they got to Mrs. Lee's house, Carol went into a full-blown cry, again! Carl walked her to the door, saying they would be back to get her that afternoon. That seemed to calm Carol down, and she stopped crying. He walked in the house with her, and she watched from the window as they walked away. That afternoon, Carol was watching through the window when Carl, Hannah, and Jackie walked up to Mrs. Lee's house. When Mrs. Lee opened the door, Carol ran outside to meet them.

Carl realized the responsibility this placed on him: Carol had full confidence he was coming to get her each afternoon. She had stopped crying in the morning when he dropped her off, and this was a relief to them.

The school year went on, and things settled down to normal. The high school girls still camped out at Rachel's place, listening to music and teaching Carl the latest dances. Central had a winter ball for students, and there was no doubt whom Carl would be asking to go with him.

That evening, Jackie handed Carl her books and he said he needed to ask her a question.

When they got to her house, he asked if she would go to the winter ball with him. Jackie quickly agreed, saying she would love to go to the winter ball with him. That evening, he told Rachel he'd asked Jackie to go to the winter ball and he needed to get her a corsage. Rachel said there was another thing he needed to do before ordering the corsage; she said he needed to ask her parents if he could take her to the winter ball. The winter ball was a big deal in Jefferson, a coming-out event for girls in the junior and senior classes at Central.

Sybil Morris beat the other girls who hung out at Rachel's house to the punch by asking Carl to be part of her court. He agreed, and Sybil was very happy, knowing this meant Rachel would be helping her raise money. Sybil wanted to win, because the winner got a scholarship to college! When Rachel was told Carl had agreed to be in Sybil's court, she explained it was up to them to raise the money. Sybil went to Rachel and explained she wanted to do something different for the ball; she would only have Carl and his date in her court.

This was a break from the past. Normally, each contestant had ten to twelve couples in her court. The idea amused Rachel, and she wanted to hear Sybil's plan for making it work. She explained that she wanted to have a spelling bee and solicit the teachers for donations for correctly spelled words. Sybil explained they could ask donations from the teachers they knew. Rachel saw the brilliance of the idea and told Sybil she was totally on board with it. She and Sybil put the spelling bee together, and both were mildly surprised at the level of support they received. They settled on ten cents a word, with a maximum donation of ten dollars.

A few days later, Carl went home with Jackie and spoke with her mother and father about taking her to the winter ball. Jackie's dad told Carl that a lot of money would be spent getting Jackie ready for the ball; she needed a dress and shoes to match. He told Carl his biggest concern was, he'd spend the money on the winter ball and Jackie would be disappointed. Carl gave Mr. Hunt his word that he would make sure Jackie had a good time. When Mr. Hunt held his hand out to shake Carl's, he remembered what Riley said.

Carl knew his word was his bond, and a handshake meant you kept your word. Jackie's dad explained he expected Carl to pick her up at 6:30 p.m. and he had to come inside to get her. Mr. Hunt explained this meant Carl would not just knock on the door and wait for Jackie to come out. He explained he should take her to the Soda Fountain for a root beer float before they went to the ball. He finished by saying Carl should have her home by ten and she needed to be smiling. Carl agreed, saying he did not have a car to pick Jackie up. Mr. Hunt laughed as he said they would work that part out.

Sybil named the spelling bee Dimes for College and sent them to the teachers she knew. Carl and Rachel did the same, sending letters to the teachers in their family. Rachel said he was on his own and needed to earn the money for Jackie's corsage and the other things he needed to buy for the ball. He went to the telephone and called Riley, explaining he needed to work with him on the weekends until the ball. Riley agreed to pick Carl up every Friday and bring him back on Sunday, even if Rachel and the girls were not going to Marshall.

Carl worked hard and earned the money to pay for Jackie's corsage and donate ten dollars to Sybil's account.

A few weeks later, the letters started to come back with donations. Carl and Rachel were surprised when they received a check for one hundred dollars from Sarah, along with a note to Sybil saying she'd help her get into college. A week before the ball, Sybil had to turn in her money, and together they had raised eight hundred dollars! They were all happy and felt Sybil would win. They didn't know how much anyone else had raised, but they felt sure this was a big number.

The winter ball arrived, and Sybil's older brother, Alfred, came to pick them up in a three-seat station wagon. She had arranged for him to chauffeur them and act as chaperone. Sybil had cleared this with everyone involved to make sure things would run smoothly. Alfred picked Carl up and dropped him off at Jackie's house. While Carl was inside, getting Jackie, he went to James Lyons's house to pick him up. Carl got out of the car and walked up the sidewalk to Jackie's house. He kept his manners in mind as he knocked on the door.

Jackie's dad answered the door and invited Carl inside. He went in and told Mr. Hunt he was there to pick up Jackie. He invited Carl to have a seat, saying Jackie would be out in a moment. Carl heard a door close, and Jackie walked out in a floor-length black chiffon dress. Carl was blown away—she looked great! He composed himself and walked over to her, placing the corsage on her left wrist. There was a knock on the door. Alfred had returned from picking up James. Jackie's parents had them pose for a picture together before they left.

Carl held the door as he and Jackie walked out, and held the car door for her to get in. Alfred seated them in the second seat, the third seat having been reserved for Sybil and her date. Jackie's parents were pleased with Carl's manners; it looked like he had things under control.

A few moments later, they were at Rachel's; Sybil had decided she'd rather be picked up there. James was in the living room, waiting on Sybil to come out. Rachel had told Sybil she should wait until Alfred came back with Jackie and Carl before she went out to meet James.

Alfred knocked on the door and announced himself, then went back to the car, waiting for Sybil and James. Rachel looked at Sybil and said she was beautiful and looked great. She also said she was proud of her and the effort she had put out to get this done. She told Sybil to enjoy herself and forget about everything but the dance. Rachel went into the living room and said Sybil would be out in a minute. A moment later, Sybil opened the door and walked into the living room, and James was blown away. Sybil also had on a black chiffon dress. She and Jackie had coordinated their outfits.

Sybil looked great, and James shook so badly he could barely place the corsage on her wrist. He opened the door and held the car door for her when they went to the car. Alfred drove to the Soda Fountain, and the guys held the door for the young ladies. When they went inside, everyone was blown away—they'd never seen a potential queen and a member of her court dressed in identical dresses! They drank the root beer floats at the Soda Fountain before they went to the ball. The atmosphere was electric as people arrived, looking at one another dressed in formal clothes.

Carl held the car door for Jackie and helped her out, then escorted her inside the gym. He and Jackie were in awe when they stepped inside—the place looked great! He found their table and held Jackie's seat out as she sat down. Jackie looked around and saw there were seven other tables for contestants. She noticed Sybil had only her and Carl in her court, while the other girls had eight or ten. The ball started promptly at seven thirty as the choir sang "Lift Every Voice and Sing." When the song was done, the program started and the caterers made their way around the gym, serving people.

While they were eating, the master of ceremonies introduced each of the contestants, her escort, and the people in her court. The master of ceremonies also outlined the young lady's life and achievements. He took his time when he got to Sybil, announcing she was the only contestant to have had a fundraiser, then went on to describe the spelling bee in detail. The master of ceremonies mentioned this had never been done before, then recognized the winner of the spelling bee. Carl grumbled when Ronnie was introduced and accepted the twenty-five-dollar savings bond.

Jackie and Sybil looked at Carl when he mumbled as the announcer said Ronnie had spelled *egregious* correctly. Carl calmed down and stopped mumbling. True, he didn't like Ronnie, but he didn't want to mess the night up. He thought to himself, *I'll beat him up later.* Carl knew this night was special. After all, he'd been given many lessons on how to behave during the ball, how to eat, how to talk, and how to walk. Sybil had taken the time to show him how to hold Jackie while they slow-danced.

After the introduction of the contestants and their courts, they announced the winners of the scholarships.

Sybil was filled with joy as her name was announced as the winner—she'd raised a total of $1,500! This meant she'd have a $1,000 scholarship! Sybil cried as she stood onstage to accept the dummy check and take pictures. Jackie and Carl were part of Sybil's court, so they were in most of the pictures with her.

When the pictures were finished, the dance started. Jackie and Carl were on the dance floor most of the night. Carl did the swing-out, and they took turns doing the tip. They showed each other how they did the tip, and they learned the dance both ways.

They had been dancing a long time when Wilson Pickett's "When a Man Loves a Woman" came on. Jackie started to walk off the dance floor, but Carl reached out to her. She stopped and told him she didn't know how to slow-dance. Sybil had prepared Carl, and he told Jackie to follow his lead. She walked back to him and into his arms. Carl was glad Sybil had showed him how to hold Jackie, because he would not have had a clue! They felt good as they danced close to each other, not saying a word.

The DJ went into a second slow song, and Carl kept her on the floor. She didn't mind. She liked being close to him like this. The song ended, however, and they went back to their seats.

A few records later, Ronnie came to the table and asked Jackie to dance. Carl sat and watched, waiting to see what Jackie was going to do. Her older sister had prepared her, telling her if she was having a good time with Carl, to not accept any dance offers from other boys. She thought she'd been having a great time and told Ronnie they would have to dance some other time. She leaned her head on Carl's shoulder as they finished the evening at the table, talking. A photographer from the yearbook staff took a picture of the young couple, and it was a favorite when the yearbook was published.

At 9:30 p.m., Alfred came to the table and told them it was time to go. Carl and Jackie did not put up any argument—they were beat from all the dancing and had thoroughly enjoyed themselves at the banquet and ball. Carl helped Jackie in the car, and Alfred drove her home. When they arrived at Jackie's, Carl got out of the car and helped her out. He walked her to the porch, and they stood for a few seconds, talking.

Jackie opened the door and walked inside the house, saying she had had a great time and danced almost the whole time. Carl went back to the car, and Alfred drove him around the corner to his house. He got out of the car and went in the house tired and ready to go to sleep. Rachel knew he'd had a good time and told him to go to sleep.

The next morning, Carl dressed and went to the kitchen. He was shocked to find Sybil sitting at the table with Rachel—she'd spent the night with them! She told Carl he'd handled himself like a gentleman at the banquet and ball.

Carl listened as Sybil explained to Rachel she did not like Jefferson and when she finished college she would not be returning there. Sybil thanked Rachel for all she'd done for her during her years at Central and asked for her help in preparing for graduation. Rachel agreed to help her prepare for both graduation and the transition to college life.

It was March, and everyone was ready for May to come so the school year could be over. The mailman came by, and Carl grabbed the mail out of the box and took it to Rachel. He was excited as he handed the mail to her. There was a letter from Bradley.

She opened the letter, and Carl saw her demeanor change as she read it. Carl didn't know what was in the letter but sensed it was not good. When he asked Rachel about the letter, she simply told him, "Your dad is being discharged from the Air Force." Hannah was standing by the door when he turned around, and the two of them went outside. She suggested they go around to Jackie's house and went inside to ask Rachel if they could go. A few seconds later, Hannah came back outside and told Carl it was okay for them to go to Jackie's house.

When they made it to Jackie's, she was outside, playing with the kids from her street. Hannah and Carl joined the group as they played softball in the street. Jackie was a great pitcher and struck out most of the players on the other team. When it was his turn to bat, Carl walked to the plate to face Jackie. The first pitch she threw him, Carl hit it right back to her. Jackie caught the ball and ran to the plate to needle Carl—he was out! This angered Carl, but he got his glove and went to the field, pretending to ignore her.

Three of the girls got base hits before it was Jackie's turn to bat. The first pitch was right down the middle, and Jackie swung hard on it. Carl heard the bat crack and was shocked when the ball sailed over his head! He ran after the ball and threw it to the pitcher at home plate, but it was too late—Jackie had crossed. He couldn't believe it: Jackie hit a home run! The girls beat the boys, and they rubbed it in. Carl realized that day that Jackie was an incredible athlete. Hannah said they needed to go home, and Jackie asked her mother if she could walk them half the way.

33

Her mother let her go and told Jackie she had better hurry up. The three of them walked together, talking about the banquet and ball and the good time they had. Jackie rubbed it in for Carl how she'd gotten him out and then hit a home run. When Hannah and Carl made it home, Rachel sat them down and told them Bradley was coming home. They didn't know what to make of it. Bradley had spent very little time with them in the past. Monday rolled around again, and as usual, Jackie was sitting on the porch when Hannah, Carol, and Carl came out of the house.

She handed Carl her books, and they walked Carol to school. Carol had stopped crying when they walked her to school; by then she was used to being left at Mrs. Lee's house when they went to school.

When Rachel and Ms. Agnes got home that evening, there was a celebration. Ms. Agnes announced she was going to marry Raymond Green and she would be moving out of the house with them. She told Rachel she'd like for Carl and Hannah to be in her wedding, and she agreed.

A few minutes later, Mr. Green knocked on the door, and the celebration started, lasting late into the night. Carl and Jackie were becoming close friends and had not argued for a while. Ronnie Simmons had made up his mind that he was going to cause problems between them; he could not accept Jackie had chosen Carl over him. Jackie wanted to be friends with Ronnie, but he wanted Carl out of the picture. Ronnie sat at the lunch table with them, and when Carl asked him to leave, he told Carl it was a free country and he did not own any of the tables in the cafeteria.

If Carl and Jackie went outside to eat, there was Ronnie right behind them. Carl and Jackie talked about it and decided they would ignore Ronnie. She didn't tell him, but Jackie thought the attention from Ronnie was flattering. Her older sister had told her to get Ronnie told she was Carl's girl, but Jackie didn't have the heart to tell him off. The teachers had been watching this and knew it would not be long before this went bad.

One day, Ronnie asked Jackie why she liked Carl but didn't like him. Jackie told him she and Carl played together, walked to school together, and were friends.

They got up from the lunch table, and Carl chest-bumped Ronnie, causing him to drop his soda. Ronnie told Carl he needed to pay for his soda and, when he refused, pushed him in the chest with both hands. Carl punched Ronnie in the mouth, and Ronnie punched Carl in the nose. Before things could escalate, Mr. Jones and one of the teachers was on them, breaking them apart. They'd been watching them and were not surprised when they came to blows. They were taken to the office, and Mr. Jones sat them down to talk about what happened.

Neither of them knew Mr. Jones had been watching the whole time as he asked Carl to tell his side of the story. Carl started by explaining that Ronnie had been harassing him and Jackie since the scholarship ball. He said Ronnie was mad because he took Jackie to the scholarship ball and she did not talk to him any longer. Mr. Jones then turned to Ronnie and asked for his explanation of what had happened. Ronnie explained Carl was only half-right; he'd taken Jackie to the sock hop and Carl had come between them. When Mr. Jones asked them who was wrong, they pointed at each other.

Mr. Jones explained that he'd been watching this play out over a couple of months and both were wrong. The boys listened as Mr. Jones gave them a life lesson about dealing with their emotions. Both felt bad when he said, "The two smartest young men in my school are fighting like common thugs." He told Ronnie, "You won the spelling bee and the prize money." Then he told Carl, "We have been trying to skip you." He looked at both boys and told them, "If the two smartest young men in my school are acting like this, how can I expect better from the other young men?"

Mr. Jones told them behavior has consequences and they were not exempt from the rules.

He laid out the discipline options for them: they could take a paddling with three licks or they would be suspended for three days. Mr. Jones complicated the situation by saying they had to agree on the punishment, and he stepped out the room. This forced them to work together and talk over what they wanted to do. Carl and Ronnie quickly agreed they would take the paddling; neither wanted to be sent home to face the wrath of their parents for fighting at school. They stepped out of Mr. Jones's office to tell him they had made their decision.

Mr. Jones walked back in the office and picked up his paddle. He asked his secretary to come in the office to witness, saying, "Before I paddle the two of you, I'm going to tell you something." He then told Carl, "You wanted to take another girl to the sock hop but found out she was related to you. Although you went alone, you had a good time dancing with the girls." Mr. Jones took a serious tone when he told Carl, "You crushed Ronnie's feelings when you took Jackie back." He admonished Carl to be careful in life when he did this because emotions are a powerful thing.

Mr. Jones told Ronnie, "You lost this one. Jackie made a choice, and she chose Carl." He went on to tell him, "Jackie might be the first girl you lost, but she will not be the last." He then gave each of the boys three licks and sent them to class.

Carl and Ronnie made up on the way to class. They both realized what Mr. Jones said was true.

Later, when they walked home from school, Carl told Jackie he and Ronnie got three licks for their fight. She smiled to herself; it was really flattering they were fighting about her. She decided to trip with Carl, saying, "Why you and Ronnie fighting about me? It's not like I'm your girl."

He thought, *Here we go again,* as he processed what she said.

Jackie taunted him, saying, "My sister's boyfriend said she was his girl, and he gave her a ring."

Carl looked at Jackie, saying, "What does that have to do with me? That's your sister's boyfriend!"

Jackie was pissed off and walked faster, getting ahead of Carl and Hannah. He was laughing now as he said, "You forgot your books!" She turned around and snatched her books from Carl, then started to run home. He ran up to her and blocked her path, saying he was sorry, that he didn't mean to make her mad. He held her and asked why she got so mad at him.

After a few minutes of jockeying back and forth, Jackie started to smile, and her anger subsided. She hated this; she could never stay mad at him!

Hannah watched, thinking her brother might be dumb about girls but sure knew how to work Jackie.

Jackie handed her books back to Carl, and they walked to Mrs. Lee's house to get Carol. A few minutes later, they were on their way to Jackie's house. He was shocked when Jackie got home and hugged him, holding him tight.

But when they got home, they were shocked to see Bradley on the porch, waiting for them.

CHAPTER 4

Bradley Stops through Texas
#BrightLightsBigCity

Carol started to cry; she didn't know the strange man sitting on their porch. Hannah and Carl tried to explain this was their dad, but Carol kept crying. She really did not know who Bradley was. They were glad to see him and hugged him, except for Carol, who was still crying. He asked if they wanted to go for ice cream, and they said yes. They knew it was not going to happen when Carol stood on the porch, shaking her head no. Bradley accepted Carol did not know who he was, and asked the kids about their day.

Hannah said she had a great day and things went very well. Carl said things were good but he had had a fight and gotten a bloody nose. He laughed as he said he did not know how he would explain the blood on his shirt to Rachel. Hannah asked Bradley if he knew Carl had a girlfriend. Bradley said he did not and asked her name. She said her name was Jackie and she lived around the corner. Bradley laughed and asked Carl how long Jackie had been his girl. Hannah butted in, saying Jackie got mad today because she wanted Carl to get her a ring. Bradley said he didn't think a ring was appropriate at their age but a charm bracelet was cool.

Rachel walked in the house and saw Bradley, the look on her face saying she was not pleased. He explained Hannah and Carl had allowed him to come in, and she rolled her eyes at them. Carol stopped crying when she saw Rachel, but she did not warm up to Bradley. Carl sensed something was wrong—Rachel did not act like she was happy to see Bradley. He told Rachel he wanted to take the kids to get ice cream and she was welcome to go. She glared at him, saying, "Sure, let's go get some ice cream." Rachel did not like the fact Bradley was riding in and making it seem he was father of the year.

While they were out, Bradley stopped at the hamburger stand and got burgers for everybody. The kids were happy, but Rachel still glared at Bradley. She was still angry at him, finding out he fathered a son in Fort Worth while he was stationed at Carswell AFB. She had a reason to be pissed: Carol was born in May, and Aaron was born the following January. It was obvious he had two women pregnant at the same time.

While they were eating, Rachel saw the blood on Carl's shirt and asked how it got there. She was shocked when he said he and Ronnie Simmons were fighting. Rachel asked why he was fighting with Ronnie, and Carl said he pushed him. She turned to Hannah, asking if she saw the fight, and she said no but she heard about it. Rachel knew they were fighting about Jackie, but since he would not fess up, she let it go. She asked if he was suspended for the fight, and he said they took three licks. Rachel mumbled, "Just like his damn daddy," under her voice. Bradley said he heard that, and she glared at him again. Bradley said Carl wanted to buy her a charm bracelet and they might do that the following day.

The next day, they all rode to Marshall in Bradley's car. He wanted to take Carl to buy a charm bracelet for Jackie. They dropped Rachel, Hannah, and Carol at Riley's house while they went downtown. Hannah could not hold it and ran to the phone to call Jackie. When she answered, Hannah spilled the beans, saying Carl was buying her a charm bracelet. Jackie squealed loudly on the phone when Hannah said Carl was buying her a charm bracelet. Hannah admonished her, "You have to act surprised when he gives it to you." Jackie promised she would act surprised and thanked Hannah for telling her.

Carl picked out a charm bracelet for Jackie, and Bradley paid for it, saying he should have it engraved with her first-name and last-name initial. He was surprised to find her last name started with *H*, the same as theirs.

An hour later, they came back and picked up Jackie's bracelet. Rachel was livid when they came back, and she realized he had been drinking. They argued, and Bradley stormed out, saying he was going to his mother's house. Rachel and Hannah looked at the charm bracelet, saying it was beautiful and he did a great job picking it out.

The following Monday, as they walked home from school, Carl gave Jackie the box with the charm bracelet. She opened the box and screamed when she saw the charm bracelet. Carl said he didn't buy her a ring; he bought her a charm bracelet instead. She saw it was beautiful and kissed him on the mouth. Jackie tried it on, and it fit perfectly. She was giddy when she looked at Carl, saying, "I'm never going to give this back to you."

Carl smiled as he said, "You're my girl. I don't want it back."

A week went by. School got out, and Bradley left for Detroit to find work.

Before he left, Bradley told Carl, when he found a job and got situated, he would send for them and they would live in Detroit with him.

Later that day, Riley showed up to take the family to Marshall for summer vacation. The days were hot and dry as Carl shadowed Riley while they sold vegetables on the street and worked in the garden. He was tired at the end of each day from all the work but took the time to read Jackie's letter and write one to her. He drifted off to sleep every night thinking how happy he was to be shadowing Riley each day.

Carl could not believe it, but after a few days of summer vacation, he started to miss Jackie. Before he knew it, however, summer vacation was almost over and they were in the store, shopping for school clothes. He and Riley made good money and Carl was able to pay for some of his school clothes. Riley told Carl he'd done a good job and bought him a blue jean suit with a pair of tennis shoes as a bonus. Riley reminded Carl he did this as a bonus because he had a great work ethic. Carl was happy and ready to start fifth grade when Riley dropped them off in Jefferson for the school year.

Shortly after they arrived in Jefferson, Jackie was sitting on the porch, waiting for them to come outside. The reunion was emotional. Hannah and Carl hugged Jackie; they were glad to see one another after almost three months. Rachel watched out the window and thought, *They* really *like each other.* Without thinking, Carl kissed Jackie on the mouth, and she kissed him back. They were hugged up when Rachel stepped on the porch and cleared her throat. They listened as Rachel told them she knew they were happy to see each other but they needed to behave.

Carl didn't know what he was feeling, but it felt good to hold Jackie and kiss her like that.

School started the next Monday, and Carol went with them. She was starting first grade. At lunch, Carl and Jackie sat together, talking about their summer vacation. Ronnie Simmons got his food tray and joined them, which irritated Carl, but he remembered what Mr. Jones said at the end of the year. Carl decided to try a different strategy and told Ronnie he was going to marry Jackie when they grew up. Ronnie was not deterred and told him, "Jackie has not said anything about that."

Jackie took the hint and told Ronnie she liked Carl and they were "mos def" going to get married when they grew up. She held out her arm for Ronnie to see the charm bracelet, asking if he liked it. Ronnie looked at her and laughed, remaining at the table with them and eating his food. He sarcastically said, "Am I supposed to be impressed he bought you a charm bracelet?" A few seconds later, Jackie and Carl got up, leaving Ronnie sitting at the table. They went out on the playground and kept talking about their summer vacation.

Ronnie was mad at Jackie and Carl because they'd left him sitting alone. Carl told Jackie he and Riley had talked about her over the summer, mentioning Riley had asked if he liked her, and he said he did.

Carl's fifth-grade year flew by, and he learned he could not beat Jackie in baseball—she was a natural. He soon realized Jackie was as fast as him; he could barely outrun her. Carl accepted the fact Jackie was a gifted athlete! This gave them peace from Ronnie, who was one of the smartest kids at Central but was not athletic as they were.

Carl and Jackie were increasingly popular with the kids at Central. They were smart and great athletes. The kids started to put pressure on Ronnie to leave Carl and Jackie alone. Ronnie got the message and reluctantly allowed them space to bond.

Meanwhile, Bradley rolled into Detroit ready to start a new life in the city. His older brother had given him the address at his house and directions on how to get there. After twenty hours of driving, Bradley was in Southwest Detroit, standing on the front porch of his brother Leonard's home. Before he could knock, his nephew Tony opened the door and welcomed him to the city. Tony was seventeen, and Bradley was more like a brother than an uncle to him. They got Bradley's bags in the house, and his sister-in-law, Sharon, prepared some food for him to eat.

An hour later, Bradley was sound asleep in the basement of his brother and sister-in-law's home. Leonard got home from work, and Sharon told him Bradley was in the basement, asleep. Leonard knew it had been a long and tiring trip, so he let Bradley sleep. There would be time to talk.

Bradley woke up the next morning, and Sharon had breakfast waiting for him. She passed along the message that Leonard wanted him to go to the Ford stamping plant and apply for a job. Bradley drove out to the Ford stamping plant in River Rouge, hoping to get an application and start work with his older brother.

He got the application, completed the union paperwork, and went home. After he had waited two weeks, there was no word from Ford on his application, so Bradley widened his search and went to the GM Fisher Body Fleetwood plant. When the hiring supervisor realized Bradley had his UAW card, he hired him on the spot! He was assigned to the swing shift and told to report the next day at 2:00 p.m. Bradley went home and shared the news with Sharon and Tony. Bradley had been in Detroit two weeks and was going to be working for GM!

He was excited and called Rachel to tell her the good news. But they got into an argument when Rachel asked when he planned to send for his family. He said he'd just started working and needed time to get everything set up for them. Rachel hung up the phone on him. She'd been listening to his excuses for more than ten years and was not in the mood to hear any excuses or explanations that day.

That evening at dinner, Bradley shared the good news with everyone. Leonard wanted him to work for Ford, but since GM had hired him, he was glad he took the job.

Patricia, Leonard, and Sharon's daughter came by the house that evening and said she would help him find a place to stay. Patricia was married and lived with her in-laws around the corner from her parents' home.

Things started to unwind for Rachel financially. Since Bradley left the Air Force, there were no monthly allowance checks. Since the kids were getting older, she needed a car to get from place to place. Rachel did not tell the kids what was on her mind, but she'd made the decision she was going to move back with Riley and Janice. She needed a car.

Money was tight, and Rachel knew she could not afford a car and keep the rent house where they lived. She became angry when she realized she would not be able to depend on Bradley to financially support the family.

A month after starting work at GM, Bradley was able to get his own place. He rented one side of a two-family flat on the east side of Detroit, spent his days at Fisher Body Fleetwood, and spent his nights living it up. After several months without any contact, Rachel realized her marriage was on the rocks. She and Bradley had been down this road, and she was tired of the drama.

During Thanksgiving break, Rachel and the kids celebrated with Riley and Janice in Marshall. She told Janice what was going on with Bradley and said she'd probably need to move back in with them. Janice let her know it was fine with her for them to move back to Marshall. Things between Rachel and Bradley got rocky when he didn't send any money to help with Christmas gifts. After Christmas break, Carl and Hannah were excited to start the new semester. With Christmas over, everyone's attention turned to the spring dance at Central.

There was no misunderstanding this time: Jackie was going to the dance with Carl. In an ironic twist of fate, Ronnie left Jackie alone, resigning himself to the fact Carl won that battle for her attention. This year, there were no chauffeured rides, no evening gowns or root beer floats. Carl and Jackie were not part of a court, so they wore nice clothes and walked to the dance. Hannah was with them this year and had promised to meet a guy at the spring dance. They had a great time, and once again, they had a dance-off, showing each other how to do the latest dances. They were a hit with the older students—they were great dancers at such a young age.

They were becoming celebrities at Central, young people who could dance, were great athletes, and were borderline genius. The fact they were both very good-looking did not hurt their popularity. Hannah was at the dance and had a great time dancing, though she didn't have an escort this year. After the dance, Hannah and Carl walked Jackie home before they went home. One thing not lost on the people was the chemistry between Carl and Jackie, how they "bounced" off each other. Nobody was surprised to learn Carl had given her the charm bracelet she wore.

The elementary students had an "everybody dance" rule, and each boy there had pulled the name of a girl he had to ask to dance. Jackie wondered who pulled her name, and Carl pulled Michelle Burns. The DJ announced the first "everybody dance" record was "Keep on Truckin'." He could not believe when Ronnie Simmons came to their table—he had pulled Jackie's name! He thought about running up on Ronnie; he felt he had pulled strings to get Jackie's name. She smiled and took Ronnie's hand when he held it out, and they went to the dance floor.

Carl had to ask Hannah which girl was Michelle Burns, and she gritted her teeth. She could not stand Michelle Burns, and her brother had pulled her name for the "everybody dance" records. Hannah pointed her out for Carl, saying she could not stand Michelle. He walked over to her and asked if she was Michelle. She smiled and said she was, not quite believing one of the most popular boys at school was asking her to dance. He held out his hand, and she smiled, took his hand, and followed him to the dance floor. She knew who Carl was; she had seen him at school.

Michelle also knew Jackie Hunt was his girlfriend—she had seen them together. She loved to dance and loved the song "Keep on Trucking." The song ended, and he went back to his table. The DJ announced the second "everybody dance" song, "Chain of Fools," and everybody went to the dance floor. He watched Ronnie Simmons dance with Jackie while he danced with Michelle. Carl had to put it out of his mind about Ronnie dancing with Jackie, realizing he was going to be in the shadows. They walked home talking about the good time they had at the dance.

Over the next couple of weeks, information about Michelle seemed to come to him. He learned she was borderline genius and his sister, Hannah, could not stand her. What shocked him was finding out Jackie was not that fond of her either.

The semester ended, and the family went to Marshall for the summer. As they rode to Marshall from Jefferson, Carl had no idea his life was about to be turned upside down for the first time. He spent the first month of the summer selling fruits and vegetables with Riley. They worked extremely hard this summer, often selling two truckloads of watermelons every day!

At the end of June, Carl was confused when Riley had him clean the hay out the bed of the truck, then sweep the truck bed clean. When he finished cleaning the bed of the truck, Rachel called him, Hannah, and Carol to her. They listened as Rachel explained she and Bradley were getting a divorce. After Riley explained what this meant, Carl asked if that meant they were not going to be a family. He said they were still a family; it just meant Rachel and Bradley were not going to be married any longer. Rachel couldn't hold her tears and started to cry as she listened to her dad.

The emotional toll of the divorce caused Rachel to be tired and unable to talk about the situation.

The next morning, Riley woke Carl up and they went to Jefferson to start moving the furniture from the house. Riley and Carl were at the house, loading furniture, when Jackie came around the corner. She was shocked to see Carl and Riley; she thought he'd be in Marshall all summer. She told him she'd just read his letter before she walked around the corner, headed to the store. When she saw them loading furniture, she asked what was going on.

Carl told her they were moving back to Marshall because his mom and dad were getting a divorce. Jackie did not know what *divorce* meant, and Carl explained his mother and father would no longer be married. Carl started to cry when Jackie asked if that meant they would no longer be friends. His emotions had gotten the best of him, and he could not stand to talk about it with Jackie. She thought about Hannah and how they would not get to talk and be friends any longer. Jackie walked off as she started to cry, saddened that her two best friends would no longer be living in Jefferson.

Riley stood on the porch, watching as Jackie walked away and Carl stood by the truck. A few minutes passed and Riley called Carl in the house to continue loading the furniture. They loaded the truck and headed back to Marshall as Riley explained things would happen in life that were out of his control. As much as he wanted to, Riley knew he would not be able to shield Carl and Hannah from the pain of Rachel and Bradley's divorce. He was not so concerned about Carol—she was young enough that the memories of this pain would fade with time.

Riley knew Carl and Hannah would carry this pain the rest of their lives. He and Carl made it to Marshall and unloaded the first load of furniture, then went back to Jefferson for the second load. Riley watched as Jackie walked to the house, then watched in silence as he and Carl loaded the truck. When they finished loading the truck, Riley told Carl to walk Jackie home. He took the truck and met Carl at Jackie's. Riley watched as Carl and Jackie stood on her porch and looked at each other, saying nothing. Riley called out to Carl to let him know they had to go.

It was a classic moment when Carl opened his arms and Jackie walked into them. They hugged, and Riley thought this was true friendship, something you did not find often in this world. Jackie asked if he wanted his bracelet back, and he said no. Carl flipped it back on her, saying, "I thought you were never going to give it back?" She walked over to him and hugged him again. She cried on his shoulder, saying she would give it back when she was not his girl any longer. As Carl walked off the porch, he looked back and told Jackie that he and Hannah would be back to talk to her some more.

When Carl got in the truck, Riley told him he should be happy to know Jackie. She was a true friend. They made the ride home in silence. He did not know what to say to his young grandson. He thought how his life was being turned upside down by factors out of his control.

Bradley had been in Detroit almost six months and was financially stable. The GM checks allowed him to have his own place and a cool car. He started to meet people, and he'd developed intimate relationships with several women. The city, the GM money, and the lure of the lights were too much for him to resist.

Late July rolled around, and Fisher Body Fleetwood had the annual shutdown to retool the plant for the new model year. Bradley decided to take this time and drive to Texas to visit his family. Riley was sitting on the porch when the blue Oldsmobile pulled in the yard and parked. He wondered who was in the car when Bradley opened the door to get out. After a few moments of pleasantries, Bradley went in the house, where Rachel, Janice, and the kids were. Carl and Hannah ran to give him a hug, but Carol clung to Rachel's leg. This made Bradley angry; he felt Carol should have been happy to see him.

He saw Carol was not going, so he took Carl and Hannah to the store to buy ice cream and snacks. They loaded up on snacks, and Hannah made sure there was enough for Carol. They took the ice cream and snacks back to the house, then rode with Bradley as he visited some of his friends. Bradley was shocked when one of his friends accused him of renting the new Oldsmobile to drive to Marshall and impress his friends. The more he talked to his friends, the angrier he became. They could not believe he made the kind of money he claimed he did.

His friends felt Bradley was bragging and rubbing his success in their faces. The ridicule by his friends and the free flow of alcohol between them led to a shoving match between Bradley and one of his friends. The guys broke them up, and Bradley had a bloody nose.

Bradley wiped his nose and called out for Carl and Hannah to come get in the car. They reluctantly left the yard and walked to Bradley's car, noticing he was trying to stop his nose from bleeding. Bradley loaded Carl and Hannah in the car and drove off hurriedly from his friend's house.

Bradley had just learned some people he grew up with were not happy he was doing good or doing better than them. As he drove to Riley's house, he told Carl and Hannah he thought his friends would be happy he was trying to do good in life. Carl listened as Bradley ranted about how people you had known a very long time could be jealous of you and hateful toward you. He stopped the car, saying what hurt him most was the fact he didn't know his friends felt this way about him. He was shocked to learn they felt he had an advantage because he was an outstanding football player in high school.

He pulled in the driveway at Riley's and sat in the car, thinking about what just went down. Hannah and Carl jumped out of the car and ran into the house, saying they'd been over to Alice and Brenda's house. Rachel listened as they said Bradley had been fighting with John Jones. This was a short but welcome relief from all the tension in the air, and Rachel started to laugh. She had a picture in her mind of Bradley and John Jones drunk as they threw punches at each other. She was sure she'd hear about it later, because she was good friends with John's wife, Estelle.

A few minutes later, Bradley came in the house complaining how John and the other guys had been disrespectful to him. Rachel asked Bradley to consider if speaking of his good fortune might sound like bragging. He was upset with Rachel, saying she never supported him. Rachel's observation morphed into a verbal altercation between them, and he slammed the door as he walked out. He got in his car and drove the two blocks to his mother's house. Bradley pulled up in his mother's yard, and she came out of the house, hugging him when he got out of the car.

Bradley was her youngest son, and she was happy to see him. They walked up the trail to Bertha's and Beulah's houses. They had a mini family reunion and celebration as Alberta, Bertha, Beulah, and their kids were happy to see Bradley. They prepared food, and Bradley answered the kids' questions about Detroit and working for General Motors. The celebration lasted into the wee hours of the night; it was clearly a festive mood with Bradley's mother, sisters, nephews, and nieces. This was not the case a few hundred yards down the street, however; the mood was anything but festive.

The next day, Bradley and Rachel made it official: they were breaking up and getting a divorce. Rachel went in the house, sat on the couch, and started to cry. Carl and Hannah sat beside her, watching their mother cry. They had no idea of the hurt Rachel felt and were sad because their mother was crying. Carl was confused. When he went down the street to visit his grandmother, aunts, and cousins, the mood was festive. He mentally compared that to the mood at his house, which was gloomy and somber. He realized Bradley's mother, sisters, and cousins were not seeing the same picture he saw.

CHAPTER 5

Carl Develops a Cool Demeanor
#NeverLetEmSeeYaSweat

Carl decided he would not go to his relatives down the street for a while. It was depressing to see them celebrate while everyone was so sad at his house.

A few days later, Bradley stopped by the house to tell them goodbye as he got ready for the drive back to Detroit. The following weekend, Riley and Carl went back to Jefferson to finish the task of cleaning out Rachel's rent house. Jackie stood quietly and watched as they loaded the truck. Carl wrote his address at Riley's on a piece of paper and handed it to Jackie.

She took a piece of paper out of her pocket and handed it to Carl. It had her address and phone number on it. Carl walked Jackie home, and they agreed to answer each other's letter the same day they got it. Jackie stood on her porch, watching as Carl and Riley got on Broadway and drove toward US 59 and Marshall. For some reason, when they crossed the railroad tracks, Carl remembered the shooting that happened there a few years earlier. They made it back to Marshall and unloaded Rachel's furniture. They used the best furniture for Riley and Janice's house and sold the rest.

A couple of days later, when Rachel woke up, she seemed to be in a better mood. She told the kids to get in the truck—they were going to get a car. Since she didn't live in Jefferson any longer, she needed a car to drive to work. They stopped at the Ford dealership, and Rachel bought a Galaxy 500, white, with a black vinyl top. There was a small problem, though: Rachel did not know how to drive a car. It was ten days from the day Riley drove the car off the lot until Rachel had to be at work. Riley wasn't sure he could teach her to drive in that short period.

Riley didn't get it done, and when school started, he rode with Rachel as she drove to Jefferson in the morning, then drove the car back to Marshall. In the evening, he drove to Jefferson and Rachel drove back to Marshall. A couple of weeks later, Rachel had the confidence to drive herself to and from Jefferson each day. Carl, Hannah, and Jackie kept their word, answering each other's letters as soon as they received them. It was a thrill for each of them, going to the mailbox to see if they had mail. School started, and Rachel enrolled Carl, Hannah, and Carol at J. H. Moore in Marshall.

Carl fell right into the groove at J. H. Moore. He knew some of the people because he'd started school as a first grader there. Hannah and Carol didn't have a problem adjusting at J. H. Moore either; they knew kids from the neighborhood who went to school there. Hannah and Carl were excited when Rachel came home with the news she was assigned to work the concession stand at Central's home football games. This would give them a chance to see Jackie while the game was going on. Carl and Hannah wrote Jackie a special letter, telling her they would be at Central's home games.

Jackie was sad when school started. Her best friends were not walking to school with her, and she could not compete against Carl. Ronnie Simmons was beside himself with glee when he was told Carl was not going to school in Jefferson. He immediately started to push up on Jackie, telling her Carl was now in Marshall and not thinking about her. So she showed Ronnie every letter she got from Carl, letting him know Carl had not forgotten about her or Jefferson. Ronnie was not deterred, however, delighted his long-standing rival was in school fifteen miles down the road in Marshall.

Mr. Jones told Ronnie he should not be so happy Carl was not in Jefferson anymore; this might not go the way he thought. This time, Ronnie did not listen to Mr. Jones. Instead, he kept pushing up on Jackie.

The second week of school, Central hosted their first home game, and Rachel had concession stand duty. Hannah and Carl were excited as they rode from Marshall to Jefferson for the game. They arrived at the stadium, and excitement was in the air. The stadium lights lit up the near-dark night as the Central High Lions prepared to play their archrival, the Daingerfield Tigers.

Riley had prepared Hannah and Carl for the return, telling them to spend most of their time with Jackie. He pulled Carl to the side and told him to not get lost in the excitement of seeing his old friends and focus his attention on Jackie. This advice was valuable, for Carl and Hannah were treated like rock stars by the kids when they saw them at the game. Carl thought about what Riley had said, reminding him who was at the truck, crying, when she found out they were moving. Carl and Hannah hugged Jackie when they found her just inside the stadium gate.

They were happy to see one another and watched the game together. This was too much for Ronnie, and he called Carl out. Ronnie told Carl he had the nerve, that he was not one of them for he lived in Marshall now. The kids stood back, expecting a fight when Carl walked up on Ronnie. To their surprise, Carl held out his hand to shake Ronnie's, then told him he was right—he did live in Marshall now. Carl then told Ronnie he was wrong because he'd *always* be a Central Lion, whether he lived in Jefferson or not.

This was not the outcome Ronnie expected when Carl walked up to him. Ronnie Simmons had squared up for a fight when Carl just wanted to shake hands.

He and Carl shook hands, and the crowd pushed back up against them. Ronnie did not know Carl had made payment number 1 on his reputation of being cool and smooth, at his expense. All the kids wanted to know why Ronnie was pushing up on Jackie and why he wanted to fight a guy as cool as Carl. The way Carl always seemed to get the best of him pissed Ronnie off in a serious way. It was a hot September evening, and Carl suggested they go to the stands to sit down, cool off, and watch the game.

With Hannah and Jackie in tow, he walked up the stairs to the stands and found a seat high in the bleachers. They were seated next to the press box, and Mr. Jones thought, *Ronnie Simmons is hard-headed and determined.* Carl was eleven years old, but it was obvious he was developing a cool demeanor. Looking at Ronnie, Mr. Jones saw he was still rough around the edges and a serious work in progress.

They cheered as the game progressed, and Jackie cuddled with Carl. The smell of fried food filled the air as Hannah and Jackie talked about girl things.

Carl was seriously watching the game, cheering when the Lions did good and cringing when they messed up.

When the game ended, Jackie asked her parents if she could ride home with Carl and Hannah. Her parents agreed, and Rachel asked Mr. and Mrs. Hunt if they could stop for a root beer float. The café was crowded, with the smell of fish permeating the air, when Rachel, Hannah, Jackie, and Carl walked in the joint. Rachel ordered root beer floats and watched as they sat and talked. She wondered how the divorce between her and Bradley would affect the lives of her young children.

The atmosphere in the café was festive—it was a big deal Central beat the Daingerfield Tigers! Carl and Jackie wooed the crowd, swinging out and showing off their dancing skills. After an hour at the café, Rachel said it was time to go. She drove the short distance to Jackie's house, then waited ten minutes while they stood at the door and talked. She marveled at how Carl and Jackie could be sweet on each other and still be friends. It got hot sitting in the car, and Rachel called them to come on, they needed to hit the road to Marshall.

Half an hour later, they were at home in Marshall. They wrote Jackie a letter, and Hannah gave hers to Riley. Carl held on to his, knowing he'd be going to the post office with Riley.

In the meantime, Bradley was back in Detroit, partying and hanging out when he wasn't working. The weather was turning cold, and there was snow on the ground. This was a fascinating time for Bradley. He was meeting lots of people, and everything was new. The differences between the Southern USA and the Midwest were stark: people talked differently, danced differently, and cooked differently.

Winter gave way to summer, and Bradley was entering his second year with Fisher Body Fleetwood. It was late July, and he'd just finished his shift at the plant. As he drove down Fort Street, headed to his place, he heard the radio announcer say Mack Avenue was blocked off. He didn't know why Mack Avenue was blocked off and tried to think of a different way to get home. He was tired, and the DJ made the announcement there was a riot going on and parts of the city were engulfed in flames. The DJ then listed the parts of the city that were off-limits.

Bradley was shocked to find the area where he lived was off-limits. The DJ announced the National Guard had been called out and it was best if everyone stayed home until order was restored. Bradley could not believe his place off Mack Avenue had been placed off-limits. He turned his car around in the middle of Fort Street and went to Leonard's house in Southwest Detroit. From the comfort and safety of his brother's living room, Bradley watched the riot on TV. He'd been in the city coming up on two years, and it was now on fire, with people in the streets.

He didn't go out the house for a couple of days; the order had been given that people should stay home. His brother, Leonard, also told him it was not safe to go outside at this point.

A week later, Bradley went to his place, and it was no surprise it had been broken into and robbed. Bradley beat his fists on the wall as he thought he had to replace everything that had been stolen. Things in the city settled into a new normal, and Bradley replaced everything that had been stolen. He started to look for a house, realizing the riots had made a lot of people feel less than safe.

Real estate agents in the city engaged in blockbusting, convincing property owners to sell for lower-than-normal prices. They did this by promoting fear that people they deemed as less than desirable would be moving into the neighborhood. The weeklong riots did not help people feel any safer in the city. After all, who expects your city to go up in smoke? This worked in Bradley's favor. He was able to buy a nice home in a great neighborhood for less than it would have normally cost. Bradley realized he might be in Detroit, but a lot of the problems he faced in East Texas were present in Detroit. He realized there was not a place you could go that did not have problems or issues.

He settled back into his routine, going to work, partying, and going to sleep. While hanging at a house party, he met a lady he wanted to know better. They traded numbers, and he promised to give her a call.

Miles away, Rachel sat in the front bedroom of her parents' home and went through the mail, taking a deep breath when she saw the letter from her attorney. She opened the letter and found the proclamation her marriage to Bradley had been ended by divorce.

Small tears welled up in her eyes, and they turned to a full-blown cry. Janice came in the room and sat with Rachel as she cried, trying to console her. Carl and Hannah came in the house, saw Rachel crying, and were saddened by her demeanor. They asked what was wrong, and she didn't tell them she and Bradley had finalized their divorce. Carl and Hannah stood by as she cried, sad because they could do nothing to stop her tears from falling. Rachel told Carl she was sad and crying because she had problems he wouldn't understand.

When the school calendar was released, they noticed they had a sock hop! Carl knew he needed a date, so he wrote Jackie a letter, hoping she'd be able to come to Marshall. He was saddened when he got her letter and found out she would not be coming to Marshall. When he read her letter, he realized Central was having their sock hop the same day as J. H. Moore. He asked Rachel about going to the Central sock hop, and she said he needed to go to the J. H. Moore sock hop. Carl realized there was nothing to keep Ronnie Simmons away from Jackie and managed to put this out of his mind.

Carl was getting close to Kendall Lewis, a girl in sixth grade with him. She wasn't a jock, but she was smart and challenged him on his classwork. Kendall kept his mind rolling, asking questions that caused him to think deeply. She was mature, and he found out her mother died a couple of years ago. He and Hannah walked to school as Carol tagged along behind them. As they walked home one afternoon, Hannah let her feelings be known, saying she did not like Kendall. It was smoking hot, and Carl thought how he really did not want to hear this, but he listened as Hannah talked to him.

Hannah felt Kendall was replacing Jackie, and she did not like it. Carl explained Kendall was his friend and they had a vibe. Hannah was not buying it and asked if he'd told Jackie about Kendall, since they were just friends. He admitted he hadn't told Jackie about her, and Hannah asked how he'd feel if Ronnie Simmons was up in Jackie's face. "Ronnie *is* always up in Jackie's face!" he screamed at Hannah. Carl walked faster, trying to get in front of Hannah and her relentless badgering. He was relieved when one of the boys in school, George Jones, caught up to them and started to spark Hannah.

Hannah was not trying to hear what George was saying, but it gave Carl peace while they walked home.

The following Saturday, Carl was helping Rachel clean the front room when the phone rang. Rachel answered, and he was shocked when she said it was for him. He answered, and it was Kendall asking when he planned to ask her to go to the sock hop. She said another boy asked but she said she already had a date. Carl took the hint, saying he planned to ask the next week. Kendall said he first needed to ask her sister if she could go to the sock hop with him.

He was a little shocked when Kendall said he should come to her house and ask her sister that day. He hung up the phone and asked Rachel if he could go to Kendall's house. Rachel knew Kendall's sister and listened as Carl said he needed to ask if he could take her to the sock hop. Rachel told him to see if Riley was able to take him to Kendall's house and called Kendall's sister while he was asking Riley for a ride. She and Kendall's sister, Lillian, worked out a plan for Carl to take Kendall to the sock hop. They knew each other very well; they went from first grade through high school together.

Lillian's mother had died unexpectedly, leaving Kendall and her younger sister in need of a place to stay. She had taken them in and was their guardian.

Rachel and Lillian finished talking as Carl sat on the porch, trying to convince Riley to take him to Kendall's house. The heat had never bothered him, but that day it was almost unbearable! After he laid out his plan to take Kendall to the sock hop, Riley asked about Jackie. He explained Jackie could not come to Marshall and Rachel had said he couldn't go to Jefferson.

Riley agreed to take Carl to Kendall's house, and Carl went in the house to tell Rachel where he was headed. It was smoking hot as they drove to Kendall's house, and Riley explained that he needed to "sit on the couch" for a few minutes *before* he asked to take Kendall to the sock hop. That seemed strange, but he listened; Riley seemed to always be right about stuff like this. Riley said he'd drop him off then come back for him in an hour or so. They pulled up in front of Kendall's house, and Riley watched as Carl walked up on the porch and disappeared inside the house.

Lillian opened the door for Carl and showed him to the couch to take a seat. He thought about what Riley said and took a seat. Kendall's sister introduced herself as Lillian Allen and asked Carl who his folks were. He proceeded to tell her that his mother's name was Rachel Hampton. Lillian smiled and said she knew his mother. Lillian asked if Bradley was his father, and Carl said he was his father. Lillian said she knew his folks and called Kendall into the room. Kendall stood by her side when she asked Carl why he wanted to take her to the sock hop.

Carl thought a few moments, then said, "I like her and want to dance with her."

Kendall smiled when she heard Carl say he liked her, and Lillian thought, *This boy is smooth.* Carl did not know that statement made payment number 2 on his cool-and-smooth reputation. Lillian left the room, leaving them sitting on the couch. Carl forgot about Jackie as he and Kendall sat on the couch, talking.

Meanwhile, Rachel was at home, thinking how her only son was maturing. She was startled by the phone ringing and answered it.

Lillian was on the other end, and Rachel thought, *My goodness, what did he do?* She was mildly surprised when Lillian gushed about Carl's good manners and how she'd love for him to take Kendall to the sock hop. She was caught off guard when Lillian said Carl was a handsome young man. At that moment, Rachel knew she had a problem and had to get out in front of it. Carl was growing up and becoming a lot like Bradley, good-looking and smooth-talking. The girls his age were swooning and falling all over him, and the older women talked about how much he was like Bradley.

Rachel knew what this meant—her hands had been full trying to keep women out of Bradley's face. She knew it did not help that he sat on the porch with Riley, listening as the older men talked about anything and everything. Rachel decided she needed to talk to Carl about the facts of life and tell him how babies were born. Carl fidgeted on the couch with Kendall, trying to find a way to ask her to go to the sock hop with him. Riley had told him he had to ask twice to take Kendall to the sock hop; he needed to ask Kendall, and if she said yes, he needed to ask her sister.

He pushed his nervousness aside and asked Kendall if she'd go to the sock hop with him. Without missing a beat, Kendall asked if she was going as a friend or his girlfriend. He was caught off guard, and Kendall said, "I'm *not* going to the sock hop as your friend!" He recovered and said she would go as his girlfriend. Carl looked at Kendall and asked if she'd go to the sock hop with him. To his utter surprise, Kendall said no! Carl was shaken and really did not know what to say. Neither of them said anything, and there was a long and awkward silence.

Carl remembered something Rachel said: If you ask a girl to go out with you, she wants to be your girl." She had told him more than once that it was a different situation with Jackie—they had a natural vibe. He coughed to clear his throat and asked Kendall, "Will you be my girl?" She smiled and told him she would love to be his girl. Kendall leaned into him, and they kissed. The next step was automatic: he asked if she'd go to the sock hop with him, and she quickly agreed.

Lillian stood by the door, observing everything going on between them. She was amazed Carl was so smooth at his age and knew he was going to be a handful when he got older and experienced more of life. She smiled as she thought, *He's going to be just like his dad.* Carl and Kendall heard the horn on Riley's truck and knew he'd come to pick him up. Kendall reminded him that he needed to ask her sister's permission to take her to the sock hop. Kendall got off the couch and went to the other room to get her sister. Lillian walked in the living room, and Carl asked if Kendall could go to the sock hop with him. She looked him in the eyes and asked if Kendall was his girl.

Carl said Kendall was his girl and he'd like for her to go to the sock hop with him. Lillian asked if he'd asked Kendall, and what she said. Carl said he did ask Kendall and she agreed. Lillian gave her permission for Kendall to attend the sock hop with him. He extended his hand to shake hers, and she shook his hand, he then excused himself to go home. The heat was smoking hot as Carl climbed in the truck with Riley, but he didn't notice. He'd gone to Kendall's house to ask if she could attend the sock hop with him and left with a girlfriend!

This was not the outcome he'd envisioned when he left home. He told Riley what went on, and Riley laughed, thinking to himself how Carl was learning to navigate life with the opposite sex. Carl told Riley he didn't know what was happening; it was not this complicated with Jackie. At that moment, he realized the error of his ways—what was he going to do about Jackie?

Riley was several steps ahead of Carl and asked about the girl in Jefferson. Carl admitted he had a problem with no idea how to solve it.

As Carl and Riley drove off, Lillian told Kendall she'd better guard her feelings. Lillian said, "He is a good boy, but he was popular, and that might be a problem."

Kendall was not listening, however, watching as Riley's truck disappeared down the street.

Lillian went back in the house and called Rachel to let her know Kendall had agreed to attend the sock hop with Carl. They worked out the details, and when Rachel hung up with Lillian, she decided she needed to speak with Carl about the facts of life. When Riley drove up in the driveway and parked, she called Carl in the house. He knew something was up—Rachel seemed so serious!

She started to talk to him about sex, how babies were born, and the need to use protection during sex. The more Rachel spoke, the more disgusted he became, with a blank stare and disgusted look on his face. He asked Rachel why she was telling him this, and she said this was information he needed to know. Carl reached his breaking point and ran out of the house to sit on the porch.

He told Riley the situation, how he'd asked Kendall to be his girl when Jackie was still his girl. Riley listened and asked how he planned to handle it.

He suggested Carl call Jackie and tell her he was going to take another girl to the sock hop.

He saw the wheels in Carl's mind turn and wondered what solution he was working toward.

He looked at Riley and said he had a solution to the problem. Riley listened as he said he would not tell Jackie about taking Kendall to the sock hop; he didn't think that would end well. Riley started to tell him to think about this but decided to let him suffer the error of his ways. He did tell Carl that was going to be a hard secret to keep from Jackie. Carl asked why it would be so hard. After all, Jackie was in Jefferson, and Kendall was in Marshall.

Carl thought, *They are not acquainted, so everything should be good.*

Riley looked at him and asked if he'd thought about Hannah and how he'd keep her quiet. Riley admonished him, "The moment Hannah is mad at you, she is going to tell Jackie." Carl used one of Riley's statements and said he'd cross that bridge when he got to it.

They sat silently as Carl thought about what Riley said about Hannah getting mad and telling Jackie. He pushed it out of his mind; he had more pressing things going on at that moment. He made up his mind; he was mos def *not* going to tell Jackie about Kendall!

The next Monday, Kendall was waiting when he left the cafeteria. She gave her books to him and they walked down the hallway. J. H. Moore was different from Central, he thought. The classes were a lot bigger!

After school, he and Rachel worked on Kendall's Corsage and the time flew by.

The night of the dance, Carl found out Riley was going to chauffeur them to the dance. He put his suit on, and Riley showed him the proper way to tie a tie. Rachel called Lillian and found out

Kendall was ready to be picked up, and she gave Carl a once-over to make sure he looked okay before he left.

On the way to Kendall's, Riley briefed Carl on how he was supposed to act. They pulled up at Kendall's and Carl got out of the truck, took the corsage, and walked to the door. Lillian opened the door without him knocking and asked why he was there. Carl was bumped off his game but recovered and said he was there to pick up Kendall for the sock hop. Lillian laughed and said she wanted to make sure and invited him in the house. Carl relaxed as he took a seat and waited for Kendall. After what seemed like an hour, Kendall came out of the room.

His mouth dropped open when he saw her—she was stunning in her red skirt-and-blouse ensemble.

He jumped off the couch and held out the corsage for her, and she held her arm out for him to put the corsage on for her. It felt awkward as he nervously put the corsage on her arm. He didn't know what it was; he seemed to be nervous around Kendall.

Lillian came back in the room and told Carl what time she expected him to bring Kendall home. He opened the door for Kendall, and they walked to the truck. He opened the truck door for her, and they made the short drive to J. H. Moore.

Carl was impressed; the cafeteria was decorated in the school colors, and everything looked great.

The J. H. Moore sock hop didn't have a DJ; instead, the kids took turns spinning records. This was cool with Carl. He'd been spinning records at Rachel's several years before they moved back to Marshall. They danced, and Carl showed her new dances he knew. A slow song came on, and he held her close, thinking, *She feels good.* He kissed her neck, and she smiled, saying, "That tickled." He kept her dancing, and Kendall had a very good time.

When the sock hop ended, Riley was waiting outside to pick them up. On the ride home, Riley asked if they had fun, and both said they did.

Carl walked Kendall to the door, and they stood on the porch, looking at each other. He pulled Kendall to him and kissed her. This caught her off guard. He kissed her before she pushed him off her.

Riley sat in the truck, watching, smiling as he cleared his throat. Kendall said he was not supposed to do that, and Carl apologized. Kendall turned to the door, and Lillian opened it for her. She saw the big smile on her face and knew she had a good time. When she asked how it was, Kendall said she had a great time. She told her sister that she really liked Carl.

Meanwhile, Jackie went to the Sock Hop at Central and was in a mellow mood. Carl and Hannah were not there, and that is who she usually danced with. Ronnie Simmons saw her walk in and thought she looked great dressed in a blue skirt ensemble. He was surprised when she danced with him when he asked and watched as she showed him new dance moves. Ronnie was having fun. For the first time, he had Jackie's attention. The DJ played a slow song, and Jackie walked off the floor. She didn't want to slow dance with Ronnie. The Sock Hop ended at midnight, and Ronnie walked her to the car. He held her hand and told her he had fun dancing with her.

He gently pushed Jackie against the car and leaned into her for a kiss. She turned her head, and he kissed her on the cheek. Jackie's older brother was driving the car and shouted for her to come on, he was ready to go. Ronnie was happy, he girl he loved had let him kiss her on the jaw! Carl had a great time at the dance with Kendall and remembered Central had their sock hop the same night. He asked Rachel if he could use the phone to call Jackie, and she promptly told him no. Carl pouted as he walked to the couch, wondering what Jackie did that night. Rachel reminded him it was after 10:00 p.m., too late to call Jackie. He talked to her, and she agreed to let him call the next day, if things with him were good. She suggested he write her a letter, in case he did not get the chance to call the next day.

Carl knew Rachel was not going to let him call, so he sat down and wrote Jackie a letter. He didn't mention he took Kendall to the sock hop in his letter. Hannah sat in the corner, stewing. She had wanted to go to the sock hop, but Rachel did not let her go. The sock hop was for sixth-grade students and their dates. Since none of the sixth-grade boys had asked Hannah to go, Rachel would not allow her to go as part of Carl's entourage. Hannah was all up in her feelings as she wrote Jackie a letter, describing in detail how she was not allowed to go to the sock hop.

She told Jackie that Carl had gone to the sock hop and took a girl named Kendall. Carl had no idea Hannah was telling Jackie what had gone on and he had taken Kendall to the sock hop. He didn't know things were about to get a little crazy and twisted with Jackie, all because Hannah was up in her feelings and snitching.

When she received the letter, Jackie asked her mother for permission to call Carl. She got him on the line and asked who he took to the sock hop. It didn't take long for him to figure Hannah had written Jackie and told her everything.

Carl asked Jackie what she did at the Central sock hop, and she asked him not to try to twist it. He and Jackie were very angry and hung the phone up on each other. Carl told Rachel what Hannah had done, writing Jackie and telling her about Kendall. Rachel was upset with Hannah for doing this but decided to discipline her later. In the meantime, she made a mental note to contact Mrs. Hunt. There needed to be some space between Carl and Jackie.

A few days later, Rachel and Mrs. Hunt spoke and agreed that Jackie and Carl needed some space. Her oldest daughter, Jennifer, overheard the conversation and said she was going to regret getting in Jackie and Carl'a way. Over the next few months, Carl and Jackie had very little contact and forged new relationships.

CHAPTER 6

I'll Cross That Bridge When I Get to It
#BradleyMakesASurpriseTripToMarshall

Eventually, Carl adjusted to his new normal, and like Riley said, he made friends at J. H. Moore. Spring rolled around, and they took pictures at both schools. Carl was surprised when he got an over-size envelope from Jackie and she had enclosed a four-by-six picture. Looking at her picture, he remembered that she was a very good-looking girl. He got one of his four-by-six pictures to send to Jackie but did not have an envelope to send it in. A few hours later, he and Riley went to TG&Y, and he bought some large envelopes.

Carl and Hannah sent Jackie four-by-six pictures of themselves. Hannah was salty when she realized Jackie sent Carl a four-by-six picture but sent her a wallet-size photo. Carl, Hannah, and Carol sent Bradley a four-by-six picture of themselves.

Spring rolled into summer, and Carl was happy to be out of school. The days were long, and the heat stifling, as he worked the fields with Rudolph and Riley. Carl seemed to take notice of the heat more now; he was covered in sweat most of the day. There was a difference when they went around the city, selling watermelons. Carl knew a lot of the kids he encountered.

They were hot and sweating when they went on Kendall's street one day. Carl didn't know they were on her street, because they came a different way. He was shocked they stopped across the street from Kendall's house; he didn't know Riley's best friend lived there. Kendall saw Carl out in the street and came out of the house. She couldn't believe he was on her street and asked what he was doing over there. He pointed at the truck and said, "We out selling watermelons." Kendall said she was making sandwiches for lunch and asked if he wanted one.

Carl was not going to turn down a sandwich and went to Riley to let him know. Riley said they'd take a quick lunch break while he ate lunch with Kendall. Riley stopped him and told him to take a four-bit watermelon with him. Carl jumped on the truck and dug down to the bottom of the stack, where the watermelons were cooler. He took a four-bit watermelon and walked across the street to Kendall's house. Riley watched as he sat on the porch with Kendall and her sister, nieces, and nephews, eating tuna sandwiches, chips, cookies, and watermelon.

Meanwhile, Fisher Body Fleetwood shut down two weeks for model year change, and Bradley drove to Texas for a few days. He drove all night, only stopping for gas, and pulled in his mother's driveway at nine thirty the next morning. When he got out of the car, the sweltering heat almost took his breath away. He'd forgotten how hot it got in East Texas, and the mild summers of Detroit had spoiled him. He went in his mother's house and said hello. Alberta was happy to see her youngest son.

It had been almost two years since Bradley had last been to Marshall. Alberta cooked breakfast while he took a quick bath. Alberta finished breakfast a couple of minutes before he came out of the bathroom. Bradley felt refreshed as he sat down to eat and talk with his mother. After he finished eating, Bradley went to his old bedroom and fell asleep. He was awakened by the sounds of kids playing outside and rolled over in the bed. He looked at his watch and was shocked it was 7:45 p.m.—he'd been asleep almost nine hours!

He lay in bed and thought about his last trip to Marshall, which ended with him and John Jones shoving and punching each other. He hoped this trip went better. He didn't want another fight with John.

He realized how little they thought of him to have them accuse him of renting a car to drive home to "impress" them. Bradley laughed when he thought about how stupid this really was. It bothered him that he and John were friends all through childhood and he felt that way. He thought how John made flip remarks, like, "Everybody wasn't a football star like you."

The one he really hated and stuck in his craw was John, saying everybody didn't have the chance to play professional football. While in the Air Force, Bradley met a counselor that told him he should not dim his light because it was too bright for others. He laughed as he thought, *I guess John is going to have to get a pair of shades.* Bradley got out of the bed, brushed his teeth, and dressed. He knew he'd never hear the last of it if he left without saying hello to his sisters, so he walked through Alberta's backyard to his sister Bertha's house.

When he stepped outside, his nieces and nephews gathered around him. Bradley was like a rock star to them, living in the big city and driving a nice car. They listened as he described the drive from Detroit to Marshall. He stood outside with them for about fifteen minutes, answering their questions about his life in Detroit. His nieces and nephews went back to playing, and Bradley walked the short distance to his sister Bertha's house. He walked inside Bertha's and saw his sister Beulah was also there. They hugged, and Bertha told him to sit down.

They were glad to see him, and after a few moments of small talk, they asked about his pending divorce from Rachel. Bradley told them the divorce had been finalized and he was single again. He listened as Beulah said she never really liked Rachel, that she thought she was better than everybody else. Bradley was up in his feelings, defending Rachel to his sister. He told Beulah she had Rachel mixed up; she didn't think she was better than any of them. Beulah kept on and said she felt Rachel looked down her nose at them because she had a chance to go to college and they did not.

Bradley asked Bertha if she felt the same way, and she said she kind of felt that way but she did like Rachel. He thought there must be something in the water; so many of the people he was dealing with seemed to be afflicted with envy and jealousy. He decided the best course of action was to allow Beulah to talk and get it out of her system. Bradley was reminded of how John had acted the last time he was home, accusing him of renting cars to impress people. He decided to keep quiet and listen to Beulah's jealous rant about Rachel.

Deep inside, he knew there was nothing he could say that would change Beulah's mind. Bradley knew he mos def did not want to argue with Beulah about this. After listening to Beulah for about fifteen minutes, he got up to leave. Bertha asked where he was headed, and he said he was headed to Rachel's house. Beulah said, "I *thought* you divorced the bitch!" Bradley drew the line and told Beulah, "The *bitch* happens to be the mother of three of my kids." He said she needed to find a way to get her jealousy under control.

As Bradley walked out the door, Bertha told Beulah she had gone too far calling Rachel a bitch. Beulah didn't back down. Instead, she said, "I call 'em like I see 'em."

Bradley walked back to his mother's house and went inside for a few minutes. He wanted to tell her he was about to visit his kids and friends in Marshall and probably would not be back that night. Alberta hugged Bradley and kissed him on the jaw, telling him he needed to go see his kids first. Bradley walked out of the house and drove to his friend Tony Campbell's house.

He drove up as Tony was getting out of the car with his wife and kids. They shook hands and hugged, glad to see each other. Bradley and Tony were very good friends and never squabbled about anything. They went inside, and Tony offered him a beer. Bradley turned down the beer and said he'd rather have a drink. Tony only had beer, so they made a run to the liquor store. The liquor store closed at 9:00 p.m., and they got there at 8:50 p.m. Bradley was drinking Johnnie Walker Red and bought two-fifths of it. As they left the liquor store, Tony asked Bradley if it was cool to go by John Jones's house.

Bradley said it was cool by him; there was no squabble, and the shoving and punching was an isolated incident. Tony was friends with both guys, and John loved Johnnie Walker Red. They pulled in John's driveway, saw his car, and knew he was home. When Tony knocked on the door, John answered and greeted them like nothing had happened between him and Bradley. John's wife, Estelle, saw Bradley standing in the yard and knew there was going to be a problem. She thought how Bradley and John were squabbling the last time he was there.

Estelle called Rachel, hoping she had a solution to the issue with John and Bradley. She got an earful, and her mouth fell open when Rachel said that not only did she not know Bradley was in Marshall but he was also no longer her problem because they were divorced. Rachel hung up the phone in Estelle's face, mumbling how she had the nerve to call her about Bradley. Rachel was pissed; she could not stand that bitch Estelle. When they were in high school and she got pregnant with Carl, Estelle was one of the people she told.

She was heartbroken when she walked up on Bradley and Estelle one day as they finished kissing. She never told John; there was no need to cause him heartbreak and pain. She had distanced herself from Estelle, and everyone wondered what happened between them. Rachel was enraged with Bradley; he'd come all the way from Detroit and had not stopped by to see his kids. Rachel smiled when she thought how the tongues would wag when Estelle told everybody she and Bradley were divorced. Rachel didn't tell the kids Bradley was in Marshall, in case he did not come by to see them.

The next day, Carl was down the street, playing with his cousin Charles. He told Carl his uncle Bradley had come by the day before. Carl looked at Charles and asked if he was sure his dad was in Marshall. Charles told him it was his uncle Bradley; he was at Mama Bertha's house. After he and Charles finished playing, Carl went home and told Rachel his dad had been at Mama Bertha's house. Rachel told Carl she heard Bradley was in Marshall but she hadn't seen or talked to him. He asked why Bradley had not come to see them, and Rachel said she did not have an answer.

Carl and Riley were sitting on the porch the next morning when Bradley drove up in his new Oldsmobile. Carl was glad to see Bradley and got off the porch to meet him in the driveway. Bradley hugged him and asked if Hannah and Carol were in the house. Carl went in the house to tell Carol and Hannah their dad was outside. Bradley spoke to Riley and said he'd been in Marshall a couple of days but didn't want to come by late at night. Carl returned with Hannah and Carol in tow. They stood on the porch as Bradley and Riley finished their conversation.

Bradley got them excited when he said they should go to the store and buy ice cream and treats. Hannah and Carl ran to the car, but Carol stayed on the porch, standing by Riley. Bradley told her to come on, that they were about to go, but Carol shook her head no. Riley sensed what was happening. Carl and Hannah knew Bradley, but Carol did not. He suggested Bradley take Hannah and Carl to the store and bring Carol something back. Bradley didn't question it as they all got in the car. Bradley backed out of the driveway, and they went to the store, buying a lot of candy and other treats. They made sure to get Carol something; they didn't want her to feel left out.

They didn't go right back home after leaving the store, instead riding around Marshall. They made several stops at Bradley's friends' houses while Hannah and Carl sat quietly in the car. Bradley seemed to be having fun as he talked with his friends. Their second stop was at John's house, which made Hannah and Carl happy. John had two daughters, Alice, who was in the same grade as Carl, and Brenda, who was in the same grade as Hannah. The kids had fun playing together as Bradley and John drank scotch and reminisced about old times together.

Estelle was tired of John drinking and wanted Bradley to leave, so she called Rachel. Rachel asked what she wanted when she answered the phone and heard Estelle's voice on the other end of the line. Estelle said she wanted to let her know Bradley was at their house, getting drunk with John. Rachel knew Hannah and Carl were with Bradley, and she didn't want him driving drunk with them in the car. Rachel agreed to talk with him, and Estelle called him to the phone. Rachel heard Estelle say, "It's Rachel," when she handed Bradley the phone.

Bradley said hello, and Rachel asked him to bring Hannah and Carl home since he'd been drinking. She was surprised when he agreed and said they'd be there in about fifteen to twenty minutes.

CHAPTER 7

The Season of Disappointment and Betrayal
#PeopleNeverKeepTheirWord

Bradley finished his drink and said he needed to take the kids to Rachel; he didn't want to make her mad. They left John's and, a few minutes later, drove up at Riley's. Carl and Hannah jumped out of the car and ran into the house. Bradley got out and walked to the porch, where Riley was sitting. He sat down on the porch, and as they talked, the conversation turned to Carl. Riley said he needed to stay in Carl's life; there was only so much he could do as his grandfather. Bradley listened as Riley told him what he felt Carl needed from his father.

Carl bounced back on the porch, and Riley changed the conversation. There was no need for him to hear what he and Bradley had been talking about. Carl asked Bradley when he was leaving to go back to Detroit. Bradley said he'd be in Marshall a few more days and then he had to go back to work. The three of them sat on the porch, talking for about an hour, and Bradley stood to leave. He asked Carl if he'd like to go to Detroit and finish his summer vacation with him. This excited Carl, and he said he would love to go to Detroit for the rest of the summer.

Riley listened as Bradley promised to take Carl to Detroit for a couple of weeks. Carl was happy because this meant he'd get to spend time with Bradley and see Detroit.

Bradley got in the car and drove off, leaving Carl and Riley sitting on the porch, talking. He listened as Carl talked about going to Detroit with Bradley, hoping he did not get disappointed. Bradley had been drinking, and that was never good; he might not follow through. Carl got up from the porch and ran in the house to tell Rachel that Bradley was going to take him to Detroit.

The next few days were a blur as Carl pumped himself for the trip, telling everyone his dad was taking him to Detroit for a couple of weeks. Riley was in turmoil. He didn't want to say anything but knew there was a possibility Bradley was not going to follow through.

That Saturday morning, Carl woke up ready for the trip to Detroit. His excitement peaked as he watched Rachel pack his bag. She didn't say anything but had a feeling Bradley was not going to pick him up. She finished his bag and watched him sit in the living room, waiting for Bradley.

A couple of hours later, the phone rang, and Rachel held her breath as she answered. Bradley was on the other end, explaining he was not coming to get Carl for the trip to Detroit. An argument ensued between them when she said she was tired of cleaning up the mess he made with their kids. She demanded he come by the house and tell Carl he was not taking him to Detroit. Bradley said that would be hard to do; he was in Memphis, getting gas. Rachel hung up the phone in Bradley's face and sat down in the chair by the phone.

She wondered how she'd break the news to Carl and went into a full-blown cry. She was furious. Bradley had blown into town, made a big promise to Carl, and left her to pick up the pieces when he didn't deliver. Rachel's chest heaved up and down as she sobbed, and Riley walked in the room. Riley saw her crying and knew what had happened. She looked up through her tears and said, "He's not coming to pick him up, and I get to tell him." Rachel felt a sigh of relief when Riley said he'd break the news to Carl.

Riley walked into the living room and saw Carl was asleep, holding his suitcase. He woke him and suggested he go to bed but Carl refused, he didn't want to miss his dad when he came to pick him up. Riley decided to let this one play out and walked back in the room with Rachel. He said he was going to bed and suggested she do the same. Rachel wiped her tears as she got up from her seat, realizing Carl would form his own opinion when he woke the next day. She fell asleep and woke the next morning with Carl standing next to her bed. Rachel decided to let Carl find out Bradley went back to Detroit; she was not going to be the heavy.

He took a bath and changed clothes as he clung to hope Bradley was coming to pick him up.

Later that day, he went down the street to play with Charles and heard Bradley was back in Detroit. Carl's world was crushed when he realized Bradley had returned to Detroit without him. He listened as Charles said his uncle Bradley had called Beulah and said he'd made it to Detroit. Carl's disappointment turned to anger when Charles said their cousin Jeffrey went to Detroit with Bradley. He told Charles he needed to go home and walked the short distance up the hill to his house.

Riley was sitting on the porch and could see Carl was visibly upset. He short-stopped him and asked what was wrong, motioning for him to have a seat on the porch. He took a seat and told Riley how Bradley had gone back to Detroit and did not stop to get him. He was in a full-blown cry when he said his cousin Jeffrey had gone to Detroit with Bradley. Riley hugged Carl and let him cry. He knew the level of pain he was feeling. He heard Bradley took his nephew to Detroit, and this added insult to injury with Carl. He finished crying and went inside to tell Rachel he would not be going to Detroit.

When he walked in the living room, Carl saw his suitcase on the couch. *I won't be needing this,* he thought and picked the bag up. He carried his bag to his bedroom as Rachel walked behind him. He put the bag on the bed and asked Rachel why his dad told him a lie. She did not have an answer and decided to let silence answer. She suggested he go back to the porch and was surprised when he asked for Bradley's telephone number. She wrote Bradley's telephone number on a sheet of paper and handed it to him. He took the paper and walked out the room to the front porch.

They sat silently on the porch as he thought about what he could say to explain the hurt he felt. Riley sensed he was sorting through his emotions and didn't say anything. When he found the words he wanted to say, Riley's first cousin Ron was standing in the yard. He was rude, crude, and obnoxious, and Carl knew he was not going to discuss this in his presence. Ron already thought he was soft, so he was not about to give him more ammunition. Ron walked to the porch with them and spoke. He shook Riley's hand and slapped Carl on the shoulder, asking, "How you feel, baby boy?"

Carl said he was feeling good and got off the porch to go inside. When he went in the house, a big thought hit him: *Call Jackie and tell her about it.* It was a long-distance call, and he made a deal with Rachel to pay for the call. She asked him to cough up the money up front; she didn't want him going back on his word. He handed Rachel five dollars, and she let him make a long-distance call. Carl picked up the phone and decided he wanted to call Bradley after all. He held his breath when the phone rang; he didn't know what he was going to say when Bradley answered the phone.

The phone was picked up on the third ring, and Carl asked to speak with Bradley. He didn't know it was his cousin Jeff answering the phone and was shocked when the voice on the other end called his name. "Uncle Bradley not here. I'll tell him you called." His disappointment turned to rage when he realized Bradley left him in Marshall and took Jeffrey instead. Carl and Jeff talked a few minutes, and then he hung up the phone. Until then, he had been able to hold himself together through the disappointment of being left in Marshall. When he realized his dad had taken his cousin instead, this was too much for him.

Carl was devastated and sat on the floor and cried. Rachel heard his sobs and went in the room, trying to console him. She'd been listening to Carl's side of the conversation and knew what he was upset about. She knew Bradley took Jeffrey back to Detroit with him; Bradley's sister Beulah had made sure to tell her. Rachel was pissed. She was picking up the pieces for Bradley again. She sat on the floor with Carl and hugged him, knowing she could do nothing to stop his tears. After he stopped crying, Carl looked at her and said he was through with Bradley.

She tried to convince Carl he should hear Bradley's side before he decided he was through with him. He looked at her and said, "Jeffrey is in Detroit, and I'm in Marshall. What is there to explain?" She did not have an answer for this and watched Carl as he dried his eyes and walked back to the porch with Riley and Ron. As Rachel watched Carl walk out the door, she saw Carl was developing the same no-nonsense demeanor that Riley possessed. She was startled by the phone ringing and picked it up. She took a deep breath when she realized it was Bradley on the other end.

Bradley asked to speak with Carl, and she said she did not think this was a good time. Rachel explained that Carl knew he took Jeffrey back to Detroit and that he had just spent five minutes crying. Bradley demanded Rachel call Carl to the phone; he wanted to speak with his son. Rachel agreed and told Bradley she was not going to whip him if he said something to piss him off. She put the phone down and went to the porch to get him, saying he had a phone call. When he said hello, Bradley asked how he was doing. Carl didn't answer; instead, he asked why he did not come by and pick him up like he said.

Bradley explained Jeffrey was old enough to babysit the kids for him. She saw him roll his eyes and knew this was not going to end well. She cleared her throat at the same moment Carl hung up on Bradley. He walked by Rachel and said, "If he calls back, I don't want to talk to him." She nodded. She knew how he felt; she'd been let down by Bradley many times. Bradley called back and wanted to know what Rachel was going to do about Carl hanging up on him. Bradley was angry when Rachel said Carl had a right to be mad and she was not going to punish him.

She hung up on Bradley and took the phone off the hook. She really was *not* in the mood to hear him rant. She walked away from the phone thinking, *Let him get a busy signal when he calls back.* Carl and Riley sat on the porch in silence, watching the neighborhood traffic. Ron was still there, and Carl knew it was not going to be long before he started to chide and make fun of him. Ron looked at Carl and said, "Baby boy, what grade you in?" He started to tell Carl who some of his nieces and nephews were, and Carl realized he was in school with several of them.

He got up and walked in the house when Ron started to go in on him. That was the only thing he hated about spending time with Riley—the older men always made fun of him. He really wanted to talk to him about what went on between him and Bradley. Jackie came across his mind again, and he asked Rachel if he could call her. She said he'd have to make it quick; after all, it was a long-distance call. Carl reached in his pocket and pulled out two dollars, then handed them to Rachel. She laughed and handed them back, saying to go ahead and call her. Carl dialed her number, and to his surprise, Jackie answered the phone. Jackie said hello, and Carl asked to speak with her.

Jackie's blunt "What do *you* want?" caught him off guard. But he regrouped and said he wanted to talk to her. She sarcastically asked, "Where is Kendall? And why do you want to talk to me?"

Carl took a deep breath, and his emotions came pouring out. He said he wanted to talk to her because she was his friend and he'd known her for a long time. This softened Jackie, and she listened to him explain how Bradley promised to take him to Detroit and left without taking him. He explained how his dad had taken his cousin Jeff to the city instead.

Jackie found herself tearing up. She could hear the sadness in Carl's voice as he told her what Bradley had done. He said the thing that bothered him most was, Bradley had lied to him. Jackie was speechless; she did not have anything to say. After he finished explaining how he felt, he thanked Jackie for listening and was about to hang up when she asked him not to hang up and said she was sorry for snapping at him. Carl started crying when he said everything was happening too fast. His mother and father had divorced, and he had to leave the school he wanted to attend.

Carl apologized to Jackie for taking Kendall to the sock hop and said he wanted to stay friends with her. He came clean and said Riley told him to call and tell her he was taking Kendall to the sock hop.

Carl said he saw how she felt since Bradley had lied to him about going to Detroit. There was silence for a few seconds as they composed themselves. Carl spoke again and thanked Jackie saying he was going to hang up. Jackie was still choked up and could only mumble, "Bye." Jackie realized she really liked Carl, she could not get angry at him when he was hurting.

She wanted to be mean to him when he called, but his pain caught her off guard. Jackie went to her sister Anna and told her about the conversation between them. Anna listened and said she was in over her head; they were kids trying to work through grown-folk problems. She advised Jackie to back away, telling her these were his problems and she was emotionally involved. She was Jackie's eldest sister, and she confided in her. She hugged Jackie as they sat on the couch in silence. Anna was twelve years older and watched Jackie work through this drama in her mind.

She knew what it felt like to be invested in a guy. She and her fiancé were going through changes. Jackie composed herself and thanked Anna for listening. Bradley called the next day, and Carl answered the phone. He recognized the voice on the other end and listened as Bradley tried to explain why he'd taken his nephew instead of his son. Carl wasn't buying the explanation and became angry with every word Bradley spoke. He could hardly contain himself when he asked, "Why didn't you come by the house and tell me? I waited all night for you."

Bradley didn't have an answer; he didn't expect Carl to grill him about being left in Marshall.

Carl finally said he had to go and hung up the phone before Bradley could say anything. He walked to the front porch and sat down, crying, because he was hurt. Riley didn't know what to do and decided to let him cry it out. He looked down the street and saw his cousin Ron walking toward the house. He thought this was the worst thing that could happen, Ron walking up to see him crying. He came up with a quick plan and stepped off the porch and walked to the edge of the yard. He short-stopped Ron and said they should go across the street to Rudolph's house—Janice hadn't finished cooking.

Ron was happy. He loved having a couple of drinks before he ate dinner. Riley called out to Rudolph, telling him to come outside; he and Ron were coming over. Riley looked back at Carl as he sat on the porch and cried out the pain he felt. Bradley called back, and Rachel answered the phone. Their talk was not warm or friendly, and Bradley demanded she discipline Carl for hanging up on him. Rachel refused and told Bradley she would not whip him because he was hurt enough already. She reminded him he was the one who caused this situation.

She was angry. Their son sat on the porch, crying, and all he could think was Carl disrespected him. She told Bradley she was tired of cleaning up his mess with the kids. Bradley was shocked when she said he should have been a man of his word and picked him up. She said it was one thing to lie to her, but it was different with his kids. The gloves came off when Rachel said she was no longer going to cover for him. It shook him when Rachel said the kids were about to see the type of man he really was. Bradley hung up the phone on Rachel. She'd never talked to him like this in the past.

Ron and Riley sat on Rudolph's porch, drinking bootleg whiskey and talking. Rachel came to the door and told Carl dinner was ready, and he got up to go inside. She hugged him and said everything was going to be fine; he just had to work through this. Carl nodded and said he knew. Rachel didn't say anything when he said he would never believe anything Bradley said again. She wanted to say something but didn't know what to say. This was a situation created by Bradley. She realized Bradley had hurt Carl to his core and there was nothing she could do about it.

Summer wound down, and Carl looked forward to going back to school. He and Riley had made a lot of money during the summer, and he'd been able to buy most of the clothes he wanted. He counted his money and realized he had quite a bit of money left over. Bradley sent Carl, Hannah, and Carol fifty dollars each to help with their school clothes. Hannah and Carol were happy to get their money, but Carl sent his fifty dollars back. Bradley received Carl's letter and the fifty dollars and immediately called Rachel. He wanted to know who put Carl up to sending his money back.

Rachel was in no mood to argue with Bradley and called Carl to the phone. She didn't tell him his dad was on the other end, just handed him the phone. Carl said hello, and Bradley asked if there was something wrong with his money. Carl said there wasn't; he just didn't want anything from him right then. This cut Bradley to his core, his eldest son speaking to him this way. He asked Carl what he needed to do to make this right. He was caught off guard and did not have an answer for this question. When he said he didn't know, Bradley followed up with the question, "Why are you mad?"

The emotional dam burst as Carl said it bothered him that he didn't stop to get him for the trip back to Detroit. Bradley listened as Carl said he waited all night and cried when he found he was not going to Detroit. Carl asked why he'd taken Jeff to Detroit but not him. Bradley explained Jeff was old enough to stay home alone and he was not. Carl did not buy this explanation but decided to let it go. He knew he'd never again trust Bradley or put confidence in anything he said. The emotional weight was lifted, and Carl went about his life, but the scar remained.

Summer wound down with Carl and Riley selling watermelons all over the city. Carl went through the motions, the incident with Bradley having left him an emotional wreck. Riley saw the pain he was in but knew there was not much he could do to help. He asked if he wanted to talk about it, and he said he didn't. He called Kendall and told her what happened between him and Bradley. She thought it was awful that his dad would do that, and listened as he talked it out with her. Kendall was therapy for him. She understood his pain because she had pain of her own.

Between letters to Jackie and talking on the phone to Kendall, the emotional load he carried eased to the back of his mind. The incident with Bradley changed him forever, and Carl built an emotional wall around his feelings. He went to Rachel, and they talked about what happened. Rachel listened to him say he was not mad but did not understand why Bradley didn't love him. Rachel stopped him, saying Bradley loved him but he would not understand some of the things going on. She hated she was once again cleaning up a mess Bradley had made with their kids.

Rachel decided she was not going to bad-mouth Bradley to his kids; they would find out who he was on their own.

Carl went to sleep with his head in Rachel's lap. She looked at him and remembered he was eleven years old and dealing with things that would make a grown person cringe. She sat on the couch with him and thought about the emotional scar this was going to leave. She hoped he was resilient enough to bounce back from this setback. Carl woke up from his short nap and went back to the porch to sit with Riley. She saw the pep was back in his step as he walked out of the room.

Riley knew Carl had turned the corner on this emotional mess. He didn't go in the house when Ron walked up. Riley was shocked when he took the verbal punches Ron threw and even threw a few of his own. Ron laughed and said loudly, "Baby boy, you trying to hang with us old heads?" They all laughed when Ron said, "You gotta be tough to hang with us." Ron looked at Riley and said he was going over to Rudolph's for a few minutes. Riley got out of his seat and said he'd join him. Carl was shocked when Riley looked at him and asked if he wanted to come.

Carl declined the offer and said he was going to go down the street to play with his friends. He saw everyone down the street playing baseball in the street and went to join them. Riley watched him play with the other kids and knew this was a great way for him to work off his frustration. Riley had been a coach for a semi-pro baseball team and really wanted Carl to play baseball. He preferred football, and Riley didn't want to steer him but knew he'd be a great baseball player. Carl was left-handed at bat, and this would cause problems for right-handed pitchers.

Riley knew Carl would be a "big bat," because he was a tall muscular kid. When Carl came to bat, Riley got Rudolph's and Ron's attention. They watched as Carl swung on the first pitch. Riley smiled and said, "The boy has a *smooth* swing!" The men sat on the porch, drinking bootleg whiskey and watching life go by. An hour or so later, Rachel came to the door and called for Carl to come home. She saw Riley across the street and asked what he wanted her to do. Riley told Rachel to fix a plate for each of them and send it over.

A few minutes later, Carl, Hannah, and Carol came out of the house with a plate of food. They took the food to the men sitting on Rudolph's porch and went back across the street. Carl sat at the table with Janice, Rachel, Hannah, and Carol, listening to them talk as they ate dinner. It amazed him, the different things the women talked about; they were nothing like the men. When the kids finished eating, Rachel told them it was time to read a few pages. She reminded them school would start in a few weeks and they needed their routine reset.

Carl and Riley finished out the last few weeks of the summer, and Carl bounced back to normal. As the school year approached, the neighborhood kids discussed what they were going to do at school. It was a transitional year for Carl; he was going to junior high school as a seventh grader. He told everyone that would listen how he planned to go out for the football team. Carl played football on a blended sixth-grade team. The coaches took boys from Dogan and J. H. Moore to get enough to make a team. They were the Bears and played several other teams from Marshall.

The summer days got hotter, and Carl started to daydream, envisioning playing football for Pemberton High and Wiley College. Pemberton High colors were purple and gold, while Wiley colors were purple and white. Pemberton's mascot was the panther, and Wiley's mascot was the wildcat. During one of his trips to Marshall, Bradley took Carl to Pemberton High and showed him the trophies he'd earned while he went to Pemberton. This stoked Carl's desire to play for Pemberton; he wanted to follow in Bradley's footsteps.

CHAPTER 8

What Is Integration?
#IshBoutToGetRealReal

Summer was winding down, and school was going to start in a week. Carl was at his friend Edward's house, playing football in the yard. A few minutes later, Edward's mother came out of the house, holding the paper. She read the headline: MARSHALL SCHOOLS TO BE INTE-GRATED WHEN SCHOOL STARTS NEXT WEEK. Edward's mother broke it down for them. "You are going to school with White kids." Carl heard what Ms. Fannie said but did not know what this meant for him or Edward.

He was going to the seventh grade, and Edward was going to the ninth grade. Carl asked to see the newspaper, and Ms. Fannie handed it to him. He read the article and realized this was going to happen. The article laid out the alignment for the school district. His mind reeled as he read the seventh grade was at Pemberton Junior High and the eighth grade was at Marshall Junior High. The article further laid out the ninth and tenth grades would attend Pemberton High School. Carl finished the article when he read the eleventh and twelfth grades would attend Marshall High School.

He ran home to tell Rachel the news and found she already knew. She mentioned a Supreme Court decision called *Brown v. Board of Education* that had been handed down in May 1954. Carl peppered Rachel with question after question, and she answered as many as she could. He was amazed as she described the civil rights movement and Jim Crow segregation. Rachel explained these were things he did not have to worry about. She said his only job was going to school and getting his education. Carl thought about this as he realized the world around him was in turmoil.

Rachel was concerned about Carl's emotional well-being. He'd gone through the drama with Bradley, and then came the news of integration. She was also concerned about Carl's physical well-being. Over the Fourth of July weekend six weeks earlier, there had been a bombing in Longview. Thirty-six school buses had been damaged or destroyed. There were some people who made threats that integration would be bloody. He didn't seem any worse for wear, but she knew this had to take an emotional toll. Carl's lone thought at that moment was, he would not get chance to play varsity football at Pemberton. Included in the article were instructions for the young men trying out for football. Carl read it and realized the first day of football practice was the next day. He told Rachel, and she read the article, realizing integration for Carl started the next day.

The next morning, Carl woke up and was ready to go to football tryouts. Rachel took a long look at him and said she hoped he made the team, then thought and prayed that everything would go smoothly. Shortly after that, the news came down that Jefferson ISD was also integrating schools. She called the office and received the instructions she needed to get ready to start school. Rachel was shocked when she found she'd been reassigned to teach government and economics. This rocked her to the core. She'd taught English for eight years at Central High School.

Rachel was shocked when she complained about the reassignment. She was told it was that or no job. She became irate when it was revealed none of the English teachers had the level of experience she did. She got over her anger, however, remembering school started in about two weeks. She buckled down and learned enough about the government curriculum to start the semester.

Carl's first day of practice went good, until he found he'd have to change positions. The coaching staff wanted him to play defensive end instead of linebacker.

Two weeks into two-a-day practices, everything seemed to be going well. Carl settled into the defensive end position even though he preferred playing linebacker. He'd become acquainted with most of the guys on the team and realized he had played against a lot of them the previous year. He remembered Charles Morgan, who played running back for the Green Wave. When the blended J. H. Moore / Dogan team played the Green Wave, Morgan scored the winning touchdown on a fullback lead play. Carl remembered the fullback block gave Morgan enough room to slide into the end zone.

The second time they played the Green Wave, Morgan was held out of the game with a high ankle sprain. He remembered the Green Wave because they had cool uniforms. Carl was a trendsetter himself, using socks that went to his knees. Everybody thought he was cool and a fashion statement when he tucked the socks under his knee-pads. The real deal was, Carl hated scratching his knees and wanted the socks as extra protection. When they broke practice, Coach Freeman called the team to him. The players and other coaches listened as he spoke.

Coach Freeman started by outlining what they should expect when school started the following Monday. The players were shocked when he asked them to rise above the foolishness they were going to witness. He told them they were the Dogies of Pemberton Junior High School. Coach Freeman said their jersey color was orange and that was what united them. He explained that the following Thursday, they would line up against the Tiger Cubs from Texarkana. Coach Freeman said he needed each of the guys to keep a cool head and focus on the Tiger Cubs during practice next week.

Coach Freeman pulled his clipboard out and gave the starting lineups for both offense and defense. Carl was happy when he heard his name called as the starting defensive end. After the starting lineup for the team was announced, they broke practice. Carl ran home and told Rachel the good news: he earned a starting position!

The weekend passed, and school started on Monday morning. Rachel could not believe all the cars she saw when she dropped Carl, Hannah, and Carol off at JH Moore. There were cars everywhere, and when she stopped to let them out, she saw the protest signs. Rachel was concerned at this point, wondering what they were protesting about. One of the women protesting came to her car and said they were protesting the landfill adjacent to JH Moore. Rachel laughed out loud, and the woman wanted to know what was so funny.

Rachel asked incredulously, "You mean the city trash dump that is across the street from the school?

The woman said, "That is exactly what I'm talking about."

She went on to say she did not want her kids going to an elementary school that had a landfill across the street. Rachel looked the woman in the eyes and asked if she knew JH Moore was there before her kids were assigned to go to school here. The woman said she did. Rachel said the parents with kids in school here had asked the city to close that dump for years, and they have refused. She asked the woman to move, rolled up her window, and drove off. As she drove to Jefferson, she thought about the irony of the situation. The city of Marshall did not have a problem with a dump across the street from the school before integration. She laughed out loud, thinking, *The first day of integration, we have a full-fledged protest asking that the dump be moved.* A week later, the Marshall City Commission held a meeting and abruptly closed the dump. When she read about it in the *News Messenger* the next day, the article said, "Flies and the possibility of airborne illnesses led to the decision." She wondered, *Where was this concern from 1954 to 1970 when JH Moore was segregated?* She shook her head as she thought, *We are in integrated schools less than a month, and the dump is gone.* She thought about the level of hypocrisy was astounding as she put the newspaper down.

It didn't take long for Carl to see what Coach Freeman meant when he said they needed to stay focused. He'd been at school less than an hour when a White boy in his homeroom called him a nigger. Carl was shocked. This was the first time he'd come face-to-face with racism. He'd seen the Jim Crow "Whites only" signs in downtown Marshall and other parts of the city. Carl looked at him, saying,

"Your mama!" They stood and glared at each other but decided to let this be. Their homeroom teacher had overheard the exchange and decided to let them settle it on their own.

The rest of the day went off without incident, and he went to football practice that afternoon. During practice, he had a hard time getting off his block fast enough to make the tackle. He made tackles, but the running back would pick up four to five yards. He knew this was not acceptable, because the goal was to hold the running back to three yards or less. He knew this system focused on power, and the system he came out of focused on a blend of power and speed. The defensive coaches told Carl he needed to step his game up.

The next day at school was uneventful; he'd learned to block out the bluster and noise from the tribulation integration had thrust upon them. That evening in football practice, the offensive coach ran leads with a lineman and fullback blocking for Charles Morgan. Carl made so few tackles the coaches alternated him with another player at that position. Carl was devastated—he'd never been benched before. Coach Lewis, a defensive line coach, came over to talk to him and asked what was wrong. Carl did not want to make excuses but told the coach these guys were so big.

It didn't help Carl's psyche when Coach Lewis said he should get used to it, that the boys were that size or bigger. He had played with Bradley at Pemberton and said he knew he was better than this. Carl remembered a move Bradley showed him, how to use his forearm as a "flipper" to get bigger opponents off him. He thought about Bradley saying, "Do *not* allow them to get into your body." He didn't know if this would work, and he learned the move from the linebacker position. When he was sent back in, Carl used his flipper and stood up the offensive lineman in front of him.

He was off his block and in perfect position a yard deep in the backfield. The fullback came at him, and he used his flipper to slide off him. A second later, the pads sounded off when Carl stepped into Charles Morgan and drove him into the ground. This shook practice up, and everyone hollered. This was a big-time move, and the coaches said, "I think we found a Hoss!" The offensive coach was pissed that Carl cleared two blocks to unload on his running back.

He yelled at the offensive line, "This is why I sent a lead blocker. We want to get Morgan in open space."

Coach Williams was even more pissed when he said Carl was not that good.

Charles Morgan stopped him, saying, "Coach, he *is* that good. I played against him last year."

Coach Williams ran the play to the opposite side and picked up a first down. He still did not believe Carl was good, let alone as good as Morgan thought he was. He ran the play to Carl's side again, and the tackle got his block, pancaking Carl. The team erupted at the sound of pads popping when the tackle pancaked Carl. Coach Freeman decided this was the perfect place to break practice.

The coaches and team stood in the middle of the field as Coach Freeman gave them instructions for Thursday's game. They played at 3:30 p.m. up in Texarkana and would leave Pemberton at 11:00 a.m. Carl got the first Dogie Pride sticker for his tackle on Charles Morgan. The second Dogie Pride sticker went to Kevin Ramsey, for the block that pancaked Carl a few plays later. A loud "One, two, three, Dogie Pride!" broke practice for that day.

The third day of school was uneventful; by then he was used to hearing the word *nigger* thrown around like it was somebody's name.

That Thursday, Carl saw Kendall on the cheer line as they loaded the bus. He was surprised, since she didn't tell him she was on the cheer squad. He broke rank and went to the cheer line, standing in front of Kendall. He hugged her and said he was glad to see her. They had talked on the phone, but he hadn't seen her during the first week of school. Coach Williams called out to Carl, telling him it was time to go. Kendall said, "I hope ya'll win," and he hustled to the bus and the team left for the trip to Texarkana. The trip to Texarkana took almost two hours, and they arrived about 1:00 p.m.

They went to the stadium field house, and the coaches passed out sandwiches, chips, and a drink for them to eat. Coach Freeman announced they should not get full; they would play better if they were borderline hungry. At 3:15 p.m., the Dogies left the field house and went to the field. The Tiger Cubs were already on the field, at the other end. The referees came to the sidelines and asked for the team captains. The Tiger Cubs won the coin toss and elected to receive. The Dogies kicked off as Coach Lewis told Carl that Ryan Jones would start at defensive end.

Carl could not hide his disappointment and wanted to cry. He sucked it up and stood on the sideline, watching when the starting defensive team took the field. The Tiger Cubs lined up, and the first play they ran was the fullback lead, and Ryan Jones stuffed it. Carl saw his playing time evaporate as Ryan Jones stuffed the fullback lead each time they ran at him. Carl was sick. He'd never been benched, and it seemed Ryan Jones had won the position. The first quarter ended, and Coach Freeman huddled the Dogies on the sidelines.

The game was tied at zero, neither team had scored. The whistle blew to start the second quarter and the Dogies lined up on defense. The first play from scrimmage, the Tiger Cubs ran a sweep with the Tackle pulling. Ryan Jones was not blocked, but he was too slow to catch the running back. The Tiger Cubs ran this play to both sides of the field, scoring the third time they ran it. On the extra point, they lined up and pushed the Dogies off the ball for the two-point con-version. The Dogie coaching staff realized they were going to have a problem with this set of plays.

Both teams scored one more time, and the Tiger Cubs went into the half leading 16 to 8. The second half started, and the Dogies were on the ball. Charles Morgan broke a long run on the third play from scrimmage, and the Dogies tied the game. After the kickoff, Coach Lewis told Carl he was going in the game for Ryan and Carl's mood changed as he ran on the field charged up. He watched the Tiger Cubs break the huddle and run to the line. Carl noticed the tackle in front of him was a big guy, and wondered how he would play him.

Carl didn't want to disappoint the coaches and certainly did not want to go back to the bench. As the quarterback called signals, Carl hoped they were not going to run the fullback lead. The center snapped the ball, and he saw the play unfold. His eyes lit up when the tackle bump blocked him. The play was going wide. When the tackle released his bump block and went to block the linebacker, he made a play on the running back. In a smooth motion, he wrapped the running back in a form tackle. The Dogie sideline erupted when the pads popped. A big play was exactly what they needed.

It disrupted the Tiger Cubs momentum for a few plays. The Tiger Cubs ran a few plays up the middle and were moving the ball. A few plays later, when the Tiger Cubs came to the line, Carl noticed the big tackle was back in the game. The center snapped the ball, and they ran the fullback lead. The tackle pancaked Carl and fell on top of him. The Tiger Cubs ran the play two more times with the same result—Carl was pancaked! Coach Freeman called time-out and sent Ryan Jones back in the game. The Tiger Cubs found their mix and scored two more times while holding the Dogies to one score.

The game ended with the Dogies on the short end of the 32–20 score. The coaching staff dissected the game during the ride home and realized they had a problem. Ryan Jones could stop the fullback lead but could not make plays on the end sweep. They knew Carl Hampton could stop the sweep but could not make plays on the fullback lead. They decided to leave the lineup as it was and work it out during the next week in practice. Coach Lewis said the Tiger Cubs were the only team that presented a dual threat. The coaching staff knew most teams played power football, running the fullback lead exclusively.

The bus pulled up at Pemberton Junior High, and Carl saw Riley sitting in the truck, waiting. He cheered up, got his gear off the bus, and put it in the locker room. Coach Freeman huddled the team, said they should forget today's game and he'd see them at practice tomorrow. Ryan Jones led them in a rousing "One, two, three, Dogie Pride!" cheer. Carl ran out the locker room to Riley's truck and climbed in. He asked if they won, and Carl said they lost, 32–20. When he asked how he played, Carl's demeanor changed. Riley saw he was not in a good place when he said he thought he lost his position.

He listened as Carl told him about the game and how he got pancake-blocked at least three times. He failed to see what was funny as Riley laughed at his "pancake block" comment. They pulled into the driveway, and Carl got out of the truck and ran inside. He hugged Rachel and told her they lost. Rachel listened as he said he thought he lost his position. He said he played linebacker last year and they moved him to defensive end, which was not fair. She stopped him, saying he needed to gut it up and learn the position.

She could not believe her son was going through the same thing she experienced on a smaller level. She asked why he thought he got beaten out for the position. Carl knew Ryan Jones was taller and heavier than him, and told Rachel that. Having watched Bradley during high school, Rachel knew a little about football. She asked if Ryan Jones was faster, and Carl said he was not. Rachel said in a matter-of-fact way, "Your speed is your advantage." He agreed, but being in a down position caused him to lose that first-step burst of speed.

Rachel asked if he wanted an excuse for being benched or a solution to his problem. Carl thought about it, got up, and walked out of the room. He knew he had work to do. He asked Rachel if he could call Kendall, and she said he needed to do his homework. Carl hunkered down and started his homework, took a break to bathe, and started on it again. He must have been tired, because after he took his bath, he went to sleep with his head in the book.

When he woke up the next morning, Rachel reminded him he had not finished his homework yet.

Carl hustled to get ready early and started working on his homework, finishing while he was in homeroom. As he walked down the hallway, he saw Kendall standing by her locker and stopped to talk with her. They had a couple of minutes before the bell rang, and she asked about the game. Carl told her they lost and he really did not want to talk about it. He asked what lunch she had and was surprised to find they both had second lunch. The first bell rang—meaning, they had one minute to get to class. Kendall didn't say anything, just walked toward her class.

Rachel sat in her classroom, thinking how fast the first week of school had gone by. It was Friday afternoon, and she thought about the highs and lows of the first week. She realized integration was tough; everyone was on edge, and nerves were frayed. She was caught off guard by the disrespect some of the students in her classes had shown. The first week, she put seventeen students out of her classes because they insisted on using her first name. As she packed her bag to leave, she thought this had never happened at Central.

Rachel was glad to make it home when she pulled into the driveway—the folks had worked her nerves, and she was happy it was over. One thing she was happy about was the fact she did not miss a beat teaching government. She'd put in the work and was far enough ahead of the students that she could master the content. When she walked in the house, Janice said she should sit down for a few minutes. An hour later, they sat at the table, eating dinner. Her mind drifted, and she wondered how the historians would write about this period in fifty years.

She put the thought out her mind and focused on eating dinner. Rachel was helping Janice with the dishes when the phone rang, and was shocked to hear Bradley's voice. She listened as he said he was coming home for a few days, explaining GM was the UAW strike target. He said they were going out on strike since GM and the union could not reach agreement on benefits. Rachel was shocked to hear Bradley say he wanted to spend time with Carl. This lowered her defense, and she said that would be a great idea, there was some fence-mending that needed to be done.

She didn't tell Carl she talked to Bradley, though; he didn't need to be let down again.

Bradley left Detroit the next morning and drove the nineteen-plus hours to Marshall. This time, when he arrived, his first stop was to see Carl. It was after midnight, and Riley didn't want to wake him up, but Bradley pleaded with him. Bradley said it would mean the world to Carl if he knew he stopped there first. He gave in and allowed Bradley to come in the house. Bradley went to Carl's bed and woke him up, saying he had come to spend time with him.

Carl rolled over and went back to sleep; he really did not want to talk to Bradley. Riley saw what happened and motioned for Bradley to come out. He walked him out of the house and told Bradley, "Get a good night's sleep and come back in the morning." Bradley took Riley's advice and went down the street to his mother's house. Alberta was glad to see Bradley again and hugged him when she opened the door.

Bradley woke up the next morning, and some of his nephews were playing outside the window.

Alberta asked if he'd like breakfast, and a thought popped in his mind. He asked Alberta if she would cook enough for Carl too. Alberta said she would, and Bradley went to get Carl. When he pulled up in the driveway, Carl was sitting on the porch with Riley. Bradley got out and walked to the porch, speaking to them. Carl stood up to walk in the house, but Riley stopped him, saying he needed to talk to his dad. Bradley asked if he'd like to eat breakfast with him—Mama Bertha was cooking. This softened Carl, and he agreed. He was waiting on breakfast.

He went in the house and told Rachel he and Bradley were going down to Mama Bertha's to eat breakfast.

A few minutes later, he sat at the table with Bradley and Mama Bertha, eating breakfast. Bradley asked how football was going, and this struck a nerve with Carl. He didn't want to talk about football, but his emotions got the best of him, and Carl told Bradley everything. Bradley listened as Carl said he got beaten out for the position of defensive end. He asked Carl if he knew why he didn't get the starting position, and he said he was the starter until he got pancaked a couple times.

Bradley could not help himself and laughed when Carl said he got pancaked. He explained the guys they played against were bigger. Bradley reminded him to use his flipper and not let the guys get into his body. He asked if he knew he had a secret weapon, and Carl looked at him like he'd lost his mind. He said he didn't know he had a secret weapon and asked what it was. He listened as Bradley described his body build as muscular but lean and said most of the guys playing along the defensive line would be bigger. Carl was shocked when Bradley said his secret weapon was speed.

He asked if any of the guys on the team were faster than him. Carl said there were several guys on the team who were faster than him. Bradley turned it, asking if any of the lineman were as fast as him. Carl said he was the fastest of the linemen. Bradley smiled and said, "That's *your* secret weapon, son, your speed."

Bradley dropped Hannah and Carol off at J. H. Moore before taking Carl to Pemberton Junior High. Carl told him what time football practice ended, and Bradley said he'd be there to pick him up. He heard a bell and ran in the school, not sure if this was the tardy bell.

He was walking to his seat when Steve Logan, who sat across from him, tripped him. Carl dropped his books as he stumbled and fell to the floor. He looked up, asking Steve why he put his foot in the aisle. Steve laughed, saying he wanted to trip him. The class laughed as Carl picked his books up from the floor. The laughter turned to gasps, however, when he put his books on his desk and dived on Steve Logan, pounding him. Carl landed several punches, and Steve Logan's face was red when they pulled him off. Steve jumped out of his seat and ran up on Carl, pounding him while the boys held him.

He broke loose, and it turned into a full-blown fight between Steve and Carl. When they broke the fight up the second time, Carl had a busted lip and Steve's nose was bloodied. The English teacher called them to the front of the room and sent both boys to the principal's office. *What a way to start the second week of school,* Carl thought as they walked down the hall to the principal's office.

CHAPTER 9

The Integration Saga Continues
#IshDunGotRealReal

While he sat in the office, Carl thought of the hell he was going to pay. Rachel was going to be beside herself with anger, and he knew she was going to whip him. She said many times he needed to learn self-control and check his temper. He knew when she found out he dived on Steve and started pounding him that it was not going to be pleasant. They were told not be lured into a fight with the White kids, and six days into the school year, he was in the principal's office for fighting a White kid. Just when he thought things could not get any worse, Coach Williams walked in the principal's office.

Carl had forgotten that Coach Williams was an assistant principal. He asked both boys why they were in the office, and neither said a word. One of the office assistants said they were fighting in English class. Coach Williams took them in the office and listened as they explained what happened. When they finished, he said he was confused why the fight started. He thought about it and sent them back to class, saying they would sort it out during football practice. Carl was taken by surprise, because he had no idea Steve was on the football team.

They did not speak as they walked back to class, and Carl wondered why he had not seen Steve at practice. They sat down, and

Mrs. Martin asked for their pass from the office. Steve said they did not have one, and she used the intercom system to call the office. The office assistant confirmed they spoke with Coach Williams and had permission to return to class. She stood up from her desk and addressed the class about the fight. "We are less than two weeks into this integration experiment, and the heathen in you little nigger kids has come out!"

Carl and the other Black kids in the class looked at Mrs. Martin as their mouths dropped open.

She continued her rant, saying, "We came here to try to *teach* you heathens, and all you can do is fight!" She sat back down at her desk and resumed teaching class.

Carl could not believe what he had just heard and tried to wrap his mind around it. He pushed it out of his mind, thinking about what Riley said about stupid people. The two-hour-block English class with Mrs. Martin ended, and Carl went to lunch. He was shocked to see Kendall at first lunch—he thought she had second lunch.

He sat at the table with her, and they talked about the weekend and his fight that morning. He told her Bradley was there from Detroit and dropped him off at school. After lunch, he walked Kendall to class and ran to beat the tardy bell for his class. He finished the day without incident and stood in the locker room, dressing for football practice. He got dressed and ran to the field for practice, lining up with the rest of the guys. The team captain led them through calisthenics and warm-up exercises. Coach Freeman ran on the field, followed by the other coaches.

They called the team together and introduced Steve Logan to the Dogie squad. Coach Freeman said he was a scatback and would compete for a running back position. It hit Carl—he played scatback for the Black Knights! He thought Logan tripped him because he was Black, but it was because he killed him last season. At the first break, Logan asked if he remembered him. Carl responded he did and said it was over. He thought there was a different reason he tripped him. Logan said he recognized him the first day of school and was shocked he did not remember him.

Toward the end of practice, Coach Williams asked Steve Logan and Carl Hampton to come front and center. He circled the team around them and formed a line on each side of them. Coach Williams said, "Earlier today, Mr. Logan and Mr. Hampton came to the principal's office for fighting." The team listened as Coach Williams explained there was a lot going on and they had to stay focused on football and school. Coach Williams said he did not paddle them because both were on the football team. He then said they had a tradition called "blood alley" they used when teammates fought each other.

Carl and Steve lined up, facing each other, and Coach Freeman blew the whistle. Carl surged and stood Steve up, pushing him back to pancake him. The squad was in awe—Carl was very quick off the ball. The second set yielded the same result: Carl pancaked Steve. After the third set and a third pancake by Carl, Coach Freeman asked if they were ready to talk. Both said they were ready to talk, and Coach Freeman asked who was going first. Carl stepped up and said he ran up on Steve because he tripped him and he fell. He said he thought Steve did this because he was Black.

Steve stepped up and said the Black Knights played the J. H. Moore / Dogan team twice last season and could not run to Carl's side. He said, when he saw Carl, he was angry because he hit him hard and his coach yelled at him. Steve said he thought about this and decided to trip Carl as payback. Coach Freeman stepped into the middle of the team and said this had to be quashed. He echoed Coach Williams when he said there was a lot going on and they needed to focus on school and football. The players listened to Coach Freeman echo Coach Williams's earlier statement.

He went a step further, saying he expected the football players to take the high road. Coach Freeman told the boys, "We are Dogies, not White Dogies or Black Dogies. We are the Pemberton Junior High Dogies!" He called everybody into the huddle and said, "Dogie Pride on three!" A loud and boisterous "One, two, three, Dogie Pride!" and practice was dismissed.

Carl ran to the locker room to shower; he was tired and had a lot of homework. When he came out of the building, he noticed

Bradley's car in the parking lot. He got in the car and said hello to Bradley.

Bradley spoke to him and started the drive home. He asked Carl about his day, and he decided to not mention the fight since that had been resolved. He was shocked when Bradley said he saw practice and the coaching staff had him out of position. He listened as Bradley explained coming from a three-point stance killed his speed. Bradley said he would work with him on how to surge from a three-point stance. They pulled up at the house, and Carl gathered his books and got out of the car. Bradley told him to do his homework and he would pick them up for school the following morning.

When he got in the house, Hannah and Carol were gushing about Bradley picking them up from school and taking them to get ice cream. Rachel held her peace, hoping Bradley had turned a page and would not disappoint the kids again. She asked how his day was, and Carl said he had a good day; there were no incidents. Rachel directed them to the table to do their homework and noticed they seemed to be happy. She was amazed how Bradley spending a little time with them seemed to lift their spirits, and she hoped against hope he would not disappoint them soon.

The next morning, Bradley dropped the kids at school and they were on time. Carl saw Kendall leaving the bus line and ran to where she was. Bradley saw him take Kendall's books and made a mental note to ask about her that evening. He walked Kendall to her homeroom, and they stood in the hall, talking. A few minutes later, the hall monitor sent him to his homeroom, and he settled in, checking his homework. At lunch, he sat with Kendall and they talked about his dad bringing him to school. Kendall was a little sad; both of Carl's parents were still alive, and hers were already dead.

He hugged Kendall, hoping she would feel better, and a few moments later, the bell sounded. Carl walked her to class and said he would see her the next day. That afternoon, the coaching staff changed the defensive scheme from four-three to forty-four stack. This move was designed to offset the fullback lead and other power running plays most of the teams in their district ran. Carl soon saw why they switched to the forty-four stack—the coaching staff introduced Matt Davis. He transferred from Texarkana and, ironically, played on the Tiger Cubs team that beat the Dogies.

During practice that evening, Matt lined up at defensive end, and it was apparent he was better than anyone on the Dogies squad. Carl's practice time took a serious hit, and he was seriously beaten emotionally. He was already on the bench, and now one of the starting defensive ends was on the bench with him. Bradley picked him up and asked how football practice went. He said not so well and explained what happened with the defensive scheme change. Carl could not believe what Bradley said next—this was possibly the best thing that could have happened.

Carl questioned him, and the light came on when Bradley said the forty-four-stack defense went through linebackers. Carl listened as he explained the forty-four stack played to his strength. It made sense when Bradley said the two outside linebackers in the forty-four stack needed to be quick. Carl knew linebackers had to be great tacklers, which he was. Bradley asked what he thought he could do, and Carl said he was going to see if the coaches would move him to linebacker. Bradley dropped him off at home and got out of the car, sitting on the porch with Riley while Carl changed clothes.

He bounced out of the house a few minutes later, and Bradley said he would show him how to get off the ball quicker. They hung out until 9:00 p.m., when Rachel came to the door and said he needed to bathe and go to sleep. Carl ran in the house and took his bath. Rachel sat him at the table to do his homework at 9:45 p.m., saying he had an hour to finish. When she came back at 11:00 p.m., Carl's head was on the table and he was asleep. *My baby is worn-out,* she thought as she woke him up, saying he needed to go to bed. Bradley took them to school again and asked if Kendall was his girlfriend.

Carl said Kendall was his girlfriend and he really liked her. Bradley said he would like to meet her, but not yet. Carl got out of the car and met Kendall at the bus line. He took her books and walked to her homeroom. The hall monitor was not having it today; she herded Carl away the moment Kendall took her books from him. He settled in homeroom and realized he had quite a bit of work to do. When he opened his history book, he found a note from Rachel saying, "Finish your work." He smiled to himself and finished his homework.

They were not hitting at practice that evening. It was the day before the game. Carl was in a great mood, even when he knew he might not play in tomorrow's game. Coach Freeman huddled them together and gave the instructions for the game the following day. Carl was not surprised he did not make the starting lineup this week. Ryan was the starter at one defensive end, and Matt started at the other defensive end. The third defensive end, Alton Smith was on the bench with him. Coach Freeman said they were playing the Robert E. Lee Rebels at 4:00 p.m. the next day in Tyler.

Coach Freeman told the guys they would eat lunch at school, then load the bus, headed to Tyler. He saw Kendall at lunch, but because they had to eat as a team, he could not sit with her. When they finished, she was in the cheer line with the other girls to send the team off. Carl went to her and got his kiss on the cheek, just like last week. The guys rubbed it in, saying he had a girlfriend. They settled down, and the bus arrived in Tyler at 2:30 p.m. One of the Rebel coaches showed them the dressing room, and they settled down for a quick nap.

They got dressed and were on the field at 3:45 p.m., waiting for the game to start. The refs called for the team captains, and the Rebels won the coin toss. They elected to receive the opening kick-off and started the game. The Rebels ran the fullback lead and dive plays. Their whole offense seemed to be between the tackles. Ryan and Matt held their own, and the Rebels had a hard time moving the ball. The Dogies took over possession, and Charles Morgan started the game at running back. The Dogies ran a fullback lead, and the Rebels stuffed Morgan in the backfield.

The coaching staff realized the defensive end on this side was going to be off his block all day. They ran the fullback lead to the other side, and the Rebel fans erupted when the defensive end got off his block and stuffed Charles Morgan in the backfield. Coach Freeman called time-out when he did not get up after the play ended. Coach Williams called Steve Logan and said he needed to go in. Logan stopped at Coach Williams's side and said, "You *know* I'm a scatback, right?" Coach Williams said he knew, and they were going to run scatback plays.

The trainers got Morgan up, and he ran off the field to applause from both sides. Steve Logan went in the huddle, and the quarterback called a toss sweep. The center snapped the ball, and the quarterback tossed to Steve Logan, going left. The tackle got his block and sprung Logan on a long run. One of the Rebel players tackled him before he could score. Two plays later, Logan plowed into the end zone on a play down the middle. This was the first score of the game, but the Dogies felt a rhythm. The Dogies then pushed the much-bigger Rebels off the line to score the two-point conversion.

Ryan and Matt held the defensive line down and stuffed the Rebels fullback lead the rest of the first half. The Dogies led the game 24 to 0 at the half. This roll came with a price: the Dogie starting outside linebackers both went down with injuries. During halftime, Coach Freeman made player changes and moved Carl to outside linebacker. There was not a starter, so the two backups were set to start the second half. The Dogies took the second-half kickoff and scored, then scored the two-point conversion. This made the score 32 to 0 early in the second half.

Coach Freeman played the linebackers a series each, allowing one set to win the position going into next week's practice. The Rebels got it together and held the Dogies to one score the rest of the game. They found a way to contain on the corners, effectively shutting down Steve Logan. Late in the game, the Rebels scored and made the two-point conversion, sending the Dogies home with a 40–8 victory. Carl could not believe the size of the Confederate flag they waved when they scored—it was *huge*! He didn't understand the meaning behind the flag, just knew that it was not good.

He was glad they only scored once—he didn't have to see the Stars and Bars being waved much that day.

Coach Freeman allowed the team to cut up. It was a sweet ride home. The coaching staff knew they had work to do. They had observed their next opponent, scouting them. The Dogie bus pulled up to the Pemberton Junior High field house, and the guys unloaded their gear. Coach Freeman said they would do stretching the next day and dismissed them. Carl ran out of the building, and Riley was waiting for him. Carl climbed in the truck, and Riley asked how the game went.

He was surprised when he said they won 40–8, and listened as Carl gave him a summary of the game. He was happy when Carl said he was switched to linebacker and got a chance to play a lot during the second half. He asked about Bradley, and Riley said he went to Fort Worth to visit his sisters for a few days. They made it home, and Carl ran in the house. He had a lot to tell Rachel. They talked about the game and his day while he ate dinner. When he finished eating, Rachel told him to bathe and do his homework. When she checked at 11:00 p.m., he was already asleep, with his head in the book.

He got a letter from Jackie over the weekend and made a mental note to write her back. When he read the letter, he realized their lives had gone in different directions. He did not know what to write about in his letter, though they had school in common when he was in Jefferson. He knew the people she wrote about, but she did not know the people he was writing about.

That afternoon, he dressed and got ready for football practice. When he ran on the field, he saw Charles Morgan with a leg cast, and both the linebackers were in street clothes.

Coach Freeman called the team together and announced they had some changes. Steve Logan was moved to running back. One of the linebackers had bruised ribs, and the other a sprained ankle. Both were expected to miss the next two games.

Practice started, and Carl played series for series with Zach Miller. The Scout offense broke the huddle and came to the line of scrimmage. The quarterback took the snap and went down the line on Carl's side. Matt got off his block and stepped across the line as the quarterback cut inside and lowered his pads.

Carl tackled Quint seven yards down the field, knowing this was unacceptable. He ran the other way on the next play, and when Ryan stepped across the line, he handed the ball off to the fullback. Five yards downfield, Bubba made the tackle. The next play, Quint handed off to Logan, and he scored on a long run. This was how practice went, Quint running plays they'd never seen, and the defense could not stop them. Coach Freeman called off practice, and the team huddled around him. He explained the new offense was the Houston Veer and they were going to run it.

Carl changed clothes and found Bradley in the parking lot, waiting for him. He asked how practice went, and Carl said the offense killed them. Bradley asked what type of offense they were running; he'd never seen it before. Carl said they called it the Veer and they were not able to stop it. Bradley said he watched practice and saw they scored every time. Carl told him about the injured linebackers with bruised ribs and a sprained ankle. Bradley was at a loss for words and said Carl had to be a "sure tackler" when he got on the running back.

At practice the next day, the coaching staff was in the defensive huddle, showing them how to play the Veer. Coach Williams emphasized the tackles had to tackle the dive back every play. Matt and Ryan were told to step across the line; the defensive ends had to tackle the quarterback. The linebackers had responsibility for the "pitch back." The offense ran the plays at full speed and was able to score half the time they had the ball. This was a tremendous improvement from the day before. Coach Freeman broke practice and said they would walk through the following day.

Carl arrived at practice the next day hyped at the way things had gone the last two days. He dressed in shoulder pads and shorts and ran on the field. The team was in good spirits; they gained confidence in the offense and defense as practice went on. The boys saw the power of the Veer, and it was something new. Coach Freeman then broke practice, and Carl dressed to go home. Bradley was waiting for him in the car and said the team looked good. They drove home, and Bradley said he was going back to Detroit the next day, the UAW and GM settled the strike.

The next morning, Bradley dropped the kids off at school. He hugged Hannah and Carol, telling them he was going back to Detroit. When he dropped Carl at school, he stood outside the car and talked to him for a few minutes. He reminded him to stay low, to keep the offensive lineman off his body. Kendall walked over, saying hello as she walked up. Carl introduced her to Bradley, saying she was a friend. Bradley excused himself. He said he had a long drive. They walked to the building with her, asking why he said she was a friend and not his girl.

Carl was excited all day because he knew he was going to get a lot of playing time. At 2:30 p.m., he went to the gym, and Coach Freeman had the players relax for forty-five minutes before getting dressed. When they took the field at 3:30 p.m., the cheer line was there. He noticed Kendall in her miniskirt, shaking her pom-poms.

The team captains met the refs at midfield for the coin toss. The Lions won the toss and elected to receive the ball. The Dogies kicked off as Coach Freeman announced his defensive starters. Chad and Danny were the starters at outside linebacker. Coach Williams told Carl to stay close; he was soon going in.

John Tyler was a team that mirrored the Dogies, small but fast players. Carl watched their quarterback take the snap from center and run the Veer. He understood why the coaches wanted good techniques—the John Tyler quarterback was a magician running the Veer offense! Carl watched as he went down the line, making his reads. Matt stepped across the line, and the quarterback pitched the ball. Chad missed the pitch back, and he ran for thirty yards before the safety bumped him out of bounds.

After six first downs, the Lions were knocking on the Dogies' goal line. The Dogie defense stopped them, and the Lions turned the ball over on downs. The Dogies took over, and the first play Quint handed off to Logan in the dive lane. The John Tyler tackle missed Logan, and he was off to the races, running fifty-five yards before a John Tyler safety was able to tackle him. The crowd loved this offense. Both teams' running backs were running in open space. Quint ran the same play to the other side, and when the John Tyler defensive end came across, he cut inside.

Forty yards later, he ran into the end zone and scored. The Dogies lined up and pushed the Lions off the ball and scored the two-point conversion. The Dogies kicked off, and Coach Freeman stayed with his defensive lineup.

On the first play, Matt stepped across the line, forcing the quarterback to pitch. Chad missed the pitch back again and the Tackle got his block on the safety. Seventy-five yards later, the Lions running back jogged in the end zone, untouched! The Lions pushed the Dogies off the ball to score the two-point conversion and tie the game at 8 to 8.

Coach Freeman sent Carl in for Chad on the next defensive series, saying, "We have to stop that pitch back!" The adrenaline flowed as he ran on the field, eager to prove himself. The ball snapped, and the quarterback came down the line. Carl saw Matt step across the line and the Lions quarterback cut inside. He stepped in the lane and met the quarterback as he lowered his pads. Carl stood him up, and the pads sounded when he ran through him with a form tackle. The Dogie sidelines erupted—Carl had made a big-time tackle!

The Lions quarterback was shaken by the vicious tackle, and his wizardry in the Veer ramped down. Carl, thought, a big hit will always slow a hot running back flow. He ran the next three plays to the other side, and the Lions were on the march again.

The veer came back to Carl's side and Matt stepped across the line. The quarterback pitched and the Scat Back was off to the races, picking up twenty yards before Carl bumped him out of bounds. The quarterback had his swag back and drove the Lions offense down the field to score two more times. The Lions led 24 to 8 and were driving late in the third quarter.

Carl saw the quarterback take the ball and come down the line to his side. When Matt stepped across and he pitched to the scatback, Carl turned on the speed and hit the scatback with a bone-jarring tackle. The ball popped in the air, and he caught it before it hit the ground. The Dogie sideline erupted again; he made a big-time hit and caused a fumble. The Dogies took the fumble, went down the field, and scored. Steve Logan was clowning! He no longer had a fear of running inside.

The fourth quarter started with John Tyler leading 24–16 and driving. The quarterback started down the line to Matt's side, and he stepped across the line, meeting him with a bone-jarring form tackle. He was in the process of pitching the ball when Matt's hit caused the ball to float. Carl made the play, intercepting the pitch in midstride. It was a footrace to the end zone between Carl and the Lions scatback. Sixty yards later, Carl sprinted into the end zone, untouched. The Dogies pushed the Lions off the line, and Logan lowered his pads to score the two-point conversion.

The game was tied 24–24, with four minutes left as the Dogies lined up to kick off.

CHAPTER 10

The Integration Saga Gets Stupid
#IshNowRealReal

The Dogies lined up and kicked off to the Lions. A few plays later, the Lions were threatening to score. The Dogies defense was nervous, for they had not stopped the Lions offense and the game was almost over. The Lions quarterback came down the line, and Matt stepped across. This time he pitched, and Carl was in perfect position to take it. The footrace was on, and eighty yards later, he ran into the end zone.

The Dogies sideline exploded. This was a huge play. The Dogies led 30–24 and lined up for the two-point conversion. The Lions defense stuffed Logan short of the goal line, and the two-point conversion failed. The Dogies kicked off, and the Lions were on the ball. The quarterback went down both sides of the line and, four plays later, pushed into the end zone. The game was tied 30–30, and time had expired. The Lions had scored before time expired and had the option to try for the two-point conversion.

The Lions pushed the Dogies off the line, and the quarterback lowered his pads. The Lions sideline exploded when the refs signaled that he scored, and the Lions won the game.

The Dogies were subdued as they lined up to shake their hands. The coaching staff told the team they should hold their heads up;

after all, they played a great game. After the Dogies shook hands with the Lions, they met at midfield to dismiss. Coach Freeman gave a game ball to Matt, and he led the cheer. With a loud "One, two, three, "Dogie Pride," they ran off the field. Coach Williams pulled Carl to the side and congratulated him on the game he played.

The next day at school, Kendell was giddy about the game Carl played. She mimicked the way he ran as he scored a touchdown on the intercepted pitch. Kendell hugged him, saying, "My friend is a football hero!" They made it to the door of her class, and Carl handed her books back to her. Kendell looked at him and said he was going to be popular, then walked in the classroom. He walked to his class and was met with cheers when he stepped in the room. They congratulated him on a game well played, and Carl basked in the attention.

When the school day ended, Carl went to the bus stop. They did not have football practice, so he rode the school bus with the rest of the kids going to J. H. Moore. He sat next to Kendell, and she asked what he planned to do this weekend. They agreed to talk on the phone over the weekend since they had not had the chance to talk much during the week. The bus arrived at J. H. Moore, and Carl found Hannah and Carol. They started the walk home with the group headed to Scotts Quarters Road. The kids from Scotts Quarters had to walk as a group, for the White kids would target them if they were alone.

Another evening walking along Norwood to the jeers of "Nigger, go home, we don't want you in our school!" Carl and the other boys in the group knew if a fight started, the girls would go home while the boys fought. It was peaceful that day. The crowd shouted racial slurs at them with no physical aggression. Carl made a mental note of the screaming of kids who went to school with him.

When he got home, Carl found a letter from Jackie. He put his books down and opened the letter, thinking he had not written her in a couple of weeks. He thought about what Jackie said; he was going to Marshall and forget her.

Carl read the letter, and Jackie caught him up on all the things going on in Jefferson. He was a little disturbed when he read Ronnie

Simmons was still trying to talk to Jackie. He finished reading her letter and sat down to write her. He was careful not to mention anything about Kendall, although Jackie had asked about her several times. He started off telling her he was benched in football, had his position switched, and then won the position he really wanted. Carl mentioned he made a big play in the game against the John Tyler Lions but they still lost the game.

Before he knew it, he had written a four-page letter to Jackie. He signed the letter and found an envelope to put it in. When he and Riley went to the store later, he planned to buy a stamp and mail the letter. He and Riley sat on the porch, waiting for Janice to finish dinner. Riley asked how school was, and Carl said it was good. Janice called them to dinner, and the family sat at the table, eating. Riley said they had solved the problem of kids fighting on Norwood, and the bus drivers had been cleared to pick them up and drop them off at Scotts Quarters and Norwood.

Carl was glad to hear Scotts Quarters and Norwood was a bus stop. This meant they no longer had to walk through the White neighborhoods along Norwood Street going to and from school. The last fight was wild—there was a lot of blood! Two boys from Scotts Quarters Road missed the bus and had to walk to the neighborhood. They were jumped by a gang on Norwood as they walked home. Knives and sticks were used in the brawl, and a couple people were cut and stabbed. This happened a couple of weeks back, and all the Scotts Quarters kids were held out of school a couple of days.

The next weekend, Carl got a letter from Jackie and was shocked to find a picture of himself making a tackle on one of the Lions players. He could tell from reading her letter Jackie was excited to find this picture in the paper. The next week, Riley bought five copies of the paper, and they cut his picture out. Carl wrote Bradley a letter and put one of the pictures in the letter. When he got the letter, Bradley showed all his friends, saying, "The boy got pretty decent form!"

Kendall saw the picture and smiled, saying he was going to be very popular at school. She didn't say anything about the conversation everybody was having about the football team. The Dogies were popular because they energized the whole school, and everyone could get behind them. There was very little everybody at the school agreed on, but everybody at the school wanted the Dogies to win!

The semester went on, and Carl had a stellar year on the football field. The Dogies ended the season with six wins and three losses. The coaching staff agreed having three strong defensive ends made their linebacker's job easy.

During the awards assembly, Coach Williams spoke on the success of the Dogie season. He mentioned Carl's and the other players' big plays during the year. Coach Williams asked everyone for applause when he said Matt Monroe was Dogie MVP for the year. He told the audience how Matt was the one player that embodied what it meant to be a Dogie player. The team stood, and Matt walked onstage to get the award. The debate started on how good Carl was as a linebacker. Some of the players believed he was very good, and others thought he was blessed to be on the same side as a stud defensive end.

The season was over, and life returned to normal. The pep rallies for the basketball games were not nearly as exciting as they were for football. Carl settled in, and the grind of studying and working with Riley resumed. Toward the end of the semester, Carl was in Mrs. Williams's American history class. They were studying the Trail of Tears, and she made the statement, "Indians had been treated much worse than Black people." Carl could not believe Mrs. Williams qualified her statement with, "I know my Black students might not agree with this."

The room went silent as Carl raised his hand and Mrs. Williams called on him. He said he did not agree with her assessment that Indians were treated worse than Black people. Mrs. Williams defended her statement, saying the Indians were driven from their home and forced to live on reservations. Carl was sent to the office when he asked how long the Indians were held as slaves in the USA. She asked Carl to go to the office since, she claimed, he had become a disruption in her class. Carl took the referral and walked the two halls to the principal's office.

The assistant principal was in and took Carl in the office to discuss the referral. A few seconds later, Coach Williams walked in the office and asked if he could be present for the discussion. Carl was admonished to keep his thoughts to himself, especially when he had no firsthand knowledge of what went on during slavery or the Trail of Tears. Carl listened as the assistant principal said he should listen to the teacher and not challenge her. At this point, he knew it was pointless to try to explain his position and sat quietly as the assistant principal spoke.

He was told to sit in the principal's office for the rest of the period, and one of the office aide's was sent to Mrs. Williams's classroom to get his books.

Finally, the bell rang, and he saw Kendall in the hall, getting ready for lunch. Carl told her he'd been in the principal's office most of last period, and she looked at him with a puzzled look. When she asked what happened in class and he told her, she was really in shock. She knew what Mrs. Williams had said was wrong, but she did not know why Carl was pushing back against her.

They went through the lunch line, and Kendall said he should let things go.

Carl felt a lot better after he talked with Kendall at lunch. He took her books, and they walked to her class. When they got to the door, he handed her books to her and pushed her against the wall. He mustered his courage and kissed Kendall on the lips. He was surprised when she opened her mouth and stuck her tongue in his. He quickly broke the kiss and backed away from her. He ran to class and was out of breath when he sat down.

After class, he was shocked when he saw Kendall standing outside the door. She handed her books to him, and they walked to the bus stop. They got on the bus and sat together. Kendall asked if she was his girlfriend, and this caught Carl off guard. He was feeling good when he instinctively kissed her, never thinking she was his girlfriend. He thought to himself and finally answered, "I guess so." Kendall was pissed and took her books back from him. He asked what her problem was, and she said it took him too long to answer. He watched as Kendall walked off, and when he turned around, the kids from Scotts Quarters were waiting for him. He looked at the buses and realized they were all full—meaning, they had to walk through the Norwood Gauntlet, as they called it. The agreement had fell apart, and the kids from Scotts Quarters were walking through the curve again.

His mind shifted from Kendall to a fighting mode. There were twelve of them, and nine were girls. They got together and started the trip to Scotts Quarters Road. When they made it to the top of the hill at Norwood and Van Zandt, the boys handed their books to the girls so they could take them with them if the fighting started. They started the walk along Norwood, and things were good, until they made it to the curve. Standing in the curve was a gang of about five to six White boys. The group stopped when they saw the White boys standing in the street and blocking their path.

Edward Johnson, a ninth grader with them, shouted over to the White boys, saying they didn't want any hassle, that they only wanted to go home. James Talley, also a ninth grader, echoed Edward, saying they did not want any trouble. Carl recognized one of the White boys in the gang, Jamie Foster, who went to Pemberton Junior High with him. Edward took the lead, saying the girls need to let them start fighting the White boys and they should run home. He said they should not stop for dropped books or anything. He knew they wanted to trap the girls and force them to fight.

Jamie Foster told Edward they had no problem with them going home; they just could not go this way. Carl heard Edward say, "I thought so," and looked at him, asking, "Are you ready for this?" Carl nodded. He knew he had to fight, because Hannah and Carol were in the group. There was no way they were going to leave any of the girls. Edward lined the girls up three deep in three rows. He then put Carl and James on Jamie's side, and he stood on the other side. As they walked toward the gang of White boys, he said when Carl and James ran up on Jamie Foster, the girls should run.

Carl felt his heart beating fast as they walked toward the White boys. When they were feet away from them, Jamie Foster balled his fists up and James looked at Carl. He knew this was the signal and waited for James to make the first move. They broke at the same moment and ran up on Jamie Foster, hitting him with a barrage of blows and knocking him to the ground. Edward hit one of the bigger guys on his side, and the girls made a break for Scotts Quarters Road. Carl, Edward, and James fought the five White boys as they made their way to Scotts Quarters Road.

Jamie Foster might have been at Pemberton Junior High, but he was a big guy. He was six foot two and looked like a grown man. After James knocked Jamie down, Carl went one-on-one with another of the White boys in the gang. He hit him as hard as he could, busting his nose. Blood splashed everywhere, and some got on Carl's shirt. He hit the guy again when he would not stop, and they started to box in the street. Carl watched the other guys as they tried to get an angle on him. The guy with the bloody nose lost his will to fight and decided to try to stop his nosebleed.

James could not handle Jamie Foster—he was too big and strong. He had gotten off the ground and was upset he'd been knocked down. They heard Edward say, "On my three!" and knew they were about to bail. Edward counted down to three, and they made a break for Scotts Quarters Road. They could see the girls were on the corner, waiting for them. The White boys chased them to Scotts Quarters Road but stopped when they got to the intersection. The trash talk started with Jamie Foster saying, "You gotta come through here tomorrow, the next day, and the day after!"

Carl felt some kind of way when Jamie Foster said this, knowing they might have to come through there since the agreement for them to ride the bus fell apart. At that moment, Carl realized there were some things in life that might not be talked through. The gang of White boys called them niggers and monkeys as they walked away. Carl knew this was not the end of it and wondered how he would handle this going forward.

They made it home, and Janice panicked when she saw the blood on his shirt. She was even more concerned when Carl said he bloodied a White boy's nose fighting and it was his blood.

When Rachel got home, he explained what happened, and she said he had a right to defend himself. She silently pondered how they were going to keep the kids safe in this cruel world of integration. She got the kids settled down, and Riley made it home. Rachel got a full explanation of the fight from Carl, Hannah, and Carol as they ate dinner. They finished eating, and Rachel spent time with each of the kids. When she asked Carl how his day was, he remembered he had another set of problems beyond the White boys blocking the street on the way home.

He asked Rachel why it was so hard to understand girls. She asked what he meant, and Carl explained how Kendall was mad at him. Carl said she asked if she was his girlfriend and he said yes, he guessed she was his girlfriend. Rachel looked at him and laughed, saying he just did not get it. He was more confused and asked what she meant. Rachel asked why Kendall chose today to ask if she was his girlfriend. Carl said he kind of kissed her after they had been talking over lunch. Rachel made a mental note that she needed to talk to Carl about the birds and the bees.

Rachel dug deeper and found Carl had been sent to the office and that led to his deep conversation with Kendall. She unpacked his day, one issue at a time. She first asked Carl if he carried Kendall's books at school, and he said he did. Rachel asked if he walked her to class at school, and he said he did. She asked if he sat with her on the bus, and again, Carl said he did. Rachel laughed, saying, "You kissed her. Sounds like *you* got a girlfriend to me, buddy!" She looked at him and saw the confusion on his face. She hugged him, saying he should apologize to Kendall for being so dumb.

Carl didn't understand it, but Rachel said girls were funny like that. When you talk to them, and especially when you kiss them, you have a girlfriend. She told Carl he should tell Kendall he did not mean to upset her and wanted to make up with her.

The next morning, Carl saw Kendall at the bus stop and walked over to her. She handed her books to him, saying, "Don't talk to me." He did not know what to say and just told her he was sorry. Kendall looked at him and said she had talked with her sister, who said boys were dumb. Carl took a deep breath when Kendall said her sister said to give him another chance.

He leaned over and hugged Kendall and said he was sorry again. Her heart melted, and her mood changed as she smiled at him. When they made it to school, Kendall was not mad any longer. They walked off the bus, and Carl walked her to her homeroom door. Kendall said he was a star football player, very smart and popular at school. He was shocked when she said she did not want him to forget about her. This resonated with Carl, since it was the same thing Jackie had said, that she did not want to get lost in the shuffle. Carl put her at ease when he said he would not forget about her.

That evening, when Carl got home from school, he had another letter from Jackie. He read her letter and got angry. She mentioned Ronnie had asked her to the sock hop and she accepted. He didn't bother to discuss this with Rachel; he already knew her answer. Carl sat down and wrote Jackie back, saying he knew Ronnie was pushing up on her and really wanted to pay him back. He threw the letter away without mailing it, remembering this was not about him. The second letter he wrote, he thanked Jackie for telling him and asked if she was Ronnie's girl.

He mailed the letter and talked with Riley as they rode home from the post office. Riley put it all in perspective, saying they were young and this was going to happen many times before he settled down. Riley advised him to not get serious about any of the girls and instead to study his lesson and enjoy life. They made it back home, and Uncle Rudolph called out to him. Riley told him to go see what Rudolph wanted, and Carl went across the street to his house. He sat on the porch with Uncle Rudolph and listened as he asked if he wanted to go to the country Saturday.

Carl quickly agreed. He loved going to the country with Uncle Rudolph. He got a gallon of water for Rudolph, collected his two-bit fee, and went home to study.

The rest of the week was uneventful, and Saturday morning arrived. Carl got up and dressed and told Rachel he was going to the country with Uncle Rudolph. She agreed and said Uncle Rudolph had spoken with her and everyone was on board. The sun was bright as Carl and Rudolph rode to the family farm. Riley was going to join them later, after he had taken Janice to the store to get groceries.

The drive to the farm took about fifteen minutes, and the roads were long and dusty. When they made it to the farm, they did not go to the garden; instead, they went to a different part of the farm. Rudolph told Carl they needed to get out of the truck and walk the rest of the way. He watched Rudolph check limbs on the ground and trip wires set up on four corners. After he was certain the premises had not been disturbed, Rudolph walked into a large clearing. Carl was on Rudolph's heels as they walked to a fifty-five-gallon drum with copper coil wires sticking out of it.

Rudolph explained this was a whiskey still and they were going to make whiskey. Carl looked at him, unaware of what he was talking about. Rudolph explained how Marshall and Harrison County were "dry," and that meant no alcohol sales were allowed. The light bulb came on when Rudolph said they would make whiskey and sell it to people. The family farm was big, over a thousand acres, and Carl could see they were a long way from the garden. He had spent a lot of time on the farm; this was where they grew the fruits and vegetables they sold.

Over the next few hours, Rudolph walked Carl through the steps to make bootleg whiskey. He was amazed how quickly Carl caught on to the process and felt he would make a great bootlegger.

A few hours later, Riley drove up, joining them at the still. Rudolph gave him an update and said he felt Carl was going to be great at this. They talked about the whiskey-making process, and Riley said the most important thing was keeping the "perimeter" clear. When Carl asked what that meant, Riley said revenuers were always looking for untaxed whiskey.

Rudolph said, "When the perimeter is set right, you know if a revenuer has been to the site."

Carl asked what a *revenuer* was, and Riley laughed as he said they were the whiskey police. He went on to explain that the revenuer would find a still but not destroy it, instead waiting for the owner to come back and arrest him.

He processed everything Riley and Rudolph told him and realized they were showing him something they both knew how to do.

On the way home later, Riley told him that he could not share this with his friends or Rachel—they could go to jail if he did. He promised Riley he would keep this to himself and not tell anyone. They arrived home just as Janice finished cooking dinner. He took

Rudolph's plate to him and came back to the table. Janice said grace, and the family was quiet as they ate.

The weather was changing. Fall was setting in, and the leaves were turning brown. Since football season had ended, Carl had a lot of time on his hands. He sat down to write Jackie a letter, curious about how the sock hop went.

The next week at school, tryouts for the basketball team were held. Carl liked basketball a lot better than football, but he was a much better football player. Things started to settle down, the fights and racial slurs slowing as the people got used to dealing with one another. Christmas break rolled around, and Carl made the honor roll for the first semester. He found Kendall to tell her the good news, and she let him know she had made the honor roll also. They talked and laughed as they rode the bus home, glad to have the two-week break they were about to get.

The bus stopped at the intersection of Norwood and Scotts Quarters to let the kids from the neighborhood off the bus. There was not going to be peace walking along Norwood, so the school board authorized all buses to transport the kids. Carl hugged Kendall as he got up from his seat and got off the bus. He was happy the days of walking the gauntlet along Norwood were a thing of the past. The school board did not really want to allow this, but there had been bloodshed, and they did not want it to get worse. The kids walked along Scotts Quarters Road, glad to be out of school.

When they made it to Kingfish, Carl stopped at the mailbox and picked up the mail. To his surprise, there was a letter from Jackie. She started the letter with, "I don't know how to tell you, but Ronnie Simmons asked me to be his girl and I said yes." Carl's heart sank as he read the rest of her letter, which said how much fun she had at the sock hop with Ronnie Simmons. Jackie ended the letter by saying she wanted to stay friends with him. He felt some kind of way when he read she was going to write him once every two weeks for she wanted to give Ronnie a chance.

Carl walked the rest of the way home, his whole day messed up. He knew this was coming; after all, he was in Marshall and she was in Jefferson. He handed Hannah her letter from Jackie and gave Janice the rest of the mail. A few minutes later, Hannah came to Carl, saying Jackie still liked him but he was not in Jefferson. Hannah showed Carl the part of her letter that said to tell Carl she was still Jackie Hampton, that that had not changed.

Rachel drove up, and Carol met her at the car, saying school was out. She told him, "I know, baby. It is time to get ready for Christmas."

CHAPTER 11

The Integration Saga Is Still Stupid
#IshNowReallyReal

Christmas was upon them, and the pressures of day-to-day living gave way to the festivities of the holiday season. Rachel sat down with her kids to help with their gift list. When Carl put Jackie on his list, she scratched her name, saying he should write her instead. Rachel gave her seal of approval when he added Kendall instead. They went shopping the next day, and Carl got gifts for everyone. After they wrapped the gifts they bought, he went out to the porch and sat with Riley until it got dark. The conversation was light, and they both went inside, laughing.

The next day, Riley's sister from Waco and her family arrived to celebrate the holiday with them. Carl liked to celebrate Christmas with them because they opened one gift at midnight on Christmas Eve. He got most of what he wanted for Christmas, and the food was spectacular.

A couple of days later, his aunt and cousins went home as the focus returned to day-to-day life. He wrote Jackie a letter and was thrilled when he got a return letter from her. The letter was light, and she told him everything she got for Christmas. He was shocked that at the end she signed, "Jackie Hampton."

Christmas break surged by, and he was back in the day-to-day grind of schoolwork. Playing basketball was not the same as football, even though he liked the sport more. He and Kendall started having problems when she said he was too popular for her. He still walked her to class and carried her books, but she was no longer his girl. He sat on the porch, telling Riley what was going on, listening as Riley suggested he hang in there with her. Riley said he had to spend enough time with her so she would believe he was her boyfriend.

Carl left the porch that day thinking how hard it was to have a girlfriend. He thought about the way he and Jackie were always able to make up. The thing that stuck in his mind was, Riley told him he should stop talking to Kendall about Jackie, and that might make things go better. He made a mental note to do this as he walked in the house. The light came on, and he thought, *I might need to stop talking to Jackie about Kendall.* He sat on the couch with Hannah and Carol, watching TV as they waited for time to bathe and go to bed.

Spring semester flew by, and they were coming up on semester finals at school. Things between him and Kendall got better, and the letters between him and Jackie slowed down. It seemed Jackie wanted a blow-by-blow narrative of what was going on between him and Kendall. School released for the summer, and Carl was happy for the freedom from having to study. He got a paper route throwing *The Marshall News Messenger* along Scotts Quarters and Norwood Streets. The only thing he hated was Sunday morning. The papers were delivered at 3:00 a.m., and they had to be thrown by 7:00 a.m.

Kendall's house was one of the first houses on his route, but her sister did not subscribe to *The News-Messenger*. He sold her a subscription to the newspaper, saying they needed to know what was going on in the community. This was a plus for him; it meant he got a chance to see Kendall every evening when he threw his route. The only problem he saw with his paper route was, he had to go through the curve on Norwood. He knew this meant he would have to fight whatever group of white boys was assembled in the curve and intent on blocking his path.

During the Christmas break, Rachel decided to buy a house and told the kids they would start looking. The home they shared with Riley and Janice had running water, but there was no bathroom. Rachel also wanted some of the newer amenities available in modern homes. There was a new subdivision being built around the corner from Kendall's house, and they started looking there. Rachel found a house she liked and started the paperwork to purchase the home. It was a new home and qualified for the FHA 235 program. The program was income-based, and her income fell inside the HUD guidelines.

The real estate agent she was working with wanted proof Bradley did not pay child support. She spoke with him, and he agreed to send a statement that he did not pay child support. Three weeks later, she received the letter, and in bold print across the top it said thus: FOR REAL ESTATE PURPOSES ONLY. She asked him about it, and he said this was added in the event she wanted to use the letter as proof he did not pay child support. She told one of her friends who had purchased a home through the FHA 235 program about this, and she said this was not normal.

She said the real estate agent Rachel was using was a "gate-keeper" who added things to the criteria/guidelines sent down from the government. Her friend told her people did this to make it harder for them to qualify for loans and homes. Rachel was surprised to find this was common in real estate and banking. Rachel listened as she said she did not have to go through this when she purchased her home. She gave Rachel the number for the bank she used out of Houston, and Rachel gave them a call. When she spoke with the bank in Houston, they gave her the name of a different real estate agent to use. She contacted the agent the bank referred her to, submitted her application, and was approved for the program.

Rachel was pissed to learn the real estate agent she used first was partners with the builder and they refused to sell her a house. The bank in Houston had her contact another builder in the area who would build a home for her. The city of Marshall informed the builder they would not release the funds needed to develop the property he wanted to build on. This killed her chance of purchasing a home on the FHA 235 program in Marshall. She went home and cried. This was a bitter pill. She was contacted by the bank, and a remodeling project was suggested.

She contacted a local contractor, and the decision was made to add two bedrooms and two bathrooms to the home. The bank in Houston funded the remodel project, and six months later, Rachel had a remodeled home with modern amenities. School was about to be out for the summer, and Riley told Carl they were not going to work as much this summer. He took this opportunity and signed up for the summer basketball program. A couple of weeks later, he was blown away when he walked on the court at Pemberton Junior High, and a squad from Jefferson was there.

He was further blown away when he saw Jackie on the other end of the court warming up with the Jefferson squad. When he walked to their end of the floor, he saw Ronnie Simmons was also there. Someone called his name when he walked past half-court, and he saw Michelle Burns standing off court. She ran out to him, and they stood at the free throw circle as she told him about the things going on in Jefferson. She made a point to tell him that Jackie was Ronnie's girl now. He smiled as he said he had heard that and walked toward Jackie and Ronnie.

He spoke to them both as the group from Jefferson surrounded him. The people from Marshall were surprised he knew the Jefferson group and wanted him to introduce them. During the six weeks of the program, Carl introduced everyone from Marshall to everyone from Jefferson. Ronnie Simmons was beside himself; he felt Jackie had pushed him aside for Carl once again. It was too cool the way it happened. Ronnie could never accuse Carl of running up to Jackie; the group simply surrounded them. The coaches used different rotations, and Carl was teamed up with Jackie.

He knew most of her moves and hit her with smooth passes that she turned into points. Ronnie was furious—Carl had been gone from Jefferson two full school years and was still upstaging him with Jackie! The rotation rolled to Ronnie and Carl defending each other. Ronnie drove to the basket, and Carl fouled him hard, forcing them to tumble into the mat behind the goal. Ronnie jumped to his feet as he and Carl were face-to-face and chest-to-chest.

"You can't come in here like that, Ronnie. This the Paint!"

Ronnie pushed Carl hard, and that was when the fight started.

The coaches got them broken up, but Carl's nose was bloody and Ronnie had a busted lip. A technical foul was called on Carl, giving Ronnie three foul shots, and his team got possession of the ball out of bounds. The coaches sat Carl down a few plays to allow the temperature between him and Ronnie to go down. The group had been watching Carl and Ronnie and could clearly see they did not like each other. Carl went back in the game and was assigned a different player to guard. The taunting between them started, and Ronnie reminded him that Jackie was his girl now.

Carl went hard on him, saying he should ask Jackie what her last name was.

Lunch came, and he sat down with Ronnie and Jackie, which irritated Ronnie to no end. He sat across from them and was surprised when Michelle Burns sat next to him. She made sure to sit close to Carl and saw this irritated Jackie. Jackie had had enough and asked Michelle to leave the table, since nobody had invited her to sit there. Michelle laughed out loud, saying, "You Ronnie girl. How you gon' ask me to leave?" Michelle rubbed salt in the wound by saying she was talking to Carl and he hadn't asked her to leave.

Carl's petty nature came to the surface. He remembered all the times Ronnie had done this to him. He hugged Michelle and paid special attention to her while they ate. Jackie felt her temper boiling over. She could not believe this girl sat down with them. The air between Michelle and Jackie was thick. There was no love lost between them. Ronnie observed there was enough shade for an eclipse as he got up in his feelings about Jackie bugging with Michelle. He went hard and said he felt Carl *and* Michelle needed to find another table to eat at.

He went real petty with Ronnie, saying, "You *don't* own this table, and you can't ask me to leave!"

Michelle smiled and said she and Carl would do just that as she stood and walked away. He knew Ronnie had won as he got up from the table and followed Michelle to another table. They sat and talked until lunch was over, and she asked him to memorize her phone number. He memorized her number and said he would mos def call her.

The rest of the program was difficult for them. He and Jackie had to deal with their feelings while competing against each other.

The games were physical, and they fouled each other hard. One play, it was Carl against Jackie, and the next it was Carl against Ronnie. Jackie stripped him at the top of the key and made a break for a layup. As she put the ball on the backboard, he crashed into her and they tumbled into the mat behind the goal. She jumped up and pushed him hard in the chest with both hands. Her emotions flooded out as she screamed, "I *can't* believe you fouled me like that!"

Carl screamed back, "This basketball, Jackie!"

Ronnie ran on the court, heading toward him, but she stepped between them.

Jackie dribbled to the side, and Carl stripped her and made a break for a layup. As he put the ball on the backboard, she crashed into him and they tumbled into the mat. There was a loud crack, and Jackie screamed in pain. He looked at her face and knew something was wrong. He helped her up and saw she could not extend her left leg. He had seen broken legs in football and knew she broke her leg when they fell. The coach ran over to them and confirmed her leg was broken. They took Jackie to university clinic, where they set her leg and put it in a cast.

Jackie's mother came in the room and was upset Jackie broke her leg. She was angry when she was told Jackie and Carl had been playing when her leg got broken. She thought, *My daughter just* can't *leave that boy alone!* She listened as Jackie described how she broke her leg, surprised when she said she was paying Carl back for his hard foul the play before. Carl didn't read anything into it when Mrs. Hunt did not offer him a ride home; he walked home, anyway.

When he made it home, Rachel was sitting on the porch, waiting for him.

She said Mrs. Hunt had called, saying he broke Jackie's leg. Carl said Jackie did break her leg, but it was in a basketball play. He threw his route from the car that day. Rachel wanted a full explanation of what happened. Rachel asked if he was mad when the play happened, and he admitted he was mad at her. Carl said Jackie was mad at him and fouled him hard. Rachel decided to let it go. She was going to call Mrs. Hunt back to tell her Carl was sorry. Jackie had told her family what happened, and when she called, they were cordial. Mrs. Hunt hung up the phone, saying, "You gon' get enough of that boy!"

Her sister, Alicia, loved seeing "puppy love," as she called it, and told Jackie to go for it with Carl. Rachel pulled up to the Hunt residence in Frog Town, saying they would stay an hour or so and then go home. She was shocked Hannah and Carl were treated like rock stars in Jefferson. The kids in the neighborhood all came to see them. Rachel knocked on the door of the apartment, and Mrs. Hunt answered. She agreed to allow Carl and Hannah to see Jackie. Alicia noticed Jackie's demeanor changed when he walked in the room, and knew she was spot-on.

Ronnie was there, and Carl decided to ignore him, speaking as he walked by him. Carl walked over to Jackie and hugged her, saying "I'm sorry, Jackie." Alicia pointed out the way they held each other, saying, "It was an accident. We know what scared women look like."

Mrs. Hunt laughed and said, "Jackie is definitely not scared of Carl!"

It shocked everybody when Carl called Ronnie over to where he and Jackie stood. The three of them stood together, and Carl said they needed to quash their beef. He looked at Jackie and said he wanted her, but he was in Marshall.

He leaned down and signed her cast, saying her leg would not be broken if they had not been beefing. Carl looked at Ronnie and said he would never give up on Jackie, but he would get out of the way. Michelle walked up and was within earshot, listening as Carl, Jackie, and Ronnie came to an understanding. Carl and Ronnie hugged, and they seemed to have quashed their beef. The sight of Jackie's leg in a cast had touched Carl's heart. Jackie's leg started hurting, and she walked in the house. Hannah followed behind; she wanted to spend some time with her best friend.

Ronnie shook his hand again and walked off, headed home. He was happy—at least Carl had said he would get out of the way. Michelle stood by Carl and said her sister Shasta lived in Marshall.

She went on to say Shasta lived on Norwood Street. When she asked if he was familiar with that street, he said it was around the corner and on his paper route. She gave him the address and said she would be there this weekend. The meds kicked in, and Jackie fell asleep with Hannah by her bedside. She left the room and told Mrs. Hunt Jackie had gone to sleep.

Rachel was happy when Hannah walked outside. She thought she was going to have to drag her out of the house. They got in the car, and Rachel drove home. When Jackie woke up a couple of hours later, Alicia said, "Sis, you might be Ronnie girl, but you Carl woman." Ironically, she understood what her older sister was saying. Alicia told Jackie she should not write letters to Carl; they had to cut ties.

Michelle went home and wrote Carl a letter, mailing it the next day.

That weekend, she was at her older sister Shasta's house and called to let him know. Shasta lived two streets over from Kendall's house. When Carl asked Rachel to stop at Shasta's house, she rolled her eyes and asked why. Carl told her he wanted to say hello to Michelle and deliver their paper. Rachel told him, "You got five minutes, buddy!" She and Hannah sat in the car, and he stayed in the house exactly five minutes. When he got back in the car, Hannah asked, "How you gon' have two girlfriends two streets over?"

He appealed to Rachel to make Hannah shut up, and she said, "Really, Carl, I was wondering that myself. You seeing two girls who are two streets over from each other." Rachel thought, *If this boy not like his daddy!* She cranked the car, and they finished his paper route, then went to the store for treats. He bought everybody something, and they went home to prepare for dinner. He sat on the porch with Riley and waited for Janice to call them in for dinner. He was surprised when Riley asked about Michelle. Riley saw he was clueless about having two girls that close to each other.

He explained, "Michelle is from Jefferson. She not going to meet Kendall."

Riley had to give it to him—he had nerves! They went in the house to eat, and Michelle called him right at 9:00 p.m. She had perfect timing—Hannah had just gotten off the phone, and Riley did not allow calls after 9:00 p.m. They talked until Hannah and Carol finished their baths and he had to take his. He didn't see Michelle the next day; it was Sunday, and they threw the paper at 7:30 a.m.

Eventually, summer passed, and he was ready for school to start, excited to be going to eighth grade.

He and Michelle wrote each other while he and Jackie continued their exile from each other. Michelle was at Shasta's house a lot, and he saw her regularly, the houses being walking distance from each other. He loved talking to Michelle. She was smart and on the cheer squad. She also kept him up on Jefferson news and gossip. He was surprised when Michelle would tell him the latest between Jackie and Ronnie. The eighth-grade team was having a crappy season, and Carl was frustrated they were losing this way.

Kendall had become distant, and they were no longer friends. She broke up with him, saying she could not handle the way people liked him. She felt small with him. He had a sympathetic ear with Michelle. The seventh-grade team she cheered for was having a crappy season too. The irony was not lost on Carl. He was popular at school, and his girlfriend lived in Jefferson. What boggled his mind was, the girlfriend was *not* Jackie! He felt like he was in *The Twilight Zone*!

The day after Thanksgiving, Rudolph was sick and had to be rushed to the hospital. Since he was a veteran, he was taken to the VA Hospital in Shreveport.

Riley went to check on him a couple of times each week while he was there, and Carl had to throw his route on his bike the days Riley went to Shreveport. He and Michelle exchanged a letter during the week and saw each other on the weekend. The Jefferson Bullpups team and the Dogies had a horrible year. Carl was glad the season was over—he hated to lose! He and Michelle had a lot in common. She was smart, with a sharp sense of humor, and talked a lot of trash. He did not know what it was, but he felt different around Michelle.

A lot of people did not understand her and wanted to fight, but he was smitten. He did not miss the letters from Jackie; she had simply been seamlessly replaced by Michelle. Riley had been making plans to visit Waco for Christmas, and it was their time to go there. The Monday before Christmas, the phone rang about 9:45 p.m., and Carl picked it up. A nurse from the VA Hospital in Shreveport was on the phone and asked if it was the James residence. He confirmed this was the James residence, and she said Rudolph James had died about an hour earlier.

Carl hung up the phone and walked in Riley's bedroom to tell him about the phone call. Riley had heard the phone ring and asked if he was sure it was the VA in Shreveport. Riley made the call to the VA Hospital, and they confirmed Rudolph had died. He hung up the phone, sat in the chair, and said, "My brother is gone." Janice walked in the room and sat next to Riley as he called his sister Anne. After he made the necessary calls, Riley went back to his room and went to sleep.

The next morning, Carl was with Riley when he went to the funeral home to make Rudolph's funeral arrangements. The funeral director and Riley were friends and made small talk as they made Rudolph's arrangements. Things went well, and when they left, Mr. Floyd walked to the truck with them. He asked Riley when he should bring Rudolph to the house for the wake and funeral. Carl thought he was hearing things but didn't say anything, holding his peace until they left. When they drove off, Carl asked what it meant to bring Rudolph to the house. Riley explained they brought the dead to the house for both the wake and the funeral. He stared out the window as this ran through his mind.

He could not let it go, so he asked Riley, "You mean we go to sleep with a dead person in the house?" Riley confirmed this was right and a tradition in their culture. Carl was taken aback at the thought that Rudolph would be in the house with them. All he could think of were the ghost movies he had seen and dead folks coming alive. When he got home, Carl called Hannah and Carol to his room. Carol was mortified when he explained Rudolph was coming to the house for his funeral and wake. She asked when he was supposed to be there, and Carl said he didn't know.

They agreed this was not a good thing as Carol went to the kitchen and got two sacks. She started to pack, saying she was not

going to be there when they brought Rudolph there. Rachel overheard them and went to Riley, saying he was about to have a mutiny
on his hands. A few minutes later, Carol came out of the house, her
two bags fully packed. Riley asked where she was going, and her
answer was she did not know. When Carl followed her out the door,
he stopped him and asked how they could settle this. He looked at
Riley, saying, "Just don't bring Uncle Rudolph to the house."

Riley almost laughed and managed to hold a straight face. He
agreed they would not bring Rudolph to the house but said he had
to tell Mr. Floyd. Carl was not hesitant and said he would be happy
to tell Mr. Floyd Uncle Rudolph could not come to the house. Riley
called Mr. Floyd and changed the plans and told him the kids were
ending this tradition in the James household. The next day, Carl and
Riley went to the funeral home and Carl spoke to Mr. Floyd. He
was direct, saying, "Mr. Floyd, you are not going to be able to bring
Uncle Rudolph to the house."

They all laughed and agreed Rudolph's funeral would be at
Macedonia Church, and the wake would be at the house, without
Rudolph's body there. Riley told Carl he and his sisters broke a long
tradition in the James household and the Black culture. He explained
how the dead normally came to the house for the wake and funeral.
Riley said Janice's father died in 1945 and he was at the house for two
days. Carl absolutely could not wrap his mind around this. *How do
you go to sleep with dead people in the house?* It was hard to believe this
was a longtime tradition.

Funeral services were normally held at 2:00 p.m., but it was
Christmas Eve. The family moved the services to 11:00 a.m. to allow
for more time to fellowship and celebrate. Funeral service and burial
for Riley was over before 1:00 p.m., and everyone went to Riley's
to hang out. It was packed. His sister Anne was there, as well as his
cousins and other relatives. The food, family, and fellowship went
into the night, and presents were opened at midnight. The mood
was a festive Christmas Day. It was hard to believe they had a funeral
the day before.

Family by family, people started to leave, and by Monday, things
were back to normal. There was still a week left in Christmas vaca-

tion, and he had his paper route to throw. He saw Michelle Monday evening when he went by Shasta's house. When he threw his route in the car, they went by Shasta's house one time. When he threw his route on his bike, he went by her house twice. He was always through with his route, and on the way home, when he passed her house the second time. Carl threw his route on his bike the rest of the week and spent a lot of time with Michelle.

He knew a couple of Michelle's nephews, and they got a basketball goal for Christmas. Michelle liked to play with them, but she was no good at basketball. Carl and her nephews worked with her, helping her get her moves down. Michelle got into it and started to get better at basketball. She was on the seventh-grade team, but her playing time was limited. Jackie made fun of her, calling her a practice dummy because she hardly ever got to play in the games. Michelle was at Shasta's house most weekends; she kept her niece and nephews when Shasta went to work or went on a date.

She was a natural for basketball, tall and limber. After a couple of months, she made her nephews stay in the house, and it was one-on-one between her and Carl. Her game got aggressive; playing against Carl was starting to pay off. It was hard seeing Kendall at school, and she barely spoke to him. Riley said she needed time to come around and suggested he speak but not try to be friends. He took the advice and focused on school, not letting the Kendall situation consume him. He was still at a loss. She just cut him off with no real explanation.

He was finally able to get past it and let it go. The semester went by, and they were getting ready for summer vacation. Riley missed Rudolph and they were not going to the garden this summer.

Over the Memorial Day weekend, Bradley called and asked if he'd like to come to Detroit for the summer. He realized they didn't go to the still the previous summer and bought the vegetables they sold because Rudolph was sick. He told Bradley he needed to work on his paper route as he normally paid for his clothes. Bradley laughed and told him he didn't need to worry about that.

He agreed to go to Detroit, and Bradley was thrilled he would get the chance to make up for letting him down. He and Rachel worked out the details, and a few days later, he was on an airplane to Detroit. He caught a Delta flight out of Shreveport, and the stewardesses were instructed to keep him on the plane until they got to Detroit Metro Airport. Rachel agreed to throw his route for him if she kept the money. Carl remembered what Rudolph told him: everything is negotiable. He hit Rachel up for 10 percent, and she flat out refused. It was all the money or give up the route. She said he should be glad she decided to not go to summer school this year to work on her master's degree. Carl gave it up. He knew she was not coming off her position.

The plane touched down at Detroit Metro Airport, and Carl was escorted off by two stewardesses. Bradley met him with Gwen, Trey, and Carlos. This was the first time he met them, and they walked out of the airport to the car. He was totally surprised when he saw the homes—they looked like cereal boxes! He also saw how close the houses were to one another.

This was new to him. He had never seen houses this close together. The plane landed at 2:30 a.m., and the ride to Northwest Detroit had taken about half an hour. He finally got a chance to lie down at 5:30 a.m. When he woke up the next morning, Carl went outside and was shocked the air was brisk, not cold air, but a cool draft.

Later that day, Bradley said it was not unusual to need a light jacket at night. As he looked around the neighborhood, Carl saw this was different from anything he had ever seen before. He was there for two months and met all the kids on the block.

He was surprised to find most of the kids were given an "allowance" to do their chores at home. He had never heard of this concept before, and one of the girls on the block had a fifty-dollar bill.

Summer flew by, and it was time to return to Texas. Carl had seen a lot of sights in Detroit. He went to Belle Isle, Northland Mall, and Canada during his summer stay in the city. He had a good time, but he was ready to go back to Texas. The kids on the block were funny to him, and he was funny to them. He laughed at their high-pitched, raspy voices, and they laughed at his Southern drawl.

Bradley took Carl shopping for school clothes before he left for Texas. Most of the clothes Carl chose were too heavy to wear—they were designed for Michigan's cooler climate. Carl caught a midday flight from Detroit to Shreveport with a short layover in Memphis. Just like on the way to Detroit, the stewardesses were told to not let him off the plane until Shreveport. Rachel and Hannah picked him up from Shreveport Regional when his flight landed at 5:30 p.m. They quizzed him about the trip during the forty-five-minute ride home.

Rachel went through Carl's clothes and saw what he bought with Bradley. She knew they would have to go shopping—the clothes he had would be better during January and February, when it got real cold. While he and Riley were sitting on the porch, talking about Detroit, he mentioned the kids there got an "allowance" for doing their chores. Riley laughed and said, "I allow you to live in my house." He hated he mentioned this when Riley kept going, saying, "I allow you to eat my food, at *my* table." It went on for what seemed like forever, Riley saying all the things he "allowed" him to do.

Riley asked what he remembered most about the city and Carl thought for a moment. He told Riley, they had been out to his uncle Leonard's house in southwest Detroit. Carl described this long bridge on I75 over a huge railroad yard.

Riley listened as Carl said they stopped at Leonard's house for a couple hours. He described leaving Leonard's house and Bradley showed them the plant where he worked. Carl said that when they left the plant, they were driving toward downtown Detroit on Fort Street. He told Riley that the view of the tall buildings downtown as they drove down Fort Street was a big memory. Riley said "Oh really" when Carl said the people there call this the skyline. Carl then told him that he had never seen big buildings like that. Carl was fascinated when he said, "Not only are the buildings big. They're really close together." He laughed as he told Riley, everything is close together there. While they talked, Carl thought out loud and asked Riley if he knew how much one of those buildings would cost. Riley said he was not sure what one of those buildings would cost, but he was sure it was into the high millions.

CHAPTER 12

People Bugging about Carl's Detroit Trip
#YouHaveAVividImagination

The first week of football practice nearly killed him—he had not worked out or run in over two months. The buzz around school was about how he had seen tall buildings and square houses in Detroit. He described his summer vacation in great detail and had no idea some of his classmates did not want to hear it. After a couple of minutes of talking about how he enjoyed the trip, his teacher smiled, saying he had a vivid imagination. He could not believe the kids did not believe him, and the teacher said he had a vivid imagination. He was stunned. That was not the reaction he expected.

Carl sat down and made a mental note to not mention what he had done to his classmates. Football practice that afternoon went great. He was working back into shape and had not cramped up in a couple of days. The first game came, and he was shocked when he saw Kendall on the cheer line. Carl ran by her and smiled, but curiosity got the best of him. He stopped and hugged her as she whispered, "Have a good game," in his ear. He thanked her and ran on the field with the rest of the team. Carl felt good; Kendall seemed to have rebounded, but he did not know life was about to get complicated.

The next morning, Kendall was at the J. H. Moore bus stop, waiting for him. She handed her books to him, and they sat together on the bus ride to school. She was quiet, and Carl did not question her about what was going on in her life. She gave him a brief explanation, saying it had nothing to do with him.

The following Sunday morning, he found himself in church at Zion Hill as they worshipped and sang hymns. During the service, Rachel said he and Hannah needed to walk to the front and ask to be baptized. A minute later, he and Hannah stood before the church, asking to be baptized.

They were not alone. There were eight or nine kids in line with them to be baptized. Pastor Allen came out of the pulpit and asked each of them why they wanted to be baptized. Carl remembered what Rachel told him to say and repeated it to Pastor Allen. Each of the kids made a short speech on why they wanted to be baptized, and Pastor Allen scheduled them to be baptized the following Sunday. They sat down, and Rachel talked to them about being "saved" after being baptized. Carl did not know what being baptized meant but understood this was expected of him.

The next week at school, he told Kendall he was going to be baptized the following Sunday, and she was excited. She told him she had been baptized during the revival last year and it was not a big deal. She outlined the experience, and he felt better when they got through talking about it. Sunday rolled around, and when they got ready for church, Carl noticed he and Hannah had clothes they could get wet. When they left the house, they did not go to Zion Hill; instead, they drove to Edwards Chapel. Carl was surprised Edwards Chapel was across the street from Kendall's house.

The choir sang hymns as Pastor Allen baptized the kids one by one. He was surprised Kendall was in the crowd of witnesses— Edwards Chapel was where she went to church. He was nervous as Pastor Allen held his nose and dipped him in the water. It went quick, and before he knew it, he was out the baptism pool. When the last kid was baptized, everyone got back in their car and drove to Zion Hill to finish the ceremony. Carl and the other kids sat in front of the church and were given the Lord's supper. As they accepted the Communion cup and cracker, they were given the Christian charge.

This caused clarity issues with Carl; it seemed everything he liked to do, he had to stop. They spoke to the kids about sin, but the focus seemed to be on fornication. He knew what *fornication* meant, as he had run across the word reading the Bible and looked it up in the dictionary. He started to notice a lot of Pastor Allen's sermons centered on fornication. The confusion started to set in with him. He had been taught God created man in his own image. When he looked at the picture of Jesus on the wall, he saw a man with blond hair and blue eyes.

He had read in Scripture that no man had seen God and lived. He reasoned, if no man could see God and live, who painted that portrait? He spoke with Rachel about this, and her eyes glazed over—he was asking things she had never thought about. She remembered he was a voracious reader and read everything put in front of him. She finally said he should pray and ask for discernment to understand the spiritual things that confused him. He read John's vision of Jesus in the first chapter of Revelation, where Jesus is portrayed as having a robe with a golden sash and white hair.

The scripture said he had eyes like blazing fire and feet like bronze. The last part of the description said he had a voice like rushing waters. Carl did not understand the meaning of "seven stars in his right hand" and a "double-edged sword coming out of his mouth." Rachel cringed when he asked if kissing was considered fornication. She did not miss a beat and asked whom he had been kissing. Carl fessed up, saying he had kissed Jackie, Kendall, and Michelle. Rachel decided she needed to have "the talk" with Carl and sat him down when they got home.

The more she explained the birds and the bees, the more disgusted the look on his face became. He finally ran out of the house to the porch, saying this was gross! When he sat down on the porch, Riley asked what was wrong. Carl looked at him with all sincerity and said girls were yucky.

The next day at the bus stop, he told Kendall he did not want to be her boyfriend any longer. When Kendall asked why, he said he thought girls were just yucky and they needed to be friends. This hurt Kendall's feelings, and she started to cry.

He hugged her, saying he didn't mean she was gross; he meant having a girlfriend was gross. This didn't help. Kendall took her books from him and ran up the steps to the bus. She side-eyed him the rest of the day and would not let him sit at the table with her at lunch. Carl was confused. Kendall was mad, and he could not figure out why. When she got home that evening, Lillian could see she was upset and finally pulled it out of her. She cried as she told her older sister Carl thought she was gross. Lillian was beside herself with anger and called Rachel to see what was wrong with Carl.

She laughed as she explained that after the baptism and sermon on Sunday, Carl was confused and now believed all girls were yucky. It became crystal clear to Lillian when Rachel said she had given Carl the birds-and-the-bees talk. When she hung up the phone, Lillian was laughing and went to Kendall. She hugged her, saying Carl was a typical thirteen-year-old boy and not to give up on him. She wiped Kendall's tears and said she should be his friend because this was not going to last long.

Carl and Hannah went to the Bulldogs games with Rachel when she worked the concession stands. Jackie was upset with him, and he no longer seemed to have a problem with Ronnie Simmons. It really stoked Jackie's anger when he seemed to pay a lot of attention to Michelle Burns. Although she was angry with Carl, she laughed when Hannah said she should look over him; he was truly bugging right then. Hannah described him as a "space cadet" and said he was very confused. Jackie could not believe this. What had happened to the smooth guy whom she knew?

It became clear to her when Hannah said Rachel had "the talk" with Carl and he now believed all girls were gross. Hannah and Jackie agreed they could not stand Michelle Burns as they watched her hanging off Carl. Through all his confusion, he forgot to give her the memo that he did not like girls and they were yucky. Ronnie Simmons loved it—he *finally* had Jackie to himself and smooth-as-silk Carl Hampton was bugging! He did not know what brought this about, but he was loving it. When Rachel called them to go home, he hugged Jackie and shook Ronnie's hand.

Michelle walked them to the car, saying she would be in Marshall the next day. She suggested Carl come by after he finished his paper route and challenged him to a one-on-one basketball game. Jackie and Ronnie walked behind them, with Hannah in tow. Ronnie did not know Jackie was seething, she was upset Michelle Burns seemed to have won out with Carl. She could not help but wonder why he was happy with talking to Michelle but did not want to talk to her. They stood around Rachel's car, and Ronnie tried unsuccessfully to get Jackie to keep it moving.

In a fit of anger, Jackie asked Michelle if she knew about Kendall. She looked at Jackie and incredulously asked who Kendall was. Jackie laughed and said Kendall was his girlfriend, adding that he had not liked Jefferson girls since he moved back to Marshall. Jackie was shocked it did not faze Michelle and she kept talking to Carl. Rachel broke up the love fest when she said they had to go, it was getting late. Ronnie walked home with Jackie and Michelle, sensing there was something on Jackie's mind.

He asked Jackie if there was a problem, and she said everything was cool. Jackie's anger got the best of her, and she blurted out, "When did Shasta move to Marshall?" Michelle laughingly said she had moved to Marshall a year ago for a job. She listened as Michelle said she went to Marshall most weekends, keeping Shasta's kids while she worked the swing shift as a nurse at the hospital. Jackie was on the verge of tears and heard her sister Alicia's voice: "You Ronnie girl, but you Carl woman." Carl threw his route on his bike the next day and stopped at Shasta's house on the way home.

He played Michelle one-on-one basketball, and she won three games to his two. They sat on the porch, resting and laughing, when Carl said he let her win because she was a girl. Michelle teased him, saying he should play her like she was a boy, and pushed him playfully. Michelle told him she didn't want him to go easy on her because she was a girl. Carl asked if she was going to be mad if it got rough, and Michelle said she could handle herself. He was about to leave when Kendall walked by with two of her nephews. She stopped and spoke to Carl, saying they were on the way to the store.

Kendall asked if he would go with them, and he agreed. He rolled his bike down the driveway to where they stood and asked Michelle to come to the curb. Michelle walked to the curb, and Carl introduced her to Kendall and her nephews. Michelle smiled, saying, "Hello, Kendall. I heard about you last night." Michelle told Kendall she had been told she was Carl's girl. Kendall was shocked a girl she did not know was saying Carl was her boyfriend. Kendall was all smiles when Michelle said Jackie said she was his girl. She told Michelle she had heard about Jackie but had never met her.

They talked a few minutes longer, and Kendall said she lived two streets over. Michelle went in the house as Carl left with Kendall and her nephews, headed to the store. Carl could not believe Rachel was right again about not lying to these girls. A few minutes later, they were at the Pack 'N Sack store, buying treats. Carl walked them to the top of the hill at Van Zandt and Norwood, then got on his bike to ride home. He knew he was going to have a problem when he came out the curve on Norwood Street and saw three White boys standing in the street.

He was on the widest part of the street and rode full speed toward the group. At the last possible second, he switched direction and rode away from them. They cursed and called him a nigger as he flipped them the bird and rode down to Scotts Quarters Road. He slowed down and heard the clicking sound of his ten-speed gears as he slowly rolled the rest of the way home. The ten-speed was a great bike, and he rode like an expert. The bike was a gift from Bradley, and he was not going to let it get taken from him. He was glad they did not show up while they were walking to the store.

He rode up in the yard, and Riley was sitting on the porch. He asked Carl where he had been saying they were starting to get concerned he had not made it home. He sat on the porch with Riley and explained he had walked Kendall and her nephews to Pack 'N Sack after he finished his paper route. Riley told him to come in the house; they had been holding dinner for him. He did not tell Riley about his near miss with the White boys. This had become so common that it did not warrant mentioning. After dinner, Kendall called him, thanking him for walking them to and from the store.

They talked a while longer, and there was no mention of Michelle. The next day, Jackie went to her sister Alicia, telling her what happened Friday night and how she got mad at Michelle Burns. Alicia laughed and asked if she remembered what she said about Carl. Jackie said she did remember what she said and understood it. Jackie helped her fix dinner, listening as she said Michelle Burns did not have a chance with Carl. This shocked Jackie, and she asked why she felt that way. She explained she saw the way he looked at her and he might like Michelle Burns but he was still her guy to lose.

Jackie tried to tell Alicia about the things happening, and she asked if Carl broke up with her. She thought about it and said he did not—she broke up with him. "Bingo!" Alicia said, then she added that she'd been listening to their mother and Rachel. Alicia knew Jackie and Hannah were friends and suggested she call her. Jackie called Hannah, shocked when she picked up the phone. They talked a while, and Hannah started to tell her how Carl was bugging. She felt better when Hannah finished her blow-by-blow detail of how Carl had transformed from this smooth young man to a bugging moron!

They laughed when Hannah said Carl was confused and thought if he kissed a girl before he married her, he was going to hell. Hannah was in tears, laughing at how confused getting baptized seemed to be for him. Hannah said their mother seemed to believe he would rebound and be okay.

The next week in school flew by, and the Dogies finished the season with another loss. Carl was happy the season was over—they went 3–5 on the year. After the game, the coaching staff thanked the guys for never giving up and told them they had tickets for the Maverick game the following night.

Carl was given four tickets and was excited when he got in the truck with Riley. When he got home, he ran in the house and told Rachel he had four tickets to the Maverick varsity game the next night. She was less than enthused and told him she would let him know the next day. The next afternoon, Rachel gave her blessing for him to go to the game. She was a little apprehensive because he and several of his friends wanted to walk to and from the game. They met at Carl's house, and Rachel spoke to them about how they were to conduct themselves.

The group was Carl, his cousin Charles, Andrew "Dru" Smith, and Byron Smith. Dru and Byron were also cousins, like Charles and Carl. Rachel explained to them they were to go to the game together and then go home together. She made sure they understood, and they all said they did. Carl gave each of them their ticket, and they left for the game. Rachel did not attempt to go to sleep; she knew it was an exercise in futility. The guys arrived at the game and were thrilled when their tickets were able to get them in. Byron and Dru had brought extra money in case the tickets were not good.

The boys had fun at the game, talking to their friends and some of the girls. When the game ended and they started to walk home, Byron suggested they stop by his sister's apartment in Bel Air Manor Apartments. Carl did not want to go but was overruled by Charles, Dru, and Byron, who wanted to stop by the apartment. Bryon's nephew Ray was at the apartment, and his sister was gone for the weekend with her boyfriend. When they got to the apartment, there were several guys standing on the balcony out front. Carl recognized all of them, and one guy was a classmate in athletics with him.

He walked over to Michael Brown, and they shook hands. They had shared a locker during the last spring's workout regimen. Michael was a distance runner and, during track season, won first place in several track meets. Carl was shocked to see him smoking a cigarette. Both knew how smoking cigarettes caused respiratory problems for athletes. He got an uneasy feeling when the twin brothers Joshua and Caleb Duncan came up on the balcony. The twins were several years older, and Carl had fought with both of them.

Joshua was the bigger of the two and had beaten Carl up when they fought. Caleb was not as big as Joshua, and Carl had beaten him up when they fought. Both the twins brushed against Carl aggressively as they walked past him. It would have normally come to blows, but since there were two of them, he let it slide. Carl told Byron he was ready to go and was blown off, saying they could stay a little longer. Caleb asked Michael for a cigarette and got mad when he did not give it to him. He pulled a .38 snub nose to show the boys he had a gun.

Carl decided it was time to go, whether Byron, Dru, or Charles was going. Caleb made fun of him, asking sarcastically, "Where you going, punk? You scared?" He had been hunting with Riley too many times and listened as he said a gun was nothing to play with. He didn't pay attention to Caleb's taunts and continued walking down the stairs. One by one the other boys with him followed his lead and left. The boys were crossing Grand Avenue when they heard a single gunshot. They looked at each other and wondered what happened.

It was not unusual to hear gunshots in North Marshall, and they did not think Caleb had shot Michael. About fifteen minutes later, Carl walked in the house and Rachel let out a sigh of relief. The next morning, Carl woke up to the news that Michael Brown had been killed in Bel Air Apartments the night before. Riley stood at the foot of his bed and asked if he knew the young man. When Carl confirmed he knew him, Riley told him to get dressed and come to the porch. Carl was in shock—the shot they heard last night was Michael getting killed.

When he sat on the porch with Riley, he asked how well he knew the young man. Carl said he knew Michael pretty good, as they shared a locker in the athletic dressing room. Riley listened as Carl said he ran the half-mile and was a good runner. Riley asked if he and the other boys had been in Bel Air Apartments the night before. Carl fessed up with everything. He knew that if Riley was asking him, he already knew something. He told Riley how they had been headed home when Byron, Charles, and Dru wanted to go by Ray's house.

Carl said he really didn't want to go, but since they were told to stay together, he went with them. Carl said they had not been at Byron's sister's apartment long when the twins Joshua and Caleb showed up. He said Joshua had beaten him up before but he had beaten up Caleb. Riley made a mental note to ask why he was fighting much older boys. His ears perked up when Carl said Caleb pulled a .38 snub nose out of his pocket, and that was when he left. He told Riley that when they crossed Grand Avenue, they heard a shot.

Riley looked at him solemnly, saying they heard the shot that killed Michael.

He asked if he knew why Caleb shot Michael, and Carl said he had no idea. Carl said Caleb asked Michael for a cigarette and he refused to give him one. He went on to say he walked off the balcony when Caleb pulled the gun out. Carl was in tears when he said he did not know Caleb was going to shoot Michael. He told Riley that Joshua was bigger than Caleb but they always started fights with people. Riley started to get a picture of the two boys and said the story he was getting was that Caleb was showing the gun to Michael and it went off.

They looked at each other, knowing this was a lie. It was next to impossible for a revolver to go off. Caleb had pulled the trigger and killed Michael on that porch.

Later that day, Rachel came outside and told Carl they would be throwing his route in the car the next few days. The ride was quiet as they threw his route; they did not talk much. He did not ask to stop at Shasta's house because he knew for the next few days, everyone was on lockdown. He called Michelle when he got home, and she was horrified he knew the guy who got killed last night. Carl told her it would be a few days before he would be back out, the same as when the guy got killed by the railroad tracks in Jefferson.

It was back to school on Monday, and it seemed surreal that Michael's locker was empty. They had lost a great athlete, and the Black kids were in mourning. Carl was shocked when he overheard one of the White teachers at lunch say a nigger kid had gotten himself killed over the weekend. This didn't bother him, since he was used to the White kids and teachers calling him and the other kids nigger. The word was used so often he thought they believed it was their name.

Life went on, and Caleb Duncan was never arrested for killing Michael Brown.

When Carl got home from school, there was a letter from Jackie. He opened it and was shocked when she said she was going to break up with Ronnie Simmons. Carl didn't know what she meant when he read that her sister told her, "You might be Ronnie girl, but you Carl woman." He talked Rachel into allowing him to call her; he really wanted to know what she meant. She agreed but said he had to keep his call under ten minutes. He dialed the number and was disappointed when Mrs. Hunt answered and said Jackie was not home.

He really wanted to talk to Jackie, but since she was not home, there was nothing he could do.

He called Kendall, and they talked about Michael's murder and how awful it was. He never said he had just left Bel Air minutes before he was killed. He felt better after talking with her and went outside.

Later that evening, when Riley got home from his bus route, he and Carl were on the porch, talking. He said he had more information about Michael's murder and Caleb did indeed shoot him about a cigarette. Carl looked at Riley incredulously, asking, "Why would he do such a thing?"

Riley shrugged his shoulder as he said, "There are some mean people in this world." He then said he had no idea why Caleb would shoot Michael over a cigarette. They had a long discussion about the reasons he needed to always protect his life. He told Carl he had done the right thing to leave when Caleb pulled the gun. He reminded Carl he'd taught him about guns and gun safety to keep situations like this from happening. After this, they sat on the porch in silence until it was time for dinner. Carl was surprised things went back to normal so fast, the adults seemed to accept he was killed.

Unlike the murder by the railroad tracks in Jefferson, this killing had a different feel.

About a week later, Ray was at Byron's house, saying Michael and Caleb had beef. Michael had beaten him up a few days earlier. Carl said that was no reason to kill him, and Ray agreed, saying he wished he had gone in the house when they walked up. Because Caleb shot Michael on their balcony, Ray said they had been evicted and had to move by the end of the month. Byron side-eyed him. He knew this meant he would have to share his room with him.

CHAPTER 13

Michelle A. Baller
#ShePlayBBallLikeABoy

Life returned to normal. Michael's death was taken in stride due to the stress of everyday life. People were dealing with the second year of integration, and the word was, Black people were heathens who killed one another regularly. Carl and Michelle were becoming best of friends, playing one-on-one basketball each weekend. Michelle was improving at basketball, and he had to step up his game to beat her. The intensity level of their games had gone way up and gotten physical. Carl and Michelle promised they were not going to allow disagreements about basketball to hurt their friendship.

Playing Michelle like a boy felt weird to Carl, but he remembered she said to play her that way. Because of the intense one-on-one play, Michelle's playing time skyrocketed. Jackie took notice and no longer teased her about being on the bench. She had no idea Michelle was able to step her game up because she spent hours playing one-on-one with Carl. The intensity level between Jackie and Michelle was high during practice.

One day in practice, Michelle went up for a rebound, and Jackie elbowed her in the face. Michelle hit her in the face with the ball, and that was when the fight started.

They went to the floor, fighting, before the girls on the team and the coaches separated them. When the dust cleared, Michelle and Jackie both had bloody noses. The coaches made them run laps for fighting, telling them they were teammates and that was unacceptable. Neither of the young women would say what happened beyond Jackie elbowing Michelle when she extended for a rebound. The girls on the team knew it was deeper than that but kept quiet. Michelle and Jackie soon realized they needed to quash the beef; they were riding home together.

When Michelle's mother arrived to pick them up, neither girl mentioned they had been fighting at basketball practice. They dropped Jackie off at home, and Michelle was quiet on the short drive home. Her mother could sense something was wrong and quizzed Michelle why she had a busted lip. She asked her mother if she ever had a boy she liked and other girls liked him too. Her mother laughed out loud as she said, "Every one of 'em!" Michelle listened as her mother explained she had to hang tough because all the girls wanted her dad.

She was shocked when her mother said she knew she was crushing on Carl. They went in the house, and Michelle's mother called her to sit on the couch with her. She told her she had eleven kids for her dad and she was the youngest. Mrs. Burns said with seven girls, she finally had the hang of helping her young daughters grow into adulthood. They had a down-to-earth talk, and her mother answered a lot of questions for her. Mrs. Burns told Michelle she knew why she was going to Marshall every weekend, and it was not to just play basketball.

They laughed together when Mrs. Burns said it was okay for her to like Carl. She was shocked when her mother said she knew about the fight with Jackie at basketball practice. She told Michelle she needed to find a different way to approach Jackie and not be mad at her. Michelle could not believe her mother understood her feelings and emotions. She talked with her mother, saying she did not understand why Carl liked Jackie more than he liked her. Michelle got upset when her mother laughed before she answered the question.

Mrs. Burns told Michelle to look at the situation between Jackie and Carl. They walked to school every day, and she was best friends with his sister Hannah. She had never thought about it that way and listened as her mother told her moving Jackie was not going to be easy. She told Michelle it was a good thing they played one-on-one basketball together on the weekends. Mrs. Burns finally said, "In other words, baby, you are building memories with him." Michelle understood now: Jackie already had memories with him from the time they had spent together.

Michelle's mother said she and her dad had been married for-ty-five years when he died ten years ago. She smiled as she told her she was her baby and a late-life child. Michelle didn't know what she was saying until her mother said she had nieces and nephews the same age as her. When Michelle asked what she should do, her mother told her she should talk to Shasta. She went to sleep that night feel-ing good and having made the decision she was not going to fight Jackie again. The next morning, Michelle waited at the entrance to the school for Jackie.

When she walked up, Michelle asked if they could eat lunch together. In a sarcastic tone, Jackie asked if she wanted to bust her lip again. Michelle reminded her she busted her lip too, then offered to buy her lunch. Jackie agreed; she didn't want a peanut butter and jelly sandwich for lunch today. They met at lunch and went through the line together. When they got to the cashier, Michelle paid for their lunch like she said. Michelle had spending change because she was getting Social Security Survivor benefits from the death of her dad ten years earlier.

Every month, Mrs. Burns had her put most of the money in an account and gave her a spending allowance. She and Jackie sat down to eat, and Michelle started the conversation. Jackie was shocked when she said she wanted to call a truce and be friends. She looked at her, asking what brought this about. Michelle smiled and said, "We compete against each other in sports. We compete against each other in school. Let's compete for Carl." Michelle kept talking and said there was no reason they should be fighting each other. Jackie was floored and did not know what to say.

144

Jackie mustered the strength and asked Michelle why they should be friends when they liked the same boy. Michelle flipped the script and said that was exactly why they should be friends. Jackie was beside herself and started to run this through her mind. Since Hannah had moved back to Marshall, she really did not have a friend in Jefferson. She knew Michelle was smart like her and a great athlete, the same as she was. Jackie asked Michelle if she was going to stop talking to Carl, and she said nope. Jackie sarcastically said, "You want to be my friend while you try to take my boyfriend."

Michelle reminded her she was not Carl's girl, that she was Ronnie's girl. Jackie said she was going to break up with Ronnie and side-eyed Michelle. They finished lunch with an awkward silence and went to the basketball courts to practice. Jackie could not believe how good Michelle had gotten in such a short time, and her game was aggressive. They learned to tolerate each other, eating lunch together each day and then playing one-on-one games afterward. The coaches watched them at lunch each day and realized their two best players were becoming friends.

A few days later, Rachel got a last-minute call to work the concession stands at the basketball games. Her principal said she was his last option, so she agreed to work. She told Carl, Hannah, and Carol to put their school clothes back on; they were going to Jefferson. On the way to Jefferson, she said they were going to the junior varsity games and they needed to conduct themselves appropriately. Jackie and Michelle's team was on the floor, playing, when they walked in the gym. Michelle was dribbling down the baseline and lost the ball out of bounds when she saw Carl.

A few minutes later, Jackie saw Carl sitting in the stands with Hannah and Carol. She looked at where Ronnie had been sitting and saw he was not there. A few minutes later, when she was going down the floor, Jackie rolled her eyes when she saw Ronnie sitting with Carl. She had totally lost her focus, and the coach called time-out to pull her out of the game. He sat her next to him and said she had totally lost her focus. Jackie's mind was no longer on the game; she saw her boyfriend sitting with the guy she loved. She knew when the game was over, Michelle was going to rub this in.

Jackie was able to focus, and the team closed out the Daingerfield girls to earn the win. The coach released them from the locker room, and they walked to the stands. There was tension and shade with Jackie and Michelle as they settled in the stands with Carl, Hannah, and Ronnie. Hannah sat in the middle of the group, with Michelle and Jackie on either side. Carl was on one end, next to Michelle, and Ronnie was on the other end, next to Jackie. Carol had gone to the concession stand with Rachel. She had no desire to sit and listen to Hannah and her friends.

Hannah congratulated them on winning the game, and the small talk started between her and Jackie. It was plain to Michelle that Hannah preferred Jackie as a friend. Carl congratulated Michelle, saying he could see the improvement in her game. He hoped Michelle would leave this alone and not mention the one-on-one sessions they had been playing. He locked eyes with her, and she could read he did not want her to mention this. She leaned into him so he could hug her, and he hugged her. Jackie felt her anger boil as she watched Carl hug Michelle a few feet away.

Ronnie put his arm around Jackie, and she didn't move. She had listened to her sister Alicia when she said she was Carl's woman. She heard her sister Joyce Ann's voice today saying, "Ronnie here. Carl in Marshall." Ronnie smiled at Carl, watching as he hugged Jackie. This was a weird scene for Hannah, her brother and best friend with other people. She thought, *If Carl and Jackie are long-distance, why aren't Michelle and Carl long-distance?* Hannah knew to shut up about Michelle and Carl playing basketball; she had been there with Jackie.

The last time she said something to Jackie about Carl, it had been major drama. Rachel said she would literally beat her ass if she made this peace-breaking move again. Hannah also knew that if she told Jackie about Michelle and Carl, that was a major peace-breaking move. She watched Jackie and Carl, feeling like she was in the twilight zone. The air was thick, and they threw shade, but the group managed to talk until Rachel told them it was time to go.

Jackie side-eyed Michelle when she got off the bleachers and walked down to the gym floor. Ronnie kept hugging her while they stood at the edge of the court and talked. Jackie was all smiles when she said to Michelle, "See you at lunch tomorrow." Hannah was stunned; she could not believe what she just heard. She told Jackie, "You gon' need to write me a letter and explain." Jackie said she would as she and Ronnie walked across Broadway to go home. Rachel dropped Michelle off at home, and she told Carl she would see him Saturday.

Half an hour later, Rachel and the kids were back at home in Marshall. Hannah ran to her room and wrote Jackie a letter, demanding she tell her what exactly was going on. She wanted to know when she and Michelle had gotten to be such good friends. She mailed the letter the next day when she got to school. That Saturday, Michelle waited for Carl to come through on his paper route. A few minutes after she went outside, he rode through on the way to finish his paper route. He stopped for a few minutes and said he would be back after he finished his route.

They played two-on-two with Michelle's nephews and beat them every game. She seemed to have a sense for Carl's moves and hit him with great passes. Shasta came to the door and called her sons in the house, leaving Michelle and Carl to play one-on-one. She hugged Carl and, when they locked eyes, said she didn't have to be his girl; they could just be friends. Michelle had baited him with that one, hoping he would say she was his girl. Ronnie had made it clear Jackie was his girl, and she wanted Carl to do the same. Their game got contentious as Michelle played very aggressively with him.

It made her even angrier when she realized he did not have a clue she was mad at him. Shasta watched out the window as her baby sister pushed Carl when he went up for a layup. They bumped chests aggressively as he walked past her to take the ball out. Michelle stole the ball as he dribbled and drove for a layup. Carl fouled her hard, and they fell to the ground behind the goal. She started to cry, holding her leg, and he saw the blood on her leg. Carl got her up and carried her to the porch as Shasta came outside. She cleaned Michelle's leg and saw she had a deep cut.

Shasta knew this was going to need stitches and called the clinic where she worked. Carl called Rachel and said he was going to the clinic with Shasta. He gave Shasta the phone, and she explained

Michelle was going to need a few stitches. Carl put his bike up at Shasta's house and carried Michelle to the car. She was feeling some kind of way. Her leg was killing her, but she loved the feeling of being in his arms. She smiled as he carried her to the car and said, "I lied when I said I didn't have to be your girl." Shasta heard her but didn't say a word. She saw her baby sister had it bad for Carl.

The doctor stitched Michelle's leg and told Shasta there was definitely going to be a scar. In an ironic twist of fate, the outline of the stitches formed a big letter C. Michelle held her arms out for Carl, and he picked her up to carry her to the car. Rachel had taught Shasta at Jefferson High, and they lamented how Jackie suffered a broken leg, and now Michelle had a scar in the letter C. They could not believe neither of the girls was mad at Carl. Rachel took Carl to see Michelle the next day, and her leg was a little swollen. He saw the outline of the letter C on her right calf.

Rachel said she was going to discipline Carl for being mean to Michelle, and Shasta said she should not. She explained she was in the window, watching them, and Michelle was goading him. Rachel looked at Shasta, stunned, and asked why she allowed them to rough-house that way. She laughed, saying, "Ms. Hampton, my sister has it bad for your son, and she would have been upset if I stopped them." Rachel rolled her eyes when Shasta said she believed Michelle loved Carl. When Shasta asked why she rolled her eyes, she said his dad had the same effect on women.

Rachel walked off, saying, "You might want to prepare your sister for a heartbreak." Shasta knew Ms. Hampton was right. Michelle and Jackie were already beefing behind Carl. The thing she observed about Carl was, he seemed to know what to say, and he was smooth. She definitely understood why her sister liked him. Michelle's leg was propped up, and Carl sat on the couch next to her. They talked and he asked if it hurt, and she said not so much. She laughed and said she had the first letter of his name on her leg. Shasta watched from the other room, and Michelle seemed so content.

She went to the phone and called her mom to tell her Michelle hurt her leg. They talked for a while, and Ms. Burns asked if she needed to come get Michelle. Shasta said she didn't think so and she should miss school the next day. Shasta told her mother she would bring Michelle home tomorrow evening. A couple of hours later, Rachel came back and picked Carl up to take him home. Before Carl left, he hugged Michelle and said, "I'm sorry, Chell." She looked at him, saying there was no need to be sorry, as it was an accident. Michelle kissed Carl and asked if he was going to come by the next day.

Shasta knew exactly how Michelle felt. She had been wild about her eldest child's father the same way. When she brought Michelle home the next day, Shasta spoke with her mother about the situation. She was shocked when Ms. Burns said she was not going to try to stand in the way. Shasta asked her mother if she was giving Michelle a license to get pregnant. Mrs. Burns looked at Shasta and smiled, saying, "I will not be able to stop her any more than I was able to stop you." Shasta was shocked when her mother said, "I knew I wanted to marry your dad when I was thirteen."

Ms. Burns looked at Shasta and said, "Michelle is a very smart girl and wise beyond her years. She has already decided Carl is going to be her man, and there is nothing we can do about that." Ms. Burns asked Shasta if she wanted breakfast, and she said she did. As she cooked, Ms. Burns laid out the plan she hoped would minimize the heartbreak if things did not go the way Michelle wanted. The next day, Michelle returned to school with a noticeable limp. She could not wait until lunch to tell Jackie she had a tattoo of Carl's initials on her leg.

At lunch, Michelle went through the lunch line and met Jackie at the table. Jackie said she missed her at lunch and basketball practice yesterday. She watched Jackie's face drop when she said she spent the weekend in Marshall and showed her the scar on her leg. Jackie half-listened, more pissed that Hannah did not tell her Michelle was spending weekends in Marshall. When they finished lunch, they didn't play one-on-one, because Michelle's leg was still sore. When they went back inside after lunch, Jackie side-eyed Michelle and said, "You got a scar, bitch. He still my man!"

Michelle smiled to herself. Jackie was pissed, and she loved every minute of it.

When she got home that evening, Jackie asked her mother to use the phone. She called Hannah and was salty when she came to the phone. When she asked why she had not mentioned Michelle was in Marshall, playing one-on-one with Carl every weekend, Hannah didn't answer. After a minute of silence, Hannah reminded Jackie of the last time she said something about Carl and another girl. Jackie rolled her eyes; she did remember that incident.

Jackie hung up the phone in Hannah's face and ran to her room to cry. She hated how she was going to lose Carl to Michelle, but there was nothing she could do about it. A few minutes later, her mother walked in the room and sat on the bed, holding Jackie while she cried, saying she hated Carl. Hannah hung up the phone and walked in the room with Carl, saying she was probably not friends with Jackie any longer. She didn't wait for a response and walked into the room she shared with Carol. She wrote Jackie a heartfelt three-page letter, saying she hoped they were still friends.

The next day at school, things were buzzing about the Watergate burglary in DC. A story had been printed by the *Washington Post* that the break-in had been ordered by the Nixon administration. The Democrat National Committee Offices at the Watergate Hotel and office complex had been burglarized. It was rumored the burglary was an attempt to wiretap the DNC offices. This allegation was explosive. The Nixon administration was in the midst of its re-election campaign, and the president had already been in the news. He had done a tour of China to open markets for trade.

This was a big deal because the USA and China had not been in diplomatic relations for over a quarter of a century. As part of a history assignment, students had to watch the news each night to see what was happening in the ongoing Watergate investigation. The nation was polarized, the Southern states were still bitter from the enforcement of the 1954 *Brown v. Board* decision. The enforcement of this landmark decision sixteen years earlier was the reason students across the South were forced to integrate schools. As a result of the allegations against the Nixon administration, the division deepened. President Nixon had a plan called the "Southern Strategy," and it pitted White voters against Black voters. This was done in an effort to control the south and win the upcoming election. There was a large number of people in the south who believed President Nixon was being persecuted, and their way of life was being threatened. This narrative was a direct result of the "lost cause" narrative that tried to paint the confederacy as fighting for a noble cause. The united daughters of the confederacy had erected statues all across the south, and as a result, this "lost cause' narrative flourished. Carl often wondered how people could find anything noble about the desire to own people. He had learned in school, "Keep your mouth shut when they talk about the lost cause and the confederacy." What he did not know, a lot of the women teachers, were members of the united daughters of the confederacy.

The following Saturday, Carl was throwing his route on his bike. As usual, he stopped by Shasta's house to play one-on-one with Michelle. Her leg was almost healed, and the stitches had started to dissolve. But there was no mistaking the big C on her leg. Carl was up in his feelings when Michelle said everyone in Jefferson thought she branded his initial on her leg. They played one-on-one, and he had a hard time playing her like a boy. He was going for a layup, and Michelle pushed him. Carl forgot about her injured leg and started to play her hard.

Michelle won the game, and he was mad when she called him a jive turkey. He thought about her, saying she lied about wanting to be friends; she wanted to be his girl. Carl was angry and remembered what Rachel said: "You don't get mad at people you don't like." He left Michelle standing in the yard, yelling at him as he got on his bike and rode off. The next morning, he and Rachel threw his route in the car, and to his surprise, Michelle was sitting on the porch. He asked Rachel to keep going, but she side-eyed him and pulled into Shasta's driveway.

She said, "You *don't* get to leave that girl hanging like that because you mad." He saw Rachel was pissed when she said he had to fix what he broke. Michelle came to the car and spoke to Rachel, then asked Carl why he ran off yesterday. Rachel listened as Michelle raked him over the coals for leaving in the middle of their argument. Carl finally said he needed to go because he did not want them to start fighting. After a few minutes of the back-and-forth, Rachel said they needed to go. A few minutes after they made it back home, the phone rang, with Michelle on the other end.

Carl promised he would ride his bike over to Shasta's house when they got out of church.

Rachel pulled Carl to the side and told him he needed to "pump the brakes" with Michelle—they were way too serious for their ages. She cautioned him that he was cruising for a bruising with Michelle and Jackie. Carl said he was good. Jackie was Ronnie's girl, and she had forgotten about him. She laughed out loud and walked away, saying he was dumb as he was cute. Carl did not know what that meant but could tell from Rachel's tone it was not a good thing. During church, he decided he would ask Michelle to be his girl. He knew that was what she wanted.

When they got home from church, Rachel sat down with Carl again. She knew she was going to have issues with her girls but had no idea she was going to have to counsel her son. He was clueless when it came to girls, and she knew that was not a good thing. Rachel told Carl he had to choose between Jackie and Michelle; he could not keep going back and forth with them. Carl told her Jackie was Ronnie's girl, and Rachel asked if he had fallen on his head. She didn't give him time to answer before she said Jackie might be Ronnie's girl but she was his woman.

Rachel felt she caused this problem. She and Mrs. Hunt discouraged them from a long-distance relationship. She had no idea Michelle was going to step into the picture and shake things up this way. Rachel could see how this was going to end: Jackie and Carl had been pushed to people they didn't like as much. At that moment, she decided to get out of Carl's life and allow him to choose whom he wanted to like. She shook her head as she thought; they were trying to break up Jackie and Carl because they liked each other too much.

She thought about the irony of the situation. There was now a girl who was just as crazy for him as Jackie. Rachel thought, *This serves me right,* when Carl said he was going to ask Michelle to be his girl. As much as she wanted to tell him not to, she kept her mouth closed. She told Carl to go ahead when he asked if he could ride his bike to Michelle's house. He got on his bike and was surprised that when he rode through the curve on Norwood, the White boys didn't challenge him about being on their turf. Michelle was standing in the yard when he rode up on his bike.

Carl put his bike down and walked over to Michelle. She was shocked when he asked if she wanted to be his girl. She didn't want to seem too eager and asked what she had to do. Carl said they would play basketball against each other. Michelle stopped him and said, "Only if you play me hard." He agreed to play her hard, and she asked what else she had to do being his girl. Carl said they could write each other letters and sit together at the games. He also said he would get to kiss her sometime. Michelle agreed, and he said they needed to kiss to seal the deal.

Carl leaned into Michelle, and she kissed him passionately. This overwhelmed him; he didn't know what he was feeling. They broke the kiss, and he did not know what to say. Michelle asked what was wrong, and he said he was okay; he just needed a moment.

CHAPTER 14

Michelle Is Carl's Girl
#SheToldErrbodyInJefferson

He was off-balance when they played the first game, and she won. Michelle beat him all that day; her kiss had bumped Carl right off his game! He had kissed Jackie, but she didn't kiss like that!

An hour later, Shasta came to the door and said Carl needed to go home because his mother called. She wanted to walk him part of the way home, but he didn't let her, saying the White boys might be in the curve on Norwood. Just as he thought, when he hit the curve on Norwood, three White boys were standing on the side of the street. He was tired and in no mood to pump hard; he was going to fight today.

He got off his bike and reached into his newspaper bag, where he kept a wooden stick he made in shop. As he pushed his bike past them, they asked where he got his ten-speed. Carl said his dad bought it and kept it moving, not breaking stride. They moved closer to him, and he showed them the stick. This backed them off. They knew he would hit them with the stick. He could hear them curse at him and call him nigger, saying they would catch him when he didn't have that stick. He was certain they would have jumped him and taken his bike if he had not had the stick.

He made a mental note to keep the stick with him when he was on his paper route. He made it to the top of the hill at Norwood and Scotts Quarters, then got back on his bike, rolling the rest of the way home. He could not help but think, *Why does it have to be this way?* He put the thought out of his mind when he rolled into the yard and saw Riley sitting on the porch. Since it was Saturday, he knew it was going to be sandwiches and potato chips for lunch and dinner. Rachel saw him outside and asked what kind of sandwich he wanted.

He asked Rachel to fry him a bologna sandwich and a pressed ham sandwich. A few minutes later, Rachel returned with a bologna sandwich, a pressed ham sandwich, chips, cookies, and Kool-Aid. He thanked Rachel and sat on the porch with Riley, eating his food. As he ate, he asked Riley why life had to be so complicated. This puzzled Riley, and he told him he had to be more specific. Between bites, Carl explained the situation coming through the curve on Norwood. He told Riley he knew those White boys would have taken his bike had he not had the stick he made in shop class.

Carl listened as Riley said, "Things are not always as they seem." He explained the ten-speed Bradley bought was expensive, and everyone knew this. Riley admitted he was concerned when Carl left the house on the bike for that reason. He told Carl to keep his guard up; the White boys were not the only ones that would lie dead and take his ten-speed. This shocked Carl and further complicated his world. He was not used to being the center of attention in this way. Riley said he wasn't concerned with the boys his age taking his bike; it was the older boys that concerned him.

Riley told him there were three ways he could come home when he finished his paper route. He suggested he change the way he came home each day so he would not be predictable. Riley laid out the three ways, and Carl was surprised each way took about the same length of time. More importantly, he could still make Michelle's house his last stop before he headed home. At school on Monday, Michelle could not wait to find Jackie Hunt and tell her she was Carl's girl. She held her speech until lunch and, when they sat down, asked Jackie what she did this weekend.

Michelle patiently listened as Jackie gave her a description of her weekend. When she finished, Michelle casually said she and Carl had played basketball all weekend and he asked her to be his girl. Jackie could not hide the shock on her face as her mouth fell open. To say she was shocked was an understatement. Michelle smiled as Jackie got up from the table, saying, "We can no longer be friends." Jackie walked off with her plate and sat at the table with the other girls on the basketball team. She couldn't hold back the tears and started crying, laying her head on the table.

A few minutes later, Ronnie came through the lunch line, and Sandra Sanders told her to get it together. Ronnie just went through the lunch line. Jackie remembered what her sisters said and got herself together really quick. By the time Ronnie made it to the table with them, she was composed. Three of the girls stood up and blocked Michelle when she tried to come to the table where they were sitting. Jackie was happy they blocked Michelle; she could not hold it together if she said something to Ronnie. Michelle smiled. She knew she was in Jackie's mind.

She understood the game and knew Ronnie would be extremely mad if he knew she was crying about Carl. Her eyes were filled with rage when she locked eyes with Michelle, and at that moment, they became enemies. Her emotions were all over the place, and she was as pissed at Carl as she was at Michelle. She told Jackie, "I'll see you at basketball practice this evening," as she walked off. Neither of them knew what this would look like, because they were on the basketball team together. Michelle was floating on a cloud the rest of the day as she thought how she slammed Jackie with her good news.

Jackie moped through the rest of the day and hesitantly dressed for basketball practice. She wanted to skip practice, but her older sister, Alicia, said absolutely not—she was going to face this little peacebreaker head-on. The rivalry between Jackie and Michelle had an edge. Michelle's older sister Shasta had a child with Jackie's sister Alicia's husband. Coach Wilson blew the whistle, and the girls lined up for practice.

Right from the start of practice, Michelle played Jackie aggressively. The contact between them was rough and boiled over when Michelle went for a layup.

Jackie hard-fouled her, and they tumbled into the mat behind the goal. Michelle jumped up and swung on Jackie, but Tosha was there to keep the fight from going further. The trash talk started, and all the girls in practice knew the back story to this drama. Coach Wilson wondered what was going on between her two best players, unaware of the drama that had taken place at lunch. Practice ended without further incident, and Alicia picked Jackie up for the ride home. She broke down and started to cry when she closed the door and Alicia drove off.

Alicia started to change her position about Carl. For a young man that lived fifteen miles away in Marshall, he sure kept up a lot of drama in Jefferson. Jackie composed herself and walked in the house, speaking to everyone as she walked in. She didn't ask if she could use the phone and made the long-distance call to Marshall. Hannah answered on the other end, and Jackie didn't ask how she was doing, instead asking why she had not said anything.

She took a deep breath and said Rachel threatened to beat her ass if she got in this. Hannah felt her heart sink when Jackie said, "I thought we were friends." Her heart was broken; she felt the hurt in Jackie's voice. This broke her down, and she didn't say anything else, just called Carl to the phone. When he said hello, Jackie asked, "Why?" Carl asked how she found out, and Jackie exploded on him. "How the hell do *you* think I found out, Carl? The bitch told me!" Jackie's emotions flooded out, and she said, "You broke my leg, Carl. I should have broken up with you then!"

Carl tried to explain, but she stopped him, saying, "We walked to school, Carl. I even have your last name on my book covers." Jackie was in a full-blown cry when she screamed into the phone. "I hate you, Carl Allen Hampton!" She slammed the phone down and walked out of the room. A second later, she fell across her bed and got her cry on. She was sobbing when her mother knocked lightly and asked if she could come in the room. Jackie nodded, and Mrs. Hunt walked in the room with her. She rubbed Jackie's hair, saying,

"I know you hurt, baby girl, and it seems like this is the end of the world."

When her mother said it was not the end of the world, Jackie asked why she felt so bad. Her mother didn't answer, just held her as she finished crying. As Mrs. Hunt wiped the tears from her eyes, they heard the phone ring. A few seconds later, Alicia walked to the door and said Ronnie was on the phone, and asked if she wanted to talk to him. Jackie said she wanted to talk to him and jumped off the bed. When she said hello, Ronnie asked how she was. Jackie said she was good, and he asked if she had heard the latest news. She played it off and said she had not heard what was up.

Ronnie took delight in telling her Carl asked Michelle to be his girl. She forced herself to laugh and asked why this would mean anything to her. He said he didn't think it meant anything to her, then asked about her day. It felt good talking to Ronnie, and as they were about to hang up, she said, "You don't have to worry about Carl. I'm over him." She could hear the sigh of relief in Ronnie's voice when he said, "It's about time Jackie, see you tomorrow." Her mother could see her mood had changed when she walked back in the room and sat on the bed.

She told Jackie, "A boy that likes you more than you like him will cry for you." She continued, "A boy you like more than he likes you will make you cry."

Jackie looked at her mother when she asked, "Who been crying tonight, Jackie?"

When she went to school the next day, Ronnie noticed she had changed all her book covers and "Hunt" was on them. He was good with this. Carl was *finally* out his way. Jackie got a chance to see what her mother meant. Ronnie went out of his way to please her. Deep down Jackie knew she had lied to herself. Carl Allen Hampton was *still* in her heart.

She knew this because she was not mad at him any longer, but Hannah was a different story.

A few days later, she got a letter from Hannah, with an explanation of what happened. She told her again Rachel was *really* going to beat her ass if she got in the middle of this. She asked Jackie to forgive her and reminded her she could not stand Michelle Burns. She immediately wrote Hannah back, saying she forgave her and they were still best friends. The next evening, Rachel got a call from Mrs. Hunt, asking she not allow Carl to contact Jackie.

She agreed and promised Mrs. Hunt she would discourage him from talking to her. Rachel said to Mrs. Hunt, "You know we setting them up for failure." Rachel reminded Mrs. Hunt this was not the first time Jackie and Carl had been hella mad at each other. Rachel was shocked when Mrs. Hunt said, when Hannah was on the bed, crying for an hour behind a boy, to holla back at her. She thought how rude it was when Mrs. Hunt hung the phone up in her face, then called Carl in the room to tell him not to have contact with Jackie.

The rest of the school year flew by, and things were running smoothly. With a couple of weeks left in May, Riley told Carl they were not going to sell fruits and vegetables this year. Carl asked if they were done. This was the second year they had not planted anything on the farm. Riley said they would have to wait until the next year to see. Since Rudolph died, he really didn't feel like planting crops. Edward and James came down the street and asked Carl if he wanted to go haul hay with them. Riley encouraged him to go, saying Rachel and the girls would throw his paper route for him.

Carl had seen bales of hay before, but he had never hauled hay before. They spent the whole day hauling hay and loaded six hundred bales in the barn. He was sweaty, tired and dusty after the long day in the hayfield. When they got paid that evening, he made twelve dollars. This was decent money, and he weighed if he preferred the dusty, hot hayfield to riding his ten-speed throwing his paper route. That night he made an Entrepreneur decision, asking Rachel and the girls to throw his paper route when he went to the hayfield.

They agreed, and Carl had a second revenue stream. Riley asked why he wanted to keep both gigs and was shocked when he said he wanted to make more money. Riley was more shocked when he laid out his plan of Rachel and the girls throwing his route while he made money hauling hay. He explained that he could make money from two gigs at the same time. Janice interrupted them when she came to

159

the door and said Bradley was on the phone for Carl. He went to the phone and was glad to hear Bradley on the other end. They caught up for a minute, and Bradley asked if he was coming to Detroit for the summer.

Carl thought for a second and said he was going to stay in Marshall—he had two hustles he needed to keep going. Bradley laughed out loud. He thought Carl was joking. A second later, he realized Carl was serious, and asked what his hustles were. Carl said he was going to haul hay and throw papers. Bradley thought, *He a hustling young man.* Bradley told him it was going to get hot and that hayfield was going to be very dusty. Carl had not thought about that but decided to stay; he wanted to make money. Bradley said he should come to Detroit for the summer and he would give him an allowance.

After the back-and-forth negotiation, Carl said he would come to Detroit for half the summer. They bounced into summer, and Carl was going good with hauling hay and throwing his paper route. He saw Michelle each evening when he threw his route on his bike— she had moved in with Shasta. They sharpened their basketball skills and talked about what was going on in their lives. Michelle was not happy when Carl told her he was going to Detroit for six weeks later in the summer. She asked why he was going, and he explained that he was going to see his dad, who lived there.

They played a couple more games, and Carl got on his ten-speed for the ride home. When he hit the curve on Norwood, he was surprised to see the hay truck—they were coming in from the hayfield. Carl stopped and, when they pulled up beside him, put his bike on back of the truck. The White boys standing on the street shot them the bird as the truck rolled slowly by them. Carl shook his head, thinking, *This is getting old,* having to fight these White boys to go down Norwood Street. When they stopped, Carl took his bike off the truck and rolled the rest of the way home.

Riley was sitting on the porch as usual when he rode into the yard and put his bike up. The next couple of weeks, Rachel worked with Carl, getting him ready for the trip to Detroit. He got luggage and several new outfits. Carl wanted tennis shoes and shorts, but

Rachel insisted he get hard-sole shoes and dress pants. He was fit to be tied because she did not get him any clothes he could play in or get dirty. A couple of days before he was to leave, Carl took money from his newspaper route and talked Riley into taking him downtown.

He bought a couple of pairs of tennis shoes, several pairs of short pants, and a couple shirts. Rachel wasn't mad at him; after all, he was using his own money so he could spend it how he wanted. She was amazed at how he was maturing. He wanted to earn his own money, and she had to admit it took a burden off her. A couple of weeks later, they all piled in the car for the ride to Shreveport Airport so they could see Carl off. He was upset when the stewardesses "tagged" him so he could not get off the plane without permission.

It was still daylight when the plane landed in Detroit, and he was met by Bradley, Gwen, Trey, and Carlos. Just like last summer, when he came to Detroit, he was amazed at how Detroit looked from the air.

They arrived at Bradley and Gwen's house just as it started to get dark, and they helped him bring his bags inside. Gwen had cooked, and Carl was glad, because he was hungry. After he ate dinner, Carl took a shower and changed into his pajamas. He loved taking showers at Bradley's—the house in Marshall only had a bathtub.

The next day, he woke up to the smell of breakfast cooking and went downstairs to see what Gwen was making. That was one thing Carl had to get used to—they cooked differently in Detroit. Rachel and Janice fried most of their food, but Gwen baked most of the time. After he finished eating, Carl went out on the block. He saw Ralph sitting on the stoop next door and went over to talk to him. They met when he was there last summer, and he remembered him. They sat on the stoop, talking and watching the neighborhood people walk up and down the block.

Carl was shocked when he realized a lot of the faces looked familiar; he saw them last summer.

Later that day, sisters Darlene and Shelia came across the street to talk to Ralph. Carl looked at them and realized he did not meet them the previous summer. When he saw them, he immediately saw how nice-looking they were. Ralph mentioned they had moved in a couple of weeks after he went back to Texas last summer. Ralph introduced them, saying he was visiting for the summer. Darlene was slim and the older of the two sisters, while Shelia was thick and the better-looking of the two.

They sat on the stoop at Ralph's house, talking, and Carl laughed at the way they talked. He was angry when he started to talk, and they laughed at him. It was a huge icebreaker, and the conversation seemed to flow smoothly from that point. Carl saw the TV helicopter hovering a few blocks over and said, "Look over yonder," as he pointed to the helicopter. The three kids looked at him, asking, "Look over where?"

He repeated himself, "Over yonder!"

They started to laugh and make fun of him. He talked funny and used funny words.

Carl had fun hanging with Ralph, Darlene, and Shelia on the block as they made fun of the way one another talked. Carl enjoyed himself and saw a lot of differences between the way he lived in Texas and the way they lived in Detroit. Other than the allowance the kids got in Detroit, he saw they had a lot of stuff he and his friends in Texas did not have. What he did not realize was, most of the parents who lived in the neighborhood had jobs that allowed them to have middle-class lifestyles. Ralph and his sisters lived with his uncle, who worked for Chrysler.

Ralph also had an aunt who worked for the Postal Service. Darlene and Shelia's dad worked for the Ford plant out in River Rouge. These automotive jobs were not available in Marshall, and Black people in Marshall were not hired to work for the Postal Service there either. He was getting a chance to see people living a middle-class lifestyle, and it was mind-boggling. During his time in Detroit this summer, Carl met everybody on Bradley's block. A week before he was going back to Texas, he and Gwen went to Northland Mall to purchase his school clothes for the coming school year.

Bradley promised Rachel he would buy Carl school clothes and kept his end of the bargain. Shopping for school clothes went much smoother this year, and they bought clothes Carl could wear immediately. Gwen was keen on the details and knew what he needed to get. She allowed him to pick one outfit on his own, but the rest, she offered her opinion. As they were leaving the mall, he thought how much she reminded him of Rachel. She was forceful in her opinion and really believed what she said should go. Just like Rachel, she had a way of influencing his decision without saying a word.

It dawned on him, being in Detroit was not much different from being in Marshall. Except for the way the people talked and the food they ate, there was a lot of similarity between the two places. On the day he was to fly back to Shreveport, Bradley took off work and they spent the day together. They sat at the Big Boy Restaurant, talking about what he had done that summer in Detroit. This was a big deal for Carl, for he had never been to a restaurant before. Gwen asked how he liked working his paper route and hauling hay, and Bradley laughed out loud when she asked what "hauling hay" was.

Carl said he liked his paper route best because he got to ride his ten-speed around the neighborhood. He told Gwen hauling hay was hot, dusty, and very hard. She laughed when he said his friend Byron bought a lawn mower and they were going to cut yards next summer. She was mildly surprised Carl had a focus on earning money at such a young age and asked if this was normal. Carl said it was normal for most of the guys in his neighborhood because they wanted their own money. Bradley stepped in and said there was a need among most of the young guys to earn money to help out.

Gwen listened as Bradley explained his childhood, how his dad had died when he was nine years old. He said that like Carl, he worked quite a bit growing up to help his mother out. Bradley said the difference between the two of them was, he worked out of necessity and Carl was working to buy stuff he wanted. Gwen asked how he was keeping his paper route when he was in Detroit. Carl explained he worked out a deal with his mother and sisters to throw his route while he was in Detroit. Bradley asked if he and Rachel were still beefing about the split from the paper route.

Carl laughed out loud and said they were not beefing any longer; Rachel had made it plain she was keeping all the money. Bradley asked how much he felt he missed by coming to Detroit for the six weeks. Carl thought about it a few minutes and said he missed about two hundred dollars coming to Detroit for the summer. Bradley made a mental note of this figure, and they finished their lunch. They left a tip for the waiter and left, headed for the airport.

On the way, Bradley pulled into a National Bank of Detroit drive-through and withdrew two hundred dollars.

Carl was shocked when he handed him the envelope with the money while saying, "Keep this so you will not lose any money coming to Detroit." He thanked Bradley, and they rode in silence the rest of the way to the airport. They pulled in front of Detroit Metro Airport and unloaded Carl's bags. Gwen and the boys went in the airport to help him get checked in while Bradley found a parking space. Later, the announcement was made that his flight was boarding, and he hugged everyone. The stewardess put his tag on, and Carl walked through the tunnel to the plane.

Bradley, Gwen, Trey, and Carlos watched as his flight taxied down the runway and took off for Shreveport. Carl was becoming a seasoned traveler; for the second summer in a row, he was flying to and from Detroit. After a quick stop in Atlanta, the plane landed in Shreveport. Rachel, Riley, Janice, Hannah, and Carol were waiting at the gate when he walked off the plane. He had fun in Detroit, but he was really glad to see everyone. They claimed his bags at baggage check and started the half-hour trip home to Marshall.

When they arrived home, Carl called Bradley to let him know he was safe.

CHAPTER 15

Drama in Algebra I
#CarlLearnsAHardLesson

His next call was to Michelle; he wanted to let her know he was back home. Michelle said she wanted to come over. Shasta dropped her off, and she jumped out of the car to greet him. It had been six weeks, and she wanted him to know she missed him.

Hannah rolled her eyes when Michelle walked up on the porch, and Rachel cautioned her to be nice. Hannah could not stand Michelle, so she walked to her room, not wanting to be part of this mess. He had not unpacked his luggage, and Rachel told him to do that later. He and Michelle went to the porch and sat with Riley.

While they were talking, Riley found her to be outgoing and smart. He liked her. Shasta picked her up a couple of hours later, and they went home. As he unpacked, Rachel saw the clothes he bought while in Detroit. They seemed to have gotten it right this year—the clothes were season-appropriate. Carl smiled and never told Rachel that Gwen had gone to the store with him and helped pick his clothes. When he finished putting his clothes up, Hannah handed him a bag of mail. He looked through the mail and was shocked to see several letters from both Jackie and Kendall.

When he read the letters from Kendall, he was shocked to find she wanted to be friends again. Her explanation was, she and her sister were having issues, and she could not handle his friendship at that time. She ended her letter by saying that they could hopefully be friends again. He went to the phone and called her. He wanted to tell her all was good. Her sister Lillian answered and said Kendall was on punishment but she could talk to him. Kendall said she was going back to the cheer line this year and the things bothering her were over.

Carl was glad to hear this and said he looked forward to that.

He hung up with Kendall and read the letters from Jackie and could not believe she had done a full 180-degree turn. Jackie said she didn't mean she hated him; what she hated was the moment she found he'd asked Michelle to be his girl. After Carl read her letters, he asked Rachel if he could call Jackie. Rachel said they needed to speak with Jackie's mother first. She had asked that he not contact her again. He showed Rachel the letter and called Mrs. Hunt. They spoke for a minute, and Mrs. Hunt said she was not in agreement but she would allow Jackie to talk to him.

He called Jackie, and she broke him down with a few short words. Jackie said she was sorry for saying she hated him, then said she could never hate him. She reminded Carl they walked to school together every day for four years. His heart was melted when she said her plan backfired when they were at the basketball game and she was hugged up with Ronnie. Carl did not say anything but listened as she said she knew he was with Michelle and she was cool with that. She stopped in midsentence, saying that was a lie, that she would just have to live with it.

He gathered his thoughts, saying he never wanted to leave her alone, but she kept pushing him away. Jackie listened when he said he thought he lost her to Ronnie when she was hugged up with him at the game. She asked if Hannah had given him any messages from her, and he said she had not. He followed up by saying Rachel forbade her to pass messages from her. Jackie wondered why Ms. Hampton had turned against her, and Carl answered the question. He said the issue they had when Hannah passed messages before, she had been ordered to let them work it out on their own.

Carl said he had to go, and Jackie smiled when he asked if they were still friends. She assured him they were and said she was going to make friends with Michelle so they could bury the hatchet.

When they hung up, Alicia saw the change in Jackie's demeanor. She asked if it went well, and Jackie said it went exactly as she said it would. Alicia hugged Jackie and said she understood she was torn between Ronnie and Carl but she was too young to shut either one out. She was determined her younger sister was not going to leave the door open for Michelle the way she left the door open for Shasta.

School started a couple of weeks later, and the first days of football practice were brutal. He had done little work this summer, and he felt it during the heat of football practice. To make matters worse, Rachel had signed him up for accelerated classes, and he had to seriously focus. He especially hated Algebra 1, and he did not like the way the teacher handled the class. There were thirty-one people in the class, and only two of them were Black. He knew the Black girl in the class, Sandra Jones, and she was having issues in the class as well.

Carl talked to Rachel, saying it seemed Ms. Smith was not explaining the concepts she was teaching. She expected the kids to read the textbook and work the problems on their own. Since the answers to the problems were in the back of the book, she also expected the kids to show their work solving problems. The thing Carl hated most about the class was, Ms. Smith gave tests with four problems. After struggling the first six weeks of the semester, they had a big test coming up. He was carrying a 75 average, and if he passed the test, he could keep his football eligibility.

If he failed the test, he was ineligible to play football the rest of the year. His heart sank when Ms. Smith returned the test papers and he made 50—he was ineligible. He sat there listening as she went over the first two problems, which he had the right answer to. The third question was flat out wrong, and he saw where he missed it. He followed as she outlined the fourth question, and they came down with the same answer. When class was over, he approached Ms. Smith and said he had the correct answer to the fourth question.

Ms. Smith said she saw that but there was an issue—he did not follow the formula. Carl showed her how he went through each step, and although the steps were different, he had the right answer. They reached a stalemate, and Ms. Smith said she absolutely would not change his grade; how could she be sure he didn't copy the answer off the person next to him? Carl knew this was Rachel's battle and went to his next class.

When he went to football practice that afternoon, he told the coach he was ineligible for the rest of the year.

Coach Williams questioned him, and he said he made 50 on a test in Algebra 1, which dropped his cumulative average to 62.5 for the class. Coach Williams knew when he took his eligibility card for signatures at the end of the week, it was a wrap. He held him out of practice and said he should not dress out until he had this situation handled. He was crushed but knew this was going to happen. You had to pass your classes.

When he got home that evening, he showed his test paper to Rachel and explained what happened at school with Ms. Smith. Rachel was not a math whiz but a teacher that worked with her at Jefferson High taught Algebra 1. When she reviewed Carl's paper, she saw he worked the problem backwards and wrote an explanation of the way the problem was solved. Rachel was shocked when she asked who showed Carl this method; it was an advanced way to solve problems normally taught in Algebra 2. That evening, when she got home, Rachel said his grade should be 75. The next morning, she called the principal's office and asked for a meeting.

The meeting was scheduled, and Rachel took off work to be there. They sat in Mr. Jones office as Rachel laid out her claim why Carl's grade should be 75 instead of 50. It made Ms. Smith very angry she was being called into the office to justify a grade she gave on a test. She was assured by Mr. Jones, this was not done to punish or embarrass her. The meeting became contentious when Ms. Smith said they wanted to change Carl's grade so he would be eligible to play football. Rachel held her cool as Mr. Jones said they wanted to make sure he received the correct grade.

Rachel was asked why she felt the grade was wrong and said he solved the problem using block theory instead of linear progression.

Everyone looked at Rachel for an explanation, and she explained he worked the problem in blocks instead of in a linear fashion.

She explained this was an advanced concept usually taught in Algebra 2. Carl was asked where he learned the block theory and said his friend in college taught him. He was asked to solve the problem and went to the chalkboard and solved the problem. Mr. Jones asked if she had ever heard of the block theory, and Ms. Smith said she had, adding, "It is a very complicated way to solve a problem." At that point Mr. Jones dismissed Carl and Rachel from the meeting saying he would let them know the decision. Mr. Jones then asked what she needed to be comfortable enough to change the grade.

The true objection came out when Ms. Smith said she felt Carl copied the answer from one of the people sitting next to him. Mr. Jones wanted to know how this was possible when he was able to work the problem using the block method. Ms. Smith stood on her assertion that they were trying to keep him eligible for football. Mr. Jones's anger rose when he realized Ms. Smith had not taken the time to find out how Carl knew this concept.

Mr. Jones asked for the test papers and seating chart for Carl's class, and she returned with them, dropping the papers off with Mr. Jones's secretary.

Later that day, Mr. Jones called the coach to let him know Carl was ineligible for the game that week. They agreed the program should stay compliant with UIL rules and not forfeit games because they played an ineligible player. When the coach asked how they got there with Carl, Mr. Jones said he did not have an answer. He reviewed the test papers and placed them against the seating chart. The first of Ms. Smith's claims fell apart when he realized every student next to Carl got that problem wrong. He was shocked Carl was the only student in the class who solved the problem correctly.

After a review of the situation, Mr. Jones met with Ms. Smith to explain his position. He asked if she was aware Carl was the only student to solve the problem, and she said she was aware. He asked why she felt he looked on another paper when none of the other students got it right. Ms. Smith did not have an answer. He sensed Ms. Smith was not going to change the grade but asked if she would.

She refused, saying Carl needed to accept the consequences and not look for special treatment. She was shocked when he said Carl was borderline genius and laid his file on her desk.

He asked her to read his file, and if she felt the same way, he would respect her decision. When he left her room, she set the file aside and went back to the work she was doing.

The next day, Mr. Jones asked if she had had time to think it over, and Ms. Smith said she stood by her decision to not change his grade. He thanked her and walked out of her room, making a mental note that she had issues. He directed his secretary to call Rachel and let her know the decision had been made. Janice answered the phone when the school called and took the message for Rachel.

When she got home and Janice gave her the message, Rachel said she was not surprised. They told Carl, and he was good. This presented an opportunity for some downtime during football season. Although he accepted the decision in stride, he could see the hatred in Ms. Smith's eyes when he was in her class. The vibe was so strong that when he had questions, he would not ask them; instead, he decided to study harder and learn to work the problems the way she put them on the board. It was hard, but he made it through and learned a valuable lesson in the process.

Coach Jenkins asked if he wanted to play basketball this season, and Carl explained he was ineligible. Coach Jenkins said eligibility cards would go out again before the first basketball game. Carl got excited. He knew he would be eligible when cards went out for the second six weeks. Algebra 1 was the only subject he struggled with, and he raised his average to 85 in the class. Carl said he did want to play and he would clear it with his mother. When he asked Rachel later that evening, she gave him the green light and reminded him he needed to keep his Algebra 1 grade up.

Carl went to school the next day and told Coach Jenkins he was ready to play; his mother had given him permission. When eligibility cards went out two weeks later, Carl saw the disappointment in Ms. Smith's eyes when she signed him off as eligible and entered his grade as 87 for her class. He had seen this look before and knew to keep it moving, thanking her for signing off on his eligibility card.

Basketball practice started, and he was placed in the guard rotation. Coach Jenkins had an idea and went with a four-guard rotation.

The gold team shared the floor with the purple team, and Carl's game went up immensely. The two teams scrimmaged each other daily. In addition to scrimmaging them each day, the purple team was on their schedule five times! Two of those games were district games, so this meant there would be high-stakes drama in their games. The scrimmages were intense, and Carl's ability to focus improved. The days were short, and night came earlier, so Rachel threw his paper route. This limited the time he was able to see Michelle, and they stayed busy writing each other letters.

Finally, though, football season was ending, and Carl looked forward to the first basketball game of the season. When they saw the schedule, the players grunted—the purple team played the gold team first! All the scrimmaging against each other every day and they opened the season against each other. The coaches passed out the uniforms, saying there had been a change of plans; they had been invited to a tournament. They were excited to learn the tournament was double elimination in Longview.

When they walked in the gym, Carl saw the burgundy colors of Jefferson. The Bulldogs were there!

He knew Michelle and Jackie were probably there, and went to the locker room to dress. He saw Jackie in the hallway and hugged her as Ronnie walked up behind her. It broke his heart when Ronnie hugged her, but he didn't let it show on his face. Jackie had to run since the Jefferson girls were about to play the Pine Tree girls. He and Ronnie went to the stands, sitting together, watching the Jefferson girls handle the Pine Tree girls. Michelle and Jackie were working together like a well-oiled machine.

Coach Jenkins called the gold team out the stands, and they went to the dressing room.

The boys wanted to know who they were about to play, but Coach Jenkins didn't know; they were still developing the brackets. Robert Williams joked that he was good with whoever it was, as long as the purple team was not on the other end of the floor. Chris Jones joked that they scrimmaged the purple team every day and had to play five games against them. They heard the buzzer ending the girls' game, and Coach Jenkins told them to look sharp as they ran out.

Carl spotted Michelle in the Lady Bulldogs huddle as he went to the floor for the shootaround.

When they broke the huddle, he went over to Michelle and they hugged each other. When she saw Jackie looking, Michelle stuck her tongue in Carl's mouth. They held the kiss a moment, and Coach Jenkins called him back to the shootaround. He felt a groove as he dribbled and shot during the shootaround. His stroke was hot! He felt good. Being ineligible the last half of the football season meant he was not banged up.

His mouth fell open when he looked on the other end of the floor and the Bulldogs were warming up. *No,* he thought, *we* not *playing Jefferson!*

The buzzer sounded for the tip-off, and the teams went to the bench. Carl didn't start the game—he was the sixth man—he watched as Jefferson won the tip. The gold team got up on Jefferson quickly. They seemed to be in sync. Carl did a mental checkup. Four of the five Jefferson players were on the football team last week. He realized this was the reason they seemed to be out of sync and rusty: they had not gotten their timing down.

A second later, Coach Jenkins called time-out and sent Carl in the game for Robert Williams.

Carl knew he was guarding Ronnie, and the whistle blew to restart the game. Jefferson threw the ball inbound to Ronnie, and he chest-guarded him. He knew this bothered Ronnie. The gold team's defense philosophy was, "We play ninety-four feet for thirty-two minutes!" Ronnie beat him to the corner at half-court and set up their offense. Coach Jenkins saw Carl was a good matchup against Ronnie and left him in the game. They went into halftime with the gold team up 32–20.

Coach Jenkins told them to shoot around and said Carl would start the second half.

Jefferson brought the ball up the floor, and Ronnie took him down low, posted him up, and got a bucket plus one free throw. He missed the free throw, and Larry Jones pulled the rebound down for the gold team. He hit Chris Washington with the outlet pass at the half-court corner, and he hit Carl with a pass at the corner of the key. Coach Jenkins yelled when he pulled up for the long-range jumper when he had a free lane for a layup. A smooth flip of his wrist, a swish of the net as the ball went down, and the rout was on as he exploded for 16 points in the second half.

Carl was hot, and everything he threw up went down! His 23 points led the gold team to a 64–46 victory. Ronnie was pissed and went straight to the locker room without shaking anyone's hand. Coach Jenkins called the gold team to the huddle and congratulated them on the season-opening win. He asked if they liked the up-tempo offense, and everybody said they did. The high-energy offense had them tired, but it was fun. Coach Jenkins led them in the gold team chant, "What's our motto?" And they responded, "Ninety-four feet for thirty-two minutes!"

The gym seemed like it shook when the boys yelled, "Panther pride!" He directed them to sit in the stands and watch the purple team, since they rode the same bus. Carl and Michelle sat together a few minutes before the coaches called her to come on; they were getting ready to leave. She made sure Jackie was looking when she kissed him bye, saying she would see him that weekend. Jackie was hella mad but hugged Ronnie as they walked out of the gym. The purple team didn't do so well; they went down to the Forest Park Dragons, the tournament host.

On the bus ride home, the gold team boys needled the purple team boys, and a fight broke out. James Allen punched Robert Washington, and the fight was on. By the time the boys got them broken up, both boys had black eyes and swollen lips. The coaching staff was highly upset that nobody seemed to know why or how the fight started. Since they had to go back to Forest Park the next morning, they decided to settle the issue at practice the next week.

The next morning, the two teams were back at Forest Park to finish the tournament.

The gold team was in the winners bracket, and the purple team was in the losers bracket, decreasing the odds they would play each other. Coach Jenkins had a copy of the brackets, and the gold team was up first at 9:00 a.m. against the host, the Forest Park Dragons. Coach Jenkins saw Forest Park was much taller than his team and told them they had to outrun this team. Coach Jenkins asked, "What's our motto?" His call was answered with the response, "Ninety-four feet for thirty-two minutes!" The booming "Panther pride!" woke up anyone who might have been asleep.

Carl recognized several of the Forest Park guys from football season, particularly since the Forest Park game was the last one he played in. They controlled the tip, and Robert Washington stripped their player as he brought the ball down the floor. Two passes put the ball back in Robert's hands, and he went for the layup. The Forest Park player fouled him hard, and he made the free throw. Forest Park had problems with the gold team press and turned the ball over several times. Forest Park did not match up well with them, and Robert Washington was going off, scoring at will.

At the half, the gold team led 40–14, and Robert Washington had scored 15 points. Carl was close behind him with 11 points. The second half started with the gold team stealing the inbound pass from Forest Park, and the second rout was on! Robert Washington led the way as they won the game 68–32. Carl chipped in 17 points in the effort. They stood in the huddle, and Coach Jenkins said this was working just as he visualized it. He congratulated them on the win, and the gym rocked again when they chanted, "Panther pride!"

The purple team was a taller team, but the gold team had shooters and speed.

The Jefferson boys were next up, and Carl spotted Michelle sitting in the stands. He went up and sat next to her, and she hugged him, snuggling up to him. She congratulated him on the win and said he was sweaty, then chided him, saying he had not shown her all his moves. They laughed and talked as they watched the Jefferson boys handle the Pine Tree boys to stay alive in the tournament. Michelle was happy Jackie decided to not come to the stands with her.

He and Michelle got to spend the day together as the tournament wound down. The gold team made the finals, and to their horror, the purple team was on the other end of the floor. Robert Washington summed it up: "It's not enough we play them five times this year. Here they stand between us and the championship trophy!" Coach Jenkins reminded them this was going to be a dogfight and they only had to beat them once. The purple team won the tip and immediately took them down low to take advantage of the size difference.

It was a dogfight, but thirty-two minutes later, the gold team held up the championship trophy! The players on the purple team were salty; they believed they were the better team.

CHAPTER 16

Kendall Is Back!
#MichelleDoesNotLikeHer

The semester was winding down, and excitement was building for the Christmas break. Kendall was talking to Carl again and allowing him to carry her books between classes. She knew he asked Michelle to be his girl, but she felt they could still be friends. Some of the time when he was at Michelle's house, she would walk over to hang out with them. She could see things heating up between Carl and Michelle, which caused her to feel a little out of place. She was still on the cheer team when the gold team played the purple team in the Pemberton Gym.

Carl could not help but like the way Kendall smiled at him when they ran through the hallway to the gym. All during the game, he looked over at Kendall, and she was looking back at him. When the game was over, she asked if Rachel could drop her off at home. Carl said she could drop her off, and Kendall walked to the car with him.

When they arrived at Kendall's house, he walked her to the door and hugged her. He didn't know Jefferson was out of school the next day and Michelle had come to Shasta's house a day early. Michelle stood on Shasta's porch, watching as Carl hugged and kissed Kendall.

He ran back to the car and got in as Rachel drove off.

A few minutes later, they made it home and the phone rang. Hannah answered and turned her nose up when she realized it was Michelle. She called Carl to the phone, and Rachel asked who was on the phone. When Hannah said Michelle was on the phone, Rachel told Hannah she saw him kiss Kendall. They both laughed when Rachel said he had to be the dumbest guy alive—two girlfriends who could see each other's front door! Michelle played it off, asking Carl how he was and what he had been doing.

Carl said he was good and asked how she was doing. Michelle couldn't hold it and asked when he last saw Kendall. Carl knew something was up and came clean, saying he and Rachel had given Kendall a ride home from the game a few minutes ago. It dawned on Carl at that moment, and he asked why she would ask about Kendall. Michelle was caught off guard and said she saw him kiss Kendall on the porch. She started crying and told Carl she did not want him to kiss anybody but her. Rachel and Hannah could see Carl was sweating as he talked to Michelle on the phone.

Rachel and Hannah were happy: Lil Romeo, as they called him, was getting exactly what he deserved! Hannah made a mental note to never talk to a guy like her brother. They heard him try to console Michelle and had to walk away to keep from laughing out loud. *He's just like his dad,* Rachel thought as she stood behind the door, listening. She smiled to herself. Michelle was capping on him. She wanted him to learn he should not play with a girl's feelings.

Carl promised to stop by Michelle's house on Saturday when he finished his paper route. He then hung up the phone.

Hannah was in her room, laughing as he walked by. She wrote Jackie a letter to let her know Kendall was back in the picture. Hannah was happy Kendall was not going away and Michelle would not have peace with Carl. Michelle talked to Shasta, and she said, "Be friends with him, and don't worry about Kendall." She took a deep breath when Shasta said Carl liked her but he was a boy and they were mixed up when it came to girls.

That Saturday, Carl threw his route and stopped at Shasta's house to hang with Michelle.

Michelle breathed deeply and played basketball, shocked at how much his game had improved. When they took a break, they sat on the step, talking. Michelle put her leg on his lap, and the C was prominent against her smooth caramel skin. She didn't know what it was, but she felt good around Carl. He rubbed his fingers along the C, asking if she was still mad about the scar. She laughed, saying she was never mad but that it hurt when it first happened. She leaned into Carl and kissed him, saying she did not want him to kiss anybody but her.

She reminded him of when he asked her to be his girl, she said he could kiss her when he wanted. Carl leaned into her, kissing her gently as she stuck her tongue in his mouth. He pulled back from her, and she laughed, saying a guy should know how to French-kiss his girl. She told him to close his eyes and stick his tongue in her mouth. They French-kissed, and he felt different. He broke the kiss, and she asked if something was wrong. He said no. They played another game of basketball, and he could not go hard on Michelle. He felt different about her.

She prodded him and pushed him, and the soft feeling passed—he went hard on her again. Michelle was twelve years old but understood passion and saw his passion build.

School dismissed for the Christmas holidays, and she spent the whole time at Shasta's house. They invited Carl for dinner, and Rachel allowed him to go. She said he needed to buy a gift for Michelle if he was going to dinner. He called Bradley and told him he needed twenty dollars; he wanted to buy a gift for his girl. Bradley asked Rachel to give Carl the money and he would send it to her when he got paid.

Rachel took Carl shopping, and he bought Michelle a charm bracelet for Christmas. When she asked if he was going to buy something for Kendall, he said he was going to get her a present also. Christmas was a few days off, but she didn't ask where he was going to get the money for Kendall's gift. She had to give it to Carl, though: the bracelet he bought for Michelle was beautiful! He went over his twenty-dollar budget when he asked the jeweler to engrave the bracelet with Michelle's name. Rachel smiled. Her son had mos def picked a great gift for Michelle.

On the way home, he asked Rachel to stop at the grocery store, and he bought treats for everyone. When they got home, he had a message to call Michelle. He went to the phone and called her, and she asked if he was going to throw his route on his bike the next day. It was Sunday, and he reminded her they threw the route in the morning. Michelle said her mother was going to be at Shasta's house and she wanted to meet him.

Carl froze. He could not think of a reason that Mrs. Burns would want to meet him. He agreed and said he would come about 2:00 p.m. the next day.

The next day, after church, he rode his ten-speed to Michelle's house and was surprised the White boys were not in the curve on Norwood. He rode up to Michelle's house, and she ran out to meet him. She dragged him in the house, and to his surprise, Michelle looked just like Mrs. Burns! Their resemblance was so strong his nervousness left him. He remembered what Riley said and stepped up to Mrs. Burns to introduce himself. After some small talk, Mrs. Burns told him there was a harvest ball coming up to celebrate the crops coming in.

Carl had heard of the harvest ball but never wanted to go because it was a formal affair and you had to wear a suit. He listened as Mrs. Burns said Michelle wanted him to be her date. Carl asked where the harvest ball was going to be held, and Mrs. Burns said in Marshall. When he said he would have to ask his mother, Mrs. Burns said she figured as much. She told him to tell his mother that if she allowed him to go, she would arrange for him to be picked up and dropped off. He did not know Mrs. Burns had already spoken to Rachel and she was on board if he wanted to go.

Carl sensed he needed to ask Michelle to go to the harvest ball with him and asked if she wanted to go. She nodded as she jumped up to hug him. Her mother saw the affection in her eyes and knew she needed to talk to her youngest daughter.

Shasta told Carl she would take him home and said he should load his bike in the trunk of her car. When they made it to the curve on Norwood, the White boys were there. They saw Carl in the car with Shasta and shot him the bird as they drove by. Shasta asked what it was with him and these boys, and Carl said they wanted to beat him up.

Shasta pulled into the driveway, and Carl got his bike out of the trunk. He spoke to Riley sitting on the porch, waiting for him to get home. Shasta and Michelle waved at him as they drove off, headed for home. He told Rachel he wanted to take Michelle to the harvest ball and asked if that was okay with her. Rachel said that was fine but he needed to wear a suit to the ball. She was excited for Carl, as this was a coming-out ball and he was taking a very smart girl. The harvest ball normally presented sixteen- to eighteen-year-old girls to society, but this year there was a junior section.

Michelle's sisters agreed to raise money for her fundraiser, and things were in place for the ball, which was scheduled for mid-January. He managed to get Christmas gifts for each person on his list, including Kendall. Michelle loved the charm bracelet and decided she would buy him one that matched hers. Michelle ate dinner with Carl and his family, and a couple of hours later, he ate dinner with Michelle and her family. He opened his gift from Michelle, a basketball and a pair of Converse All-Stars tennis shoes.

He looked at Michelle. The basketball was a Spalding all-leather gym basketball. He knew this ball was meant to be used in the gym and not on clay courts. She smiled, saying she wanted him to step his game up even more using his new gear. She walked over to him and hugged him, saying she loved her gift. He was humbled. He knew Michelle spent a grip on his gifts. He was surprised when Michelle broke out the girls' ten-speed bike her mother bought for Christmas. She laughed as she said they could ride together and play basketball together.

Kendall sat on her porch, steaming, as she watched Carl and Michelle. They seemed like they were having a lot of fun celebrating at Shasta's house.

The day ended, and Shasta took Carl home. Michelle walked to the porch with him and hugged him, saying she had fun. He felt that warm feeling again and said he enjoyed himself also. They kissed, and Michelle said she would call later in the evening. Hannah overheard her and went to the phone and called her friend Doris. She was determined to keep the phone tied up so Michelle could not get through.

Michelle ran to the phone when she and Shasta made it home, but the line at Carl's house was busy the rest of the evening. Carl forgot about the call from Michelle and went to sleep.

The next day, Carl was throwing his route and was shocked when Michelle rode her bike along his route with him. Kendall was sitting on the porch when he and Michelle rode by. They stopped for a few minutes, and Carl could sense the tension in the air. After a few minutes, he and Michelle rode off and finished his route. They spent the rest of Christmas break playing basketball and riding their bikes.

Spring semester started, and Ms. Smith was no longer his Algebra 1 teacher. He didn't know what happened; he was just happy she was not teaching Algebra 1 at Pemberton High School any longer. The new teacher seemed to be better at explaining problems, and he felt better about the class.

When he saw Kendall at lunch, he gave her the watch he bought for Christmas. She didn't want to take it, saying she had not bought him anything. He assured her it was fine, that he wanted her to have the present from him. Kendall unwrapped her present and saw it was a Seiko digital watch!

She tried the watch on, and it fit great. She leaned over and kissed him on the jaw, again telling him how much she liked the watch. She started to quiz him about Michelle, saying she saw how much time he spent there during Christmas break. Carl smiled, saying he asked Michelle to be his girl and reminded her she pushed him away and stopped talking to him. She took a deep breath and said she was going through some things at home and didn't think he needed to be involved. Carl understood and said things between him and Michelle kind of fell in place.

He asked Kendall if that meant they could not be friends, and she said they were still friends. The bell rang for fourth period, and as they walked to class, he reached for her books and she gave them to him. When they got to her class, he handed her books to her and walked to his class. For some reason, he did not feel the same about Kendall.

At basketball practice that evening, Coach Jenkins worked them hard; they had been off almost two weeks and had a game in two days. He was exhausted after practice and was happy to see Riley's truck when he walked out of the gym.

When Riley asked how his day was, he said Ms. Smith, his Algebra 1 teacher, was not working at Pemberton any longer. Riley saw he was in a good mood, and they rode the rest of the way home in silence. When they got home, Rachel briefed him on what he needed to do for the harvest ball. She said this was a big deal and he needed to make a good impression. He listened as Rachel showed him the suit she picked for him to wear and told him how to treat Michelle. He saw this was a big deal for Rachel and also wanted to make a good impression with Mrs. Burns.

The harvest ball was the coming Saturday, and Rachel said she ordered a corsage for him to give Michelle. She said, when he threw his route Saturday, they would do it by car. Rachel said she was going to drop them off and pick them up since he was the guy and needed to drive.

Mrs. Burns fitted Michelle's gown and briefed her on how to act and conduct herself as a young lady. She paused to tell Michelle she knew she wanted to marry her father when she was thirteen years old. She explained the difference was, her husband only had eyes for her, while Carl still had Jackie on his mind. She encouraged Michelle to follow her heart but be careful with her feelings and emotions. Her mother said she would go to Shasta's house that day and Rachel would pick her up there. They finished the prep for the harvest ball and went to sleep.

Carl threw his route early on Saturday so he would have time to get ready for the harvest ball. He had told Michelle he would pick her up at 7:15 p.m. at Shasta's house. He and Rachel arrived at Shasta's house at 7:10 p.m., and he went to the door to get Michelle. Her nephew opened the door and invited him in the house. He took a seat on the couch and waited for Michelle to come out. A moment later, she stepped through the door in a knee-length blue chiffon dress. Carl's mouth dropped open—Michelle was drop-dead gorgeous!

Carl stood up and handed Michelle the corsage he bought for her. He noticed her dress was formfitting and accented her long legs. She wore a pair of black platform shoes with heels that set the dress off. She gave the corsage back to Carl, saying he should put it on for her. He took the corsage and nervously pinned it to her dress. Carl complimented Michelle, saying she looked very good. She asked if he approved, and he said he did. Michelle reached on the end table and handed Carl a box, saying, "Open it." He opened the box and found a gold charm bracelet with his name inscribed on it.

The charm bracelet was a spot-on match with the one he gave her for Christmas. Carl said, "Wow! The bracelet is the bomb!" Michelle did not move when he stepped into her and kissed her passionately. He broke the kiss when Shasta came out of the back with the camera, saying she needed to take a picture of them. They stood together in different poses as Shasta took five pictures. A minute later, the pictures were developed, and they were very nice. Shasta handed two of the pictures to him, saying he should give those to Rachel.

Carl could not help himself; he felt some kind of way about Michelle. He held the door open, and she slid on the front seat, next to Rachel. Carl sat on the front seat also, next to the door. Rachel drove off, and they were headed to the harvest ball at the Wiley College ballroom. She pulled up to the curb and watched as he helped Michelle out the car, and they walked up the sidewalk to the ballroom. She could not help but think how good they looked together and decided she would get out of their way. Rachel also saw how content they seemed to be with each other.

Rachel made it home and called Mrs. Burns, saying they needed to talk. She started by saying Michelle really liked Carl and she felt he was into her as well. She continued, saying she wanted to see if they could set some ground rules to stay in control. She was a little taken aback when she heard Mrs. Burns laugh on the other end. She told Rachel, "Baby, my eldest daughter is your age, and I have grandkids Carl and Michelle's age." She said the best thing to do was let them work this out on their own. When Rachel said she felt they might be getting too close, Mrs. Burns said they would be okay.

When they hung up, Rachel felt a calmness about the situation. Mrs. Burns had put her at ease. She left at 11:30 p.m., headed back to Wiley's ballroom to pick them up. They were outside, waiting, and she thought they didn't have a good time. When they got in the car, they were smiling and said they had a great time. When she asked why they were outside, Michelle said she told them to come out at 11:30 p.m. Rachel had forgotten she told them this, and they were quiet on the drive home. When they got to Shasta's house, Carl walked her to the door and kissed her.

They were quiet on the drive home, and Rachel decided she would talk to Carl while they threw his route the next morning.

The next morning, as they threw his route, she and Carl talked about Michelle. Rachel asked if he liked her, and he said he did like Michelle, that he felt different around her. She asked about Jackie, and he said, "She Ronnie girl now." Rachel held her tongue, not telling him Jackie still carried a torch for him. She thought about the heartbreak she felt when she and Bradley broke up and the way she loved him. She hoped Carl did not put this hurt on either Michelle or Jackie.

Rachel took Mrs. Burns's advice and allowed him to "court" Michelle. He went to Shasta's house every Friday and Saturday night to watch movies and hang out with Michelle. They got real comfortable with each other, and their one-on-one games had improved dramatically. He and Kendall were hot and cold and finally went to being strictly friends. She side-eyed him when she was on the cheer line, and he ran through the hallway to the court. It didn't bother him any longer, and he realized choosing Michelle caused him to lose friendship with Kendall.

He spoke to Rachel, and she said he should have expected this, explaining Kendall felt rejected. She reminded him that before Michelle started going to Shasta's house, he stopped at Kendall's house on his route. He forgot about that, and Rachel went further, reminding him Kendall could see Shasta's house from her house. When he tried to offer his side, Rachel stopped him, saying he asked for her opinion. Carl was shocked when Rachel said he had literally thrown Kendall's heart against the wall. Rachel blew his mind by saying he replaced Kendall with Michelle and did it right before her eyes.

Carl stared blankly when Rachel said he had the nerve to ask her to be friends with Michelle. She was all up in her feelings now, and he knew to not try to stop her. He listened as Rachel said he needed to apologize to Kendall for being so insensitive. She calmed down and said, "I know you believe she pushed you away and you bonded with Michelle." She took a deep breath and told Carl he needed to fix this with Kendall. He asked Rachel how he could fix this and make it better.

Rachel took a deep breath, saying he needed to say to Kendall what she said to him. Carl noticed the change in Rachel's demeanor as she said, "You are a smooth young man. She will listen if you talk to her and ask her to forgive you." They hugged, and Carl noticed Rachel was crying. Instead of asking what was wrong, though, his intuition told him to just hold her. After a few moments, Rachel stepped back and said he should not lead Kendall on; he needed to straighten things out. Rachel told him, "If Kendall tries to walk off, gently hold her hand, look in her eyes, and ask her to please listen."

Carl could not sleep that night, thinking about what Rachel had said to him. He thought about what he would say to Kendall when he saw her and realized he was going to have to play this one from the heart. When Rachel dropped them off at the bus stop, he spotted Kendall standing by herself. He walked over to her and asked if they could talk. She said they had nothing to talk about and turned to walk away. He reached out and gently held her hand as he looked in her eyes and asked her to please listen. She stopped and looked up, saying, "What is it, Carl?"

He started by apologizing, saying he was wrong to do what he did. Kendall looked at him as he said he did not mean to hurt her feelings and he hated he did. This broke Kendall down, and she started to cry, saying he hurt her bad. He took her books, and she allowed him to hug her. Carl said he was not thinking when he asked her to be friends with Michelle. He told Kendall it was bad for him to stop at her house on his route, then stop at Michelle's house. He looked at Kendall and asked if she would forgive him. Kendall rubbed her eyes, saying she would forgive him.

The bus pulled up at that moment, and they got in line to get on board. When she sat down, he handed her books to her and started to walk down the aisle to another seat. She said it was cool and he could sit with her. Carl sat down, and they started to talk about the basketball season. Kendall said the whole school was behind the gold team and they were bad to the bone. He asked what they liked about the gold team, and she said they were exciting to watch. She especially liked their "Panther pride!" chant and loved when they did it.

Carl remembered what Rachel said last night and asked Kendall if she was cool with them just being friends. Kendall said she was good but she was not going to be friends with Michelle. She looked at him, saying Michelle liked him a lot.

They made it to school and got off the bus. He held her books while she got off the bus, but Kendall would not let him carry them. When they walked in the building, she told him he should go to class, for it would not be right for him to walk her to class. He remembered what Rachel said about not leading her on and said he would see her later.

Carl's first class of the day was American history, and the teacher had breaking news for the class. They listened as she said President Nixon was on the first leg of his China trip. As part of their assignment, they were to watch the news each night and be ready to talk about the president's trip to China. The economy in the USA was in recession, and the purpose of President Nixon's trip was to open new trade markets for American-made products. There was a sense of excitement because everyone knew if there was a new market for goods, the country would get out of the recession.

That afternoon, in practice, Coach Jenkins said they were tied for first place with the purple team. Both teams were undefeated in district, and they faced each other the next day. The intensity level was high when they scrimmaged that evening in anticipation of the game the next day. There was some shade; the gold team had beaten the purple team both times they played. There was a lot of trash talk; the purple team was certain they would win the next meeting between them. School was dismissed during the last period, and everyone was instructed to go to the gym.

CHAPTER 17

We Playing the Purple Team…Again!
#WhatsOurMotto

The gym was packed when both teams ran through the hallway to the court. Carl saw Kendall on the cheer line, and she mouthed, "Good luck." The atmosphere was electric as the purple team warmed up on the other end of the floor. The gold team shot free throws, clapping one time when they missed and twice when they made it. Coach Jenkins called them to the bench and huddled them up. He spoke, saying, "If you can't get up for *this* game, you dead!" He said they had to forget the other two games they won—it did not mean anything.

He announced the starting lineup, then led them in their call-and-response chant. The gym rocked when Coach Jenkins yelled his call, "What's our motto?" It rocked harder when they yelled their response, "Ninety-four feet for thirty-two minutes!" Coach Jenkins then settled them down, saying, "This is it, guys. 'Panther pride' on three!"

Kendall felt the chill she got when the gold team yelled, "Panther pride!" and their starters ran on the floor. She noticed Carl remained on the bench as the teams took the floor. It was clear the purple team had a height advantage on the gold team.

Coach Allen changed the purple team strategy and went with three guards to offset the gold team speed. He had his two six-foot-six players, called the Twin Towers, posted up down low. They executed their low-post game flawlessly, and the gold team had several players in foul trouble by the half. The gold team could not get their running game on track and trailed the purple team 40–36 at the half. Coach Jenkins settled them down, saying they were still in the game even though the purple team was pounding them in the paint.

He knew they would get their running game on track. There was no long strategy session; Coach Jenkins sent them out for the shootaround. This set the tone, and they were loose when the horn sounded to start the second half. The purple team controlled the tip, but Robert Washington made a play, stealing the ball and dribbling down for a layup. Two minutes into the second half, the gold team had scored 8 unanswered points and now led 44–40. Coach Jenkins was all smiles—his team was rolling!

Coach Allen called time-out. The gold team fast break had started clicking, and they were hard to stop when this happened. He changed his strategy to trap the gold team ball handlers at half-court. This worked and slowed their fast break down enough for them to tie the game. The game went back and forth, up and down the court. With twenty-two seconds left in the game, Coach Jenkins called time-out, with the gold team trailing 83–82. He designed the play and told Carl to bring the ball up the floor. On the inbound pass, the purple team did not have full court pressure.

He pushed the ball up the floor and found Robert Washington in the corner. Carl could not believe the gold team's best shooter was wide open! He passed the ball to him, and Robert got a clean look at the basket. The gym held its collective breath as the horn sounded and the ball rimmed in, bounced against the backboard, and bounced off the back of the rim. The purple team was ecstatic—they had beaten the gold team 83–82! More importantly, the purple team was in first place and had beaten the second-place team.

The scout coaches for four teams who had not played either team from Pemberton got an eyeful that day. They left the gym wondering how they could beat either team. Coach Jenkins called them to him and said they needed to shake the purple team's hands. The players lined up at half-court and shook hands, congratulating each other on a game well played. They ran to the bench for Coach Jenkins's call and response. He told them they had nothing to hang their heads about and he would see them at practice the following day.

He then did the call part, "What's our motto?"

The team responded, "Ninety-four feet for thirty-two minutes!"

Coach Jenkins dismissed them with "'Panther pride' on three," counted it off, and the gym rocked again as they shouted, "Panther pride!" There was no shade from the purple team players, for they knew they dodged a bullet. They saw Robert miss a shot he made regularly in practice. The intensity of the scrimmages picked up. The purple team knew the high-octane offense of the gold team was going to be hard to beat.

The gold team hit their stride, and the juggernaut was unleashed. They rolled through district, losing one more game along the way. With Robert Washington leading the way, they averaged 70 points a game, with an average winning margin of 20 points. They played the purple team six times during the season and won four of the matchups.

In late March, Coach Jenkins and the gold team held up the championship trophy, and he was voted Coach of the Year. Football spring training started in late April, and Carl was shocked he got an invite to try out for varsity.

This was big. Sophomores did not make varsity at Marshall High! He was especially shocked because he sat out the last half of the football season with eligibility issues. Coach Jenkins said he was having a great year when he became ineligible, and the coaching staff knew he would not be ineligible again. He went home that evening and told Rachel the good news. She was not enthused because some of the boys were three years older than him.

Spring training was brutal. Carl had never been hit this hard before. The linemen were bigger, and so were the running backs. He knew to not say anything to Rachel because she would have pulled him out of football. At the end of spring drills, he was excited to be second level on the depth chart—meaning, he would get a lot of playing time. When Bradley called to see when he wanted to come to Detroit, Carl said he was not going this year. Bradley laughed, saying, "We go through this every year, dude." After a little coaxing by Bradley, he agreed to stay in Texas for two weeks, then go to Detroit for six weeks.

He spent every day with Michelle, and she was sad when he told her he'd decided to go to Detroit. She rode her bike with him as he threw his route, and they played basketball later.

A couple of weeks later, he was at Shreveport Regional for the plane trip to Detroit. They didn't tag him this year, just said where his connecting flight was going to be. The flights Carl had taken to Detroit normally went through Atlanta, but this year he had a connecting flight in Memphis. He made his connection with no problems, and the flight landed in Detroit. When Bradley met him at the airport, he asked about Gwen, Trey, and Carlos. Bradley said they were good and he would see them later.

They made the half-hour drive to the house, and Carl was shocked when he walked in the house—there was no furniture inside, and he told Bradley they had been robbed. Bradley laughed as he said they had not been robbed, but Gwen had moved out of the home. He had a blank stare on his face, and Bradley said he would have to make a pallet to sleep on. Carl's hair was blown back but he went upstairs and got some bedding to make a pallet. He woke up early the next morning and sat on the stoop next door with Ralph. He was shocked when Ralph said Gwen had moved out a couple of weeks back.

He was giving Carl the full information when Mrs. Douglas came to the door. She called Ralph in the house, saying breakfast was ready. Carl got up to walk back to the house, and she told him to come in; she had cooked enough for him. He remembered what Rachel and Janice had said about eating at other people's house, but he was hungry. He went in and ate breakfast with them. Bradley was like a son to Mrs. Douglas, so she knew he had not gotten Carl anything to eat. She also knew the reason Gwen moved out of the home, so she told Carl he was welcome to eat there anytime.

Bradley woke up early and told Carl they needed to go shopping. They went to the furniture store, and Bradley bought a king-size bedroom set for his room. He was shocked when Bradley let him pick out the bed he wanted to put in his room. He picked out a king-size bed, two nightstands, and a chest of drawers. He was blown away when Bradley included two lamps with the purchase. He felt he had come of age.

The next stop was the hardware store, where they picked out colors for his bedroom. Bradley told him he could paint his room and the third bedroom any color he wanted.

Carl chose purple for his bedroom, and orange for Trey and Carlos's bedroom. Bradley asked if he thought he could paint the rooms, and Carl said he could. He reminded Bradley they painted the house in Marshall almost every summer. He told Bradley he needed to get several drop cloths and something to wash out the paintbrushes. They loaded the car with the paint and supplies, then headed home. He started painting the rooms the next day, doing his bedroom first. He wanted to have his room painted, and the paint dry, when the furniture was delivered.

It took him three days to paint the room and get it trimmed out. Bradley was mildly surprised when he saw the level of quality in the job. When the bedroom furniture arrived, he had them leave it in Trey and Carlos's room; the paint in his room was not quite dry. When the paint finally dried, he went about the task of setting his room up. It took a whole day for him to get the bed assembled and everything set up in his room. He was happy when he finally got it done; his room looked like a grown person room.

The next task was to paint Trey and Carlos's room, and he finished in a day.

The first few days after he finished the tasks were hard. Bradley went to work at 2:00 p.m. and did not get back until 2:30 a.m. most days. This left Carl alone, and he had never been alone for extended periods like this. He was a little rattled. The house was two stories with a basement. He got used to the different noises the house made and got used to being home alone. He did not know Mrs. Douglas kept an eye on the house and was looking out for him.

A week later, Bradley told him to pack a light bag; they were going to hang out a few days.

He packed a bag with clothes to last three days, and they left. About fifteen minutes later, they pulled into the driveway of a home, and he had no idea where he was. Some kids ran out of the house and surrounded Bradley. It was evident they knew him. Bradley introduced him to Mark, Derrick, Andre, and Nicole. They went in the house, and Bradley kissed the woman he introduced as Valerie. Carl stepped up and shook her hand, saying he was glad to meet her. She complimented Bradley, saying Carl had good manners, that somebody raised him right.

Bradley sent him to the car to get their bags, and Mark went with him, asking where he went to school. Carl told him he went to Pemberton in Marshall, Texas. Mark peppered him with questions about Texas and said he had always wanted to get out of Detroit. A few minutes later, Derrick came out of the house and they hung out on the block. This must be the thing to do, he thought, hanging out on the block. When it was time for Bradley to go to work Monday, he told Carl he was going to leave him with Valerie and her kids. Carl was okay with this; he had made friends with Mark and Derrick.

The next day, they were out on the block when two girls came down the street on their ten-speed bikes. Carl noticed out the corner of his eyes when the thin girl fell off her bike. He stood, looking for a moment, and realized she was not getting up. When he walked out to the street, he saw she was crying and her elbow was scraped. He picked her up and pushed her bike as they walked to the sidewalk. She was in a full-blown cry now, and the scrape was bleeding.

He didn't know what to do. She was holding on to him and crying. He looked at Mark, and he said she lived two doors down at the house with the double driveway. Carl let her lean on him as he pushed her bike toward their house. Her sister Marsha was with them as they walked and said her sister's name was Felicia. When they got to the double driveway, Carl saw what Mark was talking about and pushed her bike as they walked up the double driveway. He asked where her mother was, and Marsha said she was at work. This was a first for Carl: there were no adults at home with these kids. Felicia was a tall and thin chocolate girl. Her hair was flat ironed and Carl heard how funny she talked. He didn't want to leave Felicia like this and asked Marsha to get a towel.

A few seconds later, Marsha came back with the towel, and he ran cold water from the hydrant over it. He applied it to Felicia's elbow, and she cringed from the sting. He assured her it would not sting long, so she let him keep pressure on her elbow. A minute or so later, Carl took the towel off, and her elbow was not bleeding. He handed the towel to her and said if her elbow started to bleed again, she should hold it against it. Felicia asked where he learned to do this, and he said Boy Scouts. He walked away, headed back to Mark's house down the block. Carl and Mark went back to hanging out. The excitement was over.

Later that night, Bradley got off work and picked Carl up from Valerie's house.

It had been three days since they had been home, and the next morning, Mrs. Douglas asked if things were good. He assured her they were as he ate breakfast. He normally did not talk about what went on in the house, but he felt different with Mrs. Douglas. He also had not been told this by Bradley; this was the rule in Texas. As he ate breakfast, Mrs. Douglas got the information she wanted to know. She knew Bradley loved women and shook her head because he was so irresponsible. She could see Carl had been taught manners; he was not like the kids in Detroit.

He finished eating and left the kitchen, headed back to the block. Carl knew they cooked differently in Detroit, but Mrs. Douglas cooked a lot like they did in Texas. The six weeks he committed to Detroit flew by, and it was time to go back to Texas. Bradley told him he was going to help him with his school clothes and arranged for him to go to Northland Mall to shop. He got dressed and was waiting for whoever was going to pick him up to take him to the mall. He was surprised when Ms. Valerie pulled up with her kids. They came in the house, and she went upstairs to Bradley's room.

A few minutes later, she came back downstairs with the keys to Bradley's Cadillac, saying they were ready to go. Valerie drove to Northland Mall, and they picked clothes for Carl to wear at school. She did the same as Gwen, helped him pick clothes he could wear in

Texas. Valerie told him she knew the weather was different there. She had visited some of her relatives in Tennessee.

A week later, Carl was at Detroit Metro Airport, waiting for his flight to Shreveport. Bradley asked him to not tell Rachel he and Gwen had split up; he wanted to be the one to tell her.

Carl boarded the plane for the flight home. It was the same as the flight to Detroit, a layover and change of planes in Memphis. The layover was two and a half hours in Memphis, and he decided to get something to eat. Bradley had given him two hundred dollars in cash, what he called train riding money. He was hungry. He had not eaten all day and bought a hamburger at one of the airport hamburger stands. He heard about barbecue in Memphis but settled on burger and fries. Carl finished the burger and fries and saw he had two hours left before his flight.

Bored from the wait until his next flight took off, he stopped at a magazine stand and bought stationery and an envelope. He wrote Michelle a letter, knowing she would get the letter after he got back to Texas. He described the airport in Memphis and what he did while in Detroit for six weeks. He sealed the letter and handed it to the clerk at the stationery store, who mailed it for him. He boarded the plane for the second leg of his trip and landed in Shreveport two hours later. Rachel, Hannah, and Carol met him at the airport and gave him big hugs.

They talked while making the half-hour drive to Marshall, and he thought about his agreement with Bradley. They pumped him for information about his vacation in Detroit. Hannah wanted to know if Bradley had bought his school clothes. Carl told her he did get school clothes and they were in his suitcase. He was happy when they arrived home, glad to be back in Marshall. He loved going to Detroit, but there was no place like home. Riley was sitting on the porch and he hugged him, then went into the house to hug Janice. He unloaded his suitcases from the car, then called Michelle.

She was happy to hear from him and asked when he got home. Her heart perked up when he said he had been back about an hour. She asked about his six weeks in Detroit, and before he knew it, they had been on the phone an hour. When they hung up, he went in the bathroom to take a bath and knock the travel dust off. He and Janice sat down to talk so she could catch up on the things he did while he was there. She knew Bradley was basically irresponsible and wanted to make sure everything was okay. Carl assured her it was all good and he stayed safe while he was in Detroit.

The conversation changed to his paper route, and Rachel said she was happy to turn it back to him. She asked what he was going to do in the fall when football season started. Rachel told Carl she was going to work some of the games for extra money. He knew she was asking about his plan for dealing with the problem he had with the White boys in the curve on Norwood. She suggested he might need to give up the route, but he had time to think about it. Carl said he would think about it and went to his room to go to sleep.

When they watched the news the next day, the lead story was about the burglary of a hotel in Washington called Watergate. There had been five arrests, and it seemed some people in the Nixon admin-istration had authorized the burglary. This was significant because President Nixon was up for re-election in November. Carl put it to the back of his mind and thought nothing else about it. It was early August, and he decided he was not going to the hayfield; he would throw his route. When Ed found out he was not hauling hay, he asked Carl to help him cut yards.

He closed the deal with Carl when he said they could work like they wanted. Ed had a second lawn mower, and they were on their way, cutting yards a few days each week. Carl liked this better than hauling hay; he made more money and did not work nearly as hard. He threw his route on his bike and was astonished the beef between the neighborhoods had been quashed. It took a second meeting of the grown-ups to bring this about, and only after one of the Black guys had shot at them with a .22 pistol.

Carl and Michelle were honing their basketball game playing one-on-one against each other.

Michelle's game became more masculine, and she was aggres-sive in her style of play. Her demand that he not take it easy on her was paying off. They were bonding in their relationship. He French-kissed her when he arrived and when he left. His hormones raged, and when he kissed her, he felt different. He saw her every day, and she rode her bike with him as he threw his route. Since a truce had been called with the White boys on Norwood, it was safe for her to ride her bike to his house. The more Hannah saw Michelle, the more she was reminded she did not like her.

Two-a-day football drills started in mid-August, and he was ready, excited because he was going to be on varsity. The first day of practice, he went to the varsity field house and was told he had been demoted to JV! There had been fourteen ninth graders who worked out with the varsity and only one made the team. Carl was pissed, having gone through those brutal three weeks of spring training only to be sent back to JV. When he got home that evening, he mentioned it to Rachel, and she said he knew he would be a starter on JV. He sucked it up and went to the afternoon practice.

Just like Rachel said, he was a starting outside linebacker on the junior varsity. He got a chance to take his frustration out on the running backs, hitting them hard on every tackle.

Practice ended, and he was on the way home, stopping through Bel Air for a few minutes. He didn't ride his bike because he needed the walk home to loosen his muscles and wind down off the contact. He got his papers and headed to throw his route, slowly riding down Norwood. He went to Michelle's house and got her so they could ride and talk.

He sat on his bike as she kissed him, saying how it made him feel funny, but in a good way. As they rode and threw his route, she told him Ronnie Simmons made varsity for the Bulldogs and was their starting quarterback. He stopped his bike, asking Michelle if he heard her right. She said he did hear her right; Ronnie Simmons was the starting quarterback for the Bulldogs. Carl cursed under his breath, and Michelle then told him Jackie Hunt made the varsity cheer squad. He knew what Michelle was doing and let this little piece of information slide by without a reaction.

He listened as Michelle went on about how Jackie would be cheering for her man on Friday nights. Carl remembered something Bradley had said: never lose your cool. He looked at Michelle, saying he was happy for them. They finished the route and stopped at

Michelle's house. She asked about going one-on-one, and Carl said he had been to football practice twice, plus threw his paper route, so he was tired. She thought about it and realized he should be tired. They sat on the porch a few minutes, and Carl said he was about to go home; he needed to rest.

Michelle leaned into him and kissed him, saying he was the man and she would be at all the JV home games. School started, and the JV opened the season with the Nacogdoches Dragons. When they ran out of the rock house to the field, Carl noticed Michelle by the fence. She pounded his shoulder pads when he stopped to say hello. He could not put his finger on it, but when he looked in her eyes, they seemed to sparkle. The team was fired up, and the Dragons won the coin toss for the kickoff.

Coach Walker got them in the huddle and said, "This is where we start our season. Let's go out and get it done."

The stadium rocked when they shouted the team chant. The Mavericks got up on the Dragons, and the game was well in hand by the half. When they ran off the field at the half, Carl saw Kendall on the cheer line. He waved to her and was shocked she smiled and waved back. Carl had a monster game, a tackle for a fumble and a fumble recovery for a defensive touchdown. He might have been on JV, but he was making noise!

CHAPTER 18

Reality Sets In
#RonnieABaller

As Carl was folding his papers the next day, he saw his picture when he made the tackle for the fumble. It was an incredibly clear picture, and he cut it out. He looked further down the page and saw an article about the Jefferson game. The headline was this: BULLDOGS LED BY SOPHOMORE PHENOM RONNIE SIMMONS. Rachel startled him when she drove up, saying he had better get rolling on his route. They were leaving at 6:30 p.m. sharp. He looked at his watch. It was 4:30 p.m., and that meant he had an hour and a half to throw his route.

When he went by Shasta's house, it was funny not seeing Michelle in the yard. She was in the varsity pep squad, so she was getting ready for the game. He finished his route and slow-rolled home. He was really tired. Rachel packed them up, and they headed for the Jefferson game. The atmosphere was electric, and the early-September heat was searing.

Carl went to the stands and found a group of people he knew. He was no longer a rock star among them. Everyone was instead talking about Ronnie Simmons. They listened as the announcer introduced the starting lineups for both teams.

The stadium rocked when Ronnie Simmons was introduced as "The Sophomore Phenom." He saw Jackie on the cheer squad as they did splits and cheered for the Bulldogs. He felt slighted. Things had gone straight downhill. Jackie was a varsity cheerleader, Ronnie's girl, and he was the starting quarterback for the Bulldogs varsity squad. They were opening the season with their archrival, the Daingerfield Tigers. The Bulldogs won the coin toss and took the opening kick-off. He watched as Ronnie ran on the field and called signals for the "Dawgs."

The Ronnie Simmons era at Jefferson started with a bang. He took the third play from scrimmage for a fifty-five-yard touchdown. The crowd went wild, and the stadium rocked—he energized the fans! Ronnie ended the night with a solid game, and the Dawgs beat their archrival 40–14. Michelle rode to Marshall with them, and Hannah went into her peacebreaking mode, chiding Carl for being a loser. He seethed inside but managed to hold it together, not wanting Michelle to see him and Hannah clown.

Rachel dropped Michelle at Shasta's house and made the short drive home. When they got out of the car, he swung on Hannah and she ducked. Rachel got between them and ordered them inside, saying she was going to talk to them both. Rachel got inside and wound down, then called Hannah and Carl in the room with her. She asked Hannah why she said Ronnie took Carl's girl when Michelle was in the car with them. Hannah said she could not stand her and Jackie was her friend. Rachel asked her, If Jackie was Ronnie's girl, why did she not like Michelle?

Carl listened as Hannah said she did not want Michelle with Carl, period. She repeated that she did not like her and mos def did not want her as a sister-in-law. Hannah told Rachel she knew he was going to swing on her, and that was why she was able to duck. Rachel looked at her, saying she needed to take her butt to bed and she would figure out how to discipline her later. When Hannah left the room, Rachel told him it was good, until he swung on Hannah. He apologized and said he lost it. Rachel smiled and said, since he did not hit her, it was no harm.

He hugged Rachel, and she told him she understood how he felt. Rachel said it would get worked out and he had to cover Michelle because Hannah could be cruel. Carl said what hurt the most was Hannah saying he was not good enough to make varsity and Ronnie was a star. She did not say anything; instead, she listened as Carl said this bothered him. Rachel hugged him closer. She could feel his hurt but could do nothing about it. She noticed he did not cry, just said he was hurt behind it all. Rachel knew he was maturing when he asked why he was salty instead of happy for Ronnie.

She took this one and said it was only natural since they had been rivals for a long time. Carl laughed out loud when Rachel said this and told him to go to bed. This was something he did not need to worry about. When Carl woke up the next morning, he was shocked Hannah apologized for being cruel to him and Michelle. He took the hint, apologizing for swinging on her. He got his breakfast plate and went to the porch with Riley. He wanted to hang out today. He almost went back in the house when he saw Ron standing in the yard. He was always needling him.

Ron saw him come out of the house and hollered at him, "How ya doing, baby boy?" A moment later, he said, "Riley told me you were playing football for the school." Carl was pleasantly surprised. For once he was not talking about how soft he was. He ate his breakfast, listening as Ron told Riley he needed a ride to Macedonia Cemetery; he had to dig a grave for a 2:00 p.m. funeral. Riley told Ron he would take him to Macedonia Cemetery when Carl finished eating his breakfast.

They dropped Ron off and did a quick cleanup of Rudolph's grave, then talked on the ride home. Riley said things had a way of working themselves out and asked what the problem was. Carl said he didn't make varsity but Ronnie Simmons did. He listened as Riley said he could not gauge his life based on what other people did. He told Carl they needed extra players and that was the reason he and the other guys practiced with the varsity. He listened as Riley said Marshall High was a much bigger school than Jefferson High and there were more kids to choose from.

He had never thought of it like that and laughed when Riley said, "If Ronnie were in Marshall, he would be on JV with you."

When they got home, he got his bag and papers, then rolled out. He didn't roll the papers; he was going to do that when he got to Michelle's house. A few minutes later, he was at Michelle's, where she was standing in the yard, waiting for him. He got off his bike, and she locked her arms behind his neck as they French-kissed. They broke their kiss, and he grabbed the bag with his papers and threw them on Shasta's porch.

While they rolled the papers, Michelle said she felt funny when they kissed. He laughed, saying Rachel told him their hormones were raging. Michelle laughed and asked why Hannah did not like her. He told her to not worry about that; Hannah did not like anybody. She reminded him Hannah was best friends with Jackie, and he let the conversation go silent.

A few minutes later, they rolled the last paper and started the route by leaving Shasta's paper in the front room. They threw his route and rolled around the neighborhood on their ten-speeds.

The other kids thought they were a big deal—those ten-speed bikes were expensive! They finished the route and were rolling back to Shasta's house when Michelle asked him why he still liked Jackie Hunt. He looked at her, saying he did not like Jackie, but she did not believe him. She said Jackie was in love with Ronnie Simmons; she liked being the star quarterback's girl. His emotions were all over the place, and something inside said to come clean with her.

Carl stopped his bike, looked at her, and took a deep breath. He told Michelle that for four years she walked to school with them. He admitted he liked her, but said he knew she was Ronnie's girl. She listened as Carl said there was something about them that separated her from Jackie. Michelle held her breath and asked him, "If she quit Ronnie Simmons, are you going to take her back?" Michelle's heart pounded as she waited for his response and looked in his eyes. He said he would not take Jackie back if she quit Ronnie Simmons. He got off his bike and walked to her, kissing her intimately. Michelle started crying and put his hand on her chest.

He felt the beat of her heart as she said, "You in my heart, Carl." He kissed her again, and that funny feeling came over him once more. He smiled, saying he felt differently about her than he did about Jackie. She asked him to explain, and he said he felt good when he was around her. She smiled through her tears, saying, "That was a *really* good answer, Carl." Michelle kissed him again, and they held each other for a few moments. He tried to let her go, and she asked him to keep holding her, that it felt really good. He leaned into her and kissed her again; it felt like the thing to do.

Michelle whispered she believed he would not take Jackie back and promised to not ask about her again. They were startled by Rachel's voice saying, "Here you two are." She explained they were worried since it had been over an hour since they left Shasta's house. Rachel knew she had seen an intimate moment between them and her mind was racing. She wanted to get out in front of this but was not sure how to do it. She told them to load their bikes in the car; she would give them a ride. Rachel went to Shasta's house, and Carl took Michelle's bike out the trunk.

Rachel told them to wait outside while she went in the house. She asked Shasta if she could use her phone to call Mrs. Burns. Shasta said that was fine with her and dialed the number for her mother. When Mrs. Burns answered the phone, Rachel identified herself, saying she wanted to talk to her. She started by saying she wanted to talk to Carl and Michelle about sex and babies. Rachel was stunned when Mrs. Burns laughed out loud, saying she had talked to Michelle about sex. She told Rachel nothing had changed since the last time they had this conversation.

She gave Rachel permission and her blessing to speak with Michelle about her raging hormones. They ended their call when Mrs. Burns said she knew Michelle liked him; she talked about him constantly and spent every moment in Marshall. When Rachel hung up the phone, Shasta said, "The girl don't like to ride bikes, but she had our mom buy her one so she could ride with him." She looked at Rachel and said there was nothing to do; Michelle's mind was made up about him. This was crazy to Rachel. It seemed they had given up and were going to allow her to run straight into a heartbreak.

Rachel looked at Shasta, saying, "I know that boy, and he is going to break her heart."

Shasta smiled, replying, "She will do what each of us women has done when the man we love broke our heart, deal with it and make excuses for him." Shasta shook her head, saying they all had one and he was Michelle's. She described Michelle as a homebody who spent all her time with their mom, until she started liking Carl. She told Rachel their mother talked to her and she knew about sex and babies. The light went off, and she realized she was living her heartbreak behind Bradley through Michelle.

She calmed down and told Shasta she was absolutely right, then decided to allow them to enjoy their "puppy love." Shasta sat Rachel down for a moment, saying, "Michelle is very smart and talks about finishing school early." Shasta continued, "She wants to go off to college with him." She did not tell Rachel about Michelle's plan to get an apartment for them to live together. Rachel pulled herself together and made a mental note to call Bradley and tell him their son was getting serious about a young lady. She had a hard time accepting these kids being this serious.

Shasta came up with an idea that made a lot of sense, saying they should work together to watch them. They agreed to have a talk with them to work this out. They relaxed and laughed as Shasta walked Rachel to her car. She told Carl they needed to go and get in the car.

The next morning, when Carl got his papers ready, Rachel didn't let Hannah go with them. After they finished throwing the route, they stopped at Shasta's house. He thought he was in trouble when they walked in the house and Shasta was sitting at the table with Michelle.

He took a seat across from Michelle, and Rachel took a seat across from Shasta. Rachel said they were not in trouble but there were some things they needed to talk about. She started saying she sat there about ten minutes yesterday, watching and listening to them. Rachel told Michelle she reminded her a lot of herself at her age. She really liked Carl's dad, Bradley. She turned her attention to Carl, asking, "Do you like Michelle?" He looked at Rachel, saying he did like Michelle. He was stunned when she asked, "Would you marry her right now, Carl?"

He looked at Rachel and excitedly said, "I'm too young to get married right now!" Shasta saw where Rachel was going and asked Michelle, "Would you marry him right now?" There was no surprise when she emphatically said yes. Rachel looked at Michelle and said she was going to tell her a brutally honest story. She related how she knew at thirteen years old she wanted to marry Bradley. They were together, and he did like her, but the other girls would not leave him alone. Rachel said, "The same way you wonder about Jackie Hunt, my nemesis was Ella Chalmers."

Rachel's voice broke when she said while she was pregnant with Carl, she saw her best friend kissing Bradley. Michelle listened as Rachel said she knew Bradley loved her but the attention from the other girls was too much to resist. She asked if this sounded familiar and reminded her they were being totally truthful. Michelle looked at Rachel and said it did sound familiar. Shasta stepped in, saying she was wild about the dad of her eldest son, Trey. Carl stopped her and asked why they were doing this. Rachel laughed out loud, asking, "Are you mad, son?"

Carl said he was not but it seemed they were trying to scare them. Shasta laughed and said they were not trying to scare them; they wanted them to know what they were getting into. Shasta looked at Carl and said they were trying to help them. She told Carl, "You are going to get her pregnant, and all her little supposed-to-be friends will be running up in your face. They know she pregnant and feeling bad, so they invite you to parties and dances. The next thing you know, you involved with one of them, and that is just the way they planned it."

She shocked Carl by saying, "When your friends find out Michelle having sex with you, they will be hitting on her." She summed it up for them by saying, "These other girls and boys are not going to let ya'll have peace."

Shasta said, "This how we are going to handle the situation." She asked Carl if he had asked Michelle to be his girl, and he said he had. Rachel took a deep breath when Shasta said, "Since Michelle your girl, we are going to show ya'll how to court each other."

Rachel made eye contact with her. She thought this was brilliant. She saw they could chaperone them and decrease the chances of their hormones running amok.

Shasta asked Carl, "How did you ask her to be your girl?"

He said they had been playing basketball and he asked her to be his girl. He could see the look in Shasta's eyes and knew he needed to keep explaining. He said, when he asked Michelle to be his girl, she wanted to know what she had to do. They listened as he said he told her he could kiss her and they would play basketball together.

She looked at Michelle, and she said that was right; that was how they did it. Carl and Michelle were surprised when Shasta said that was great and a good starting point. She told them that was what she and Rachel would do, show them how to get along with each other and figure out if they should be together. Rachel's heart softened toward Michelle, realizing she was just a girl that really liked her son. Shasta finished by saying they wanted them to do this correctly and they should not be sneaking around. Carl asked them what it meant for them to show them the proper way to "court" each other.

Rachel said she would explain that later and asked if he had any other questions. Neither of them did, and they stood to leave. Rachel knew she had a decision to make: Should she ask Bradley to talk to him, or should she get Riley? Since he spent so much time with Riley, she decided to get him to talk to Carl.

Later that day, she spoke with Riley, and he agreed to speak with Carl about courting girls.

The weeks flew by, and the Maverick JV had a horrible season. Everyone looked forward to Thanksgiving break, when they turned in their pads.

The Bulldogs in Jefferson had a stellar season, led by Sophomore Phenom Ronnie Simmons. He had followed them during the season because Ronnie got major press in *The News-Messenger*. Ronnie's popularity soared, both in Jefferson and the region. He was a great athlete, and the sports reporters from both the *Jefferson Jimplecute* and *The Marshall News Messenger* called him a magician with the football. The guys from Marshall asked if he was really as good as the papers made it seem. Carl had to take a deep breath before confirming Ronnie was fast and had a strong arm.

Envy was working in Carl's head. Ronnie Simmons was popular as an athlete, and he won the battle for Jackie. He remembered how she barely spoke to him when he saw them at the Jefferson playoff game.

Basketball season started, and Carl was behind in practice time. His chances of making the JV were complicated because he was not in basketball shape. Marshall had so many good basketball players that the coaching staff created a tenth-grade team. The purple and gold teams from Pemberton each had twelve players, and the tenth-grade team was only going to carry twelve guys. This meant half the guys who played basketball the year before would not make the team this year. When the dust settled, he made the team, but he was not in the starting rotation.

When he threw his route the following Saturday, Michelle was beaming. She greeted him with a wet kiss, saying she made the girls varsity basketball squad. She thanked him because their one-on-one play together had moved her game to another level. They continued to play, and he noticed she was good. Her strength was the ability to use both her left and right hands equally.

Michelle had a classic move that threw Carl every time. She would move the ball from her left to right hand and drive for a layup. She made the move on Carl, and they crashed to the ground after she made the layup. They laughed together as she reminded him that was how she got the C scar on her leg. He didn't want to tell her he was on a tenth-grade team and not in the starting rotation. Carl went to her next Friday-night game and watched as she and Jackie led the Lady Dawgs to a big victory. He was fit to be tied when the boys team came out, and Ronnie Simmons was on varsity!

When Michelle came out the locker room, she said Shasta was waiting to take them to Marshall. He was good with that; there was nothing else in Jefferson he wanted to see. He was quiet on the drive to Marshall, listening as Michelle went on about how she was on in the game that night. He had to give Michelle her props; she had stepped her game up, and Jackie was forced to play second fiddle. The following Monday, Mrs. Burns received a request from both the *Jefferson Jimplecute* and *The Marshall News Messenger*—they wanted to interview Michelle.

The papers were doing a segment called "Freshman Phenoms," and Michelle was their choice for the girls basketball segment. She called Carl to tell him, and Hannah answered the phone. She could tell Michelle was excited and asked what was up. She excitedly told Hannah about the interview request and asked where Carl was. Hannah was rude, saying, "And…?" then said she would give him the message. As excited as she was when she made the call, Michelle was brought back to earth by this. Her mom could see she was upset and asked what happened.

She opened up to her mom, saying Hannah did not like her and she'd never done anything to her. Michelle was stunned when her mom said she needed to gut it up and forget about Hannah. After all, she was Jackie's friend. She listened as her mother laid out the relationship between Carl, Hannah, and Jackie. She reminded Michelle they walked to school together for four years and it would be a minute before she warmed up to her. Michelle cheered up, realizing her mom was right—she should focus on Carl. She knew Hannah would not give Carl the message.

She called Shasta and asked her to stop Carl when he came by on his route. Half an hour later, Carl rode by on the way home, and Shasta stopped him, saying Michelle wanted to talk to him. She called Michelle on the phone and handed it to him. She came on the line, and he could tell she was happy. He listened as she said she had been selected to be interviewed by the *Jefferson* and *Marshall* newspapers. Carl asked why, and she said she was a "Freshman Phenom" because she made the girls varsity basketball team. He was happy for her and congratulated her.

Michelle asked if he would sit with her during the interview. He asked if that was possible; they wanted to interview her. She assured him they would do it, and said she wanted him there with her. They hung up, and Carl started the ride down Norwood Street, headed home.

A week later, he found himself sitting at a table with Michelle as they asked her questions. They asked how she felt being the star of the varsity as a freshman. She downplayed the question, saying it was no big deal. One of the reporters asked how it felt to be starting on varsity as a ninth-grade player when she barely got playing time on the eighth-grade team last year. Michelle smiled and said she had worked hard to get there. She then introduced Carl, saying he helped with her game, playing one-on-one against her.

The reporters were curious and asked if he was her brother. Michelle smiled, saying, "No, he my boyfriend." They asked more questions, and Michelle said he showed her how to drive to the basket and shoot jumpers. One of the reporters asked how much credit she would give his playing one-on-one with her for her high-level game. She told them, if Carl had not been playing one-on-one with her, she would not be a "Freshman Phenom."

The reporter from the *Jimplecute* said he checked the school records and found she was a straight-A student. He followed up, asking how she kept her grades up with a vigorous basketball schedule. Michelle said she studied all the time and made sure her work was always done.

Carl looked at Michelle when she said her long-term goal was to finish school a year early. She said she wanted to finish early so she could go off to school with Carl when he graduated. *The News-Messenger* reporter walked through the open door, asking if they had plans to be married. This caught Carl off guard, and the surprise showed on his face. One of the photographers took his picture, and his surprise was evident.

He was asked for information on himself, and he told them he was a sophomore at Marshall High School. The reporter from *The News-Messenger* said he thought he knew him. Carl said he was a starting linebacker on the Marshall JV football team. To his surprise, the reporter asked what he saw for Marshall in the next football year. Carl declined to answer, saying his only concern at that point was making varsity next year. The room broke up in laughter; the way Carl said it made everyone laugh. They finished the interview with Michelle saying she wanted to be valedictorian of her class.

She respectfully ended the interview when one of the reporters asked if marriage would happen before she finished high school. Rachel and Mrs. Burns stood off the set, beaming with pride. Michelle and Carl had handled themselves with both poise and class. Rachel made a mental note: she knew for sure Michelle's endgame was being married to Carl.

CHAPTER 19

Carl and Michelle Are Courting
#JackieFeelsLeftOut

The interview hit the paper, and the pictures of him and Michelle were great. They became instant stars at school, and his friends wanted to know how he met Michelle. Jackie saw the interview and pictures and wondered why Michelle was being showcased. Ronnie Simmons saw the interview and thought, *Only Carl would be able to do nothing and be celebrated for it.* Ronnie called Jackie and asked if she saw the bullshit interview with Carl and Michelle. She confirmed she read the interview, and they started talking about Carl and Michelle.

Jackie ended the conversation by saying, "The bitch forgot she *still* on the team with us." She slammed the phone down, fighting mad with Michelle and Carl. She started to cry. The facade she put up was a front. She could not believe Michelle had the top spot on the basketball team, was the top student in school, and had the guy she wanted. Jackie heard her sister's voice say in her head, "You Ronnie girl, but you Carl woman!" She lay across her bed, crying, when she heard the phone ring. She mustered her strength and went to the phone, surprised to hear Hannah's voice on the other end.

Hannah said she couldn't talk long but wanted to give her a heads-up that Carl and Michelle were in the paper. Jackie said she saw them and was pissed. She and Hannah had a hate fest, with Hannah saying Rachel would whip her if she caught her bad-mouthing Michelle. She could not believe it when Hannah said Rachel was in Michelle's corner. Hannah said she had to go; Big Mama Janice was coming, and she hung up the phone. Janice asked Hannah whom she was speaking to, and Hannah said, "A girl from school." Janice didn't believe her but accepted the explanation.

That weekend, Carl sat on the porch, talking to Riley, looking for a segue into the conversation about dating. He asked if dealing with girls was always going to be hard. Riley asked what he meant, and he said they wanted to always talk about love. He listened as Carl said he and Michelle had an interview where she said she wanted to marry him. Riley asked how he felt about that, and Carl said he was too young to get married. Riley picked up the conversation, saying he should be careful how he handled her. He had a puzzled look on his face when he asked Riley what he was talking about.

Carl listened as Riley said Michelle liked him a lot. "And you should never do a girl bad when she like you." Riley asked if he really liked Michelle or if he was just infatuated with her. He paused, saying he did like her and felt different when he was around her. Riley told him, "When a girl likes you the way she does, they become attached to you." Riley said the way Michelle looked at him, he could see she had deep feelings for him. He said if his feelings changed, he should tell Michelle and not lead her on. Riley asked him what it meant to lead a person on, and he said it was acting like you like somebody when you don't. *That was close enough,* Riley thought and said he was right.

Carl asked him if he should tell Michelle if he did not like her any longer. Riley said he should tell her that as soon as he felt that way. He saw Carl was confused and said, "Playing with her emotions is a no-no, son." He was starting to get the message and said he understood. Riley said they were going to chaperone him and Michelle as they courted each other. He asked why there was so much energy being given them. Riley leaned back in his chair and said girls and boys have a physical attraction, and that was why he felt different around Michelle.

Riley explained the feeling he got with Michelle was a natural attraction.

He explained the adults expended a lot of energy because when a young girl and young boy are attracted to each other, the girl can get pregnant. This hit home. He understood what Riley was saying and knew at least five girls at school who were pregnant. Riley explained that there was nothing wrong with being attracted to girls; they were trying to control the babies. Carl had a mortified look when Riley mentioned babies. He had had this talk with Rachel but forgot most of what she said. He listened as Riley said, with chemistry like he and Michelle shared, it was a small distance to a big mistake.

He backed up, saying love is a great thing when two people share a loving bond. Carl asked how he should handle Michelle and was shocked when he said, "Always tell her the truth." Carl knew this was going to be hard; Riley would not be talking to him if it were not.

Michelle capped an incredible Freshman season for the Lady Bulldogs with a 23-point-per-game average. The Lady Bulldogs won district and went three rounds in the playoffs, with her leading the way. Jackie could only watch as Michelle outhustled and outplayed everyone on the court.

Jackie was envious that Michelle was in the spotlight and made sure she shared it with Carl. He did not go to the last playoff game for the Lady Bulldogs; he went to the Marshall High playoff game against John Tyler instead. He was sitting with his good friend Edward as the game progressed. Edward looked up in the stands and saw a tall thin exotic-looking young lady. He leaned over and asked Carl who the girl was. He looked in the stands, asking whom he was talking about. He saw Edward was asking about Sandra, one of his friends.

Carl told Edward that was Sandra Wynn, his classmate. Edward asked him to introduce them and was beside himself when Carl said no. Edward reminded him he had been with him all his senior year, going to parties where there were no other sophomores. He still refused to introduce them and told Edward he should buy him a hot dog, chips, and soda if he wanted to meet her. He could not believe how quick Edward bolted to the concession stand and got the hot dog, chips, and soda.

Carl called Sandra, and she sat next to him, asking what was up. He pointed to Edward, saying, "This my friend Edward, and he want to meet you." Sandra held her hand out to shake Edward's, listening as Carl said, "This is Sandra Wynn, my friend and classmate." He saw Edward and Sandra make goo-goo eyes at each other and said, "Don't ya'll get married!"

The game ended on an exciting note, with Marshall High winning on a last-second jump shot that went down as the buzzer sounded. Track season started, and Carl loved to go watch the sprints and the sprint relays. He was fast enough to be on the track team but hated the workout they went through at practice.

A few weeks later, Jefferson had their sports banquet, and Michelle invited him as her guest. He jumped at the invitation because he wanted to see what awards were going to be handed out. He had a gut feeling Michelle was going to get a trophy for Most Valuable Player (MVP). He wanted to be there to support her when she received her award.

They were seated, and the meal was served as the master of ceremonies announced the award winners.

The players cheered when he called Michelle's name and said, "Most improved player." It made sense, since she was a substitute on the eighth-grade team the previous season and was now starting on varsity as a freshman! The real stunner was his next announcement: Jackie Hunt was Most Valuable Player (MVP). Coach Harris explained she chose Jackie as MVP, saying it came down to Jackie and Michelle. Coach Harris summed it up by saying, "We can win without Michelle, but we can't win without Jackie."

She was crying as she walked to the podium to receive her trophy.

It was a sweep for Ronnie and Jackie when he was named Most Valuable Player, (MVP) for the varsity football team. At picture time, Jackie and Michelle were in the middle, with him and Ronnie on either side. Ronnie leaned forward and said, "You do know second place is the first loser." Carl listened and side-eyed him as he said,

"You on junior varsity, and your girl most improved player." He felt the shade when Ronnie said they both needed to practice more and laughed out loud. Ronnie *always* did this, found a way to make an incredible experience about the rivalry between them.

Ronnie had a point; it seemed he and Michelle were a step behind them. She looked at him, and he could see she was well pleased, so he held his tongue. The photo shoot was over, and he leaned into Ronnie, saying, "Man, fuck you!" He gently touched Michelle's arm, holding her as they walked back to the table. She noticed he was talking under his breath to Ronnie and side-eyeing Jackie. As they rode to Marshall with Shasta, she kissed him, thanking him for holding his tongue. She said she knew Ronnie was being mean saying the things he said, but there was no need to spoil the night.

Shasta dropped him off at home, and Michelle kissed him again. She asked if she could go in and speak to Ms. Rachel. He didn't know why she wanted to but said sure and walked in the house with her in tow. Rachel was sitting on the couch, and Michelle went over and hugged her. She said they had a good time and asked if she could call Carl when she got home. Rachel asked why, and she said to let him know they made it home safely. She laughed out loud, saying she sure could call him when she got home. Michelle hugged her again and thanked her before Carl walked her to the car.

Ten minutes later, the phone rang, and he picked it up. Rachel said she was going to bed; she would talk to him in the morning. She thought to herself, *Michelle is going after what she wants.* She was warming up to Michelle; her manners were great, she was very smart, she was a great athlete, and she seemed to really like her son. Michelle said she had a great time at the banquet and he treated her great. Carl had to ask if it bothered her being Most Improved Player instead of Most Valuable Player (MVP), but it did not surprise him when she said she was not upset and asked if she could tell him something.

She told him about the conversation with her mother and explained she understood the relationship between him and Jackie. She continued, saying she knew they walked to school together for four years. He listened as she said they had to be good friends and

Hannah's dislike for her was part of that relationship. He was not shocked when Michelle said she was good with being Most Improved Player. She told Carl to think about it; she went from being a substitute as an eighth grader to "Freshman Phenom" in one season. He could not believe Michelle said Jackie felt she took her place with him.

She asked, "Didn't you and Michelle use to play basketball together?"

Carl thought about it. They did play basketball together. She mentioned the fall when Jackie ended up with a broken leg. "She did not stop crying until you picked her up." Michelle asked if he remembered that, and he said that of course he remembered that. She asked if he knew how to dance, and he laughed, saying he could dance. She asked whom he danced with, and he mumbled, "Jackie." He was a little irritated and asked how this had anything to do with the All Sports Banquet and Jackie winning MVP.

She laughed, saying it had everything to do with the All Sports Banquet. Michelle said she was happy Jackie won MVP; she was, after all, the best player on the team. She said, "Coach was right when she said they can win without me but we can't win without Jackie." She went on to say she knew Jackie was going to rub it in her face when they went back to school. He asked why they were talking about Jackie, and she said, "So he would see why Jackie is salty with her." Michelle asked whom he played basketball with now, and he paused as he said, "You."

Michelle said he didn't break her leg, but she had a big C scar on it. They laughed when she said it took longer for the C scar to heal than Jackie's broken leg. He listened as she asked whom he danced with tonight, and he said they were dancing. Carl saw where she was going and said he could see why Jackie felt replaced. She said, "I have a ten-speed bike to ride with you on your paper route, Carl, and she found out." He told her Hannah told Jackie she rode with him on his route. She broke it down. "For four years, ya'll did everything together, and now you have gone your separate ways."

He reminded her it had been almost two years since they broke up. Michelle asked if he knew when she wanted to be his girlfriend, and he said he did not. She laughed, saying, "When you picked me off the ground when I got the C scar." Michelle said she stopped crying, and he laughed when she said Shasta heard her scream and cry. She said Shasta still teased her because when she got outside, Michelle was in Carl's arms, looking in his eyes.

He was amazed the older women said she and Jackie were both crazy; he had done broke one leg and scarred the other one. He listened as Michelle said the feeling she had when he picked her up, she knew what Jackie felt. She described it as a warm feeling, and she felt an aura of protection, even if her leg was bleeding. Michelle said she knew he did not mean to knock her down and scar her leg.

She came back to the banquet, saying why it was good for Jackie to be MVP. Michelle said, when they took pictures earlier, Jackie eyes said she still had feelings for him.

Carl was shocked when she said looking in his eyes said he still had feelings for her. He took a moment, and Michelle didn't say anything. He spoke, saying he did have feelings for Jackie and she was right. She asked what he would call Jackie, and Carl said she was his friend. She asked what he would call her if they were no longer friends. He thought about it a minute and said, "I guess you would be my ex-girlfriend." At that moment, he got it and said he saw her point. He saw the difference between the two of them as Michelle said she had to get comfortable knowing Jackie was in the background.

Carl realized they had been on the phone almost an hour and said he was going to bed. Before they hung up, Carl said he did like her and was happy she was his girl. Michelle said she felt the same way about him.

At school Monday, Michelle saw Jackie sitting with a group of basketball girls and decided to sit with them. She knew it was coming when Jackie sarcastically said, "She might be Freshman Phenom, but I'm MVP, bitch!"

Michelle let the air out Jackie's balloon by saying she deserved to be MVP.

This shocked Jackie, and she said, "Say what?"

Michelle repeated herself, saying she deserved to be MVP and she was a better player. The other girls listened when Michelle said, "Coach got it right, I am the Most Improved Player." Lacey agreed, saying she barely got playing time on the eighth-grade team last year and she was now the leading scorer on varsity. They all laughed when Lacey said, "You stepped your game *way* up, gurl!" Michelle knew she could use her wits on Jackie and the other girls to keep the peace. She was going to keep Jackie close, knowing Carl still had a soft spot for her.

She had taken the shade out and given Jackie the spotlight, making everyone happy. Before they left, Jackie apologized for being mean and calling her a bitch. She accepted her apology as they walked to class. Spring Football started in Marshall and Carl made Varsity as a linebacker. He noticed Kendall was not on the cheer line when they went out on the field for the Red / White Game. The Red / White Game was on Tuesday and the rest of the week he did not see Kendall at school. He was throwing his route that Saturday and her sister Lillian was out in the yard.

He stopped and asked if everything was all right, because he had not seen her at school. His mouth fell open when Lillian said Kendall had been in Arizona a week. She went to Phoenix with her sister. He asked if she was coming back, and Lillian said she doubted it. He got back on his bike and rode to Michelle's house. She met him at the door and let him inside. He was still in shock that Kendall had moved to Arizona and did not mention it to him.

He really liked talking to Michelle. She helped him understand things. She mentioned she wanted to go to summer school and get half-credit on another year at school. He looked puzzled. He knew she had not flunked. He asked, and Michelle said she wanted to graduate with him so they could go to college together. Her plan was to go next summer, too, and they would start their senior year at the same time. Carl looked at her, saying, "You have this all planned out." She smiled, saying she did have it planned out. She got up from the couch and walked to her bedroom and returned with a book.

She opened it to a page and handed it to him. He took the book and read the caption on the page, "My plans with Carl." He read that she planned to use summer school to graduate at the same time he did and they would go off to college, get an apartment together, and he would be her boyfriend. He kept reading to see she knew they would need jobs, and her SSI check would help with the bills.

Carl asked what would happen if it did not go out this way. Michelle said she read a quote that said, "The best-laid plans of mice and men often go awry."

Carl smiled when she said she would rather have a plan and fail than to not have a plan at all. His eyes popped wide open with the thought that hit his mind. He asked Michelle if getting an apartment together meant they would be in the same bedroom. She didn't answer directly but said the plan was for a one-bedroom apartment. His mind raced as he thought about sharing the bed with her. He could not say anything; he was literally stunned she had put this much planning into her vision. He again mentioned how much planning she put into this, and Michelle said this was two years away.

Carl thought about it, and she was right. In two summers, he would be out of school. He started to seriously think about summer in two years, when he would be ready to go off to school. He thought how brutal football was and was not sure he wanted to play in college. While he was thinking, he mentioned to Michelle he was going to Detroit when school was out. She asked if he was going to stay the summer or a few weeks. Carl gave it some thought and said he and Bradley agreed he would stay six weeks. He said he wanted to come home and work with Edward the second half of the summer.

She loved the attention he gave her when they played one-on-one. It was up close, personal, intense, and she learned a lot about him while they played. They finished playing, and he went home to take a bath and dress. He and Michelle had a date at seven thirty. Edward called and gave him a number to call. One of his classmates wanted to invite him to a party. Rachel laughed to herself as she listened to him tell Edward he was going to ask if he could go to the party. She thought, him getting dressed for a date with Michelle and about to call another girl about a senior party invitation.

Rachel shook her head, thinking how he had forgotten all about Michelle even though he was getting dressed for their date.

She listened to him dial and ask for Marsha. She must have answered, because he said, "This is Carl Hampton. My friend Edward Marshall said you were having a senior party." She could hear Carl's side of the conversation, and Marsha must have asked why his number was not in the phone book. She heard him explain their number was in the name of Riley James, his grandfather. Marsha must have given him the invite. He wrote an address down. He called Michelle next and asked if she wanted to go to a party, because he had an invitation.

She hated to spy on her son, but this was too good to pass up. She listened as he tried to explain to Michelle why they should go to the party. After a short conversation with her, he hung up the phone. He called Edward back, saying he would not be going to the birthday party. She stepped back when he hung, up and he walked to his room to finish dressing. At 6:30 p.m., he came out of his room and walked to the porch with Riley. They were about to get in the truck for the ride to Michelle's when Edward pulled up with a couple of friends.

They talked for a few minutes, and Edward said there would be a lot of girls from school at Marsha's birthday party. What Carl loved about these parties was, all these people at the party would be seniors, two grades ahead of him. He knew Marsha, who was on the drill team. He met her at a party he went to with Edward. Riley cleared his throat, and he knew that meant, "Let's go." Carl said he had to bounce and said bye to Edward and his boys. When Edward asked where he was going, he said he had a date and climbed in the truck with Riley.

They made the short drive to Michelle's, and Riley said he would not be able to go to parties with Edward. Riley laughed out loud, saying he either had to take his girl with him or he was going to argue with his girl when he saw her again. He thought, *Oh wow,* as they pulled up in front of Michelle's house. Riley said Rachel would pick him up when he called and he should start thinking about coming home at 10:30 p.m. He sat on the couch, waiting for Michelle, and was blown away when she walked in the room. Her hair had been hot-combed, and she looked great!

He remembered his manners and stood up to let her take a seat. They had the living room to themselves and ate popcorn as they watched TV. He went back to the conversation about getting an apartment when they went off to college. He admitted he was not good reading between the lines and asked if she could be clear about what she was planning. She smiled and kissed him as she got her book from the end table next to the couch. She opened to a page with a letter to him.

The letter started with Michelle saying she was putting her cards on the table. She said they would share a bed and she would be his woman in every way. He got a little nervous reading that they could find out if they wanted to get married. Carl asked what happened if they decided to not get married. She asked if he would *intentionally* have sex with her and *not* marry her. She didn't give him a chance to answer, saying he needed to read the rest of the letter.

CHAPTER 20

Carl and Michelle Are Really Serious
#JackieAndCarlStopSpeaking
#RonnieSimmonsIsAnAllWorldAthlete

Carl was reading in Michelle's journal, and the letter was deep. He read a few more lines, and Michelle said, "When I give you my chastity, always be truthful with me. If you don't want me, let me go." He paused, and his next thought was, *I will do the same for you.* The letter was signed, "Michelle Hampton." He looked at her, and they locked eyes. He really did not know what to say and instead leaned over and kissed her. The kiss was passionate and intense as they felt each other's energy. His feelings were all over the place; he was young, but he and Michelle had a vibe he could not explain.

After they broke the kiss, he and Michelle sat close to each other on the couch. He asked if she had music, and Michelle remembered Shasta's mixtape. Carl turned the TV down so they could listen to music while they watched TV. Courting felt familiar. He remembered the girls coming to their house when they lived in Jefferson. "Dancing Machine" by the Jackson 5 came on, and he pulled Michelle off the couch. It felt like old times, playing music and dancing with a girl. Michelle knew the robot, and he showed her how to add the Harvey steps.

He did the Harvey, crossing his legs and spinning, then mixing the tip in with it. They worked on it, and Michelle learned this dance move and was smooth with it. Marvin Gaye's song "Let's Get It On" came on, and he pulled her to him. She rested her head on his chest and shoulder as she followed his lead. Michelle felt great in his arms, and they were lost in the moment. He whispered in her ear that he would be truthful with her all the time. She nodded to acknowledge that she heard him. They sat on the couch and kissed each other again.

Without trying, he ended up on top of her as he kissed her. He had a flashback to the night he was in the doorway, watching James Alexander on top of Judy Allen, the babysitter. He realized they were having sex! He got off Michelle and sat up on the couch. She pushed him back and lay on his chest as they kept listening to music and watching TV.

He asked, "What if we break each other's heart?"

They laughed when she said, "I'll have another scar you gave me."

He asked, "What if you break my heart?" She looked at him, saying she would never break his heart.

She kissed him and said she liked him too much to hurt him. They laughed when she said, "I couldn't get mad at you about the scar on my leg, so you good." Carl asked if he would ever be able to live that down, and they laughed when she said no. The phone ringing startled them, and Michelle picked up. It was Rachel on the other end, asking to speak with Carl. She said, "Just a minute, Ms. Rachel," and handed the phone to him. He said hello, and Rachel said it was 11:30 p.m., time to come home. When Rachel said she was on the way, he said he was waiting.

They kissed and both said how they enjoyed their date. Carl said he would make a mixtape for them to listen to next week. The following Monday at school, the focus was on Watergate and the break-in. The drama had been unfolding for a couple of years, and now the Nixon administration was being implicated in the burglary. The homework assignment in American history class was to watch the news to see what went down in the Watergate hearings.

The Nixon administration maintained that they had done nothing wrong, but Congress seemed to not believe this version of the story.

Carl planned to work in Marshall the first half of the summer and visit Detroit the second half of the summer. He wanted to haul hay and cut yards with Edward to earn some cash before going to Detroit. He saw Marsha Davis at school, and she went on about how he missed the greatest senior party in the world. She wrote his number down and said she would call him later to tell him where the party was this week. Since he was such good friends with Edward, everybody took for granted that he was a senior. He had several honors classes, and this made people think he was a senior.

During the week, he made a mixtape for the next date with Michelle. His mixtape had songs Rachel liked and songs he liked, including some blues. There was a café across the alley from his bedroom, and he went to sleep most nights listening to the blues from the jukebox. He got the call from Marsha that Thursday to tell him it was going to be a house party on university. He realized he had a problem when he thought about his date with Michelle. Carl made the decision to get out in front of it and ask her to go to the party with him.

He waited until the next night when he and Michelle were on their date. She was suspicious when he asked if she was going back to Jefferson the next day. He came clean when she said she was staying at Shasta's until Sunday evening. He remembered what Riley said about courting and a girlfriend; he should ask her to go with him to parties. When Michelle said she wanted to go to the party with him, he felt deflated. He wanted to go by himself. He pulled himself together and made plans to pick Michelle up the following evening.

He talked to Rachel, and she agreed to drop them at the party and pick them up when the party was over. They were excited going to a senior party. When Michelle asked how he got invited, Carl said his friend Edward worked it out for them. Rachel dropped them off and he saw Edward standing in the yard with Sandra. He took Michelle by the hand and walked over to where they were. He introduced Michelle to Edward, saying this was his girlfriend that he told him about. He introduced her to Sandra, saying he had introduced the two of them.

Sandra smiled and said, since he introduced them, he should be the first to know. His mouth fell open when Sandra said she was pregnant and they were going to get married. He pulled himself together and said, "This is exactly what I told you guys not to do, go get married!" They laughed together as Michelle made friends with Sandra and they talked about her pregnancy. Edward said he and Sandra were going to get married when he came back from Army boot camp. He could not believe what he was hearing—they just met in February!

It was now mid-May, and they were talking about her being pregnant and them getting married. More than anything else, his boy was going to the Army when he graduated in a couple of weeks. Carl thought how this disrupted his plans. With Edward gone, he had no respite from hauling hay. Not only that, but one of his revenue streams was drying up. They walked to the house and went inside for the party. The atmosphere was festive. Marsha and her crew had the black lights turned on, with Eddie Kendricks's "Keep on Truckin'" blasting from the DJ booth.

One of the reporters who interviewed Michelle for the "Freshman Phenom" piece spotted her and walked over to say hello. He held his hand out to shake hers, saying he was Charles Davis. She asked if they had met, and he said he was one of the reporters for *The News-Messenger* that interviewed her for the "Freshman Phenom" piece in the newspaper. He explained he was a senior at Marshall High and worked part-time at *The News-Messenger*. Michelle smiled when he asked how she knew about the party and said she was there with her boyfriend.

He looked at Carl, saying, "I forgot you were dating this guy."

"Boogie Down" by Eddie Kendricks started to blast, and Carl pulled Michelle on the dance floor. He could not believe this guy was bold enough to try to talk to Michelle with him standing there. The DJ transitioned to "Let's Get It On" by Marvin Gaye, and Charles walked on the floor and asked Michelle if she would dance with him. Carl said she was dancing with him, and Charles said he didn't ask him, that he asked her. Michelle smiled politely and refused, saying she was dancing with her boyfriend.

Carl heard him mumble, "What does she see in that loser?" as he walked away.

Carl made a mental note to address this with Charles when he saw him at school on Monday. Edward walked to Carl and told him to keep his eyes open, as several of the guys were looking at Michelle.

A few minutes later, Marsha came over and asked if he and Michelle wanted to be on the Soul Train line. Carl and Michelle got separated in the Soul Train line and were dancing with other people. The DJ spun into "She's Gone" by the Tavares, and Charles pulled Michelle up on him.

Marsha had Carl's attention, asking if he'd dance with her. He looked back to see Michelle slow-dancing with Charles and pulled Marsha close. When the second record came on, he let Marsha go and walked over to Charles and Michelle. He posted up next to Charles, saying, "If you don't let my girl go, you about to find out why they say brothers from the North Side stupid." He didn't know anything about Carl, but he knew the reputation of the North Side, so he let Michelle go. Carl thanked him as he walked off, hugged up with Michelle.

He rubbed it in, kissing her on the mouth as they walked away.

The party ended, and Marsha stood at the door, saying goodbye as everyone left. As he and Michelle walked by, she said, "You invited to the next party but leave your girlfriend at home." Michelle braced herself, and he hugged her tighter, a sign to just let it go. They walked outside and saw Rachel parked, waiting on them. They got in the car, and both sat in the front seat with Rachel. Michelle started talking, saying, "Ms. Rachel, this guy and girl tried to separate me and Carl tonight."

Rachel asked what she meant, and she said this girl Marsha was all up in Carl's face while this guy named Charles was all up in her face. Rachel drove while she talked, saying they were both very attractive and people were going to hit on them. Michelle listened when she said they had to be strong enough to work through it. She said it would not be this bad all the time; they were a freshman and sophomore at a senior party. That was one thing Rachel loved about Michelle: she was an open book and talked to her about what was on her mind.

Rachel went on to say Charles and Marsha felt they were up for grabs. She thought, *They have* not *met this young lady!* Michelle settled down when Rachel said that and was quiet the rest of the way home. They arrived at her house, and he walked her to the door, holding her for a few moments before kissing her good night. He didn't know why, but he was not upset with Michelle because she slow-danced with Charles. He walked back to the car, and Rachel drove them home.

The first stop he made the next day was at Edward's house.

Graduation was two weeks away, and Edward was leaving for the Army the following Monday. As they talked, Carl asked about the lawn mowers and yards. Edward said he sold the lawn mowers and his customers to another kid in the neighborhood. Edward said he didn't tell him about it because he knew he was going to Detroit. He thought about it and let it go; he was not going to buy the lawn mowers, anyway. Edward started to question him about his girl, saying she was very good-looking and fine. Carl said she was from Jefferson and she went to Jefferson High.

Edward said part of the reason the guys tripped with him was, he seemed to know all the girls! He asked how he met Michelle, and Carl said they were in school together in Jefferson. He spent a couple of hours with Edward, then went home to get ready to throw his route.

Michelle and Shasta were having a serious conversation. She had confided that she wanted to have sex with Carl. Shasta kept her cool. Her mother said Michelle would probably come to her about this. Shasta asked if she had ever had sex, and she confirmed she was a virgin. She asked Michelle why she felt now was the time and Carl was the guy. She said she felt different around Carl and it just seemed right. Shasta had been prepared by Mrs. Burns, telling her to listen and let Michelle talk. Shasta was glad Michelle had come to her and was truthful with her.

When Michelle asked how to keep from getting pregnant, Shasta said there was no way that was 100 percent accurate. Michelle laughed when Shasta said her allergies might keep her from being able to use condoms. Shasta held her hands and asked if Carl felt the same way about her that she felt about him. Michelle said she did not know but she was going to ask. Shasta wanted to say he would like to have sex with her but remembered her baby sister was in love. She asked if she was prepared emotionally if he did not feel the same way about her.

Shasta threw it out, asking if he would be willing to marry her if she was pregnant, to make her his "forever girl." Michelle admitted she did not know but would find out. She remembered her mother said, "Don't bust her bubble. Let love bruise her the same way it bruised us." She did not know why her mother seemed to have so much confidence in Carl.

An hour later, he was knocking on the door to let Michelle know he was there. Michelle came to the door and told him to hold up as she was almost ready.

A couple of minutes later, they were riding and throwing his route. She asked if Edward and Sandra were really getting married, and he said they were. She asked when they were going to get married, and Carl said it would be when Edward got out of Army boot camp. He said they were invited and he was Edward's best man. They stopped at their spot and kissed each other while they talked, and she asked if he would marry her if she got pregnant. Michelle was shocked when he said he had been thinking about that. He said that since he found out Edward got Sandra pregnant, that had been heavy on his mind.

They sat looking at each other, having a deep conversation as they kissed and hugged each other. He whispered to her, "I don't know if we would get married if you were pregnant. That is the best I can do." Michelle could not get mad; he had told her the truth. She was blown away when he said he would not break up with her if she got pregnant. She did not know whether to be thrilled with him or get mad at him. They kissed again and got back on their bikes to ride to Shasta's house. They had a date that night, and they could finish talking about this then.

He thought about the conversation with Michelle as he rode home.

The truce with the White boys seemed to be holding. They had not met him on the Norwood Street curve in a couple of months. When he got home, he sat on the porch with Riley, telling him about Edward and Sandra. Riley listened and told him they were at the age when they would get their lives started. He explained that Edward and Sandra were doing what most people do, get married. He asked how he would know it was time to get married. He laughed, saying, "You just get a gut feeling she is the one."

He asked Riley if there was a step between being one's girl and getting married. Riley told him there was a step in between, a promise ring. Carl looked at him and asked what that meant. Riley said it was the next step in courting, a promise to be serious with her. He cautioned him to not give her this ring if he was not serious about her. Carl assured Riley he was serious and wanted to give her a promise ring. He told Carl he needed to tell Rachel this was what he wanted to do. Rachel knew already; she was standing in the door, listening to their conversation.

Riley had seen her standing there, but Carl had not. He got off the porch and went inside the house with Rachel. She answered when he called out for her, saying he needed to talk to her. Rachel listened as Carl said he wanted to give Michelle a promise ring. She said okay and asked if he knew what making a promise to someone meant. Rachel didn't give him chance to answer, saying a promise ring meant he could not take any other girl serious. She told Carl to not give Michelle this ring if he was not serious about her.

Rachel could not believe her thoughts; she knew he was about to be having sex with Michelle. She also knew she had to call Mrs. Burns and tell her Carl wanted to give Michelle a promise ring.

While Carl was bathing and getting dressed for his date with Michelle, she called Mrs. Burns and spoke with her. She could not believe how unconcerned this woman was. Her daughter was on the verge of losing her chastity, and she was nonchalant about it! They agreed that nobody would say anything, allowing Carl to tell Michelle. This rubbed Rachel the wrong way, as Mrs. Burns seemed more concerned with making sure Michelle had some fairy-tale love story going on in her head rather than her getting pregnant.

When Carl had gotten dressed, Rachel drove him to Shasta's house for his date with Michelle. She told him he did not have to rush; if he did not want to tell her tonight, he didn't have to.

Rachel watched her son walk in Shasta's house, thinking, *This is some surreal shit going on.* In a way, she felt Mrs. Burns was pushing Michelle off on Carl. He had the mixtape he recorded and put in the cassette player. They turned the sound down on the TV and turned the tape deck up. The conversation they had earlier came back up, and he said he wanted to give her a promise ring, to show he would be serious with her as his girl. Her eyes lit up as she said she would accept his promise ring. He asked if she wanted to go with him to pick out the ring, and Michelle said she did.

He laughed, saying it might be a minute before he could buy the ring since he needed to get the money up. She barely heard a word he said. She was on a cloud and excited that he wanted to give her a promise ring. Carl took a deep breath, saying, "You asked if I'd marry you if I got you pregnant." He kept talking. "The promise ring will be my promise that I will not break up with you if I get you pregnant." Michelle was all over him, kissing him passionately. The entire time they had been talking, he always seemed standoffish and nonchalant about her.

His statement removed any doubt from her mind that he had feelings for her. She whispered in his ear, "I'm cool with that." They watched TV, listened to music, and danced until midnight.

Then the phone rang. It was Rachel saying she was on the way to pick him up. She told Michelle and did not bother to ask to speak with Carl. She hung up the phone, saying, "Ms. Rachel is on the way to pick you up."

Michelle asked if he was going to take his mixtape, and he said he was leaving it with her.

A few minutes later, Rachel drove up and Carl kissed Michelle good night as he walked out the door. She was giddy and felt a sigh of relief. She finally knew how he felt about her. She thought about the way she had been crushing on him since elementary school, but

Jackie had him wrapped up. When Jackie broke up with him, she let it be known she liked him and hoped he would like her. She even resigned herself to the fact that as long as she was with Carl, Jackie would be standing in the shadows.

He and Michelle went shopping and picked out a promise ring she liked. It cost $59.95, and he put it on layaway, paying ten dollars down. His plan was to pay the rest before summer was over. He spoke with Edward, and he said he was going to marry Sandra on Labor Day, when he got out of Army boot camp. Carl went home and looked at the calendar—his birthday fell on Labor Day! He worked out his schedule for the summer and decided to go to Detroit the day after school was out. He called Bradley and asked if it was okay if he came to Detroit the day after school got out. Bradley said he thought it was great he was coming the day after he got out of school.

Carl told Rachel of his plans, and she was okay with it. She really wanted to talk to him about Michelle but did not know what to say. When he said he and Michelle picked out her promise ring, Rachel said he needed to ask Mrs. Burns if that was okay with her. She said he needed to do it before he went to Detroit. Rachel's mind was going very fast, but she could see her son had matured. He picked up the phone and called Mrs. Burns, asking if they could sit down and talk.

He was surprised when she invited him and Rachel to Sunday dinner the next day. He held the phone and asked Rachel if that was okay with her. When he went back to the phone to tell Mrs. Burns that was good, she invited his whole family. Rachel accepted for the family, and Mrs. Burns asked them to be there at 2:00 p.m. Carl and Rachel got everyone together and said they were going to Sunday dinner in Jefferson the next day.

The next day, Carl and his family ate dinner with Mrs. Burns, Michelle, and Shasta. They talked about Carl and Michelle, saying they were about to take a serious step. Carl didn't flinch when Mrs. Burns asked if he knew what giving a girl a promise ring meant. He explained to Mrs. Burns his promise to Michelle was he would not break up with her if she got pregnant. Rachel almost fell out of her chair, but Mrs. Burns, Riley, and Janice handled it in stride.

Carl continued, saying his promise to Michelle was that he would work with her to make her his wife. He was shocked when Mrs. Burns asked if he and Michelle were having sex and smiled as he answered, "No, ma'am, we are not having sex." Rachel was beside herself, she saw her son and Michelle headed down the same path she and Bradley had walked a few years earlier. She maintained her cool as they kept eating dinner. They listened as Mrs. Burns segued into her own life experience. She said she married Michelle and Shasta dad when she was seventeen years old. She smiled when she said everybody thought it was scandalous because he was twenty-five years old.

She explained she and her husband had seven kids over the next twelve years. Everyone laughed when Mrs. Burns said she was thirty-seven and came up pregnant with Shasta. She said she was downright mortified when she came up pregnant with Michelle at forty-seven. She explained she and her husband were an older couple with a newborn baby. The mood was solemn when Mrs. Burns said her husband went to work one day, had a massive heart attack and died. She had to take a moment as her feelings overwhelmed her.

They listened as she said her husband was fifty-seven when he died, leaving her with a two-year-old and twelve-year-old to raise. She said she shared her story to bring clarity to this situation. She wanted them to know she was thirteen and her husband was twenty-one when she decided she wanted to marry him. Mrs. Burns smiled as she said everyone thought she was crazy and he was running from her. She laughed out loud, saying, "Four years later, we were standing at the altar to be married, and I was pregnant with his child."

She kept talking, saying Michelle was exactly like her and had made up her mind that she wanted to marry Carl. She looked at Carl and asked if he was ready for that. Riley was a little uncomfortable with the conversation but waited to hear more before he said anything. Mrs. Burns asked Carl what turned him toward a promise for Michelle. He seemed to be going in a different direction. At that moment, Rachel had an epiphany: Mrs. Burns was not as nonchalant as she thought! They listened as Carl said he really had not given it much thought until the last couple of weeks.

CHAPTER 21

Carl Gives Michelle a Promise Ring
#JackieGoesIntoDeepDepression

Carl explained that when his best friend Edward announced he was going to marry Sandra, he started thinking about him and Michelle. Carl continued, saying, "I introduced Edward to Sandra at a basketball game in February and at the end of May. They making plans to be married in September." He said they had been talking a lot longer than that and he did like her. Rachel couldn't help herself and asked if he was trying to get married because Edward was about to be married. Carl said that was not the case; he was not in a rush to get married.

He segued into his point and said, since they were courting, they needed to have a plan for their future. Rachel asked what if they broke up and went their separate ways? Carl looked at his mother, saying he was going to let Michelle answer because he asked the same question. She looked at Rachel, saying, "I told Carl the best-laid plans of mice and men often go awry, and if we break up, I understand." Rachel said this sounded good in literature but they were dealing with human feelings and emotions. Michelle said she knew this and was prepared to deal with the heartbreak if it came.

Riley spoke for the first time, saying he understood Michelle and Carl's dilemma. Everyone listened as he said they were young people who had feelings for each other. Riley said he had spoken with Carl and believed he did like Michelle a lot. Everyone laughed when he said Michelle was a good girl and he believed she would keep Carl in line. He complimented Mrs. Burns on the dinner and said his vote was that they allow them to keep courting. Riley mentioned how one of his sisters was about Michelle's age when she said she was going to marry her husband.

Rachel had enough and exploded. "Why am I the *only* person who does not see this train wreck about to happen?" She stood up at the table, saying, "Mrs. Burns, it *seems* you are offering up Michelle to the first young man that would have her!" Rachel was in tears as she sat down. She saw herself and Bradley in Michelle and Carl. Everyone was stunned as Mrs. Burns said she had not given Michelle to Carl. She continued, saying she knew how futile it was to try to stop them from seeing each other. She turned to Shasta, asking how that worked for her.

Shasta took a deep breath, saying, "I was Michelle's age and went crazy behind a young man, and Mother did everything in her power to stop us." She continued, saying, "She forbade us from seeing each other, and I sneaked around to see him." Shasta then summed it up by saying, "Long story short, he is the father of my four kids and we are divorced."

Carl's eyes were glazed over, and he wondered why everyone was making such a big deal out of this. He spoke up. "I like Michelle a lot and feel different when I'm around her." He said he would never do anything to hurt her.

Rachel laughed at her son, saying, "Oh, you are going to hurt her in a way she has never been hurt before." She then stood again, saying, "I have a problem because Michelle has bled for Carl and still looks at him with goo-goo eyes!" She looked at Michelle. "I like you a *whole* lot, Michelle, but I do not want the two of you to make the same mistake his father and I made."

Michelle stunned everyone when she said, "I watched Carl and Jackie for three years, all the while liking him." They listened as she talked about Carl walking Jackie home and carrying her books at school.

Michelle laid out how when Carl and Hannah moved back to Marshall, she lost contact. She said it piqued her curiosity when she heard Jackie broke up with him, but she didn't believe it. Michelle said she knew for sure Jackie had broken up with Carl when they were at the gym and she got her leg broken. She smiled when she said, "The way Ronnie Simmons looked at Carl when he picked Jackie off the floor was priceless. When Carl handed Jackie to Ronnie, I knew the breakup between them was real." Michelle said she never said anything to Carl while he and Jackie were talking.

She went back to her explanation, saying she was young, but not foolish. Hannah grunted when Michelle said she knew Jackie Hunt was going to be in the background for a long time and she was willing to accept this. Rachel was uncomfortable when Michelle said she was not giving Carl back to Jackie Hunt. Carl sensed he needed to shut Michelle down; he could see Hannah wanted to say something, and he did not want that. He looked at Mrs. Burns and asked if she would give her blessing to him giving Michelle a promise ring. He listened as Mrs. Burns asked him to explain his promise to Michelle one more time.

Carl took a deep breath and said he promised Michelle he would be serious about being her boyfriend. He kept talking, saying he also promised Michelle he would not break up with her if she got pregnant. This caused Mrs. Burns to raise her eyebrow, and she asked why he made Michelle that promise. Carl looked at her and said they talked about it and he promised to not run out on her. Everyone took a deep breath, realizing Carl seemed to have this under control. Rachel hung her hope on the fact that Carl seemed to be able to control Michelle.

When Mrs. Burns asked if they left room for dessert, Riley said he thought she would never ask. Janice side-eyed him. Riley seemed to be a little too friendly with Mrs. Burns for her liking. The dessert hit the table, and Mrs. Burns asked Carl when he planned to give Michelle the promise ring. Carl said he wanted to give it to her around Labor Day. He explained he was going to Detroit for a few weeks and planned to work while he was there. Rachel was shocked when he said he was coming back in mid-July; he could throw his route and haul hay to make the money to pay the ring off.

The look on Mrs. Burns's face said it all, and she asked who was in Detroit. Rachel explained that his father lived in Detroit and Carl went there for a few weeks each summer. Mrs. Burns said she had no idea Carl's father was in Detroit. Rachel quickly said Bradley was Hannah and Carol's father also but Carl was the only one going to Detroit. Carl told Mrs. Burns he was leaving for Detroit in a week, flying from Shreveport.

The dinner wound down, and Mrs. Burns said they should do this when Carl gave Michelle the promise ring. She looked at Michelle and Carl, saying, "Take the time between now and Labor Day to really get to know each other." They listened as Mrs. Burns said he should not give Michelle the ring if his heart was not in it. She said the same thing to Michelle. "Do not take the promise ring from Carl if your heart not in it." Carl hugged Mrs. Burns and said he would not give Michelle the ring if his heart was not in it. Michelle agreed, saying she would not take the ring if her heart was not in it.

The next week flew by, and that Friday night, he attended the Marshall High graduation. Edward was about to graduate, and he was there with his clique. They shouted when his name was called, and he walked across the stage. Michelle was there with them, and she had made friends with Sandra. Carl and Michelle went to the graduation party, and Charles Davis saw them when they walked up. He could not believe this North Side loser had this fine, good-looking girl hanging off him. He and Michelle walked in the house, and Marsha walked over to them.

She welcomed them to the party, and he congratulated her on having finished school. Michelle was about to say something, but he squeezed her hand and she thanked Marsha instead. Marsha was feeling herself and said, "I know you a damned sophomore and this bitch a freshman." She laughed, adding, "I also know you one of those North Side boys, so I'm gon' chill." Carl looked at her and thanked her, saying they just wanted to dance and have fun. Michelle made a mental note to run up on Marsha if she ever saw her by herself.

The night went by, and they danced a lot. Marsha and Charles tried the same bullshit with the Soul Train line, but Michelle was on it this time. She ended up dancing with Charles, but when the DJ spun into a slow record, she walked off the floor and left him hanging. Carl did the same for Marsha, and this pissed them both off. They gathered themselves and did a toast for all the seniors who were about to start their lives. The atmosphere was light as the party went on, young people about to start their lives. The rest of the night went great. Charles and Marsha got the message and backed off.

The next day, Carl's flight left at 4:00 p.m., and they rolled into the airport at 3:00 p.m. Michelle was with them on the drive to the airport. Hannah looked at Michelle. She still did not like her. She felt Carl would go back to Jackie if she were not in the way. It did not help the situation that Jackie kept saying she would break up with Ronnie if Carl broke up with Michelle. After the dinner the previous Sunday, Hannah knew for sure Michelle was not going away. The feeling was mutual—Michelle felt the bad vibe from Hannah and knew she would be feeding Jackie information.

Rachel found a spot close to the airport, parked, and walked in the airport with Carol in tow. Carl breezed through check-in, and they sat at his gate, waiting for the flight to board at 3:15 p.m. They talked, and Michelle asked how often he would call. Carl said he was not sure; Bradley was sensitive about his phone bill. They agreed to write every day, and he wrote Bradley's address down for her. Hannah looked on, thinking, *Can I puke?* as Michelle sat close to Carl while she talked to him. The announcement was made the flight was boarding, and Michelle kissed Carl before he walked to the plane.

He hugged them and walked to the gangway. They stood at the window and watched as his flight left the gate, taxied down the runway, and took off. They couldn't explain it, but they were in tears when his flight took off. This was one of the rare times he had a non-stop flight from Shreveport to Detroit. His flight landed at 7:30 p.m. Detroit time, and he was met at the gate by his cousin JD Hampton. He said Bradley had to work and asked him to pick him up at the airport. They made the half-hour drive to Bradley's house, and Carl got his bags out of JD's car.

He noticed the car sitting in the backyard driveway and thought, *Somebody has a really cool car.* It was a '72 SS 396 Chevy Chevelle, deep blue, with Cragar wheels. Carl told JD, "That is a sweet ride," as he took his bags in the house. He was shocked when JD said it was Bradley's car; he bought it a few weeks back.

Carl called Rachel to let her know he was safe at Bradley's house, then called Michelle. She reminded him she started summer school the next day, and he said she would do just fine. They talked for half an hour, and Carl said he had to go; long-distance charges were no joke.

Bradley called home and said he was glad he made it. He told Carl there was twenty dollars on the nightstand and JD could take him to get something to eat. Bradley asked if he saw the car in the yard, and Carl said he did. He was shocked when Bradley said he should check it out and told him where the keys were. He asked if he could drive a stick, and Carl said he could; he had been driving tractors and trucks in Marshall and knew how to shift gears. Bradley knew he had a hardship/farm license and told him he could drive around with JD to get some food.

He went back to the den and told JD he had some money and wanted to get something to eat. When JD backed his car out of the driveway, Carl saw they had a problem. He knew he could not back the car out without hitting the fence or the house. He decided to turn the car around in the backyard and drive out. He missed the fence but skinned the back portion of the car against the house. When he got past the house, he looked and saw it was a minor scratch. He could not believe it; he had not driven fifty feet and *already* hit the house.

The car was a three-speed on the floor with bench seats. When he got in the street, he popped the clutch, and the Malibu turned the tires. He shifted into second gear and coasted to the stop sign at Curtis and Sorrento. JD had suggested Wendy's by Northland Mall and Carl turned right on Curtis and Outer Drive to head that way. It was frustrating driving the short distance along the city streets and shifting gears. JD watched as his fifteen-year-old cousin shifted gears.

Carl hit the service drive on the Lodge and Seven Mile, popped second gear, and went down the ramp.

He was rolling seventy-five miles an hour when he hit the freeway headed to the Greenfield / Eight Mile exit. They hit the drive-through at Wendy's and made the trip back home. They were eating, and Carl told JD, "That car is sweet!" JD was ten years older and asked how he liked coming to Detroit every summer. Carl said it was cool; he got to get away from Texas and see something different. JD said he always liked coming to Texas because things were so much different there.

He took a shower and went to sleep about 11:30 p.m. Bradley's car between the houses woke him up at 3:15 a.m. He remembered that sound. Bradley turned the light on in his room and said hello, telling him to go back to sleep, that they could catch up in the morning.

The next morning, he and Bradley were in the yard, piddling with the Chevelle. Carl could not get it out of his mind how cool the car was. They washed and shined the car as Bradley laid out the ground rules for driving. He had a grid formed by Seven Mile, Wyoming, Six Mile, and Greenfield.

Bradley said he could not go outside that grid, and no freeway driving. He told him if he went to Northland Mall, he had to catch the bus. The last thing Bradley said before they drove off was, "If someone take this car, give it to them. We can replace the car, but we can't replace you." Bradley drove out the yard and told Carl he needed to watch the way they went; he was dropping him off at work. They drove to the Fleetwood Plant, and Bradley asked if he could get back home. Carl said he could; he remembered the freeways and streets he needed to turn on.

When he came up on the Wyoming exit where the Jeffries ended, he knew where he was. This was the freeway where they rode ten-speeds last summer. He drove down Wyoming, noticing landmarks that let him know he was going the right way. When he crossed Six Mile and passed Mumford High School, he knew he was in the neighborhood. Curtis Street came up, and Carl made the turn to go home. He pulled into the driveway and drove into the back-yard. He locked the car, set the kill switch, and went in the house.

He wrote Michelle the letter for today like he promised, and when he called her on the phone, she was happy to hear from him. He asked her to set a timer for ten minutes and they would be good. He told Michelle, if they talked for ten minutes or less each day, that would keep the bill low and Bradley wouldn't be mad. He told her about the Chevelle and that Bradley let him drive.

Later that evening, Carl went next door to Mrs. Douglas's house to let her know he was back in Detroit. She said Bradley had told her he was coming but didn't say when.

Carl fell asleep watching TV, and when he woke up, it was 11:00 p.m. He took a shower and went to bed at midnight. Bradley called about 11:00 a.m., saying he spent the night at a friend's house and he would be home that night. Carl told him he was going to put some gas in the car and look for a job. Bradley said he didn't need a job; he should just hang out and have fun. Carl went to the Sunoco station at Seven Mile and Outer Drive to put some gas in the Chevelle. There was a "Help Wanted" sign in the window, and he inquired about the job opening.

The owner said he needed someone to pump gas, wash cars, and do general chores around the station. Carl asked what the job paid, and Mr. Johnson asked if he was interested. He followed up, saying the job paid 150 dollars a week and he would have to work five and a half days. Carl did the calculations in his head and realized that was a little low. He asked if there was a way he could make 200 dollars a week for five and a half days of work. Mr. Johnson instantly liked him and said sure and gave him the job. He told Carl to be at the station at 7:30 a.m. the next day.

Mr. Johnson knew he had a winner when he drove up the next morning and Carl was sitting in the parking lot. He worked each day from 7:30 a.m. to 6:00 p.m. and 8:00 a.m. to noon on Saturday. The job was a great fit, and he didn't get a chance to hang out like he would have liked. Bradley insisted he save his money from working and gave him an allowance of fifty dollars a week. A month later, Carl was happy; he had saved eight hundred dollars! Bradley got ahead of the game this summer and took Carl school-clothes-shopping at the end of June.

The stores still had summer clothes out, and this was a great fit for the Texas weather. At the end of July, he had saved sixteen hundred dollars.

Carl's whole mindset changed. He was now thinking about a car. He thought how hard it would be back in Texas riding a bike when he was driving a car in Detroit. He decided to stay and work three weeks in August so he would have twenty-two hundred dollars. He also wanted to go to the Father-Son Day GM was hosting at the Fisher Body Fleetwood plant in mid-August. Michelle was not happy when he said he was not coming home as planned.

He was at work, looking at the TV, when the news broke in with President Nixon's picture on the screen. He and Mr. Johnson were listening as Walter Cronkite, CBS news anchor, announced the president would be on shortly. There was a sense of importance; each of the networks had blocked out time for the president. A few minutes later, President Nixon came on TV to announce he was resigning as president of the USA. It was August 8, 1974, and Carl had just witnessed history. They had been studying Watergate in school the last couple of years, and now President Nixon had resigned!

Two weeks later, Fisher Body Fleetwood was preparing for the model year changeover. Carl went with Bradley to the annual Father-Son Day that was hosted by Fisher Body Fleetwood. This event provided the kids of people working in the plant an opportunity to see the process of building cars. It was helping to develop the next generation of UAW members and auto workers. He met Richard "Rick" Miller. His dad and Bradley worked together at the plant. Rick knew Bradley and was shocked when he met Carl. He didn't know Bradley had a son his age.

Carl spent the day hanging with Rick, and they became friends. After the day watching Fleetwood Cadillacs being assembled, they knew the auto industry was not for them. It was interesting, though, how the car started on the fifth floor as a chassis. When it arrived on the first floor, it was a Fleetwood! That was awesome, and they enjoyed watching the process.

Rick called Carl later that evening; he knew Bradley's phone number. Carl said he was leaving to go back to Texas in the next couple of days but they should stay in touch.

Rick asked about the Chevelle, and Carl said he had been driving it since he got to Detroit in late May. Rick wanted him to pick him up, but Carl said his house off Puritan was out the grid Bradley assigned him. The friendship between them was a natural. Rick's Dad, Albert, and Bradley not only worked together but were also in a social club called the Eldorado Club. He started packing for the trip home the next day, and Bradley reminded him to get everything. He felt good about Carl's visit this summer; they spent time together and got to know each other on a deeper level.

Bradley was shocked that Carl was so much like him, although they had not spent a lot of time together. On the drive to the airport, Bradley told him he sent Rachel a cashier's check with the twenty-two hundred dollars he earned working at the Sunoco station. He handed him an envelope with three hundred dollars and said he should get Michelle a really nice promise ring.

Carl's flight left at 2:00 p.m., and they arrived at Detroit Metro Airport at 1:15 p.m. Bradley sat in the terminal with him as they waited for his flight to board.

Carl looked at Bradley when it was announced there was a two-hour delay of his flight. He took the time to sit and talk while they waited on the flight to board. Carl listened as Bradley said Rachel told him about Michelle, and he asked his son to tell him what he liked most about her. He thought for a minute and said he could talk to her—they talked about everything. He said they were friends and played basketball together. Bradley asked how he ended up with his friend and his girl being the same people. Carl laughed as he said it just kind of happened.

He was shocked when Carl described his and Michelle's one-on-one basketball games as being intense. Rachel sent him some of the clippings Carl had collected of Michelle. When Carl told him how he helped turn her game around, Bradley thought they bonded over basketball. One of the pictures of Michelle in the air showed the

C scar on her right calf. *The boy done marked her!* he thought as he laughed to himself.

Bradley's birthday was the day before, and Carl's birthday was six days away. He told Carl he was going to send him another two hundred dollars for his birthday. During the conversation, Bradley asked Carl if he could forgive him and that they build their relationship going forward from there. He was caught off guard but said he was fine with that. He enjoyed sitting there, talking with his son, and was startled when they announced his flight was boarding.

Bradley stood watching as Carl's flight taxied off the runway and took off. He got to know him this summer, and the father realized that his son was a kid with a deep thought process.

CHAPTER 22

Edward and Sandra Get Married #LookAtTheSizeOfMichelleRing

When Carl's flight landed in Shreveport, he was met by Rachel, Michelle, Hannah, and Carol. They were glad to see him since he had been gone for over eleven weeks. He hugged his mother and sisters, then hugged and kissed Michelle. They were happy as they walked through the airport and picked up his bags. Carl told them how he spent most of his time working and didn't do a lot of sight-seeing and visiting this summer. He bought gas for Rachel's car, and they made the short drive back to Marshall. Michelle didn't go home; instead, she stayed with them and helped Carl unpack.

He and Michelle sat on the couch, and he fell asleep. Rachel watched as Michelle lay across his lap, watching TV. After about an hour, Carl woke up and they got a big laugh at the dribble on the side of his mouth. At eleven that evening, Shasta pulled up to pick Michelle up. She asked Carl what time he was coming over the next day and suggested 8:00 a.m. He said that was early, but Michelle said she was going to cook breakfast. He agreed, saying he would be there, and took a bath when she left.

Rachel woke him up at seven thirty the next morning and reminded him of the breakfast date he promised Michelle. He shook out the bed, brushed his teeth, and washed his face. Carl dressed and stood on the porch at 7:50 a.m. Rachel was shocked when he got his bike; she thought he was going to ask for a ride. She watched him ride down Kingfish and disappear on Scotts Quarters Road. Exactly ten minutes later, he rode his bike into Shasta's yard. Michelle opened the door and invited him in the house. He walked in and was told to go in the dining room.

He sat with Shasta's kids and listened as she said Michelle was cooking breakfast every Saturday morning at eight. She told Carl, "When ya'll get your place together, this girl needs to know how to cook." She scrambled eggs, fried bacon, and toasted bread. It turned out great, and she did not burn anything. Shasta told them to get their plates and come in the living room. They ate breakfast and listened as Shasta said, "This is a standing date that you don't get to call off." She told Michelle, "I don't care if you mad as hell at him. Saturday morning at eight, have your ass on that stove!"

She looked at Carl, saying, "Nothing comes between you and this 8:00 a.m. date. Use this time to work out your issues over break-fast." They agreed to this, and Carl said he would be at breakfast each Saturday morning.

The following Monday was Labor Day and Carl's birthday. Rachel cooked a chocolate cake and invited Michelle to come over and celebrate with them. Riley bought ice cream to go with the cake, and at 1:00 p.m., they celebrated his birthday. Michelle was beside herself; some of the girls in his neighborhood were just too friendly!

She was happy when everyone left and it was just them. She was no longer angry and gave him her present. He opened the box and saw the gold chain inside. Michelle said this was his birthday present and clasped it around his neck. He thanked her for the chain. It was a great present! Football season had started, and he missed two-a-day practices the last two weeks of August. He lost his starting position because the coaching staff heard rumors he was going to Mumford High School in Detroit. When he didn't show up for two-a-day prac-tices, everybody knew he was not coming back from Detroit.

The Mavericks got hammered in the Friday-night game, and the linebacker corps especially took a beating. Carl rotated in and out at each of the four linebacker spots as they were banged up. The

Saturday-morning stretch session was called off so the trainers could take care of injuries. He went to Shasta's and watched as Michelle cooked breakfast for them. They listened to Shasta and ate breakfast on the couch while they talked. He said they would go get her promise ring when they finished breakfast. She perked up and asked how they were going to get downtown. He smiled as he said they were going to ride their ten speeds.

They finished eating, and he got her ten-speed off the back porch. They rolled out and saw the White boys in the street when he hit the curve on Norwood. "Gear your bike down and pedal hard," Carl said to Michelle as he worked the minibat off the bar of his bike. He stepped his speed up to match hers and rolled along. Jamie Foster hollered at him, saying he could put his bat up, that nobody was thinking about his nigger ass. He and Michelle rode by them, going across the bridge toward Grand Avenue.

They rode to the jewelry store where the promise ring she picked out was on layaway. Michelle looked at the ring she really wanted while they waited for somebody to help them. He asked if the money he paid on his layaway could be used on a different ring. The lady said he could, and he remembered the ring Michelle wanted. It cost $149.95, and he paid for it. The ring was beautiful, and it was *big*! She could not believe it when Carl pulled out enough money to pay for the ring.

After that, they stopped at JCPenney to look at outfits while waiting for her ring to be sized.

They bought matching blue jean suits and tennis shoes, and Carl spent almost one hundred dollars. He had saved four hundred dollars of the weekly allowance money Bradley gave him. When he added the three hundred dollars Bradley gave him, that was seven hundred dollars! They picked up her ring and rode home with their packages. They went to Carl's house and showed Rachel the blue jean outfits. The next day, he and Rachel got in the car and drove to Shasta's house. He was shocked they changed the location from Jefferson to Shasta's house.

He and Rachel went inside and sat at the table with Mrs. Burns and Michelle. They talked while eating, and Mrs. Burns asked Carl how Detroit was. He said he worked all summer and didn't do much sightseeing this year. When dinner was over, Rachel and Mrs. Burns left the room. This meant it was time for him to give Michelle the promise ring. He reached in his pocket and pulled the ring out, opening the box. He held it out to Michelle, saying he was making a promise to her. Carl said he would be serious with her and would not run out on her if he got her pregnant.

He slid the promise ring on her finger and kissed her. She asked him to sit down and pulled a box out of the cabinet. He opened it, and there was another gold chain, this one with a capital letter *C.* She clasped the necklace around his neck, saying, "When things get tough, I'll go twice as hard." He looked in Michelle's eyes as he added, "I know this not going to be easy, but I promise to work hard at being good to you."

Michelle teared up when he said he was going to stand on his promise, and he *really* liked her.

Carl listened as she said that when things got tough, to remember the C scar on her leg.

She smiled, saying, "I was bleeding but felt secure in your arms, and I don't ever want to lose that feeling." They locked eyes as she said, "Your eyes said it all that day. I saw your feelings in them." They talked and knew they needed their mother's blessing. So they decided to ask their mothers to bless them. She took her ring off and put it back in the box, and he took off the gold chain and put it back in the box.

Rachel and Mrs. Burns came back in the room and sat down. Rachel asked if Carl had given her the ring, and Michelle said not quite.

She handed Mrs. Burns the box with the gold chain, and Carl handed Rachel the box with the ring. He looked at Rachel, saying, "Mama, I'm going to ask you to bless me and Michelle." He said the ring he bought for Michelle was in the box. Rachel listened as he asked her to give him the ring if she would bless their courtship. She knew exactly what he was asking; he wanted her to "cut" for him and Michelle. Rachel smiled as she thought about it. This was his way to neutralize Hannah's interference. Rachel called Michelle to her and hugged her, crying because she was happy.

Rachel had deep respect for Michelle, and she made it known she auditioned to be Carl's wife. Rachel added up her factors: she was smart, was a good athlete, and had made plans for her future. She handed him the ring, saying he had her blessing. While Michelle hugged his mother, he slipped the ring on her finger. Michelle stepped away from Rachel and asked her mother to bless them. Mrs. Burns looked at Carl, saying, "You don't have to treat her bad. If you don't want her, bring her home." He hugged Mrs. Burns, saying he would never treat Michelle bad.

Mrs. Burns looked at Rachel, saying, "They are young, and we just need to get outta the way." She looked at Michelle and added, "Baby, this young man put a ring on your finger, and that means you his girl."

Michelle looked at her mother, saying, "I know, Mama, I'm his girl."

She kept talking, saying, "You can't talk to the other boys just like he can't talk to the other girls."

Carl said he didn't talk to other girls; it was him and Michelle.

She handed Michelle the box, saying she had her blessing. Michelle took the gold chain outta the box and clasped it around Carl's neck.

She explained to her mother and Rachel that she bought two chains for Carl, to let him know she was going to work twice as hard. Rachel spoke to Carl, saying, "Michelle has made it known she wants to be your wife." Carl said he knew this and he wanted to see if he wanted to be her husband.

Mrs. Burns broke the tension by asking, "Who wants dessert?"

They all went for dessert and had light conversation for the next hour. Rachel said she had to go and asked Carl if he was coming with her. Before he could answer, Michelle said she and her mom would bring him home.

Rachel called Bradley when she got home, saying Carl had given Michelle a promise ring. He was not surprised and said he would hope for the best. He was shocked when Rachel said they reminded her of them, two young people trying to find their way in life. Bradley agreed; he had never met Michelle, but from all he heard, she was a solid young lady. They laughed together and said he needed guidance at this moment.

The next week was better for the Mavericks football team. Carl found himself again bouncing from linebacker position to linebacker position. He was a better outside linebacker but was effective in the 4–4 defense as a middle linebacker. The Mavericks won the game, and one of the linebackers went down for the year with a broken leg.

They were stretching the next morning when the coaching staff said they made a change on defense. Carl was moved back to outside linebacker and given his starting job back. The coaches knew he was a solid player, and he managed to avoid getting hurt in this high-contact position.

He was walking home from stretching and practice when he passed Sandra's house and saw Edward getting out of the car.

He ran to the car and hugged his boy. He was glad to see him. He had just gotten off the bus from Leesville, Louisiana, and Army boot camp at Fort Polk. Sandra ran out the house and into his arms, welcoming him home. Edward announced that he and Sandra were getting married the following Saturday and said Carl was his best man. Edward had a thirty-day pass and had to go back to Fort Polk for AIT after that. Sandra said she would call Michelle and tell her about the wedding the following Saturday.

The nation woke up on September 8, 1974, to learn President Ford had pardoned President Nixon.

This was the topic at school on Monday, how President Ford issued former president Nixon a pardon—on a Sunday, at that! This dominated the conversation all week, the culmination of a two-year investigation. Former president Nixon was about to be impeached and tried in the Senate, so he resigned to keep this from happening. President Ford issuing a pardon was something that no one had talked about or seen coming. That Friday night, Michelle was on the Bulldogs cheer line, watching Ronnie Simmons have a career night against Gilmer.

He was on track to throw for over one thousand yards and rush for over one thousand yards. Every Sunday morning, when he picked up the Sports section of *The News-Messenger*, Ronnie had top billing. The Mavericks pulled out another win that Friday night, and Carl returned an interception for a touchdown. The next day, he threw his route early. Edward and Sandra were getting married at 6:00 p.m. He was riding through the curve on Norwood when he noticed a white Cougar slow down. Carl put his minibat in his hand as the Cougar pulled up beside him.

He looked in the car and noticed Edward was driving. "How you like my car?" he asked as Carl stopped and leaned in the car. He asked when he got it, and Edward said he bought it the day before. Carl said he was going home and to meet him there. He climbed back on his bike and rode home, Edward pulling up at the same moment. They talked for a few minutes while Carl looked his car over. It was a 1972 Mercury Cougar with bucket seats. It was white, with Cragar rims. Carl *loved* this car! Edward said he would see him shortly; he was going to get dressed for his wedding.

At 5:30 p.m., Rachel drove him to Shasta's house to pick up Michelle. He went to the door to get Michelle, and she was drop-dead gorgeous. She had on a blue miniskirt that accented her curves. Rachel looked at her and thought, *She is cute!* He looked at her, saying, "Michelle, you look great!" She thanked him as he opened the door and she climbed on the seat next to Rachel. She complimented her on her dress, saying she looked great. A few minutes later, they were at Sandra's sister's house. Edward and Sandra were getting married in her older sister's backyard.

He and Michelle walked in the backyard, and Edward came over to meet him, saying he was glad they made it early. He handed Carl the ring and told him what he wanted him to do. Carl asked how he felt, and he said he was a little nervous but would be okay. He mentioned he loved Sandra and wanted to marry her. Michelle stepped from behind him and said hello. He spoke and noticed the ring on her finger. He asked Carl, and he confirmed he gave her a promise ring. She held out her finger, and Edward got a good look at her ring.

"That is a serious rock," Edward said and was curious how much it set him back for.

The wedding started, and Edward was asked for the ring. Carl saw the ring when he passed it to him and realized it was a *huge* rock! He knew Edward dropped a grip on this ring. Michelle's ring was 150, and this rock was a lot bigger! Sandra stood with Edward in front of the pastor, and Carl saw the baby bump. His mind wondered to his childhood babysitter, who got married with a baby bump, and wondered if this was a shotgun wedding.

Carl could not believe he remembered something like that and it would cross his mind at this moment. His mind then went to the promise he made Michelle. He would not run out on her if he got her pregnant. Carl thought how the things he had seen, he was now a part of. He and Sandra were in the same class, and she was about to have a child.

At the reception, Carl joked how, back in February, he introduced the bride and groom, and they were now married. Everyone laughed when he said he told them, "Don't go get married."

The wedding and reception ended with Carl's best friend now being a married man. His mind was bent—two people who met in February were now husband and wife.

Edward dropped him and Michelle at Shasta's house as he and Sandra rolled out for their honeymoon trip. Michelle asked where they were going, and Carl said they were headed to Dallas. She and Carl sat on the couch, watching TV and listening to music. Michelle lay in his arms and asked if he had thought about them getting married. He admitted that since the wedding, he had thought about them getting married.

They switched topics and talked about the football season. He could not believe Ronnie Simmons was having the year he was having. Since she was on the Bulldogs cheer line, she was watching down by down as Ronnie put up obscene numbers. Carl was having a decent year in Marshall; he had one interception and two fumble returns for touchdowns at the midway point of the season. Between Ronnie in Jefferson and Simon Bennett in Hooks, he could not get a lot of print in his hometown newspaper. This kept Carl humble when he got the big head about how good he was.

Edward's leave was over, and it was time to go back to Fort Polk for Army AIT. He did not want to catch the bus back to Fort Polk and could not bring his car. Sandra did not have her license, so Edward asked Carl if he would drive to Fort Polk and bring his car back to Marshall. He went in the house and asked Rachel, and she wanted more information. She called Edward in the house and talked to him about the trip. She reluctantly gave permission for Carl to drive him back to Fort Polk, and Edward asked if they could leave the next morning.

The next morning, Carl, Michelle, Edward, and Sandra left at 8:00 a.m. for Fort Polk. Edward made the drive down, and they arrived in Leesville at 11:00 a.m. They had Edward on post and were headed back to Marshall at 1:00 p.m. Everyone breathed a sigh of relief when Carl called at 4:45 p.m. to say they were at Edward and Sandra's apartment. Rachel got in the car and picked them up, dropping Michelle off at Shasta's and driving home. Carl was worn-out; they had been riding and driving for almost nine hours. When they made it home, he went to his room and took a nap.

A couple of hours later, Hannah was at his bedside, shaking him to say Jackie was on the phone and wanted to talk to him. He should have known she would not wake him up if it had been Michelle. He heard Jackie's voice on the other end asking how the wedding was, and he said it was great. He asked how she knew he went to a wedding. Jackie said the flower girl's mother was her cousin and saw him there, saying he was the best man. He didn't know where this was going, so he listened as she talked. Hannah had told Jackie about Michelle's promise ring, but she wanted Carl to tell her himself.

She could sense he was not going to tell her and knew if she said anything, he would know Hannah told her. To her shock and surprise, he said there was something he needed to tell her. Jackie took a deep breath and asked what that was. She was numb, listening as Carl said he gave Michelle a promise ring. She couldn't help herself and asked what he promised her.

Jackie was angry when he refused to say what he promised Michelle, and hung up the phone. She then went to her room, laid across her bed, and cried.

She could not believe Michelle had taken Carl away from her that easily. Her sister, Alicia, stood in the door, saying, "I mentioned you were Ronnie's girl but Carl's woman. This is what I meant." She sat on the bed and said she had to make a choice: either she was going to stay with Ronnie or she was going after Carl. Jackie hugged her, crying and saying she felt like a fool. Alicia didn't say anything but thought, *I've felt that way a few times.* She hugged Jackie as she cried, hoping to comfort her. Jackie jumped off the bed and bolted out the apartment, headed to Michelle's house.

When she knocked on the door, Mrs. Burns answered. Jackie asked if Michelle was home, and Mrs. Burns said she was there. She said she would get her but asked Jackie to not fight her daughter. She turned and walked away, and a second later, Michelle appeared in the door. She asked Jackie what she wanted, and without saying a word, Jackie stepped on the porch and punched her in the face. Michelle said, "Oh, hell no!" and punched Jackie back. They fell off the porch, fighting, and Mrs. Burns managed to break them apart. Alicia walked up as Mrs. Burns got them broken up.

She told Jackie she needed to come home, and she agreed and walked off with her. Michelle and Jackie both had a bloody nose, and they knew this was far from over. Her mother looked at Michelle, saying, "You have the ring. Now you have to defend it." They walked in the house, and Mrs. Burns put a cold, damp cloth on Michelle's nose.

The next day at school, Jackie and Michelle glared at each other over lunch. When the basketball girls asked what was wrong, neither of them would say anything.

Michelle kept her hand below the table; she did not want the added drama of explaining the promise ring. When she got up, how-ever, Gina Jones saw the ring on her finger and screamed, "Look at the rock on Michelle's finger!" The basketball girls circled Michelle, demanding all the sultry details. She played it down, not wanting beef with Jackie. She saw the hurt in Jackie's eyes as everyone talked about her promise ring. Michelle thought about what Shasta said, "You and Jackie will never be cool. You like the same guy." She watched Jackie walk away and wondered why it had to be this way. Her mother had said, "You don't have a beef with her because you won!"

Michelle did not say anything about the time she spent watching Carl, Jackie, and Hannah. Jackie was cool in her demeanor toward Michelle from that point forward; she knew she had won.

Friday night rolled around, and Ronnie was having a gangbuster night against DeKalb. Jackie was cheering, but her heart was not in it. She wondered why she was not into Ronnie the way Michelle was into Carl, and thought, *Because he my man!*

Jackie started to have angry feelings about Michelle as she thought how she replaced her with Carl.

She thought how he *used* to play basketball with her and now he played with Michelle. She thought about how they studied together and now he was studying with Michelle. She thought how she made big plans to give Carl her virginity, and now Michelle was going to give him hers. Jackie was in a rage as she walked off the football field to the restroom. She needed a moment. She was beside herself. Everything she planned with Carl had turned to shit! She knew she could not go out like this, but at this moment, she had no idea what to do.

Then the thought hit her: *Keep your friends close and your enemies even closer!* Jackie decided at that moment she and Michelle were going to be best friends. She pulled herself together, washed her face, and walked out of the restroom.

The second half of the game was starting, and everybody said Ronnie finished the first half strong! Jackie perked up as she looked over to the cheer line and saw Michelle. She thought, *The girl so naive. She not going to know what I'm doing.* Jackie shook her pom-poms as Ronnie led Jefferson past DeKalb.

Carl and the Mavericks did not fare so well and got spanked by the Texas High Tigers. They were as fast as Marshall, and the Mavericks could not stop the outside sweep. Carl made sixteen tackles and was worn-out when the game was over. The Tigers won the game 24–12.

The Mavericks held Saturday-morning stretch practices from eight to ten, and this was mandatory for Carl. To offset this, he and Michelle moved their Saturday-morning breakfast date to eleven o'clock.

Michelle was worn-out and tired when she woke up the next morning. Michelle told her mom she did not want to go to Marshall to make breakfast for Carl; she was tired. Mrs. Burns said, "Tired or not, you going, and it is not making breakfast *for* Carl, it's having breakfast *with* him." She ended by saying, "If you don't want to go, you don't have to go."

Michelle thought she had to gut it up; basketball season was about to start. Since she went to summer school, she had not picked up a basketball since late May. She told her mom she was going to Marshall and dug her basketball out of the closet. A few minutes later, Michelle and Mrs. Burns were headed to Marshall.

Her energy level surged during the ride to Marshall, and she was no longer tired. They arrived at Shasta's house about 9:30 a.m., and everybody was still in bed. Shasta made it to the door and let them in, saying she thought Michelle wasn't coming this morning. Mrs. Burns said, "She changed her mind," as she walked past her.

CHAPTER 23

Jackie and Michelle Play Nice
#TheyTryingToWinDistrict

Michelle followed her mother in the house and went to the kitchen to set up and cook breakfast. Carl walked home and got his ten-speed to ride to Shasta's house. He rode up in Shasta's yard at ten minutes before eleven. Michelle's attitude changed when she ran on the porch to meet him. He stood half on and half off his bike, with Michelle standing up on him. She said she was ready to cook as they walked in the house. She cooked eggs, bacon, and toast, again, but it was better. Riley had told him to eat her cooking and not complain, that she would get better.

They took their plate into the living room and talked as they ate breakfast. Michelle said she was mentally and physically tired; school and after school activities had worn her out. Carl told Michelle about the game last night, saying Texas High wore the Marshall High line-backers out. He said they blocked the corners exceptionally well and he was beaten up from the contact. He thought about Michelle being tired and realized neither of them had a summer break. He told Michelle he had worked all summer in Detroit, and she was in summer school.

Michelle agreed, saying they had not had a break in almost a year. Carl said they would have to wait until Christmas for a break. He mentioned basketball, saying he was not playing this year. Michelle asked why not, and he said he knew he would be on the bench. They laughed when he said that by the time football season was over, he would not be able to get playing time on either basketball team. He asked Michelle if she was looking forward to the season this year, and she said she was. They relaxed on the couch and fell asleep watching Saturday-morning cartoons.

An hour later, they woke up and Carl said he needed to go home. Michelle asked what time he was going to throw his route. It had started getting dark early, so he said he was going to throw it about 4:00 p.m. Michelle asked if he could throw his route early so they could play one-on-one. Carl said he would and got on his bike for the ride home.

His papers were being dropped off when he got off his bike in the yard. It was 2:00 p.m., and he knew if he was going to play one-on-one, he needed to roll his papers and leave. Carl rolled his papers and rode off to throw his route at 3:00 p.m.

He asked Rachel to call Michelle and tell her he was on the way. Ten minutes later, he rolled up in Shasta's yard, and Michelle was waiting for him. They then rolled his route, and an hour later, they rolled back up in Shasta's yard. They took a short break, and Michelle got her basketball out of the house. She walked to Carl, kissed him, and handed him the promise ring. Michelle said, "You *not* playing your girl. I'm just a random player going one-on-one against you."

The longer they played one-on-one, the higher their intensity level went. Carl showed her a move, helped her work her steps in the move, then blocked her shot when she took it. Michelle loved it when she walked through the move; it was a shooter's move. She had to get up to speed on the move because it would create space between her and the defender. She was working the move, and it created space between her and Carl, but his four-inch height advantage allowed him to block the shot. Michelle got the mechanics of the move down, but she could not get the shot off over Carl.

He hugged her, saying she should not worry, that she would get it off over the girls she was playing against. They closed out their three-hour-plus practice session with an intense one-on-one.

Carl won 20–12; he refused to let Michelle win, and she loved it. When they finished, she held out her ring finger and he slipped the ring back on her finger. Michelle kissed him again, saying she would never tire of watching him slide that ring on her finger.

The following Monday at school, Jackie stopped Michelle, saying practice for basketball would start the next week.

Michelle said she had heard and wondered why Jackie was being nice to her. Coach Allen found them at lunch, saying *The News-Messenger* and *Jimplecute* wanted a dual interview with them. She said they wanted to interview the Most Valuable Player and Most Improved Player from last year. She was shocked at Jackie's answer when asked if she and Michelle were friends. Without missing a beat, Jackie said they had their issues but they were teammates and friends. The reporters asked Michelle what she expected from the upcoming season, and she said their goal was to win district.

The interview lasted an hour, and it seemed Jackie and Michelle were best friends. The reporters thanked them for the interview and wished them well on the upcoming season. When they left the interview table, Jackie apologized for punching Michelle and said they should find a way to be friends. All kinds of alarm bells went off in Michelle's head, and she knew she had to feed Jackie out of a long-handled spoon. She laughed out loud, saying, "I don't trust you as far as I can throw you, Jackie!"

Michelle thought, *Last week she was punching me, and now she want to be friends.*

She knew Jackie was planning something and was surprised when she said she should not trust her.

Jackie laughed, saying, "Just because you can't trust me doesn't mean we can't be friends."

Practice started the next week, and the move Michelle had been practicing with Carl was a winner. She used it on Jackie, and like he said, there was space between them. Carl had shown her how to transition into the move off the dribble, and she could see how hard it would be to stop her.

She ran in the house when Mrs. Burns picked her up from practice, saying she wanted to call Carl.

Hannah answered the phone and said Carl wasn't there, then hung up. Michelle knew she was probably not going to tell Carl she had called, and so she wrote him a letter. Hannah was being petty and kept the line tied up until Riley's 9:00 p.m. "quiet time" rule kicked in. When Carl asked to use the phone, she refused, saying she was working on her homework.

Meanwhile, Michelle practiced the fadeaway shot and got good with it. Coach Allen noticed how smoothly she came off the dribble into the fadeaway shot. This was good. She knew Michelle was going to be hard to stop with that shot. Michelle was a pure shooter, and this move was a bonus.

The next Sunday, Carl opened *The News-Messenger* and saw a close-up picture of Ronnie Simmons on a touchdown run. He folded the paper, thinking, *The boy is all-world!* Rachel drove as he threw his route and asked if he had thought about giving up the route. He said he had and asked when she thought he should give it up. She said she needed to think about it and would get back to him. Carl knew it would be hard to give up the route; he was used to the spending change he got from throwing papers.

He loved the Saturday-morning breakfast and talk times between him and Michelle. Just like Riley said, however, things got better and Michelle learned how to cook pancakes. They had pancakes one Saturday, then eggs, bacon, and toast the next Saturday. He loved talking to and studying with Michelle. They were friends and talked about a lot more stuff than dating. Football season ended for the Mavericks, and they did not make the playoffs. In a way, he was glad they were done, he had taken a beating during the last half of the season. The linemen had gotten bigger and harder to shake to make a tackle.

On the way home, he was listening to the radio and heard the announcer say the Jefferson Bulldogs had beaten DeKalb to advance to the playoffs. He listened as the announcer said Ronnie Simmons led the Bulldogs attack with 116 passing yards and 119 rushing yards. The announcer continued his analysis of the Bulldogs, saying they had a running back who rushed for 144 yards during this game and had over 1,100 yards for the year going into the playoffs. The announcer said the Bulldogs could make noise in the playoffs if the coaching staff kept the team settled down.

Carl went to the last stretching practice for the year and turned in his pads. He then made it to Shasta's house at 10:30 a.m. and asked Michelle if she knew whom the Bulldogs were playing in the first round of the playoffs. She said they were going to play Gladewater at a site to be determined. Michelle said the cheer line would be there since the basketball season had been put on hold until the Bulldogs playoff run was done. Carl said this was actually a good thing; it gave her time to work on her moves.

For the second Saturday in a row, she cooked pancakes, and they talked about what was going on in their lives. Carl said he was glad the football season was over—he was tired of taking a beating on Friday nights. He was angry the defensive ends of the Mavericks could not hold the linemen off the outside linebackers.

It was mid-November now, and it was dark by 6:00 p.m. Carl wanted to show Michelle the second half of the fadeaway move, the part where she drove to the basket. He rode back up to Shasta's house at 1:45 p.m. and told Michelle he was ready. She got her bike, and they threw the rest of his route. They stopped for a few minutes at their spot and kissed each other. They didn't stay long, though; Carl reminded her they needed to go back so she could practice.

Carl showed her the drive move off the fadeaway shot and walked her through it. He told Michelle, "You have to sell this move for it to work right." She asked what that meant, and he said the defender had to believe she was going to take the fadeaway jump shot for it to work right. He walked her through the move and showed her the places she had the defender beaten. Michelle saw it instantly, how the fadeaway and driving to the basket worked together. She realized he was showing her moves that boys made on the court.

He walked her through the decision-making process, when to take the shot and when to drive to the basket. She listened as he said, "If the defender is close enough to block your shot, drive." They walked through several scenarios of this, and he flipped it, saying, "If the defender play off you, take the shot." Michelle laughed when he said the whole thing was predicated on her making the fadeaway. He emphasized that she had to get good at knocking down the fadeaway jump shot for the move to work. He pushed her on her jump shot, saying she needed to elevate and shoot.

He emphasized that her ability to shoot the regular jump shot would make the fadeaway even more effective. Michelle knew she had to work on her strength; it was hella hard to elevate and shoot. They played the one-on-one, and their intensity level was high as usual. Michelle drove past him and was pissed when he blocked her shot from behind. They played longer, and she drove again, this time doing a reverse layup on the other side of the goal. He could not block her shot because she used the rim to shield him. Carl could not believe it—Michelle had beaten him 16–14!

She jumped in his arms and kissed him, celebrating her win. He celebrated with her, saying she was getting better. He congratulated her on the reverse layup, which was a thing of beauty. She looked at him, saying she would use the same logic for the fadeaway shot or drive. He put the promise ring back on her finger, and they walked in the house. They talked and she rubbed it in, kissing his neck as she asked if he wanted to take his girl to the movies that night. He thought about it a second and jokingly said, "No, she beat me."

Michelle playfully punched him in the arm, saying she wanted to see Uptown Saturday Night with Bill Cosby and Sidney Poitier. Carl said he was going home to ask Rachel if she would drop them off and pick them up from the movies. Michelle took things in her own hands and, when Carl rode off on his bike, called Rachel and asked if she would take them to the movies. Rachel said she would be glad to take them to the movies. Michelle thanked her and hung up the phone.

A few minutes later, Carl walked in the house and Rachel asked how long it would be before he was ready to go to the movies.

Rachel laughed to herself, thinking, *Michelle is going to be just fine. She knows how to get out in front of him.* He said he would be ready in about an hour, then asked how she knew about the movies. Rachel told him to bathe and get dressed, and to not worry about how she knew.

Forty-five minutes later, Carl was dressed and ready to go. He and Rachel got in the car and headed to Shasta's house. He got out of the car when they got there and went to the door to get Michelle. She came out and jumped on the front seat next to Rachel. She spoke up, saying, "Thank you, Ms. Rachel, for picking us up."

It was at this moment Carl realized his mother liked Michelle and would listen to her. He also figured out Michelle had called and asked if she would take them to the movies. Rachel dropped them at the movies and said she would be back in two hours to pick them up. Michelle thanked her as she jumped out of the car and they walked to the ticket booth.

Later, when they got out of the movies, Rachel was already there. He and Michelle were so hyped about the movie Rachel decided she would go see it.

The following Friday night, he was in the stands as the Bulldogs played the Gladewater Bears.

The game was being played at Lobo Stadium in Longview, and this meant he could not wear the Maverick school colors. Longview High and Marshall High were bitter rivals. Although neither of the teams were playing, he knew some of the Lobo players would probably be at the game. He rolled with the Jefferson entourage to avoid a misunderstanding. It was late November, and the weather had turned off cool. He did not bring his jacket, and by halftime, he was cold. He watched as Ronnie and the Bulldogs drummed the Bears from Gladewater. Carl watched Ronnie Simmons single-handedly put a stop to the shouts of "This bear country!" coming from the Gladewater side of the field. He had a chance to watch Ronnie Simmons in action, and he was a magician with the football.

The Veer offense was perfect for Ronnie's speed; he could run or pitch. As he watched the game, Carl realized Ronnie was the real deal. He thought how chasing him, trying to tackle him would be a nightmare. Jefferson won the game, and Ronnie Simmons had another good night. He stood at the gate, leaving the field to congratulate the Bulldogs players and coaching staff. When Ronnie came by him, he shook his hand and hugged him, giving him props on the great game he played. Ronnie looked at him and said he was glad he was supporting the Bulldogs.

Carl was surprised he knew most of the Black players on the team, and he told Ronnie, "You bad to the bone, dude!" The players went into the dressing room, and Carl went to find Michelle. He turned around when he heard his whole name, "Carl Allen Hampton." He locked eyes with Jackie Hunt and walked toward her. He didn't know what he was going to say, and it was a little awkward when they reached each other, but they hugged. He said he was so glad to see her, and Jackie said the feeling was mutual. The awkward feeling didn't last long—they were talking like they saw each other every day.

Michelle watched from a distance for a moment. She wanted to see the dynamic between them. After a few minutes, she walked up behind Carl and asked what they were doing. He said he and Jackie were catching up, talking about old times. Michelle could see what Jackie was up to and gave Carl a long, wet kiss on the mouth. She was going to show Jackie this was her boyfriend and she was not going to give him up without a fight. Jackie looked off for the few seconds they held the kiss. Jackie knew she could not walk away; she would reveal her hand to Michelle if she did.

Instead, she stood there watching as her behavior with Carl grinded her gears and worked her last nerve! They broke the kiss, and Michelle asked if she was catching the bus back to Jefferson. Jackie knew this was a catty question and answered, saying she was going to ride the bus back to Jefferson. *Oh, this bitch!* Jackie thought as she stood there, watching Michelle hugged up with Carl. Jackie was glad when she looked up and saw Ronnie coming out of the field house. When he walked over to them, Jackie gave him a wet kiss and said he played a great game.

They stood talking for a few minutes before the bus was ready to leave. He and Michelle walked to the parking lot and got in the car with Shasta, who had also gone to the game.

The next morning, she cooked pan sausage, scrambled eggs, and made toast for breakfast. Carl made it to Shasta's house at 7:55 a.m. and took a seat on the couch, watching cartoons. Michelle was normally dressed when she cooked breakfast, but today she had on her pajamas. They ate breakfast and talked about the game and how Jefferson killed Gladewater.

The next opponent was Center the following Friday night. Carl ate breakfast and left; he and Riley had some work they needed to do before he threw his route. He told Michelle he would be back about 2:00p. Riley and Carl were in the truck riding to the country, he wanted to clean the graves of his sisters and brothers. He and Carl took a couple of hours and cleaned the graves in the James tract.

As they were headed home, Carl asked Riley what it was like being married. He answered him by saying, "You have a person whom you love that gives you orders."

Carl looked at him and wanted to ask more but let it drop. Riley said they would talk more about it later. Carl said, "That was cool," and he wanted to hear more about it.

The News-Messenger delivery driver was dropping his papers off when they drove up at 1:30 p.m., Carl took his papers, rolled them, and headed out to throw his route. He made it to Shasta's at 2:00 p.m., and Michelle was sitting on the porch, waiting for him. When they made it back, they got the basketball for her practice session. She handed her ring to him, and they started practicing the fadeaway and drive-to-the-basket moves.

After an hour, they went to one-on-one play and he drummed her. They laughed together when she asked if he was mad that she beat him the previous Saturday.

The following Wednesday, Carl got a call from Sandra saying Edward was graduating Army AIT that coming Saturday. She asked if he could drive her to Leesville; she was big pregnant and could not drive. Carl said he would have to ask Rachel and got the details from Sandra. Graduation was at 11:00 a.m. Saturday, and they could leave at 7:30 a.m. and make it on time.

He spoke with Rachel, and she said she needed to think about it. She called Mrs. Burns and asked what she thought about this, knowing Michelle was going to go with them. Together, Rachel and Mrs. Burns decided, since it was a turnaround trip and he had driven it before, they would let them go. When Rachel said he could do it, he immediately called Michelle to ask if she wanted to go. She did want to go and asked her mother. Mrs. Burns did not let on that she knew about the trip and gave permission for her to go. Carl then called Sandra to tell her they were on—he could drive her to Leesville.

Michelle and Carl were not allowed to go to the Bulldogs play-off game against Center since they were leaving at seven thirty the next morning. They wanted to minimize the number of stops the next morning, so Mrs. Burns allowed Michelle to spend the night at Carl's. She knew Riley, Janice, and Rachel would be watching them.

The next morning, Rachel took them to Sandra's apartment for the trip to Leesville. When Sandra came out, Rachel was concerned she was ready to drop the baby at any moment. Sandra assured her she was just big; she still had a month before her due date.

Rachel sat in the apartment parking lot, watching as they loaded up the Cougar and rolled out for Leesville. It was 8:00 a.m. when Carl pulled out of the apartment parking lot, heading for Fort Polk. A couple of hours later, they were rolling through Leesville and headed out to Fort Polk. They arrived on post at 10:45 a.m. and were shocked to learn Edward's Army AIT graduation ceremony was the next day at 11:00 a.m. Sandra had somehow gotten the days mixed up!

They went to a McDonald's and sat down, thinking about what they were going to do. They all had money but were worried about what they should do. Carl decided to call Rachel and Mrs. Burns so they could make a decision. He found a pay phone and got some change, then made the call to Rachel. He explained that Sandra got confused and the AIT graduation ceremony was not until the next day, and he asked what she wanted them to do. Since Michelle was with them, Rachel knew she needed to call Mrs. Burns. She told him to give her half an hour and call back.

Rachel called Mrs. Burns and explained what had happened, then asked what she thought they should do. Without hesitation, Mrs. Burns said they should stay in Louisiana until the AIT graduation the next day. She explained Carl was an inexperienced driver, and having him drive back to Marshall and go back to Leesville the following day would be extremely dangerous. At first, Rachel was beside herself; it seemed Mrs. Burns was giving them a license to have sex. When she thought about it, she knew he would want to drive Sandra back the next day for the graduation ceremony.

Rachel wondered about Sandra's ability to take all the riding in her pregnant state. She took a deep breath and told Mrs. Burns that was a good idea. Mrs. Burns said they had enough money. Michelle had 150 dollars she gave her before they left. Rachel thought about it, and since they had money, it made sense for them to stay until the ceremony was over. Rachel called the command office to find out what happened and was told the ceremony was originally scheduled for Saturday. The liaison said it had been rescheduled because the venue was not available.

She listened as the liaison apologized, saying they had not been able to contact everyone. She took a deep breath when she realized they had no idea the ceremony had been rescheduled. A few minutes later, Carl called back and Rachel told him they should get a room and stay until tomorrow. She told him that when they got the room, they were to park the car because he did not need to be driving all over the place. Rachel cleared her throat, took a deep breath, and told Carl he should buy a box of condoms. He thought, *Here we go again,* as he listened to Rachel explain that things happen.

He promised he would buy a box of condoms as they hung up the phone.

Rachel's mind raced, a sixteen-year-old and a fourteen-year-old, alone in a hotel room. She started to rethink her decision to let him drive Sandra to Fort Polk. She realized it was too late; they were already in Leesville, with no supervision, and were about to spend the night in a hotel room. Rachel took a seat. This was too much to her. She still could not understand how Mrs. Burns stayed so calm in a situation like this.

She decided to call Bradley and tell him Carl was about to spend the night with Michelle.

CHAPTER 24

Carl and Michelle Spend the Night Together #TheyNotVirginsAnyLonger

Carl hung up the phone and said they needed to get a room. The local hotels all provided a discount for military personnel, and Sandra had her dependent ID card. They got a room at the Ramada Inn in Leesville, then stopped at a 7-Eleven to buy a toothbrush and tooth-paste. Edward was not able to go off base and be with them, so they had to wing it on their own. Sandra's back was hurting from the ride, so they found a park where they could hang out. The air was brisk, so not many people were at the park, and at 4:00 p.m., they went back to the Ramada Inn to check into their room.

Sandra had a room by herself, while Carl and Michelle planned to share a room. They were surprised when they went in the room and there was a king-size bed instead of twin beds. Michelle called Sandra and asked if her room had twin beds. Sandra's room also had a king-size bed, so they called the front desk. They were told there were no other available rooms; they were sold out for the night. They looked at each other, not sure what to make of the situation. Carl volunteered to sleep on the couch, but Michelle said no, that they would have to control themselves.

She laughed, saying they should not miss the opportunity to see what it felt like to spend the night together.

The phone rang at 6:30 p.m. It was Sandra, asking where they wanted to get something to eat. They went to Burger King and got their food to go, coming back to Sandra's room to eat. When Sandra fell asleep, Michelle woke her up, saying they were going to their room. When they turned on the TV, it was a surprise Leesville had the same channels they had at home. He took the alarm clock radio and turned on the music and turned the TV down.

They listened to music and cuddled, the same as they did at home. They danced, and when a slow song came on, Carl felt the funny feeling he got when he was around Michelle. As his heart raced, he thought it might not be a good idea for them to be alone. His mind raced when he remembered he did not buy the box of condoms like he told Rachel he would. They kissed sensuously and broke it off, turned off the music, and turned the TV up. When the news came on, Michelle said she was going to take a shower and Carl said he would shower when she finished.

A few minutes later, Michelle exited the shower in one of the robes provided by the hotel. Carl got up and took his shower and wore the second robe supplied by the hotel. He climbed in the bed next to Michelle, rubbing her body, realizing she did not have on clothes. They kissed sensuously, and in a second, he was on top of her, just like when they were on the couch at home. This time, however, there were no clothes between them as he settled between her open legs. It felt natural as he kissed her neck and thrust. Michelle grunted sensuously as he pushed past her hymen to claim her virginity.

They felt great as they moaned and rocked their hips together.

A few moments later, they exploded in orgasmic bliss as they experienced their first climax. Carl tried to roll off her, but she held him in place, kissing his neck and saying it felt too good for him to move. Her kisses seemed sweeter as they loved on each other. It wasn't long before his excitement built and they shared each other's love for the second time. He felt his feelings toward Michelle grow deeper, more passionate as they continued to make love. They were spent and fell asleep as the TV was signing off for the night.

A couple of hours later, the noise from TV static woke Carl, and he got up and turned the TV off, then climbed back in bed on top of her. Michelle woke up and kissed him as they made love once again, then fell asleep cuddling each other. She again woke up at 5:30 a.m. and went to the bathroom, not believing this did not wake Carl. She rolled over on him, and he slowly woke up. He woke all up when he realized he needed to use the bathroom. A few minutes later, he was back in bed and on top of Michelle.

In the other room, Sandra had woken up and could hear the unmistakable sound of them making love. *I hope he doesn't get her pregnant,* she thought. She didn't really think Michelle was ready for married life.

Carl and Michelle showered and were out of the room at 10:30 a.m. Sandra was standing by the car. Sandra noticed Michelle's hair was sweated out and she was sporting a fro. She looked at them laughing and asked if they enjoyed themselves. Carl looked at her, wondering how she knew.

They rolled on post and were already seated when the graduation ceremony started. An hour later, Edward was a full-fledged soldier, and they were on the way back to Marshall.

They stopped for gas, and Edward asked if he and Michelle had sex last night. Carl reluctantly said yes, and Edward said he hoped he used a condom. Sandra was talking to Michelle the same way, saying she did not want to have kids yet.

Three hours later, Edward dropped them at Carl's house, and as soon as Rachel saw Michelle, she was livid! She put them in the car, drove to the Spring Street park, and told them to spill it. She looked at Michelle, saying, "Your hair was flat-ironed when ya'll left, and you come back with a fro. Michelle was in tears as she and Rachel locked eyes.

Her voice rose when she asked Michelle, "Did you play basketball and sweat while you were there?" Carl tried to interrupt, but Rachel told him to shut up, that she was talking to Michelle. He listened as Rachel said they were too young to be doing this. Carl wilted in the seat as Rachel turned her stare to him and bluntly asked, "Did you use condoms?" He had never seen Rachel like this and saw the fire in her eyes when he said he forgot to buy condoms. Rachel banged her hands on the steering wheel, saying, "That was the *last* thing I said before we hung up, Carl Allen!" She told them she was disappointed with them and she should beat both their asses right then.

Michelle broke Rachel down when she went into a full-blown cry and, through her tears, said, "Ms. Rachel, I'm sorry, it just happened."

Rachel could not get mad at Michelle, so she hugged her, saying, "It's all right, baby." She then turned to Carl, saying, "If she pregnant, you *will* marry her, young man." She cranked the car, saying she could not believe they just decided to spend the night having sex. Michelle cried all the way to their house, and when Rachel pulled in the driveway, she said she needed to get herself together. She looked at Michelle and said, "I see myself when I look at you, baby."

She encouraged her to dry her eyes; everybody did not need to know she had been crying. She apologized again, and Rachel said she was good with her; it was her son she was pissed off with. Michelle said, "Ms. Rachel, don't be mad at him. I was there too."

Rachel laughed out loud, and her anger subsided as she said, "Girl, you got it bad!" She told her to come on in the house, then she told Carl to sit his hot ass down on the porch. He walked up to the porch and sat down with Riley and laughed when he said, "If I were you, I would not go in that house for a while."

He listened as Riley reminded him he had not seen anybody who could work Rachel's nerves the way he worked them. Riley asked if he remembered when he was a boy about seven or eight and got a whipping every day. He surprised Riley by saying he remembered him saying he should just get his whipping first thing in the morning. Carl said he knew he meant he should get his whipping before Rachel or Janice got mad. Riley laughed as he said what he and Michelle did was not wrong; it was just the wrong time. Riley said her emotions would be all over the place now.

He listened as Riley said he had to be mature enough to step up and handle her. Riley knew she had deep feelings for him, and that meant she would listen to him. Riley dropped a bomb, saying he could forget about breaking up with her; she was his woman now. Carl looked at Riley, asking what he should do now. Riley said he should keep everything as normal with her as possible. He told Carl she was going to question the decision to have sex with him every day and she was going to trip with him. He told Carl he should hope and pray she was not pregnant.

He was shocked when Riley said the best thing he could do then was to play basketball with her. Riley didn't wait for Carl to answer but called Rachel to the porch, saying to bring Michelle with her. She heard her dad calling and went to the porch to see what he wanted. She went back inside and got Michelle when he said he wanted her as well. When Michelle walked out of the house, Riley told her to close the door; this was for their ears only. He said they were going to walk to Shasta's house and play a few games of basketball.

Rachel listened as he said they needed to be alone and talk as they walked to Shasta's house. They took a deep breath when Riley said they should forget last night and focus on going forward. Rachel hugged Michelle again and said she was not mad at her.

Michelle looked at her and asked, "How did you know we had sex?"

Rachel looked at her, saying, "Baby, we all been fourteen before. Besides, your hair was sweated out."

Michelle laughed at the thought, saying, "I guess my hair is nappy."

Carl returned with his ten-speed, and Riley said he should head home by 5:00 p.m., well before it got dark.

Riley looked at his watch and said, "It's 3:00 p.m. now, so you have a couple of hours to play basketball and talk."

Carl pushed his bike as he and Michelle walked to Shasta's house. Their conversation gradually went back to normal as they pushed last night out of their minds. He was happy when they went through the curve on Norwood Street—the White boys were not outside to harass him. When they walked up in Shasta's yard, she said, "I like that 'fro," and walked back in the house. Michelle got her basketball and held her hand out for Carl to take off the promise ring.

They practiced her move and were soon playing one-on-one at an intensity level they never had before. Michelle had gotten smooth enough with the fadeaway shot that Carl had to defend her hard. She felt some kind of way. She would beat him by a step, and because of his height advantage, he would still block her shot. After about forty-five minutes of playing, Mrs. Burns drove up in the yard. She knew Michelle had lost her virginity to Carl the moment she saw her sweated-out hair. She got out of the car and walked over to them and hugged Michelle, saying she was glad they made it back safely.

Michelle knew her mother would not make a big deal of it and she would talk to her later. Mrs. Burns saw Carl was nervous and said he should relax; she already knew what happened. He looked at Michelle, wondering how her family was handling this so much better than his family did. Carl was shocked when Mrs. Burns said they would not be flat-ironing Michelle's hair for a while, especially since basketball season was back in. Carl got the message and realized Mrs. Burns's attitude did not change from the dinner where he gave Michelle the promise ring. She said he should put his bike in the car and she would take him home.

Friday night rolled around, and the Bulldogs were facing Lindale in the regional round of the playoffs. Ronnie Simmons led the way as they won the first two playoff games. The game against Center was a pyrrhic victory, with their best running back going down in the third quarter. The medical verdict was a high ankle sprain that would keep him out of action for two to three weeks. With DJ out, the Bulldogs' offense was not the high-octane machine it had been all season and through two rounds of the playoffs. Without DJ, Ronnie did not have the option to pitch, and this limited their offense.

The Bulldogs pulled it out to advance to the fourth round of the playoffs.

The next morning, Michelle and Carl had breakfast time to talk. Today was awkward; it was their first breakfast together since they claimed each other's virginity. He sensed the awkwardness and, when they finished eating, just held Michelle. This was the right thing at the right moment, and a warm feeling radiated over them. They felt each other's vibe and energy as they cuddled without saying anything.

A few minutes later, Michelle told Carl she loved him, then asked if he loved her.

She was livid when he said he wasn't sure if he loved her; he wasn't even sure he knew what love is. They argued and she pushed away from him. After a few minutes of silence, she said he should leave. He didn't say anything, just walked out the door, got on his bike, and rode home. He rode in the yard, and Riley was sitting on the porch, talking to Ron. Riley saw Carl's demeanor was not normal and guessed he and Michelle had been arguing. Ron said he was waiting for Janice to finish cooking breakfast so he could get a plate. He was digging two graves that day and needed the energy from a good breakfast.

A few minutes later, Janice said breakfast was ready and they should come eat. Ron went in to eat, but he and Riley stayed on the porch. He asked what went wrong, and Carl said Michelle put him out of Shasta's house. He listened as Carl said she asked if he loved her and didn't like his answer. Carl said he told her he wasn't sure if he loved her, and she got pissed! He listened as he said she started crying and pushed him away. Riley thought, *Oh no, he did not,* but said, "Last week you were having sex with her, and today she put you out."

Carl fell right into it, saying, "I know!"

Riley understood his grandson was clueless and didn't know what to do. He asked if she gave the promise ring back, and he said she did not. He told Riley he didn't want to lie to her, saying he loved her when he was not sure. He reminded Carl that when they came back with his mother last week, Michelle was crying. The light came on in Carl's mind, and he thought about what Riley said. He told Riley, "I guess I didn't handle that too good." Riley laughed out loud, saying, "Nope, you did not." Hannah was standing by the door and heard the conversation between her grandfather and brother.

She could not believe what she'd just heard—Carl and Michelle were having sex! She walked to the kitchen and saw Rachel at the table, eating. She went to the phone and called Jackie, saying she had some hot-off-the-press news. Jackie pressed her for the news, and Hannah said, "Michelle gave it up—she having sex with Carl!" Jackie could not believe what she heard and asked Hannah if she was sure. Hannah said she was positive they had sex; now they were arguing and she put him out of Shasta's house. Jackie listened and repeated, "So she gave it up and now they broke up?"

Hannah said, "Exactly! Last week they were boning, and this week they hate each other. "Jackie asked how Carl felt about it, and she said he was sitting on the porch, talking to their grandfather, but he sounded pissed! Hannah said she could hear Rachel coming, then said bye real quick and hung up. Jackie was blown away. They were sophomores in high school, and Michelle was having sex! She and Ronnie had talked about sex, and she knew it would happen, but Michelle had gone and done it! She realized that if she wanted Carl back, sex would be part of the deal!

Ronnie Simmons and the Bulldogs were in round 4 of the playoffs, facing the Troup Tigers in Longview. Not only were the Bulldogs' big back, DJ, out, but their best linebacker, Rickey Jenkins, had also stretched his hamstring in practice. The defense was weakened when they were facing a Troup team with two 1,000-yard backs and a QB coming into the game with 975 yards. Ronnie had a career night, rushing for 137 yards and throwing for 115 yards. There were scouts there to see the Troup running backs, and Ronnie hit their radar. Scouts from Tulsa, Oklahoma, and Texas Tech took Ronnie's contact info.

Troup advanced in the playoffs, and the Bulldogs went home to play basketball. Carl caught a ride to the game with Rachel; she had concession stand duty. He saw Michelle headed to the cheer line bus and caught up to her, asking if they were on for breakfast the following morning. Jackie saw them and went over to be messy, knowing they were having problems. She walked up just as Michelle was about to answer him, and she changed the subject. Carl caught on and rolled with it; he did not want her to be angry with him about this.

Michelle asked Jackie if she would give them a moment, and she said, "Hell no!" and stood there. Carl knew the bus was going to be leaving soon and asked Michelle if they were going to practice basketball the following day. She cheered up and said she needed to think about it. Jackie chided them, saying, "Oh, that's so cute. They gon' be playing one-on-one!" At that moment, Michelle had

had enough and said, "Jackie, I'm having sex with Carl, and we need to talk about something."

She was shocked when Jackie laughed, saying, "It seems to me, you two are having problems."

Michelle slapped her and ran up on her as they punched each other and rolled on the ground. Carl managed to break them up before any of the teachers or coaches saw what happened.

Jackie yelled at her, "This not over, bitch!" as she wiped the blood from her nose.

Michelle said, "Bring it, bitch!" as she wiped the blood from her nose. She then looked at Jackie, saying, "You right, we *were* arguing, and I was about to break up with him!" She waved her finger at Jackie, saying, "I got the ring, bitch!"

Michelle turned to Carl, saying, "Yes, we having breakfast in the morning, we practicing after you throw your route, and we having sex tomorrow night." She again looked at Jackie. "Everybody said my heart was going to be broke having a boyfriend that other girls want." She shrugged her shoulders, saying, "I guess this what they meant." She kissed Carl sensuously as Jackie stood watching. She broke the kiss and told Jackie, "I know you want Carl, but you going to have to step your game up, bitch."

Michelle mused, *I wonder if Ronnie know you pining behind* my *boyfriend?*

Carl felt he was in the Twilight Zone, wondering what the hell just happened. Jackie walked off. Michelle had clearly won this round. She looked up at him, saying, "I've given you everything I have, and you have the nerve to not know if you love me."

He looked at her, saying, "I promised to never lie to you." He leaned down and kissed her gently, saying, "I told you the truth, and you mad at me." He kissed her again, saying, "Think about it. I told you the truth. I did not lie to you."

She laughed, saying, "My mother said there would be times I hated you and loved you at the same time."

They laughed together as she said, "I guess this is one of those times." She kissed him again and said, "I love you, Carl." She laughed, saying he did not have to say anything. She wanted him to know. At breakfast the next morning, they agreed their argument was silly, and they made up. He apologized, and Michelle stopped him, saying, "You told the truth." He asked if she was serious when she told Jackie they were going to have sex that night. She laughed as she said, "Yes, I was serious, we are going to have sex, but you have to use a condom."

When Carl left to get his papers and throw his route, she talked to Shasta about sex. Shasta told Michelle she was glad she came to her and gave her pointers on protecting herself.

Shasta emphasized she wished Michelle had kept her chastity, but since she crossed that physical line, she had to deal with it. Michelle listened as Shasta said she should try to keep from falling in love with Carl. She laughed out loud as she said it was too late for that; she saw love in her eyes. Shasta said she should study ovulation in her biology class and use condoms. Michelle hugged and thanked her. Shasta looked at her, saying, "I know how it feel to be in love with a man you like, and you two have mad chemistry."

Meanwhile, Carl loaded his papers on his ten-speed and rolled toward Shasta's house.

When he pulled up in the yard, Michelle kissed him and got her ten-speed. She was ready to go.

An hour later they were in the yard, and he was showing her a couple of new moves. Michelle's game was aggressive; working with Carl had her playing like a boy. After two hours of practice, they played one-on-one. Carl could barely beat Michelle now, and they laughed together when they were done. She held her finger out for him to put her ring back on, and she smiled when he did. He asked what time she wanted him to come back, and Michelle said about 7:30 p.m.

She told him to not eat; she was making hamburgers for them. Rachel dropped him off at 7:30 p.m. on the dot, and watched as he walked on the porch. She could not believe her sixteen-year-old son was dating and involved in a full-fledged romance! Michelle directed him to the kitchen; she had waited for him to arrive to fry the burgers and fries. As they ate, Michelle said Sandra called, saying she had her baby earlier in the day. He looked at her, saying he had not heard the news and Edward was overseas in Germany. Michelle said that was why Sandra called; she wanted them to know she had the baby.

They finished eating and went to the couch to watch TV and talk. They turned the TV down and turned on the music, a mixtape Michelle had made. They cuddled as they talked, and Carl said they did not have to have sex. This was a shock to Michelle; she could not believe he did not want to have sex! He was anxious and wanted them to get their emotions under control before they got out of hand.

The following Monday, Michelle was at basketball practice. The Lady Bulldogs were about to kick off their season. The first game was the next night, and she was clicking on all cylinders.

First up was Gilmer on their home floor. The Lady Bulldogs looked rusty, except Michelle—her game was tight. She saw the time spent practicing with Carl was paying off. She kept them in the game with her fadeaway jump shot and drive to the basket. Michelle had 19 points at the half, and Coach Jenkins hoped her shot did not go cold in the second half. She ended the game with 34 points, but the Lady Bulldogs lost the game 53–49. Everyone hugged her after the game, giving her props for the stellar performance.

Jackie hugged her, asking if they could talk for a minute. They walked to midcourt and talked about things that affected them. They agreed Michelle had the guy Jackie wanted and Jackie wanted the guy Michelle had. She suggested they stop fighting and work to be friends. Michelle reiterated she did not trust her and had seen this movie but she would try.

Jackie congratulated her, saying that was a hell of a game as they walked back to the bench. Their teammates took a deep breath; it looked like they worked it out! Coach Jenkins knew this was a great sign; she needed both on top of their game. Jackie made friends with Michelle because she could not be MVP if she was up in her feelings and not playing well. The next evening, she called Hannah and said Michelle was on their good list. Hannah could not believe what she was hearing and asked what happened. Jackie explained she needed Michelle's points to help win games.

They laughed when Jackie said, "She can't focus when things are not running smoothly."

Hannah threw shade, saying, "The basketball court is the only place she functions under pressure."

She agreed to stand down and be nice to her. They understood her emotions would be all over the place—having sex with Carl was going to do that.

Michelle got her period after the Friday-evening game and was not feeling breakfast the next morning. She called Carl to cancel and was shocked Hannah was nice to her before she called him to the phone.

CHAPTER 25

Jackie and Michelle Are Still Friends #RonnieAndJackieMakeItOfficial

Christmas Break came, and everyone was happy. They were about to be off for two weeks. Carl, Hannah, and Carol worked together to surprise Rachel with a great Christmas gift. Things were different this year. Carl saved his money and set aside some for them helping him with his paper route. They decided to get her a nice Seiko watch for Christmas. Michelle went with them when Riley drove them to the jewelry store and helped pick out the watch. Carl thought about Michelle and what to get her for Christmas. Riley said, since he already had given her a ring, he had set the bar kind of high.

He settled on a Timex watch for her. He splurged on the promise ring, so he spent modestly on the watch. He got a present for Mrs. Burns too. He wanted her to know he was thinking of her.

He and Michelle agreed they would spend Christmas at his house and visit all her relatives. He could not believe Rachel allowed him to drive the car so he and Michelle could visit everybody. Her mother came to Shasta's house so he didn't have to drive to Jefferson. Rachel was limiting his driving; she had no idea he had been driving on the surface streets and the freeways of Detroit.

Basketball resumed after the Christmas break, and Michelle led the Lady Bulldogs in scoring, assists, and steals. Jackie was also having a great year, and her game complemented Michelle's. Coach Jenkins knew how to use both girls' talent to get the best result for the team. Jackie and Michelle together led the Lady Bulldogs as they rolled through the district. It was late March, and Michelle's birthday was coming up, but they were in the middle of their playoff run. Michelle turned sixteen on March 25, and she wanted to spend the day with Carl.

They planned to skip school and hang out together all day. Jackie heard her talking at school about her birthday and knew they had a game that night. If Michelle skipped school that day, she would not be eligible for their game that night. She had a great read on Michelle and knew she would be off her game behind this. Jackie went to Michelle, saying she wanted to talk about the game Thursday night. Michelle listened as she said the team needed her to be at the top of her game that night. Jackie said she knew she wanted to spend her birthday with Carl and asked her to invite him to the game.

Michelle agreed, saying they could push her birthday celebration to the weekend. She did not know why, but for some reason, she really wanted to be friends with Jackie. Everybody said she should watch Jackie, but Michelle wanted peace with her. She loved playing basketball, and their styles of play complemented one another. If the defense shut Jackie down, Michelle's game blew up. If the defense shut Michelle down, Jackie's game blew up. The teams that beat the Lady Bulldogs while Jackie and Michelle played together shut them both down.

When Michelle got home that evening, she called Carl and asked if he would go to the game instead of them skipping school and spending the day together. He agreed, saying he would find a way to Jefferson for the game that night.

When Carl talked to Rachel later, she said she would work the concession stand so he could go to the game. In a rare Thursday-night playoff game, the Lady Bulldogs hosted Center and Carl was in the stands. It was Michelle's birthday, and she was struggling in her game; the young lady defending her challenged every shot she put up.

Carl watched as Jackie made layups and pulled up for jump shots. She did the wrist flip he had shown her when she sank jump shots. Michelle watched as he flipped his wrist to acknowledge her. He saw Jackie had a fadeaway shot, like the one he taught Michelle. He knew she had watched Michelle do the move; she could catch on this way. He remembered when they were dancing together, she could watch a dance move and mimic it.

Jackie ended the game with 23 points while Michelle chipped in a hard earned 23 points.

The dynamic duo led the Lady Bulldogs as they cruised to a 75–65 victory over Center.

Carl and Michelle talked while Rachel and the teachers/students closed the concession stand. As part of her birthday celebration that weekend, she wanted to go to the Paramount Theatre and see *Jaws*, but Carl said he was out of money. Michelle said that was not a problem; she had them covered. When they left for the show that night, she handed Carl $20 and leaned into him. He laughed when she said nobody had to know his girl gave him the money for the movie.

After the movie, Carl said he was not going near the beach, and Michelle laughed, saying there was not a shark like that in real life. Rachel picked them up from the movie and, on the way home, asked Michelle if she still thought she wanted to marry Carl. She said she was sure she wanted to marry him; they had spent time together, and she loved the way he treated her. Rachel turned the question to Carl, asking if he still thought he wanted to marry Michelle. He leaned forward, saying they were still auditioning but he had not taken his promise ring back.

They laughed. He had lightened the situation with his flippant comment. Michelle said he had another thought coming if he thought she was giving the promise ring back. Rachel dropped her off at Shasta's house and drove home. The Lady Bulldogs were eliminated in the next round of the playoffs; the Gladewater team was taller and quicker. The Lady Bulldogs offense sputtered when they shut both Jackie and Michelle down. Carl couldn't believe the semester was almost over and football spring training was about to start.

Spring training was brutal. He had minor bruises and bumps the whole time they practiced. The hitting was harder, almost like two years ago when he was a freshman. He made big plays on both interceptions and fumble recoveries. He didn't know why, but he never felt good about going full out on his teammates. In the annual Red / White Game, he turned in a stellar performance. Carl scored a touchdown on a pass interception, and on a fumble recovery, he returned for a touchdown. The coaching staff wished them a happy summer, saying they should stay injury-free.

They collected the equipment, and the guys left for the summer. He went outside and found Michelle so they could get ready for the walk to his house. Carl convinced Rachel to let them walk from the Stadium to the house. She agreed: this side of Norwood was not rowdy like the other side.

Carl and Michelle walked home, talking about summer plans. Half an hour later, they walked up in the yard. Since she was going to summer school, Carl said he thought a few weeks in Detroit might be good for them. They didn't get a consensus on his summer plans, and Michelle assumed he was going.

School was out for the summer a week later, and Bradley sent him a ticket. Michelle got him to agree to stay three weeks in Detroit, then come back to Marshall. When he told Bradley he was going to stay three weeks, he said that was cool. Carl flew out of Shreveport Regional the first day of June, with a connecting flight in Memphis. While they were waiting for his flight to leave, he and Rachel talked about his paper route. He planned to give his route up, but she felt he should keep it through his senior year. He was going to miss everybody, but he wanted to hang out in Detroit this summer.

Bradley met him at the airport, and when they got outside, Carl was shocked to see he drove the Chevelle. Bradley threw him the keys, saying he thought it would be good to break him in driving home. A half-hour later, they pulled up at Bradley's house and Carl stopped the car in the front half of the driveway. He could not get the car out of the backyard part of the driveway—he either hit the fence or the house. Bradley gave him keys to the house and said they would talk about his grid later.

The next Monday, he went back to the Shell station where he worked last summer.

The station had been sold. Mr. Johnson was no longer the owner. The new owner, Bill Smith, asked if he worked there before. He said he did and explained he worked for Mr. Johnson last summer.

Carl explained he pumped gas and washed cars for Mr. Johnson during the summer last year. Bill liked what he was hearing and decided to hire him to wash cars and pump gas. Carl agreed to $150 a week, until he saw the number of cars he was washing. With Mr. Johnson, he would wash two or three cars each day. With Bill, he washed cars all day and pumped gas in between. When he and Bill sat down, he ended up with $275 dollars a week! The days went fast as he was always busy, the station—was booming!

Bill Smith added body work to the services at the garage and he was a gifted body man. He rebuilt a Ford van to look like a Greyhound bus, and this turned eyes all over the city. Carl was out delivering a customer car and thought there was a car following him. He did a couple of dummy turns and lost the car, but he could not shake the eerie feeling. He told Bill he had a funny feeling when he delivered the car, and Bill said he should shake it off. Bill also sold cars at the station, and some people asked if the deep blue Chevelle was for sale.

He knew he was driving a cool car and knew why people were looking when he drove by. He was a seventeen-year-old driving a car like this, and that drew attention. About three weeks into the job, he was doing the windshield for a group of three girls. He could hear them giggle, and one of them said she thought she knew this guy. The girl sitting in the back seat asked if he was from Texas. This got his attention, and he looked in the car, saying he was from Texas. He was about to ask how she knew when she asked, "Whatever happened to the girl who fell off her bike and you walked her home?"

He was saying they lost contact when he snapped and asked, "Was that you?" Felicia said it was her and she remembered him. Her friends could not believe she had met this guy, let alone that he was from Texas. They exchanged numbers and promised to call and catch up.

She called him when he got off work that evening, and they talked for a minute. He heard a beep in his ear and said the phone was beeping. Felicia said he need to click Over; there was another call coming in. He clicked the receiver, and sure enough, there was another call on the line.

He said hello and was a little startled when Michelle said hello. He asked her to hold on; he needed to get off the other line. He clicked back over and told Felicia he had to go as he had another call. She ragged him, saying, "Is your girlfriend on the line?"

He paused for a second and said, "Yes, my girlfriend is on the other line."

He was shocked when Felicia said, "Call me tomorrow." He didn't know what to say, so he agreed he would call her. After they got over the marvel of call-waiting, Michelle wanted to know whom he was talking to.

She listened as he said a couple of summers ago, he met this girl over on Lauder Street and she crashed her ten-speed. He told her how she was scratched up and he carried her home. Michelle was getting pissed as he told her whom he was talking to. She cut him off, asking, "How did she get your number? How did she know you were in Detroit?" Carl explained they had lost contact until today, when she was with two of her friends and they stopped at the Shell station to get gas. She remembered he told her they rode ten-speeds on the slab of a freeway that was extended but not open.

Michelle asked again, "How did she get your number, Carl?"

He took a deep breath and said he gave her his number. The phone went quiet as Carl processed what he should say next. Michelle asked her name, and he said Felicia Barnes. Carl said he had no idea he was going to bump into her and he had not been to her neighborhood. Michelle breathed deeply. She knew she was going to have to trust him. They talked about missing each other and summer school. She mentioned the work was challenging and she needed a break.

Carl laughed and said this time next year, it would be behind her.

At that moment, a reality hit him: he was about to graduate high school. Michelle said she had turned in applications to East

Texas State, Texas Southern, and University of Houston. Carl said he was going to see if he got a scholarship to figure out where he was going. He didn't know Rachel had been working with Michelle and turned in an app for him at the same schools.

The ten-minute timer went off, and Carl asked her to set it again; they could end their call then.

They hung up when the timer sounded the third time, but Michelle did not take her mind off Felicia Barnes.

The weekend rolled around, and Carl called Steve to see what he had planned. He said several girls at school he liked said they were going skating. Carl could skate, but he did not want to go skating; fights usually broke out at the skating rink. He decided to go see Cooley High at the Mercury Theatre on Schaefer. He and Steve were in the lobby, buying snacks, when he saw a girl he thought he'd seen before. He spoke and asked if he had met her before.

She smiled, saying, "We kind of met the other day. I was in the car with Felicia when we stopped at the station where you work." She held out her hand, saying her name was Debra McAdoo.

He shook her hand, saying, "I'm Carl Hampton."

She asked how he remembered her, and Carl said it was that he remembered her freckles. The other girl with her introduced herself as Van Howard. She was driving. He was about to ask about Felicia when she walked into the lobby, all hugged up with a guy. He saw the shock on her face when she saw him.

Steve cleared his throat, and Carl said, "My bad. This my friend Steve." The girls introduced themselves, and they stood in a group, talking. They decided to sit together when the movie started, and Steve loved this. They asked what school they went to, and Carl said Marshall High. They had heard of Marshall, Michigan, about ninety-five miles away on I-94, but had not heard of Marshall, Texas.

Van was surprised and said, "Oh my god, you *really* do live in Texas!"

Steve said he went to Redford, and they asked how he pulled that off—his hood was zoned to Cooley.

Steve laughed and said his mother took him to school every day. The girls said they went to Cooley and wanted to see the movie named after their school. Steve had gone to Cooley for a year, and they knew some of the same people. Van asked why he was in Detroit, and Carl said he was visiting his dad. McAdoo asked where his dad lived, and Steve answered, "Right around the corner from here, and he at work." Steve made sure the girls knew Carl had a car and was home alone until three in the morning. Since Van had the car, Steve asked if they would come by Carl's house. Van said no since they had to go home to make an 11:00 p.m. curfew.

Felicia's boyfriend, Eric, went to the restroom, and McAdoo told Steve to write the address down. He asked Carl the address and wrote it down, 18293 Sorrento, between Pickford and Curtis. Eric came out of the restroom just as Steve handed Van the address. They walked out of the Mercury to the parking lot. Van was driving a Chevy Nova with Cragar rims, and they saw the Chevelle Carl was driving. Eric said, "Wow! That is a cool car!" Carl was feeling himself and turned the tires when he pulled out of the parking lot.

A white Duster with slot rims pulled up beside them, and Carl geared the Chevelle down. The Duster sped up and tried to cut them off, swerving into his lane and forcing him on the curb. Carl realized what was going down and slammed on the brakes. When the door opened on the Duster, he popped the clutch and the Chevelle turned those tires as it Leapt off the curb! This caught the guys in the Duster off guard, and they had to get their guy back in the car. Carl watched in the rearview mirror and saw the Duster come off the curb.

Steve asked how he knew they were jackers, and he said there was just a funny feeling. Carl said he wasn't going home until he got rid of 'em. Steve told him to go down on the Lodge; he knew just the exit to get them. They drove on the Lodge at ninety miles per hour, with the white Duster behind them. When the Elmhurst exit came up, Steve told him, "There is a hard right at the top of this exit, then we lose them." Carl hit the ramp for Elmhurst and saw the hard right coming up. He slowed and geared the Chevelle down, then shifted up when he hit the right turn.

He had to squeeze the Chevelle into the traffic. It was back-to-back. They got in, and the Duster got cut off. They saw the smoke from the tires where they slammed on their brakes! Carl got his bearings when he saw Livernois Avenue. He turned on Livernois and got on the Lodge service drive when he crossed the freeway. When he crossed Wyoming, he looked down on the Lodge and saw the white Duster. They held up their guns as they went under the bridge and rolled out of sight. Carl decided to go over to Seven Mile, just in case they got off at Six Mile.

Fifteen minutes later, he drove into the yard at Bradley's house. Carl was panicked when a car pulled to the curb, and ran in the house to get the gun. He looked out a window and saw it was Felicia, Debra, and Van. They came over! He put the gun down and went back downstairs to greet them. Steve looked at him—they were alone with three girls! They talked and watched TV in the den at Bradley's. He looked at Felicia and said, "You *didn't* tell me you have a boyfriend." Felicia looked at him, saying, "You *didn't* ask!" They laughed, but both could see there was chemistry.

Van asked to use the phone at midnight and called her mother to say she was headed home. She said they needed to go; she did have a curfew of 12:30 a.m. The time they spent with them, Carl found out Felicia and McAdoo were ride-or-die, while Van was a friend. He noticed the way Felicia side-eyed Van when she left her number with him. He left at the same time the girls left. He had to take Steve home. Steve said, if he stayed away from the Six Mile and Schaefer area, he should be okay. He told Carl he was sure the white Duster was stolen.

Carl went around Outer Drive over to Greenfield and over to Puritan. Steve lived on Ferguson off Puritan. He took the same way home and rolled into the backyard part of the driveway. He would ask Bradley to get the car out tomorrow morning. He was startled when he walked in the house and the phone rang. He picked up the phone, and Felicia asked, "Did you tell your girlfriend you were talking to me?"

Carl laughed, saying he did tell her whom he was talking to. Felicia listened as he said he told Michelle about carrying her home when she fell off her bike. Felicia said, "You know she mad at you, right?" Carl laughed, saying he didn't think she was mad at him. He asked if her boyfriend knew they dropped him off and came by his house. Felicia laughed and said he didn't know but that bitch Van might tell him. He was shocked when Felicia said, "Van likes you, in case you didn't know." Then she went on saying, "She will probably tell him, thinking I'll back off."

Felicia asked what time he got off work tomorrow, and he said they closed at 6:00 p.m. She said he could pick her up at 8:00 p.m. tomorrow night and they could ride to Belle Isle. He suggested McAdoo and Steve come along and they could double-date. Felicia said she didn't know how they did things in Texas but girls in Detroit didn't double-date. She laughed, saying, "If you got a boy you like, don't bring him around these girls—they will talk to him!" Felicia laughed when she said, "Eric probably already know we came by your house."

The next evening, at 7:,55 p.m., he pulled up in front of Felicia's house on Lauder Street. He saw Mark down the street and said he was going to holla at him when he got Felicia out of the house. He knocked on the door and asked for her, and her mother asked who he was. He introduced himself as Carl Hampton. She asked whose car he was driving, and he said it was his but his dad bought it for him. She introduced herself as Alice Barnes and asked how he met her daughter.

Carl said, "A couple of summers ago, she fell on her bike and I carried her home."

Alice snapped, saying, "You the young man from Texas that carried her home when she banged herself up." She looked at him incredulously, adding, "I thought you guys lost contact."

Carl explained that they *had* lost contact, until earlier in the week, when her friend Van stopped at the station where he worked to buy gas.

Her mother said, "Felicia has a serious boyfriend. I don't know if she told you that."

Before he could answer, Felicia walked downstairs, saying, "He has a girlfriend back in Texas, Mama." She continued, "It's just two friends riding to Belle Isle to hang out and talk."

Alice threw shade, saying the last time they talked, she went fifteen rounds with Michigan Bell to get the long-distance phone charges removed. They walked out of the house, and Carl asked her to hold up a couple of minutes while he went down the sidewalk to talk to Mark. He got an earful about Felicia from Mark, and he said their families had fallen out. He thought, *Well, dayum,* as he listened to Mark prat on. They were glad to see each other, and he said he would be back to hang out with him. He got in the car, and they made the drive downtown to the Riverfront and Belle Isle.

They got there at 9:00 p.m., and the park closed at 10:00 p.m. They found a secluded spot and lay on the hood of the car, talking. Carl laughed when Felicia said she crashed her bike that day because she was looking at him. She said she was really hurt and crying but she stopped crying when he picked her up. Felicia leaned over and kissed him, saying she could still remember how she felt when he held her. He kissed Felicia and she reminded him that he had a girl-friend. He reminded her she had said his girlfriend was in Texas and he is in Detroit. They talked and kissed some more, he could not believe how he was feeling.

When they rode their ten-speeds on the freeway slab, he never knew Felicia felt this way about him.

It was close to time for the park to close, and they got back in the car for the drive back to Northwest Detroit. Felicia suggested they go to his house; she wasn't ready to go home yet. She sat close to him on the seat, and his arm rested on her leg. He had to rub her legs to shift the gears—she sat so close to him. While they were riding to Northwest Detroit, Felicia asked if he would give her the phone number in Texas, and he gave her the number.

They pulled up in the backyard, locked the car, and went in the house. They showed each other the popular dances and hung out until midnight. He remembered what Alice said and told Felicia he was going to take her home. She asked if he was sure he wanted to pass up this opportunity, and he said he was. They got in the car and pulled up in front of her house at 12:25 a.m. He walked her to the door, saying he had a great time. They did not try to kiss, just hugged, and he left.

The next day, Carl got a call from Van and wondered how she got the number. He was shocked when she said she cross-checked the address in the Polk directory and got the number. Carl was impressed, although everything she said went right over his head.

After talking to Van a few minutes, he knew Felicia was in a sexual relationship with Eric. She made it a point to say she did not have a boyfriend and would like to hang out with him. When Carl said he had a girlfriend in Texas, Van said, "This Detroit. You not in Texas."

CHAPTER 26

Carl and Van Have Great Chemistry #VanIsANerd

Carl could not put his finger on what it was with Van; she seemed to be on his level mentally. When he and Felicia talked, it seemed she was only interested in parties, going to Belle Isle, and having fun. When Van started to talk about the Watergate scandal and how it took over everything, he was shocked. He had talked to Van over an hour and was about to hang up when she asked if he was going to Belle Isle the next day. He said he and Steve had planned to hang out at Palmer Park. Van said she wanted to ride out with them, and he agreed to let her know.

The next day, Carl picked Steve up, and they were on the way to Van's house. When he told Steve where they were going, he asked why they were taking a girl with them—there would be plenty of girls at the park. He laughed when Steve said taking a girl to the park was like taking sand to the beach. Carl said his word was his bond and he promised Van he would pick her up. A few minutes later, Carl pulled up in front of Van's house, got out the car, and went to the door. She answered and introduced him to her mother, who asked where he lived and where they were going.

He explained he lived on Sorrento and they were going first to Palmer Park and to Belle Isle later. Her mother caught his accent and asked how long he had lived in Detroit. She side-eyed her daughter when he said he was there for the summer and was going back to Texas. Mrs. Howard took a polaroid of them together and let her go.

A few minutes later, they rolled into Palmer Park and things went bad. The white Duster from the other night was parked, and Carl got a good look at the guy driving. He told Steve they were going to roll farther; he saw the guys that tried to jack them.

Steve asked how he knew that was the car, and Carl said he would recognize that car anywhere. Steve saw he was right. As they rolled out of the park, one of the guys saw the Chevelle and pointed at it. Steve asked Carl if he saw them get in the car, and he said he did. He rolled out onto Woodward and decided to go over to Seven Mile. Carl knew, if he took them to his cousin's house off Mack Avenue, they had his back. When he rolled on Mack Avenue, he saw the Duster in his rearview mirror. Carl turned on his cousin's street and hit the side street to go into the alley behind his cousin's house.

The guys standing outside with his cousin checked him until DJ said he knew him. Carl pulled up, and the Duster stopped when the driver saw the group of guys standing ahead. He had accomplished his goal: the guys in the Duster would think this was where he lived. They stayed at DJ's house with his crew for an hour or so, and Carl said he was ready to go to Belle Isle. DJ insisted one of his guys roll with him to the Fisher Freeway, saying, "It's not that safe for you guys over here in that ride." He hit the Fisher Freeway ramp, rolling full speed, headed for the Lodge Freeway Exchange and downtown Detroit.

A few minutes later, they rolled through the tunnel off Jefferson and into Belle Isle Park. They found a park, and while Steve walked around, he and Van found a table. They sat and talked, asking each other questions and answering the questions. She was shocked when Carl said he gave Michelle a promise ring. She coquettishly asked what he promised her. He smiled when he said he could not say what promise he made Michelle. He asked Van how she would feel if he made her a promise and told everyone what that promise was.

Steve walked back to the table, accompanied by two girls. He introduced them, saying they lived in Northwest Detroit and went to Henry Ford High. Carl and Van introduced themselves, and one of the girls asked if he was really from Texas. Carl said he was from Texas, just in Detroit for the summer, visiting his dad. Steve asked if it was possible for Diane and Julia to catch a ride back to Northwest Detroit with them. Carl looked at him and said sure, they could ride with them. Diane thanked him, saying they rode the bus to Belle Isle and it would be nice to have a ride home.

They loaded up and, a few minutes later, were on the Lodge Freeway, headed to Bradley's house. Carl pulled up in the back driveway, and Diane asked who lived there. Carl laughed, saying this was his dad's house and it looked like he was not home. They went inside, sitting at the bar, talking about school and Texas. They seemed to have a thirst to know what life was like in Texas, and he assured them everyone did not have cows and a ranch. After talking to them for a couple of hours, he dropped everyone at home. He dropped Van off last; she lived closest to him.

When he pulled up to the curb at her house, she asked him to hold up. She wanted to tell her mother she was okay. A few minutes later, she came back out, saying she was going to meet him at his house. He pulled from the curb, watching as she got in the Chevy Nova and backed out of the driveway. When he pulled into the backyard driveway, Van was pulling up at the curb. They went in the house and spent the next three hours talking. Van filled in the blanks with Felicia that he had no idea of. When he said he met Felicia several summers ago and they had not had contact, she thought he was lying.

Carl said they rode ten-speeds on the freeway slab, but other than that, they had had no contact. Van related how when they met the other day, Felicia made it seem like they were long-lost friends. They talked and he found out she was also about to be a senior in high school. She was on the cheer squad at Cooley and loved football. She asked if he had given any thought to going to school in Detroit. Carl laughed at this suggestion, saying his mother would *not* go for him going to school in Detroit. He said if he did go to school in Detroit, he was in the Mumford zone.

Van laughed, saying she was on the school zone line, so she could go to either Mumford or Cooley. She said she went to Cooley because most of her friends were at Cooley. She asked what it was like going to school in Texas and was shocked to find Marshall High School was bigger than Cooley.

The phone rang while they were talking, and Carl picked up, shocked it was Michelle on the other end. He looked at the clock and saw it was 7:30 p.m. They had agreed to talk every day at that time. He asked Michelle if he could call her back in about an hour, and she agreed.

Van laughed when he hung up, asking, "What if I'm not gone in an hour?" He laughed out loud and said she had to be gone; he needed to call her back. Van knew she had to leave shortly, since her mother had asked her to come home by 8:30 p.m. She was not going to tell Carl this; she wanted to leave him hanging. She said she needed to go and stood to leave. He walked her to the door and out to her car. Carl said it was nice talking to her and she should call when she got home. He wanted to make sure she got home safely, but Van read it wrong; she thought he wanted to continue their conversation.

He called Michelle back, and they talked about her summer school woes. The curriculum was killing her. Carl encouraged her, saying this was her plan, that she wanted to be a senior when school started. He told her she needed to take a deep breath and put the books down for a few days and her focus would return. She agreed and started laughing when he said life was more than school.

The next few weeks went by quickly, and while working, Carl could not shake the eerie feeling somebody was watching him. Business was booming, and he learned basic bodywork while he pumped gas. He was talking to Michelle every night and hanging out with Van. Felicia called him regularly, but he backed off her because she had a stupid boyfriend.

It was mid-July, and Carl was scheduled to return to Texas, but he wanted to stay the rest of the summer. He and Michelle had their first real argument when he mentioned he was not coming home until late August. He explained Bill had given him a raise to three hundred dollars a week and he wanted to make the extra money.

Michelle was incensed and told Carl the money was cool but she really missed him.

After a few cross words and her accusation of him boning Felicia, she cursed him out and hung up. He could not believe it and called her back, shocked when Mrs. Burns answered the phone. She told him Michelle did not want to talk to him and to let her know when he decided to come home. He said he would do that and hung up.

The phone ringing startled him, and he was shocked when it was Felicia on the other end. She asked if he wanted to come to her sister Marsha's birthday party. He asked if Steve could come, and Felicia said he could bring him. She said the party was this coming Saturday and started at 7:30 p.m. Carl said he would be there with his friend Steve after he got off work and got cleaned up. The conversation turned personal when he asked what Eric was going to think. She asked what he meant, and Carl asked, Didn't she think Eric would be mad if he was there? She knew Van probably told him everything—she was a bitch like that. Felicia said they could be friends because they had something in common. He couldn't believe what he heard and asked what they had in common.

She laughed, saying she had a boyfriend she had sex with and he had a girlfriend he had sex with. He was shocked she went there and asked why she believed he was having sex with Michelle. She shocked him again when she said he told her. Carl laughed, saying he had not said anything about them having sex. Felicia asked if he didn't tell her he had given Michelle a promise ring. Carl remembered that and listened as she said she had relatives in Birmingham. She talked to them, and they said when you give a girl a promise ring, she is expected to have sex with you. Felicia said Eric hadn't given her a promise ring, and she didn't expect him to.

Carl was totally confused. The Southern culture was bumping against the Detroit culture. He remembered what Riley said: when you're not sure of what to say, don't say anything. This was one of those moments when he did not have any idea what he should say. A few seconds later, Felicia said she needed to go; they had probably said too much. She asked if he was still coming to the party, and he said he would be there. Saturday evening, he pulled up at Felicia's house at 8:00 p.m. and saw a few people in the yard.

He was mildly surprised to see the blue Nova Van drove sitting out front. He walked into the backyard, where they were playing music and dancing.

He saw Van when he walked past the DJ booth and Felicia stood in the back door. He scanned the yard for Eric and saw him standing behind Felicia, inside the back door. Van walked over to him, and they hugged, glad to see each other. When she asked where Steve was, Carl said he was riding solo tonight. He saw the birthday girl when she walked out of the house to the backyard. Carl got on the Soul Train line when they played "Boogie Down" by Eddie Kendricks. He watched to see what dances they did and did a two-step tip that fit right in.

Marsha turned twelve, and most of the kids at the party were her age. About 8:45 p.m., he and Van decided they were going to leave. She asked if he would come by her house to pick her up. Felicia came out with Eric and talked to them a few minutes before they left. He met Van at home, and she invited him in. He saw Mrs. Howard was sitting on the couch, and she invited him to sit down. Van sat down and asked if she could ride to Belle Isle with Carl. She asked where they were going after Belle Isle since it was 9:15 p.m. and Belle Isle closed at 10:00 p.m.

Van said they would go by the movie to see what was playing. She asked for his phone numbers, both in Detroit and Texas. Carl wrote down Rachel's number in Marshall and Bradley's number in Detroit. They left, and Van stood by the passenger door until he came and opened it. She slid across the seat so she would be sitting close to him. He drove to Belle Isle, and they talked about her life. She had three brothers and a sister, all more than fifteen years older than she was. Her dad got killed three years ago in a robbery working in the restaurant his family owned.

He was shocked to find out the Nova she was driving was hers! She didn't tell anyone; everybody assumed it was her mother's car. They rode through Belle Isle and headed back to Northwest Detroit. She watched him shift gears and got a feel for shifting gears and using a clutch. It was a little after 10:00 p.m. when he hit the Lodge, headed for the Wyoming exit. When he came up on Wyoming, he said he was not going over to the Mercury; they might see that Duster. He was starting to feel some kind of way with her sitting this close to him and decided he was going home.

He pulled up at the house, and there was not a park in the driveway. He parked on the curb, set the alarm/kill switch and walked inside. Van held his hand as they walked up the sidewalk to the backyard. He walked in the den and knew most of the people there. The music was loud, alcohol flowed, and he could smell the weed being smoked. Bradley was having a party, and he did not know it! Van asked if he smoked weed and, when he said he did, asked if he would get some for them to smoke. Carl went to Bradley to see if he could have one of the joints they were smoking.

Bradley gave him a joint, and he introduced Van, saying they were going to hang out at the party. After a few minutes, she said she was uncomfortable; all the people at the party were so much older. They went upstairs to his room, turned on his component set, and listened to music. He left the door open, and they sat on the bed, talking. Bradley startled them when he came upstairs to tell him they were getting ready to leave. Carl went downstairs to make sure everyone was gone and all the doors were locked. When he locked the den door, Van startled him when he turned to walk upstairs.

"I hope you don't mind. I like wearing men's shirts."

Carl's mind started to race. She was standing in front of him with a shirt on! He might have been slow on the way they did things in Detroit, but he was pretty sure she was naked under that shirt. He walked up to Van and kissed her full on the mouth. They broke the kiss, and he picked her up, carrying her up the stairs to his room. He closed the door and saw her clothes on the chair in the corner. He turned off the light and undressed, then slid in the bed next to Van.

She still had the shirt on, and he kissed her on the mouth again. She asked, "If we do this, am I your girl?" He kissed her and said she knew he had a girl he gave a promise ring to. She pulled away from him, and he rolled over, thinking she was about to put her clothes on and ask him to take her home. The bed rocked when Van rolled over on him—she had pulled off the shirt! She said she wanted to see if he would lie and kissed him on the mouth. He rolled over on top of her and settled between her legs. They rocked their hips together and were now intimate friends.

At 1:30 a.m., Carl asked what time she needed to go home and was shocked when she said she was spending the night. Van laughed, saying he was really not up on the way they did things in Detroit. She said her mother got his address and phone number because she had already asked to spend the night. He asked if this was something they could do again, and she said she could spend the night as often as he wanted. Carl was a little shaken when she said she didn't know if she could keep quiet when Michelle called. She laughed and said she was joking, then said she was serious.

Carl said she played too much and started laughing, making a mental note that Van was a little jealous.

When he dropped her off the next day, Mrs. Howard was standing on the porch. He got out of the car and walked Van to the porch. He spoke to Mrs. Howard, nervous because this was not normal to him. She told him to pull his car in the backyard and invited him in. He pulled into the backyard driveway and walked to the kitchen door. Carl was shocked when he went inside and there was a full meal cooked. The table had meatloaf, yams, macaroni and cheese, and corn bread.

Van said her mother cooked dinner for them and hoped he would stay and eat. He jumped at the idea; he was starving and thinking about where he could go to get something to eat. He sat down, and Mrs. Howard said grace over the food. She asked him a lot of questions, and he learned a lot about Van's family in the process. Her mother was from Memphis and had been in Detroit a little over seventeen years. Her husband moved them there to help his brother run his restaurant. Van's mother said she could tell he was raised right and was a solid young man.

Carl finished eating and thanked Mrs. Howard for dinner. She invited him to be there every Sunday if he wanted. He said he would think about it, and Mrs. Howard said he could tell Van. He walked out of the dining room and to the porch, standing there talking to

Van. She asked if he would pick her up when he got off work the following day. He didn't commit, instead saying he would give her a call. Van knew he talked to Michelle at seven o'clock every night and wanted to get in the way of that. She had already caught feelings; she liked him and did not regret spending the night with him.

The next day at work, Carl could barely keep his focus because he was so sleepy. All he could think about was going to sleep when he got off work. When he drove up to the house, he could see someone sitting on the front porch. He saw it was Felicia and wondered how she got over there. He pulled into the backyard and parked, then walked around front. Felicia ran over to him and kissed him on the mouth. He broke the kiss, asking what she was doing there. He was shocked when she said she caught the bus to see him, hoping he would take her home.

Felicia was shocked when Carl said he was tired and wanted to go to sleep. He offered to take her home then, but she wanted to stay a little while. Carl said he would take her home because when he went to sleep, he was done.

Eric was standing on the porch, about to knock on the door, when he pulled up to the curb. When he saw Felicia in the car, he walked out to the curb, where they were. He asked Felicia what the hell she was doing in the car with him. He listened as Felicia said she was at Van's house when he came by and gave her a ride home. She jumped out of the car, thanked him, and said she would see him later.

Carl popped the clutch, and the Chevelle leaped from the curb. Fifteen minutes later, he was back at home, taking a shower. The phone rang as he came out of the bathroom, and he let the machine pick it up. He was shocked when Michelle's voice come over the machine, and picked up. She asked what he was doing, and he said he just finished his shower and was really tired, so he was going to lie down. She asked if he was mad at her, and he said he was not.

Michelle said she wanted to make up for hanging up on him and apologized. He accepted her apology, and they talked about a lot of things. He was glad to hear she had summer school under control and was passing her classes. They talked for about thirty minutes and hung up when Carl fell asleep on the phone. He didn't know how to approach the situation with Michelle since he had sex with Van. This was on his mind when he woke up, and he did not know what to do. He knew he sure could not ask Rachel—she was going to freak out if she found out.

He decided to keep this to himself; that was the path of least drama and blowback.

The phone ringing shook him out of his thought process, and Michelle sounded happy when she asked if he woke up. It was 11:30 p.m. He had been asleep four hours. He and Michelle talked about things in Detroit, and she was curious about what he was doing. When she talked about how big the city was, Carl said the city got real small some of the time. He told her about the white Duster and how he had seen it several times. He told her most of the people buying gas where he worked were regular customers.

The next morning, he went to work and Van drove through with Mrs. Howard. He pumped their gas, and Van stood outside, talking to him, wanting to know why he didn't pick her up the day before. Carl explained that he went home and went to sleep because he was tired. He asked if he could pick her up when he got off work that evening. She smiled and said she was waiting for him to ask. He stepped to the window and asked Mrs. Howard if he could pick Van up when he got off work. She smiled at him, saying he could, and thanked him for pumping their gas.

Van called later in the day, and Carl thought she was canceling the date, but she said he should pick her up before he went home.

When Carl got off work, he picked Van up, picked up Chinese food takeout, and rolled home. They ate the Chinese food and played dominoes. Van was a good domino player; she had learned in Memphis during the summers when she went there.

The next four days, Carl went to work, picked Van up, and went home. They spent the evenings hanging out and spent the nights having sex. She cooked three of the days, and she was a decent cook.

He was dog-tired when he got up Friday morning, getting ready for work. Bradley called him to his room and asked when Van moved in. He explained she had not moved in, and Bradley interrupted, saying she was squatting. His hair was blown back when Bradley said,

"The lil hooker needs to go." He agreed and said he would figure out a way to handle it. Bradley went back in his room and closed the door, and Carl finished getting ready for work.

When he dropped Van off at home, he cut the car off, saying they needed to talk. She looked at him as he said he was not going to pick her up tonight. Van didn't ask why and said, because he had been enjoying her all week, the weekend was their time to hang out. She looked at him, saying he *really* needed to pick her up tonight and tomorrow night. He gave in and said he would pick her up at 7:30 p.m. She said, "Pick me up when you get off work like all week." He popped the clutch and, ten minutes later, drove up at work. His energy level picked up, and the day passed quickly.

Bill closed the station at 5:00 p.m. He had some repairs he wanted to focus on. Carl went to Van's house, and she met him on the porch, smiling. She had just gotten out of the shower and had her robe on. They went in the house, and he spoke to Mrs. Howard. He was shocked when Van told Mrs. Howard his dad was mad at him and he needed a place to stay for a few days. She smiled when her mother agreed he could stay a few days. She dressed, and they went to Bradley's house so Carl could shower and dress. When he came out of the shower, Van was in the bed, and he slid in next to her.

They dressed and headed out to Belle Isle at 8:30 p.m. Van had tickets to a concert at the Amphitheatre. When "Dream Maker" by New Birth came on, he showed her how they danced in Texas. She laughed and called it "grinding" on each other, saying they did the same thing in Tennessee. After the concert, Van yawned when she said she knew he was tired. She suggested they go to sleep. He hit the Lodge Freeway, wondering what he should do. Van's mom had asked them to spend the night with her. Van smiled as she said her mother really liked him, and she liked him a lot too.

He pulled up in the yard at Van's house, and she directed him to the backyard driveway. They got out of the car, and he set the alarm/kill switch on the Chevelle. Van stuck her head in her mother's room to let her know they were back and went to her bedroom.

They woke up the next morning to pancakes and pan sausage. Carl and Van went downstairs at 10:30 a.m. and thanked her mother for breakfast.

CHAPTER 27

Carl and Pam Meet for the First Time
#ISHBoutToGetMessyII

Carl cranked the Chevelle and backed down the driveway to the street. A few minutes later, he pulled into the backyard driveway at Bradley's house. He and Van watched TV in the den for a couple of hours, then rode out to the house of one of her cousins. She was shocked he could play basketball as she watched him play her cousins. Later that evening, they were at Bradley's house, getting ready for a party. She told him Felicia and Eric would probably be at the party they were going to. He said he might not need to go; he and Eric might be beefing.

Van knew what the drama was about and asked what it was with him and Felicia. She said, "It seems you guys are old friends, but you also seem to barely know each other." He explained how they used to ride ten-speed bikes together several summers ago and he'd known her for, like, five years. Van's expression changed as she said, "You guys really did ride ten-speeds together?" He looked at her, saying they rode on the slab from Schafer to Greenfield and back. She looked at him and asked, "Have *you* had sex with Felicia?"

Carl laughed, saying, "A gentleman does not kiss and tell."

Van was mad she did not get an answer to her question, and his expression did not give him away.

They went to a matinee at Northland Mall, then on to her house at 3:30 p.m. They took a nap, waking up at 8:00 p.m., showered, and were rolling toward the party at 9:30 p.m. He told Van if Eric started beefing, they would have to leave. They pulled up to the party at 9:45 p.m., and Felicia was standing on the sidewalk. Carl laughed, saying, "I need to ask what it is with you and Felicia. Are you friends or what?" His reaction was "Oh" when Van said she tried to have sex with all her boyfriends.

Van said, "Felicia has been telling anybody who would listen about this guy in Texas, and everybody thought she was lying. The day we pulled into the Shell station where you work and she said she thought she knew this guy, we knew she was tripping." Van said she and McAdoo listened as she said, "Ya'll remember that guy from Texas I told ya'll about? That's him." She said they were shocked again when he remembered her and told the same story she did about the fall off the bike. Van laughed as she said, "And you were every bit as good-looking as she said you were!"

Van said she had been off her game since the moment he shook her hand. She said, "What sealed the deal for me was when you had the name she said, Carl." They got out of the car and walked up the sidewalk to Felicia. She hugged them, saying she was outside because there was nobody at the party. Fifteen minutes later, Felicia got in the car with them and they left the party. When Van asked where she wanted to be dropped off, Felicia said she was riding out with them. Van rolled her eyes at Felicia and said he should head to Lauder Street.

Carl decided he didn't want to be in the middle of this and rolled by a house party Bradley invited him to. They pulled up to the house on Freeland, off Six Mile. They walked in the backyard and saw people of all ages. There were a lot of people at this party, and Carl had met a lot of them. Felicia and Van knew a couple of people there and danced with a few of the young men. Carl watched Van talking to a guy when Felicia walked over and said, "She having sex with him." He looked at her, asking how she knew, and Felicia said she knew all the guys Van was having sex with, including him.

His mouth fell open, and he didn't say anything. She kept talking, saying Van wanted every guy she talked to and tried to have sex with them. Felicia laughed when she said the day they saw him at work, she knew Van was going to have sex with him. Carl watched as the guy French-kissed Van, and thought, *I was riding that a couple hours ago, and now he tongue-kissing her!* Felicia saw this and asked if he still thought she was tripping. She looked at him, saying, "Truth be told, she not your girl." He thought about it. She was not his girl, *and* he had a girl in Texas.

Van walked over to them with the guy in tow, introducing him as Derrick Dunlap. Carl shook his hand, and Derrick mentioned Van said he was from Texas. He said he had a cousin who attended Wiley College. Carl said he was from Marshall, and Derrick wanted to introduce his cousin to him. Although Derrick was having sex with Van, the more they talked, the more Carl liked him. He said his cousin would be at the party later; this was where she lived. Carl found out Derrick was first cousin to the host and he was there to help celebrate her birthday.

He spoke to Felicia, saying it was good to see her. Felicia was hanging off Carl as they danced and had fun. Bradley showed up at the party a little after midnight, and Carl found out he was dating Derrick's aunt Janie! He was ready to leave about 1:30 a.m. when Pam walked in the backyard. Derrick saw her and stopped him, saying his cousin who went to Wiley had come home. Derrick came around the corner with his cousin Pam, a tall slender young woman with a muscular build. She stood next to Derrick as he introduced her, holding out her hand, saying her cousin said he went to Wiley.

Carl corrected her, saying he didn't go to Wiley and he lived in Marshall. Pam asked where he went to school and was shocked when he said Marshall High. Derrick asked if she knew where Marshall High was and she said it was right up the street from Wiley. He told her he would be a senior when school started and he played football. She laughed, saying, "Ya'll didn't do too good last year." He laughed, saying they didn't and he got beaten half to death before the year was over. They all laughed when Carl said they planned to do better this year.

Pam said Derrick played for Mumford and asked what position he played. Carl said he was a linebacker and smiled when Derrick said he was a running back. He listened as Derrick said he had 1,283 yards rushing last season as a junior.

Bradley came over to the group and introduced himself as Carl's father. Pam said she never knew he had a son this old. Pam said she saw they were leaving and was not going to hold them up. He rolled away from the curb, trying to get his bearings down.

He had been beefing with Van about riding with them, saying she needed to stay at the party with Derrick. She insisted she was going with them and got in the car when he opened the door. Felicia sat on the front seat under him, and Van sat next to the door. He wanted to get to Greenfield and Grand River so he could take Felecia home. Felicia asked him to stop at one of the party stores so she could get a pack of cigarettes. When he stopped at the store, Van let her out and slid under Carl. Ten minutes later, they pulled up to the curb in front of her house. Felecia laughed, saying she wasn't ready to go home. Van laughed sarcastically, saying she didn't have to go home, she just had to get out the car with them.

They were startled when she screamed—Eric had walked up on her in the dark. Felicia yelled at him, saying he scared her. She asked why he never made it to the party. Eric said he couldn't get a ride and didn't have a way to tell her, so he came to her house. Van said he needed to get help, waiting for people in the dark. Eric in the dark had rattled Carl, and he sat there a moment to get himself back together. Van snuggled up to him, saying, "I know you glad I was with you now. It would have been drama with just you and her."

He didn't acknowledge her but knew what she said was right. He cranked the car and headed to Van's house and dropped her off. He pulled up to the curb and waited for her to get out of the car. Van kissed his neck, saying she was not going in the house alone. Carl mentioned she just got through slobbing Derrick down. She laughed, saying she would brush her teeth and then she was going to slob him down.

When they woke up the next morning, she asked what Felicia had told him. He looked at her saying Felicia told him she and

Derrick were having sex. Van admitted she had sex with Derrick in the past but said he was not her boyfriend.

He followed his instinct and paused, listening as Van explained her relationship with Derrick. He smiled to himself. She gave up way more information than he would have asked. She melted down, saying how much she hated Felicia and the way she always tried to fuck the same guys she was fucking. Carl laughed and said Felicia said the same thing about her. She lost it, saying that was a damn lie. Felicia really could lie!

That evening, Van wanted to ride out to Belle Isle, just to see if there were a lot of people there. Carl didn't want to ride out; he wanted to go home and get ready for work the next day. Van was pissed when he would not let her go with him, asking what was wrong. She looked at him as he said everything was good; he just needed a minute to himself. A few minutes later, he pulled into the backyard driveway on Sorrento and locked the car. Bradley was in the den, watching TV when he came in. They talked, and Bradley said the women in Detroit were very aggressive; Carl needed to get used to it. When Carl asked why he said that, he laughed, saying he saw the two "little hookers" he had with him last night.

Later that evening, Carl and Van rolled back to Bradley's house from Belle Isle. Bradley pulled him to the side saying, "It is evident that both Felicia and Van are feeling you." He reached in his pocket and pulled out a sheet of paper, saying, "Pam sent her number and said to call her tonight." He told Carl Pam was a nerd girl and she did not date—that he knew of. He took the number and said he would give her a call.

At 7:00 p.m., he called Michelle and was shocked she had an attitude. It hit him a second later: he hadn't talked to her in a week! She questioned him, and the best Carl could come up with was that he'd been working. Michelle wanted to know why he could not tell her what he had been doing for a week.

Carl assured her he was working and the days just ran together. Michelle was crying and said he was having sex with Felicia. She stopped crying when he changed the conversation to summer school. For the first time, he saw the vision Michelle laid out. If things worked out, this time next year, he and Michelle would have an apartment together. He told Michelle he was looking forward to being home in a few weeks.

He called Pamela later that evening and was surprised how direct she was with him. He thought about what Bradley just said about Detroit women being aggressive.

He found out she was going to be a sophomore at Wiley in the fall. He asked if he could pick her up after work one day this week, and Pam said he could. She called her soror who was from Marshall and got the full info on Carl. When he picked her up Thursday, they rode to Palmer Park and parked. Pam said he was quite popular; he had two girlfriends in Detroit and one in Texas. They went back and forth about an hour when Carl cranked up and headed up Seven Mile. He pulled in the driveway on Sorrento and invited her inside, laughing when she said they were not going inside to have sex.

They played Spades and talked for a couple of hours. It was getting late, and he needed to take her home; he needed to sleep for work. She asked if he was kicking her out, and he laughed, saying if she wanted to look at it that way, she could. They walked to the car, and Pam said she did not really want to go home. She called her mom to say she would be gone for a few days, then went upstairs with Carl. Bradley had bought groceries and told Pam what Carl's favorite foods were. While he dressed for work, she asked what he wanted her to cook that evening.

She got an invite to a yard party on Saturday night and asked if he would take her. He picked up the cue and said he would be happy to be her date for Saturday night. He asked what the dress code was, and she said jeans were fine. He could barely focus at work. Another girl was in his bed, and he knew he needed to call Michelle at 7:00 p.m. It was a busy day, and he was tired when he got off work at 6:00 p.m. It felt good to have a home-cooked meal, and he enjoyed the meatloaf, yams, corn bread, and Kool-Aid. He took a hot shower and lay across the bed about 7:30 p.m.

He woke up when Pam rolled over on top of him and kissed him on the mouth, smiling when he rolled over on top of her, kissing her neck. He looked at the clock, and it was 11:30 p.m.—he had forgotten to call Michelle! He worked all day Saturday and got off at 5:00 p.m. Pam cooked burgers and fries and asked him to shower while she cooked. He noticed she was already showered and wore a duster while she set up the kitchen. They pulled up to the party at 11:30 p.m. and saw there were a few people there. There were a lot of Pam's friends there, and she introduced him as her "friend" from Texas.

She hung off Carl, wanting her friends to know he was her date. They hit an after-hours joint when they left the party, and it was 5:00 a.m. when they made it back to Bradley's house.

The next morning, she woke up and cooked breakfast. She felt herself falling for Carl. When he came downstairs, Pam asked if she was his girl. He was not expecting this and did not know how to tell her he had a girlfriend. Carl didn't answer and instead fixed a plate. Pam pushed him for an answer; she really wanted to know. She went the other way, asking if he had a girlfriend in Texas.

He blurted out that he did have a girlfriend in Texas and they were serious. Carl told her he had given her a promise ring and they were making plans to get an apartment next year when they went to college together. The room went silent when she asked why he did not tell her this before she had sex with him. He shrugged his shoulders and said he did not know. He said he was not trying to deceive her; things just happened so fast he forgot to tell her. She asked if his girlfriend went to Marshall High, and he said she didn't. Pam let it drop, her feelings having been hurt enough.

Carl intuitively got up and went over to Pam, kissing her sensuously as he said he never meant to hurt her. Pam was crying. She had let herself catch feelings for him. She fell in his arms and followed him upstairs and dropped the duster to the floor as she climbed back in his bed. He took her home that evening and sat with her family for a couple of hours. Everyone was shocked. Pam didn't date, and she had fallen headfirst for this guy! When he left at 6:30 p.m., she asked if he was going to call his girlfriend. He said he was, and Pam said she understood.

The next week went great. Carl talked to Michelle every evening and did not speak to Pam or Van.

He got off work Friday evening and pulled into the backyard driveway and yelled, "Fuck!" when he saw Felicia sitting on the steps to the den. He saw her bag when she walked toward the car. When he got out of the car, Felicia told him she was *not* going home. "So don't mention that." He asked where Eric was, and she said forget about him since she had broken up with him. She followed him in the house, asking why he was so cold to her. He told her having a boyfriend who acted like he was crazy would do that. Felicia asked him to let that go; she had broken up with Eric.

He asked why she acted like she didn't know him when they stopped for gas. Felicia said she felt like if he was in Detroit, he would call her; that was why she was unsure. At that moment, she said, "If you in Detroit, *always* call me."

They watched TV, and at 9:30 p.m., she called her mother to tell her she was not coming home. He could hear Alice screaming in the background when Felicia said she was staying with Carl. He was really shocked when she asked, "Are you with that boy from Texas whose daddy used to fuck the bitch two doors down?" He listened as Felicia gave her the address and phone number.

She asked her mother to not come for her; she was not going home. Felicia said she would call every day and let her know she was okay. Felicia handed Carl the phone, saying her mother wanted to speak with him. He got an earful from Alice, including her saying she was going to call his mother. She slammed the phone down and found an old phone bill with Rachel's number and immediately called her. Hannah answered the phone, and Alice asked to speak with Rachel. She called Rachel to the phone and listened for her to pick up.

When Rachel picked up and said hello, Alice screamed, "Your son kidnapped my daughter!"

Rachel said, "Hol' up. First off, who is this?"

Alice identified herself, and Rachel immediately remembered the drama she had with her about the long-distance phone bill. She said there was not a chance he kidnapped the "lil hooker," and Alice didn't appreciate her saying that. Hannah's mouth fell wide open when Alice said Carl was having sex with Felicia and her best friend, Van. This was too much for Hannah, and she said, "Oooohhhhh."

Rachel yelled at her to hang up the damn phone and bring her nosy ass in there with her. She went back and forth with Alice for an hour before she said she would call Bradley and let him handle it. When Alice said she doubted Bradley would handle it, Rachel asked why she didn't just go get her daughter. They cursed each other out and hung up. Rachel called Bradley's house, hoping Carl would pick up the phone. When he picked up, Rachel cursed him out, and Felicia heard his mother call her a "lil hooker." Carl side-eyed Felicia when she started to scream in the background.

She heard every word when Rachel said he needed to take her ass home before this bitch forced her to come to Detroit and clown. He had never heard his mother talk this way. It made him nervous. He agreed to take Felicia home, and she shook her head to say she was not going home. She politely took the phone and said hello to Rachel. Felicia said she didn't want her son to lie to her, so she was telling her she was not going home. She told Rachel she wanted to put them on three-way with her mother to get this worked out.

Felicia put Rachel on hold and dialed her number at home. When Alice answered the phone, she said she was going to put them on three-way. She clicked Rachel back on and said they were all on the phone. Rachel was shocked when Felicia told Alice she was going to stay at Carl's house for the next few days. She told Rachel he did not kidnap or force her in any way. Amazingly, Felicia was able to get both women settled down, and they hung up the phone.

Hannah heard every steamy detail of what her brother was doing in Detroit; it sounded like he was working and having sex with two girls. Rachel was shocked to find Bradley had given Carl total access to the Chevelle. She cursed louder when she realized Bradley had little to no supervision of Carl. When Rachel cooled down, she looked at Hannah and said, "What goes on in *this* house, stay in *this* house." Hannah knew this meant she better not tell Jackie, but they both knew she could not keep this.

Rachel started to cry when she realized Carl had broken Michelle's heart. She was overwhelmed and went to her room to cry, not able to wrap her mind around her son having sex with two girls in Detroit.

When Hannah saw her go in her room, she immediately called Jackie. When she came to the phone, Hannah filled her in on the salacious details of Carl's mess. Jackie was shocked and her mouth fell open when Hannah said he was having sex with two girls in Detroit. She asked if Michelle was still a friend, because this was something they could *really* smack her with. Jackie laughed, saying they were not that friendly and she needed to know.

Jackie had an ulterior motive for wanting Michelle to find out and figured this was still summer. "We can get her back before basketball season starts."

Meanwhile, he and Felicia laughed as they ate dinner and remembered riding the ten-speeds on the freeway slab before it opened.

They watched TV and fell asleep on the couch. Carl woke up at 11:30 p.m., saying he was going to take a shower. Felicia took a shower after he finished and slid in the bed beside him. He listened as she said she had wanted to do this since he carried her home when she fell off her bike. He rolled over on top of her and kissed her neck as she cried tears of joy.

The next morning, he woke up for work and told Felicia he needed to drop her at home. She said she was going to stay and would be there when he got off work. She smiled, saying he could call Michelle at 7:00 p.m. She would be quiet.

Rachel had calmed down and told Hannah she had better keep this to herself, her brother in Detroit acting a fool. She thought to herself, *Too late. I've already told Jackie.*

Later that day, when Rachel was throwing Carl's route, she called Michelle. She listened patiently as Michelle told her about the challenges of summer school and Carl not calling her. Hannah could not hold it any longer and said he couldn't call because he was too busy with Felicia and Van. By the time she finished, Hannah had provided Michelle with every salacious detail of Carl's behavior in Detroit.

When Carl got home from work, Felicia had cooked pork chops, yams, corn bread, with mac and cheese. He was not shocked when she said Bradley had not been home all day. He called Michelle at 7:00 p.m., and his hair was blown back when she cursed him out and hung up. When he called back, she asked why he lied about fucking Felicia. At that moment, he knew Hannah had told her every detail. When he didn't say anything, Michelle cursed him out again and hung up. Felicia had witnessed the argument and thought this was the best thing that could have happened for her.

The week flew by, and on Saturday, Carl was ready to go home. He told Bradley to get his ticket so he could fly home. He was arguing with Michelle and didn't want her to break up with him. Bradley said that was cool and he would get his ticket and leave on Tuesday. He took Felicia home, and her dad was standing in the yard when he pulled up to the curb. Ray walked to the car and cursed her out, saying she needed to go in the house. He asked why he kept her nine days, and Carl said she would not come home.

He had met Carl in the past and believed him when he said this. He invited him in the house, and they played a couple hands of dominoes. Carl was nervous. He felt Ray was pissed with him. Ray said he needed to make a run and asked if he would stay until he got back. He agreed, thinking Ray wanted to talk to him. An hour later, Ray walked back in the house and sat down, talking to Carl. Ray offered a beer, but Carl refused and kept playing dominoes. Ray lit a joint and offered him a drag, and he took it. He smoked weed with him and played dominoes for a couple of hours. Carl got the feeling that something was going on, but he could not put his finger on it.

Alice walked in the house about 6:30 p.m., and Ray pulled out a joint, lit it, and took a deep drag. Carl could not help but think this was getting really weird really fast. Ray asked Alice how she did bowling in Chicago over the weekend. Alice said things went well but she didn't win any trophies. Ray asked about Terri, Diane, and Shelia, how they were doing. Alice looked at him and said they were fine and asked where he was going with this.

Ray walked up on Alice and slapped her, saying, "They in the hospital. Try again, bitch!" Alice started crying when Ray said Terri,

Diane, and Shelia crashed Friday evening in Gary, Indiana, and were in ICU at a hospital in Chicago. He slapped her again, saying, "Bitch, I drove five hours Friday night thinking you were in the wreck!" Everybody listened as Alice said she left Friday evening with Allen, a guy on the bowling team. He slapped her again when she said she and Allen spent the weekend together at a hotel in Detroit.

Carl tried to stop Ray from beating Alice and finally got him pulled off her. He slapped her one last time, saying this was why he asked him to stay; he knew he would eventually stop him from beating her. He looked at Carl, saying, "If you wonder where our daughter got her hoe tendencies, she got it from her mother!" When Ray opened the door to go outside, Eric ran in the house and ran up on Carl. Blows were passed, and Carl knocked him down. Eric got up, and Ray said they needed to take that shit outside; he didn't want his furniture broken.

They went outside, and blows were passed again. Carl could see Eric was a better boxer than he was. They were pounding each other when Ray stopped the fight.

A second later, the Detroit Police drove up. Marsha had sneaked and called 911 while Ray was beating her mother. The police tried to sort through it and finally gave up. They took everybody's ID, and when they ran Eric, he had outstanding warrants. Carl thought it couldn't have happened to a better guy as they cuffed Eric and put him in the cruiser. He told the officers, if it was all right with them, he would like to go home.

The officers cleared him and he walked to his car. He popped the clutch, and the Chevelle leaped from the curve. As he drove home, he could not believe what he just witnessed. It was surreal. After the drama with Ray and Alice, he got run up on by Eric! Insult was added to injury when he realized he had a bloody nose and busted lip. He had had enough of Detroit this summer, he decided. He was going to tell Bill he was going back to Texas tomorrow. The ongoing argument with Michelle meant he had fires to put out when he got to Texas.

When he said it was his last day working, Bill asked if he would work until 2:00 p.m.; he could handle it after that. Business was brisk. It was car after car from 10:00 a.m. on. Before Carl knew it, 3:00 p.m. had come. Carl started to balance the register when a guy dressed in black with a ski mask ran in the office. He saw the gun and almost panicked until he said he was a US Marshal. Carl dropped the money and put both his hands in the air. The guy cuffed him and led him outside to the cruiser. The news was there, and this was the lead story at 6:00 p.m. and 11:00 p.m.: CHOP SHOP BUSTED IN NORTHWEST DETROIT.

It was August 11, and Carl planned to fly home the next day. When he was released into the general population, the first person he saw was Eric, and he ran up on him. Over the next hour, the officers separated them four times. When the guys asked what their beef was, they couldn't believe Eric was pissed because his girl spent a week with Carl. The guys in the pod with them put the brakes on the beef, telling him that was the game. Carl did a twenty-four-day stay at the Beaubien Hotel and was released the day after his eighteenth birthday on September 3.

CHAPTER 28

Carl Is Out of Jail
#HeStuckInDetroit

The court agreed to a release from jail but placed a fourteen-day administrative hold on Carl. Rachel was furious when she found Carl had been released from jail and placed on a fourteen-day administrative hold. Bradley's friend Norma, who was acting as Carl's counsel, told them this was normal. The court asked he be enrolled in school during this time, and Bradley enrolled him at Mumford.

Carl could not believe he was stuck in Detroit. His first day at school, he bumped into Derrick in the cafeteria. He said he'd seen the news and was glad he was out.

Derrick told the coaches they had a guy from Texas enrolled who said he was a linebacker. He gave them Carl's name and got the full history of why he was at Mumford. They found out he was on an administrative hold and made the decision to give him a tryout. They played their first game on Saturday, and linebacker was one of their concerns. When he walked in the gym to the coach's office, they were impressed. They noticed he was tall, about six foot one, and a little light at about 155 pounds. The coaches were impressed with his physique—he was cut to shreds!

They sent him to the team MD, who gave him a clean bill of health, clearing him to play. That evening, he called Michelle, and she was truly concerned for him; she could not believe he spent twenty-four days in jail. She was devastated when he said they placed an administrative hold on him and he could not leave Detroit until the court released him. She was mad at him for the drama with Felicia and Van but wanted him home in Texas. After the small talk, she asked why he was still talking to Van and Felicia. At that moment, he knew what Riley meant: his mess was all the way in Texas.

Michelle said she was going to break up with him and hung up.

The next day, the principal at Mumford cleared him for football practice. The coaches looked at themselves when Carl said he was an outside linebacker in a 4–4 stack defense. They worked him out and found he ran a consistent 4.5 in the forty-yard dash. He was given instructions on where to be and what time to be there.

The next day, he reluctantly got up and got ready to play football. He talked to Rachel on the phone, and she was livid the court would not release the hold on him so he could come home. She wished him well in the game, saying she knew he was going to do good.

Bradley took him to the stadium, and the coaching staff breathed a collective sigh of relief when he ran on the field. He had not played football for Mumford, but the staff had a feeling he could play. They quizzed him about outside linebacker responsibilities, and he seemed to understand the position.

Carl listened as the announcer gave Derrick stats from last year. Carl didn't start, and after a couple of plays, it was clear Northwestern planned to run the ball on them.

The off-tackle dive was killing Mumford, and after the second score, Coach Hollins put Carl in the defensive lineup. He ran out on the field, the only player with his socks under his kneepads. After a couple of run plays up the middle were snuffed, the Colts ran a toss sweep and Carl read the play. He made a big time hit and forced the running back to fumble. Carl caught the fumble in midair and was a blur as he ran down the sidelines to score. This rattled the Northwestern players—a game they were firmly in control of had swung Mumford's way.

The coaching staff could not believe Carl's first tackle caused a fumble, which he recovered and returned for a touchdown! The Mumford sidelines were ecstatic, and one of the coaches yelled, "He a Hoss!" This energized the Mumford players. Northwestern had owned them for years! The Mumford players talked about Northwestern with respect, but Carl did not have that respect; he'd never played them. He turned in a stellar performance, twelve tackles, a forced fumble and recovery for a touchdown, and an interception return for a touchdown.

He hit the radar of scouts who had come to the game to see Derrick Dunlap. His performance was also stellar, rushing for 217 yards on sixteen carries and three touchdowns. After the game, three scouts stopped Carl as he was on the way off the field. They got his name and wanted to know where he played before he got to Mumford. He gave them his name and number, then ran to the field house. He saw Van on the way but remembered she was Derrick's girl and kept running. Bradley was waiting on him when he came out and congratulated him on the hella game!

Two cheerleaders waited on him and introduced themselves when he walked by. He stopped and talked to them, saying he would see them at school. He made it to the parking lot in time to see Van drive off with Derrick in the car.

Carl was a hit at Mumford. Anybody who kept up with Mustangs football heard about the standout linebacker from Texas. A few days later, he was watching the 6:00 p.m. news and was shocked when the sports segment came on and they profiled him. They led saying the Mumford Mustangs seemed to have landed a blue-chip linebacker in a move from Texas. The announcer profiled his stats from Saturday, saying he did not believe this was a fluke performance.

Felicia called, saying he was a celebrity; she saw the segment during the sports broadcast. She said her dad saw him on TV and called her in the room to watch. She asked what he was doing for the night and could not believe his mother had grounded him from Texas. She asked if he still thought she was lying about Derrick being Van's boyfriend. Carl laughed when Felicia said Van tried to make her look like a hoe when she was the hoe.

He didn't say anything, just kept his mouth closed.

The phone buzzed, and he told Felicia he needed to go; there was another call coming in. She asked if he was going to call her back, and he said he wasn't sure. He answered, and it was Rachel saying he better not let any of those fast-ass girls come over either. She started in on him, saying she could not believe Bradley had not supervised him better. Carl tried to remind her he got arrested for working in a chop shop. Rachel said she knew this. "And stop trying to turn it around!"

When Carl told her he made the news tonight, she said the only news she wanted to hear was that they released him to come home. Rachel settled down, and he mentioned Michelle broke up with him. He got pissed when Rachel said she told her to break up with him. Carl asked why she did this, and she said it was the thing to do. Rachel told him he was lowdown for having sex with *two* girls in Detroit knowing how Michelle felt about him. Rachel said she *thought* Bradley was bad, but he was going stronger at a younger age! He could sense she was pissed at him and asked why she was mad.

Rachel told him she raised him better than this and she hoped he would not be like all the rest. She said he might have had fun, but he crushed Michelle's whole world. Before she hung up, Rachel told him, "You *might* get her back, but the Michelle you fell in love with, you will never get her back."

An hour after he had hung up with Rachel, Carl was still thinking about what she said. He picked up the phone and called Michelle, and Mrs. Burns answered the phone. When he spoke and asked if he could talk to Michelle, Mrs. Burns said she did not want to talk to him.

He asked if he could leave her a message, and Mrs. Burns said he should give her time to come around. He asked Mrs. Burns to tell her he was sorry. He knew he had messed up; he had *never* called Michelle, and she wouldn't talk to him.

Monday afternoon in practice, Derrick turned upfield and lowered his pads on Carl, knocking him down. *Well, dayum,* he thought as he got off the ground and saw Derrick was smiling. Practice was different here; they went hard all practice instead of just during scrimmage. The offense ran the toss, and Carl lowered the boom on Derrick when he turned upfield. It got personal between them, and both knew it was behind Van. Derrick had never seen anyone with Carl's speed who hit like he did.

Watching Carl go head up with Derrick, one of the best backs in the state, let the coaching staff know the level of Carl's talent. One of the coaches thought out loud, "How the hell does this guy have to fight for playing time in Texas?" They realized there must be a deep talent pool for football in Texas.

The next week in school, his teammates quizzed him about playing in Texas. They were shocked when he said they faced a back like Derrick every game. They found it hard to believe he was an "average" player in Texas. Carl was shocked Marshall High had more students than Mumford; he thought the school was much bigger.

The Henry Ford Trojans were up this Saturday, and he was in a football-playing mood. Coach Hollins said he could read Carl pretty good and he seemed to have a vibe today. Derrick Dunlap had a big day, and Carl Hampton led the defense as Mumford rolled to a big win. Derrick turned in 277 yards, on nineteen carries and three touchdowns. Carl rolled up sixteen tackles, two fumble recoveries, and an interception for a touchdown. Carl was nicked during the game with a slightly bruised rib. This win by Mumford set the stage for an early season showdown with Cooley.

Pam called her aunt Janie and said Carl was a big deal in Marshall and people wondered why he was spending his senior year at Mumford. Everyone knew he was out of jail, but they didn't know there was an administrative hold on him. *The News-Messenger* picked up the stories from the *Detroit Free Press* and *The Detroit News*. It seemed he was making a lot of noise in Detroit.

Michelle started to soften her position, thinking he might not be coming home. She called Rachel and asked her to let Carl know it was okay to call her. Carl noticed he had not been cursed out in a minute; they were missing him in Texas. Before Rachel had chance to tell him, he called Michelle and she took his call. She said she was still angry with him but she wanted to talk to him. Carl said he was sorry again and said he hoped they could get past this. Pam told her cousin Derrick that Carl had a reputation as a hard hitter in Marshall.

The game against Cooley was a classic, and Carl turned in another stellar performance. He ended the game with fourteen tackles and a fumble recovery. Mumford got away with the victory, with Derrick scoring as the final horn sounded.

Everyone in Mustang Land was giddy. The Mustangs were 3–0 for the first time in a long time.

Felicia called to congratulate him on beating Cooley, and they talked for over an hour. She laughed when he said he was still grounded to the house. She said she quit Eric; he got sent to the penitentiary for the case he had. Carl asked how her mother and father were doing, and she said they were getting a divorce.

Felicia said she had seen it coming for a while and they seemed to be cool.

Carl said Bradley and Rachel had been divorced eight years. He said his court hearing was the following Tuesday, September 23, at the court downtown. Felicia wished him well, and he said he hoped they released the administrative hold on him. Felicia was not surprised when he said he wanted to go home; she knew he was homesick.

Later in the week, Carl stood in front of the judge and listened as Norma pleaded his case. The state had had the chop shop under surveillance since December, and Carl did not come to work there until June. The judge handed down his ruling: the administrative hold would be transferred to Texas. Carl smiled when the judge said he could pick up the paperwork on Friday.

They left the court, and Carl thanked Norma for handling his case. She reminded him it was not over; there was still going to be a trial. What they had to determine was whether he was going as a material witness or a defendant.

Bradley and Carl were home, talking, when the phone rang that evening. It was Janie, saying her mother died earlier in the day. Later that night, he called Pam and spoke with her. Pam said she was coming home and asked if he would pick her up from the airport. He was still grounded, but he agreed to pick her up from Detroit Metro the next day.

Pam caught a midday flight out of Shreveport the next day. When her flight landed, she was glad to see him waiting at baggage claim. He took her home, and she asked him to come inside with her. Her mom said she had everything set for Saturday morning at ten. Pam was hungry and asked if they could get Chinese takeout. They got the food, and she said her mother's house was full, then she asked if she could stay with him. She got the whole story of his case, and he said he was getting his case transferred to Texas on Friday.

When Carl said he was leaving Saturday, she asked if she could ride back to Texas with him. He agreed, saying they could work out the time they needed to leave. She cooked every day as they spent all their time together. They liked being around each other; they seemed to vibe together. She was standing next to him when the court handed him the paperwork to transfer the administrative hold. He was so happy he kissed Pam sensuously, and she knew they were having sex that night. She laid out her clothes for the funeral the next day and helped him with his.

They were showered and in bed by 9:00 p.m., rolling over on top of each other.

Mama Ruby's funeral was at 10:00 a.m., and they pulled up at the church at 9:45 a.m. Her mother thanked him when they walked up, saying she felt comfortable when Pam was with him. Van was there with Derrick, and Carl said hello as he walked by. After the funeral, he and Pam went to her mother's house to eat. Derrick came over and shook his hand, saying they needed to be safe on that trip back to Texas. He told Carl that Chevelle was one of the coolest cars he had ever seen.

He and Pam changed clothes and got ready for the trip to Texas. At 2:00 p.m., he and Pam rolled out of the driveway and he popped the clutch on the Chevelle. He was excited to be leaving. It had been over seventeen weeks since he was last in Texas. They pulled up to Six Mile and Freeland, then went east on Six Mile to the Lodge. He stopped at the light and went down the ramp to get on the Lodge. He hit the ramp at full speed, and they were on the way to Texas. Pam was good company and could read a map.

He hit the Ford Freeway interchange off the Lodge, headed west. When they passed Metro Airport, Pam said she saved $40 by getting a one-way airline ticket. She smiled when she said they were going to spend that getting a room tonight. He looked at her, asking, "We not going to drive all night."

Pam flipped it back on him, asking, Would he rather drive all night or roll over on her all night? His eyes said everything, and she slid closer to him. The first one hundred miles went quick, and they got off I-94 and on to I-69 in Marshall, Michigan. An hour and a half later, they pulled off in Fort Wayne, Indiana, for gas and rest their legs. They were on the schedule Pam set up for them, roll two hundred miles every three hours. It was 5:30 p.m., and they were just under two hundred miles out of Detroit. At 7:30 p.m., they rolled through Indianapolis and caught I-70 west.

At 10:00 p.m., they rolled into Effingham, Illinois, and stopped for gas. They had been driving eight hours, and Carl was tired. Looking at the map, they figured they were less than two hundred miles from Sikeston, Missouri. They called Bradley collect to give them a progress report. They rolled out on I-57 for the last leg of their trip at 10:30 p.m. At 1:00 a.m., he popped the clutch to downshift and rolled into Sikeston, Missouri. They found a room at Holiday Inn and got checked in. The desk clerk told them checkout was noon. Carl thanked him, saying he planned to use every minute of that time.

Carl went in the shower first and was shocked when Pam opened the door to join him. He felt refreshed when they stepped out of the shower to dry off. They climbed in the bed together, and he rolled over on top of her.

They were dead asleep when the alarm rang at 11:00 a.m. He turned the alarm off and rolled on top of Pam, kissing her sensuously. They showered and ran out of the room at 12:05 p.m. She put the map up and said she was ready to help him drive. He was more than happy to hear this—he could come off hyperfocus for a few hours.

He got Pam on I-55 and lay back for a while. He was surprised when she drove through Memphis; she had the hang of shifting gears. She said the Chevelle was a sweet car and she liked the way it handled. Carl was startled out a half-snooze when she shifted down and caught an exit, saying they needed gas. It was 5:30 p.m., and they were in Little Rock, Arkansas. She asked what his girlfriend was going to do when he got back to Marshall. Her ears perked up when he said she already broke up with him. She asked him if they could be friends even if they were not having sex.

They left Little Rock at 6:00 p.m., headed for Texarkana, Texas. Carl was back driving and asked Pam what being friends meant. She thought about it a second and said, "Come over to watch TV, play cards or dominoes, just hang." Carl said they could be friends but he was going after Michelle. Pam smiled, saying she knew this and that was cool.

At 8:30 p.m., they hit the I-30 and US 59 exit for the home stretch. At 10:00 p.m., they rolled on Wiley Campus and unloaded her bag at Dogan Hall. Pam held him for an hour, hugging and kissing him as they talked.

Carl smiled at her and asked, "Why you going to make me make a choice, Pam?" She laughed, saying she was not going to walk away or make it easy; he would have to push her away. She kissed him, saying she wanted to make sure he knew there was another girl who wanted to be his girlfriend. Carl gave her a grown-man answer when he said she should not do anything to break him and Michelle up, to let it run its course.

He pulled up in the driveway on Kingfish at 11:15 p.m. Rachel ran out of the house and hugged him. She had not seen him in over four months! She saw the difference in his demeanor and realized circumstances and the city had changed her son.

When Carl woke up the next morning, Riley was sitting on the porch. He smiled when he said, "That car is cool." Carl had to laugh when Riley said he left here riding a ten-speed and came back driving a cool Chevelle.

After football practice that evening, Carl drove to Jefferson and pulled up in Michelle's yard. She came out on the porch, standing with her arms crossed. He asked how she knew it was him, and she asked, "Who else would it be?" She asked what he wanted, and he said he wanted to talk.

He walked to the porch and stood on the steps, saying he was sorry for everything. Carl said he really messed up and didn't blame her for breaking up with him. Michelle started crying and opened her left hand to show Carl the ring box. He took the box and opened it to see the promise ring he gave her inside. Through her tears, Michelle managed to say, "The sad thing is, I still love you." He closed the box and took her hand, saying he would be a fool to take this ring back. Michelle looked at him when he said it was hers then, and it was still hers now.

She listened as he said, "It's up to you what you do with it, but I'm not taking it back." He put the box back in her hand and closed it. Michelle took the ring back and sat down on the steps, still crying as she looked at him. They sat there, neither of them saying anything. It was dark, and Carl knew he needed to head home. He asked Michelle what he should do with the chains. She mustered the strength to say he should keep them and do what he wanted with them. Carl walked down the steps and stood on the ground. He tried to read Michelle but couldn't see what she was feeling.

He pulled her to him, and she fell in his arms. Carl kissed her, and she opened her mouth to French-kiss him. Michelle sobbed as he held her, saying she needed some time. She walked up the steps and was in the house as Carl drove off.

The week flew by. September changed to October, and he was thankful Marshall High had an open date. He went to the Jefferson vs. New Boston game and watched Ronnie Simmons work his magic with the football. The shade started when the Bulldogs came off the field. Ronnie laughed, saying, "Oohh, lookee, it's the Michigan High School player of the year, *not!*"

When that fell flat, Ronnie said he was glad he was out of jail. Carl said he was glad to be out too, then asked if he had seen his cool car. Michelle said she had seen it and it was a cool car. This got Ronnie's goat, and he ran to the locker room, his attempt to shine Carl on totally backfiring. Jackie walked over to them and said hello. Carl hugged her. He was really glad to see her. Jackie said she was glad to see him, and he thought that, for a brief moment, the world made sense. The one person he went all the way back with was the only one not pissed at him.

He laughed and walked over to Michelle, whispering in her ear to ask if she wanted to go to Marshall. She looked up at him, saying he needed to talk to her mother. She got in the car, and he drove to her house and went inside. He spoke to Mrs. Burns and asked if Michelle could go to Marshall. Michelle had told her mom what she wanted her to do, and she agreed. He was shocked when Mrs. Burns asked if her baby was going to be crying when she came home. He said she was not going to be crying when she came back and he was sorry he made her cry before.

Carl looked at her, saying, "I made a mistake, Mrs. Burns, and I want to make up for it."

Mrs. Burns asked how he was going to unbreak her daughter's heart. He listened as she said, "We sat at my table, and I allowed you to court my daughter." She continued, "The two of you made the decision to take your courtship physical." Carl felt really bad when she said they were too young and she knew this was going to happen. She turned the tables, asking how he would feel to find out Michelle was having sex with two other boys.

This brought it home for Carl, and he understood how Michelle felt. He knew he would be up in his feelings if he found out she was having sex with two other boys. When Mrs. Burns said Michelle was confused right now, he understood because he was mixed up. When Carl said he was not going to do anything to make Michelle cry, Mrs. Burns said she had heard that from him before. Mrs. Burns turned and said Michelle was too weak to even think right now. She told him the next time Michelle came home crying, he was no longer welcome at her house.

He said he understood and asked if that meant Michelle could go to Marshall. Mrs. Burns didn't answer him, and Michelle said she could go. She explained her mother said what she was too weak and emotional to say. She grabbed his hand and said, "Let's go," and walked to the car with him.

As he drove to Marshall, she said her sister, Alicia said she should not give him away. Michelle started crying again when she said her sister told her not to break up with him until she was sure she was through with him. He listened as she said she was going to take her sister's advice and give him a second chance.

Michelle said he had to buy a broken-heart medallion and a chain to hang it on. They went to the Spring Street Community Center, but Michelle didn't want to go in, so they left and parked in Shasta's yard. As they talked, Carl said he was sorry again and leaned into Michelle to kiss her. When she didn't resist, he rolled over on top of her. She cried as she kissed his neck while they rocked their hips together.

The next day, Carl went to the jewelry store and bought a broken-heart medallion with a chain. When he called Michelle to ask about bringing it over, she said 7:30 p.m. at Shasta's house.

When Carl pulled up in the yard, Rachel asked when Bradley was coming to get the car. He looked at her, asking what she meant. She changed it over, saying, "When is your daddy coming to get his car?" Carl said he was not coming to get the car. Rachel asked how he was going to get back to Detroit. It dawned on him at that moment that Rachel did not know he drove to Marshall by himself. He thought, *This is about to get real weird.* He told Rachel he drove from Detroit on Sunday. She jammed him up. "I *thought* you left Saturday."

Carl backed up, saying he did leave Saturday and got there on Sunday. Rachel did not like what she was hearing and went in the house to call Bradley. He picked up the phone, and she screamed, "Why the *hell* did you allow our eighteen-year-old son to drive to Marshall by himself?" Bradley blew the lid off everything when he said Carl was not alone; Pam rode with him. Rachel asked who the hell Pam was, and Bradley said she was a sophomore at Wiley. She cursed him out, saying he let Carl drive all that way with a girl he did not know.

CHAPTER 29

Rachel Is Pissed Carl Drove from Michigan to Texas #ThatsABigConfederateFlag

Rachel cursed louder when Bradley said Carl met her before they rode to Texas together. The light came on when she remembered he spent the night on the road. She cursed Bradley out again and said she was not done with him about this. She slammed the phone down and called Carl in the house. When he walked up to her, she grabbed him by the collar and pulled him close to her. He was really nervous. She pushed him against the wall, saying, "I'm gon' ask you about your trip to Marshall, and *you* need to fess up."

When she was done questioning him, Rachel knew what time he left Detroit, everywhere he stopped, and whom he was with. She was beyond pissed when she found Pam spent four nights in bed with him. He screamed, "Mama!" when she said, "Give me the car keys." Hannah laughed when Rachel said, "Set 'em out, son, right now." Carl reached in his pocket and got the keys to the car and handed them to her. She called Bradley to scream and curse some more, asking, Didn't he think she should know Carl had a car?

Rachel cursed again when Bradley asked if Carl told her. She screamed in the phone, "Of course he did not tell me! If I hadn't asked, I *still* wouldn't know!" Rachel was livid but lowered her voice and said he really should have run this one by her. She asked Bradley if he knew the young lady Pam, and he said he did. He went on saying she was smart and planned to be an attorney when she finished Wiley. Rachel yelled at Carl to go get this girl; she wanted to meet her. Carl asked if they could do this some other time because he really needed to go to Shasta's house to see Michelle.

Rachel screamed again, saying she didn't care what he *thought* he needed to do; he needed to go get the "lil hooker" like she said. He asked about the car keys, reminding her she had taken them. She caught her breath and thought better of having him get the young lady. Carl asked if he could go to Michelle's house. He had something he wanted to give her. She told him, "Sure. Take the ten-speed." At first, he thought she was joking, but her expression said she was not.

Ten minutes later, he rolled up in Shasta's yard and pushed his bike to the porch. Michelle came outside and sat with him on the steps. She smiled when he showed her the broken heart medallion and chain. When he put it around her neck, she paused him long enough to put the promise ring on the chain. They went inside, and she explained the broken heart is her heart, broken because a promise was broken. Michelle said she wasn't mad and would not change anything about the way things happened. They sat on the couch and watched TV until Rachel called and said he needed to come home. Shasta gave him the message, and ten minutes later, he rolled into the yard.

When he walked in the house, he was happy Rachel seemed to have come to herself. She told him, "These last few months have been hella tough, and just when I thought it was about to get easier, the ride sped up." She handed him the keys, saying he could keep the car. She talked to him and said he was about to be really popular. "That is a really cool car." Rachel accepted the fact her son had matured and girls found him attractive. She hoped all the conversations about condoms had sunk in with him. Rachel turned to Hannah and said she better not mention Pam to anyone.

A couple of weeks later, basketball practice started, and Michelle was working into basketball shape. Their one-on-one sessions were more intense than ever. Michelle had learned to control the basketball and flowed smoothly into her moves. Carl had to play hard to beat her—her game was solid. The Mavericks closed out the season with the Tyler Lee Rebels, and neither team was going to the playoffs. It was a meaningless game.

The Black players on the Maverick team were shocked at the size of the confederate flag Tyler Lee flew. It took four people to handle the flag, and the game was a constant skirmish between the Black players from the Mavericks and the Tyler Lee players. Marshall built a huge lead, and the coaching staff benched the Black players after the half. They had never been called nigger so much in one game, and he was glad when the game ended.

When he walked off the field, Pam was standing by the gate. He forgot how cute she was until he saw her standing there. She smiled when she asked, "Where your girlfriend?" He looked at her, saying they played an out-of-town game in Hooks.

She invited him to a party in Seven Keys Apartments that one of her friends was having. He said he would go but needed to shower and change. He gave her the car keys so she could sit down while she waited. When he came out a half-hour later, the car was running. Pam had cranked it and turned the heat on. It was mid-November, and the temperature was in the mid-forties. He got in on the passenger side, and Pam shifted into gear and popped the clutch. The Chevelle jumped forward, and Pam headed to her friend's party. She wanted to show her friends the guy she was dating in Marshall.

They went in the apartment, and there were seven or eight girls and three guys at the party. They stayed an hour, and Pam said she was ready to go. He wanted to take her to the dorm, but she was not ready to call it a night. They parked at the juke joint around the corner from his house. He knew the spot, and they would have privacy there. They rolled the windows halfway down, and Carl leaned into Pam, kissing her. A second later, he rolled on top of her and she moaned as they rocked their hips together. Carl got her back to the dorm at 2:30 a.m. and rolled in the driveway at home at 2:45 a.m.

He ignored Rachel when he walked by her and she asked which one of the "lil hookers" he had out tonight. He asked if he could tell her tomorrow and closed the door to undress. Rachel yelled, "I got your 'Can I tell you tomorrow?'" then shook her head and went to bed.

Carl finished the football season with solid numbers, but the mumbling about his stay in jail bothered him. The police stopped him regularly, a Black kid with a cool car. Some of the people around him insinuated he might have stolen the Chevelle he was driving.

The kids at Marshall High didn't know what a kill switch was and had never seen a car with one. The girls at Marshall High heard about his girlfriends in Detroit and were curious. He had a cool car and a cool reputation, and like Rachel said, his popularity exploded. When he went to his car for lunch, there was always one or two girls hanging around, saying they wanted to "ride out." He remembered what Rachel said and kept them at arm's length; he really wanted to get back with Michelle.

His life had finally slowed down, and he took the time to enjoy his senior year in high school.

Ronnie and the Bulldogs didn't have the deep playoff run this year, so the girls basketball season was not interrupted. Michelle went with her family at Thanksgiving break, and Carl did not get an invitation.

Pam knew how to talk to Carl when it came to Michelle, to get him to give her the real deal. She asked if he was spending the holiday with Michelle, and he said no. She asked if she could come to Thanksgiving dinner with them, and he said yes. Thanksgiving Day, he picked Pam up at noon, and they rode around. He pulled up in the yard, and Riley was sitting on the porch, waiting for them to finish dinner. It was a good day to be outside. The temp was a great seventy degrees. They sat on the porch with Riley, and Carl introduced her as his friend from Detroit. Riley talked to them and realized this was the girl that rode from Detroit to Marshall with Carl.

Rachel came out to the porch to tell Riley dinner was ready and saw the young lady sitting next to Carl. She turned around, and Rachel saw it was her soror Pamela Matthews, who had just gone over the Friday before! She said, "Wow!" several times, unable to wrap her mind around the fact her son was having sex with a college girl. Rachel knew about Pam. She was a line sponsor in the sorority!

She never called Pamela "Pam," so it did not click with the similarities. Pam's mouth fell open when she made the connection that her boyfriend was her soror's son!

They walked in the house, and Rachel eased up next to Pamela, saying, "Don't get pregnant!" They walked in the dining room and enjoyed Thanksgiving dinner.

Carl went to the Jefferson girls basketball games on Friday nights. Michelle was having a hella season, and the Lady Bulldogs were rolling again. While Jackie provided stability for the Lady Bulldogs offense, Michelle was that wild card going off for between 20 and 30 points most nights. Coach Jenkins said in one of her interviews, "Michelle gets her points very quietly."

At the Christmas break, Michelle averaged 23 points a game and was being celebrated everywhere. The reporter who did the "Freshman Phenom" interview got an interview just before school dismissed for Christmas. He asked about Carl Hampton, her boyfriend from Marshall. Michelle smiled and said she and Carl were still friends and he was probably in Marshall. He followed up by saying, "You gave Carl credit for your game. Do you still feel that way?" Michelle said she felt very strongly that it was the one-on-one play with Carl that elevated her game to the level it was now.

The line of questioning changed, and the reporter mentioned she was on pace to be valedictorian of the senior class. They fleshed out during the interview how she had gone to summer school to graduate early. The question was, "Is this plan still working the way you wanted?" This was a hard question, but Michelle said the plan was still working; she was going to finish school a year early. When the next question came off, "Are you and Carl Hampton going to college at the same place?" she recognized the reporter.

This was Charles Davis, the guy they met a couple of years back at a senior party. She refused to answer any more questions about her personal life and said she would take a couple more questions. One of the reporters pulled out a publication that listed her as one of the top girl prospects in the region. Michelle said she had not seen that and had no comment. She ended the interview and went into the locker room. This was the last game before Christmas break, and Coach Jenkins said there were several big-school scouts in the stands.

Michelle went into Christmas break with a bang, putting up 31 points in the final game of the fall semester.

The next day, she called Carl, saying he should not get her a present for Christmas, to take her off his list. They talked for a few minutes, and he could not shake the gut feeling Michelle was letting him go. He talked to Riley about it, and he advised him to try to court her if he wanted her back. He told Riley that Michelle was keeping space between them. Riley reminded him how much his popularity had soared and the fact she knew he had sex with two other girls. He said that was *not* a good combination.

Carl was shocked when Riley said he was not surprised that he was right where he was. He asked Carl if Michelle was still having sex with him, and when he said she was, he said that was not a good sign. Riley explained that if Michelle was going to stay with him, she would shut him down until she was over this. He listened as Riley said that because she was still having sex with him, she was deciding to stay or go. He told Carl, "The girl is smart. She having sex with you, so there is no excuse to have sex with another girl." Riley told him that if he wanted to keep Michelle, he should *not* have sex with any other girl!

Carl took his advice and wanted to break it off with Pam, but she had already left for Christmas break. He called her in Detroit, and she was chipper when she answered the phone. When he said he and Michelle were getting back together, she asked why he was telling her, since they were just friends. She smiled, saying she was serious about her desire to be his friend. Pam said she understood his situation and was not going to complicate it. He thanked her, saying he was confused right then.

Spring semester started with a bang. Jackie had five consecutive games where she scored at least 30 points. Carl still went to the games but gave Michelle as much space as she wanted. He wanted to see Jackie play, but when Michelle got mad and asked him not to come, he respected her wish.

During mid-January, Michelle flip-flopped and seemed to be cool again. They started the Saturday-morning breakfast and talk sessions and went on dates every weekend. He shut Pam down and stopped taking her calls, and Bradley's attempt at intervention did not change his mind.

Michelle was feeling Carl again. Things were starting to feel normal. Tongues had stopped wagging, and the rumor mill had found another target. It was a plus he had this sweet Chevelle that was a borderline race car. The talk about him centered on the sweet ride he was driving instead of his time in jail or the girls he was boning. Michelle asked him to come back to the games, and they planned a big celebration for Valentine's Day. Carl's world seemed to level off, but he had a gut feeling he and Michelle were not going to make it.

Valentine's Day came, and they celebrated in Dallas. It was a Saturday, and they made reservations at the downtown Dallas Holiday Inn. Everybody was mad as hell when he and Michelle drove off, saying they would be back the next day. Carl called Rachel when they made it to Dallas to let her know he was safe. Michelle and Carl went by her sister Alicia's house in Oak Cliff. Their room was ready at 4:00 p.m., and they followed her downtown so they would not get lost. She hugged them when she left them to check in their room. They ate dinner at a Bonanza restaurant and went dancing at a downtown club.

They were having a really great time and felt really good. They got to the room at midnight and slid into bed, watching TV as they talked. Carl started to kiss her and rolled over on top of her. Michelle moaned and cried as she rocked her hips against his.

To their surprise, there was no drama when they went home; everybody was just glad they made it back safely.

Michelle finished the year gangbusters, and the lady Bulldogs made the playoffs. Mid-March came, and Michelle flip-flopped in a major way—she wanted to break up with Carl.

She called him, saying they needed to talk, and he knew what was up: she had made the decision to break up with him. Carl picked her up at Shasta's house, and they drove to the Spring Street Park. They sat on one of the benches in the park, talking. She started saying she loved him but she wanted her freedom. Carl listened as she said she loved the guy she got back from Detroit; he was aggressive and had experience having sex. But Michelle said she hated he got that experience with other girls instead of with her.

He took a deep breath, saying he felt they would end up doing this, and apologized for messing them up. He asked if it was okay to hug her, and she playfully slapped his arm, saying yes. They hugged, and she kissed him as the tears started to fall. Carl said he was going to miss her, and Michelle said she knew she was going to miss him too. She held up her leg, saying she would never have the C scar taken off her leg. They got up from the table and walked back to the car.

When Carl pulled from the curb, she asked if he would take her to Jefferson.

He listened to Michelle as he drove her to Jefferson. She invited him to her graduation. He drew the line there, saying he did not know if they could be friends since she had broken up with him. Michelle cut him to the core when she said, "I know. You can only be friends with Jackie." She thought out loud, "I wonder what she is going to do when she finds out we broke up." Michelle looked at him and asked if he thought Jackie would be happy.

Something Riley said to Carl hit him now: "Have class in everything you do, and remember, you messed this up."

He walked Michelle to the porch, and when Mrs. Burns came to the door, he said Michelle broke up with him. She didn't say anything; she was shocked Michelle broke it off with Carl. He apologized for making Michelle cry, and Mrs. Burns said she understood.

When Jackie walked by and spoke to them, Michelle got really petty. She called her over to them and said she had just broken up with Carl. This caught Jackie off guard, and she said, "You lying ya'll broke up!" Michelle nodded and walked in the house.

Jackie jumped in the car, and Carl asked her to get out. She knew it was real when she saw the tears in Carl's eyes. She asked him to take her home, and he asked her to let him go home; he was not feeling good. Jackie could see he was serious, but before she could get out, he cranked the car and backed out of the driveway. He dropped her at home and popped the clutch, and the Chevelle leaped from the curb. He blew as he passed Michelle's house, headed for US 59 and the fifteen-minute drive home. He saw her in the window waving as he passed by. What he did not see was, Michelle was in a full-blown cry.

The news that Michelle broke up with him beat him home. Jackie had called Hannah to ask if she had heard. Jackie knew she had hot-off-the-press news when Hannah did not know they had broken up. They talked a few more minutes, and she told her to ask him to call her. Jackie could not believe this. After all the drama and Michelle hanging on to Carl for dear life, she broke up with him! *I hope this bitch can keep her game up,* Jackie thought, as she was still in shock.

Hannah was finishing telling Rachel that Michelle broke up with Carl when he drove up in the yard.

Riley could see his demeanor was not good when he locked the car and walked on the porch. He looked close at Carl's face and could see he had been crying. He said, "She broke up with me," as he walked in the house. Rachel hugged him when he came inside, saying she just heard. Carl went to his room and lay across the bed. A few seconds later, the tears started to flow, and he cried himself to sleep. He missed the entire next week of school; he had no desire to go. He went to the bathroom, ate very little, and cried all the time.

Things were not any better at the Burns house. Michelle did not go to school the next week either, lying in her bed, crying. The Lady Bulldogs squeaked out the two games they played, and Jackie knew they needed her for the playoff run. She wondered, *Why this dizzy bitch break up with him now?* On the way home after practice, Jackie stopped by Michelle's house, and Mrs. Burns asked if she had come to gloat. She assured Mrs. Burns she had not; she was truly concerned about Michelle. She was cut when Mrs. Burns said, "You wondering if she going to get it together in time for the playoffs."

Jackie did not try to hide it and said, "Yes, ma'am. We are all concerned. We need Michelle for the playoffs."

Mrs. Burns called Michelle out of her bedroom, and she stepped out and saw Jackie. She asked Jackie what she wanted; she had already broken up with Carl. She cut right to the chase. "We need you to get it together, Michelle."

She looked at Jackie and asked, "Why? Ya'll can win without me."

Jackie took a deep breath and said, "No, we *can't* win in the playoffs without you, Michelle."

Her heart was melted; she was looking at Michelle, and Carl was not taking her calls.

She came from the heart, saying when she happened to walk by and found out she broke up with Carl, she was happy. She admitted it was petty of her to jump in the car with him at that moment. Jackie said she saw him crying as he dropped her off at home. Mrs. Burns listened as Jackie emptied her heart to Michelle, saying she was wrong to not allow them to have peace. Jackie said she did everything with Carl she had hoped to do. She wanted to give him her virginity. Jackie admitted she was mad at her and jealous of her; she felt she had taken everything she wanted.

Michelle listened as Jackie said she remembered the other time she saw him cry, when they were loading Ms. Rachel's furniture on the truck. She related how she played basketball with him, walked to school with him and Hannah, and them hanging out together. Michelle stopped her, saying, "Jackie, I was crushing on Carl then, but I let ya'll have peace. It was only after you broke up with him that I started to talk to him." Jackie said she knew this, and she respected her for that. She went a step further, saying they were different kinds of people.

Jackie finished by saying Carl was not taking her calls and he was in Marshall, doing what she was doing, trying to die. Jackie shocked Michelle and Mrs. Burns when she apologized and asked her to forgive her. Both their mouths fell open when she asked her to call Carl; she wanted to apologize to him too. Michelle picked up the phone, and when Janice answered, she caught her voice. She called Carl to the phone, saying Michelle was on the line. He jumped out of the bed and ran to the phone. When he said hello, Michelle said, "*Your* friend Jackie Hunt is on the other line and has something she wants to say."

Carl listened as Jackie apologized and said she had sown discord between them since he made her his girl. Carl accepted her apology and listened as she said they needed to get it together. He asked what brought this on, and Jackie said it was time to grow up. When they hung up, she hugged Michelle, saying the whole team wanted her back.

When Jackie left, Mrs. Burns said she believed her. She cautioned Michelle, though, saying when it came to Carl, all bets were off.

Rachel called Bradley and asked if he knew what they could do to help Carl bounce back. He was at a loss, saying perhaps it would wear off.

Janie was at Bradley's house when he had the conversation with Rachel and made a mental note to tell Pam.

The following Monday, Carl pulled himself out of the bed and went to school. Michelle did the same, went back to school the following Monday. Jackie embraced Michelle when she saw her at school, and the basketball girls said they were glad to see her. She started to feel much better, and her mind went to basketball. Coach Jenkins was happy to see Michelle at practice; she knew they needed her at the top of her game for their playoff run.

When Pam called home on Wednesday, her mom told her to call her aunt Janie. She wanted to talk to her about something. She rushed her mom off the phone and called Janie collect. She could not believe what she was hearing, that Michelle had broken up with Carl and he was sick behind it! Pam asked when this happened, and she said it was about two weeks ago.

That Friday, after her 11:00 a.m. class, Pam walked the five blocks to Marshall High School. She found Carl's car in the parking lot and was going to leave a note on it. Before she could leave, though, the bell rang, and he came outside. He saw her and hugged her, asking what she was doing at Marshall High. Pam said she heard Michelle broke up with him and she wanted to remind him there was another girl who wanted to be his girl. She asked him to take her back to the campus, and he said, "Cool." He dropped Pam off at Wiley and said he would call her that evening when he got out of school. When he got home, he spoke to Riley about his situation and asked what he should do. Riley suggested he call Michelle to make sure she was done before he started up with Pam.

He went in the house and called Michelle to find out if she was done with him. He knew it was over when Mrs. Burns would not call her to the phone. He called Pam and asked if that girl was still interested in being his girlfriend. She said yes, but only if he was sure he was not going back to his old girlfriend. Carl laughed, saying he did not think that was going to happen.

The playoffs started, and the Lady Bulldogs offense sputtered because Michelle was off her game. Coach Jenkins was concerned her team was in the playoffs on less than a hard roll; they were not play-ing their best ball. This was exacerbated by the fact Michelle was not getting her points. She knew about the breakup with Carl and won-dered how to get Michelle going again. Nobody believed Michelle when she said she was not feeling the best the last few weeks. The second round of the playoffs started, and Michelle found her stroke. The Lady Bulldogs rolled through the playoffs and were at the state tournament. They drove to Austin the day before the tournament, and Michelle was car sick. She thought of Carl when they stopped at a Bonanza restaurant in Austin to eat. Coach Jenkins felt good when Michelle ate a full meal, maybe it was carsickness.

The coaching staff got the girls bedded down early; they had an eight o'clock game the next morning. It was early April, and the girls had on their burgundy wind suits to fight off the morning air. Michelle felt queasy but didn't say anything. They tipped at 8:00 a.m., and this Houston-area team had their best defensive player guard Michelle. She was exploding and had 10 points by the end of the first quarter. During the time-out for the quarter change, the trainer gave Michelle a cup of water. She took one gulp and had to find a bucket to throw up in.

Coach Jenkins held Michelle out the second quarter, hoping she would be together by the time the third quarter started. When the horn sounded for the third quarter, Michelle had her strength and was ready to go. The Lady Bulldogs rolled through the tour-nament and won state! Michelle could barely stand for the awards ceremony—she was exhausted! Charles Davis, the reporter from *The News-Messenger*, asked for an interview, and Coach Jenkins stopped him, saying she needed some time. She said she would make the team available for interviews shortly. He knew something was up; Michelle did not seem to be herself.

He stopped her when she walked by him and asked for a date, saying he knew she broke up with her boyfriend. Michelle pulled away from him and cursed him. She looked at Jackie, saying, "That guy is creepy."

The next day, Jackie called Hannah and said she believed Michelle was pregnant. When Hannah asked why she believed this, she said she had all the symptoms she saw with her sisters when they were pregnant. The throwing up, not being able to hold food down, and feeling lethargic.

Carl heard about the state championship and sent Michelle a letter to congratulate her. She read his letter and called him, asking why he didn't call. He said, since his other calls did not go through, he didn't think she would take this one. They talked briefly, and he congratulated her again before they hung up. When he got word of the Jefferson sports banquet, Carl was sick Michelle did not invite him. Jackie broke up with Ronnie Simmons and invited him, but Riley would not let him accept. He was angry with Riley, but he promised he would thank him later. When he saw the Jefferson sports banquet pictures in the paper, neither Jackie nor Michelle had a date.

The Marshall sports banquet was a week later, and Riley said he should not take Pam; it was just too soon. He didn't take a date and was shocked to see Michelle in the audience. She had come to tell him she accepted a combination academic/athletic scholarship to SMU in Dallas. She hugged him, saying she was going to be right in Dallas, and asked him to not give up on them. She asked if she could kiss him, and he pulled her to him. Michelle felt the warm feeling in his arms as he French-kissed her. They broke off the kiss, and he reminded her she broke up with him.

Michelle smiled and pointed to the broken heart and promise ring around her neck. He said cool, that he would stay in touch.

The following Monday, Carl got two very important letters. The first was from Wayne County. A court date had been set. He was still confused about that. They had not announced charges against him, but he had to be in Detroit the first week of June. The second letter was from Wayne State. They wanted to offer him a combination academic/athletic scholarship. He showed the letters to Rachel, and she was happy about the scholarship offer.

CHAPTER 30

Carl's Girlfriend Name Is Pam
#HisCourtDateHasBeenSet

The information about his court case was so vague Rachel wondered if the folks knew what they were doing. She believed what he said about having no idea the gas station was the front for a chop shop. His court case was set for June 7, and she knew he needed to be in Detroit a couple of days early to prep with his attorney. Marshall High released seniors on May 25, so he had a few days before he had to leave for Detroit. Carl called Pam to let her know he would be coming back to Detroit; the court had notified him of the June 7 court date.

Rachel and Bradley worked together to get things worked out, and he left Marshall at 6:00 a.m. on the twenty-ninth, a Saturday. Rachel stood on the porch, crying, as he finished packing the Chevelle and cranked the car to leave. She could not believe that for the second time in less than a year, her eighteen-year-old son was about to drive over a thousand miles by himself. They worked out a system where he would call every five to six hours, when he stopped to get gas.

He walked back in the house and went to the phone. He called Michelle, and Mrs. Burns answered the phone. He asked to speak to Michelle and held his breath, hoping she would let him. He was surprised that after a short delay, an obviously sleepy Michelle said hello. He said hello and told Michelle he was getting ready to roll out to Detroit. He held his breath and asked if it would be okay if he stopped for a few minutes. Carl was happy when Michelle said she would be glad to see him before he left. They hung up, and fifteen minutes later, he drove up in Michelle's yard.

Michelle was standing on the porch when he pulled up and got out of the car. She invited him inside, and they stood in the hallway, talking. He apologized for hurting her and said he was really going to miss her. Michelle changed the subject, saying she hoped his court case turned out okay. He was moved when she said that and pulled her close to him. He whispered in her ear, "When you asked if I loved you and I said I didn't know, I didn't know what love was." She listened as he held her and said he knew what love was and he did love her.

Michelle asked him what love was, and he said it was being hurt because you hurt somebody. Carl said love was being sad because you wanted to call that person but you knew they wouldn't talk to you because they were hurt and angry. She kissed him and said she know he loved her, and that was why what happened hurt her so bad.

They heard the phone ring, and Mrs. Burns wondered who was calling this time of morning. Carl heard her laugh and say, "Yes, Rachel, he is here." A few seconds later, Mrs. Burns came in the room, saying Rachel wanted him to roll as he had a long drive.

Michelle said that if things went right, they might get chance to make the drive together. He pulled her to him and kissed her again and walked out the door. She stopped him on the steps, saying, "I don't hate you. And I still love you." He looked at her, saying he loved her too, and kissed her again.

The drive was going smoothly, and at 7:30 a.m., he rolled through Texarkana, Texas, and hit I-30. A lot of people complained about shifting gears on a long trip, but he loved the sound of the pipes as he gunned the Chevelle. Riley had taught him how to drive a stick when he showed him how to drive a tractor. When Riley saw he was responsible, he trusted him with his classic '56 Chevy Bel-Air Coupe, which was also a stick.

He rolled into Little Rock at 10:00 a.m. and filled the Chevelle with gas. He called Rachel, and she wanted to know where he was and how everything was going. Carol had a map, and he told her to color in Texarkana and Little Rock; he had gone through those cities. They talked a few minutes, and he stretched his legs. At 10:30 a.m., he hit the I-40 interchange and was on the way to Memphis, Tennessee. It was a warm Saturday, and traffic was not bad when he rolled through at 12:45 p.m.

He caught I-55 out of Memphis and headed north. At 3:00 p.m., he rolled into Sikeston, Missouri, and stopped for gas. He called Rachel to let her know he was okay, and she asked if he had eaten the sandwiches she packed. He said he had eaten the sand-wiches and was hungry again. He saw a Burger King across the street from the gas station and told Rachel he was going there to get a Whopper. She told him to be careful, and they hung up the phone. A few seconds later, Carl pulled up in the Burger King parking lot and saw a candy-apple-red Chevy Nova SS.

He parked a few spaces over from the Nova and went inside to get a Whopper. When he came out, he noticed there were four White guys standing close to his car. He left the alarm/kill switch on and stood watching them. One of the guys said the Chevelle was sweet and they especially liked the Cragar rims. He turned off the alarm/ kill switch and opened the door to get in. He located the .32-caliber pistol Riley had given him and saw it was loaded. He was very famil-iar with the gun as he had shot it numerous times with Riley.

He put his food on the passenger seat and said they had a sweet car too. One of the White guys walked toward him, and he made eye contact, saying, "*Don't* walk up on me. I *don't* know you like that." The White guy stopped in his tracks, saying he didn't mean any harm. He asked if Carl was from Detroit; he saw the Michigan license plates on the car. Carl was not in any mood to talk but said he was actually from Texas; the car just had Michigan plates. When he asked where he was headed, Carl said he was done talking and closed the door.

He had read the guy right. When he pulled out of the Burger King parking lot, they pulled out behind him. He stopped at a red light, and the passenger rolled down his window and asked if he wanted to run that shit. Carl laughed, saying, "You want to run a SS Nova against a Chevelle SS." He laughed harder when he said, "That SS Nova has a 283, and this Chevelle SS has a 396 with three hundred horses." The driver leaned forward, asking if he was insulting his car. Carl looked at him, saying he could take it any way he wanted. The light changed, and Carl popped the clutch, turning the tires on the Chevelle.

The SS Nova popped his clutch and turned his tires too, spinning off from the light. The Chevelle jumped five car lengths on the Nova off the light, and Carl saw the police car on the other side of the street. He saw the lights come on but also saw he was blocked by traffic. He mashed the Chevelle and ran up to ninety-five miles an hour when he saw the ramp for I-55 north. He hit the I-55 ramp, with the Nova SS a few car lengths behind. It dawned on him that these guys might not be locals, and he gunned the Chevelle down the ramp. He was rolling down I-55 at ninety miles an hour.

When the SS Nova got to the bottom of the ramp, he saw the police car at the top of the ramp. Carl knew this could be a bad situation, so when he rolled over the next hill, he hit the exit ramp. When he went across the bridge over the freeway, he saw the SS Nova go under on I-55, with the police car close behind. He kept driving west and ran across a big street that ran north and south. He took the big street and rode it for about fifteen miles.

He saw an interchange that said I-57 and I-55. Carl knew he had to go down here; this was a major intersection on his route. He stopped for a second, took a deep breath, and hit the I-55 and I-57 interchange. He was beside himself when he rolled on the I-57 ramp off the interchange and saw the candy-apple-red SS Nova. *I guess they really were not locals,* he thought as he went down the ramp to get on I-57 north. When he got close enough, he saw the SS Nova had Indiana license plates, and the four White guys were still in the car.

He gunned the Chevelle and rolled by them, watching in the rearview mirror as the driver pointed at him. For the next hour and a half, the SS Nova and Chevelle SS took turns chasing each other, often at speeds of ninety to one hundred miles an hour. Carl saw the sign "Effingham, 15 Miles" and was glad—the gas hand was riding empty. He saw the clock in the gas station where he stopped say it was 6:30 p.m. and filled up. He looked across the street at the Marathon station and saw the SS Nova. While he was on the phone with Rachel, the SS Nova came across the street and pulled up next to him.

The driver, the guy he had told to not walk up on him, asked where he was headed. Rachel heard the conversation and asked whom he was talking to, and he said they were guys admiring the Chevelle. She asked if everything was okay, and he assured her it was. A few seconds later, they hung up and he turned his attention to the White guy in the SS Nova. He kept talking, saying, "You got Michigan plates on your car and headed north, so you probably on the way to Detroit." Carl was shocked when the guy said they wanted to roll the rest of the way with him; they were headed to Fort Wayne.

The White guy in the SS Nova said, "I got a ticket, and that cop is looking for that black Chevelle."

Carl laughed, saying he got off the freeway before the cop could catch up to him. They introduced themselves, and the driver said his name was Robert. The SS Nova pulled out of the gas station first and hit I-70 east, headed to Terre Haute, Indiana. Carl saw an Illinois State Trooper sitting at the on-ramp for I-70 and waited a few minutes. He didn't have to wait long before the state trooper had a target and activated his lights to stop them.

He smiled to himself as he popped the clutch and went down the ramp to I-70 east. The SS Nova had a good five-minute start on him, but he felt the Illinois State Troopers were out there. He rolled the speed limit of fifty-five until he hit the Indiana state line, then ramped up to seventy miles an hour.

Half an hour later, at 9:00 p.m., he was rolling through Indianapolis, Indiana, and could feel Detroit getting closer. When Carl got on the interchange from I-70 to I-69, he saw a line of cars on I-69. Traffic rolled slowly for a couple of miles, and he spotted the SS Nova—he had caught up to them!

He rolled slowly with the traffic and pulled up beside the SS Nova. He read Robert's lips saying they were about two hours out of Fort Wayne. Traffic cleared, and they rolled hard right into Fort Wayne at 11:00 p.m. When he pulled off I-69 for gas, he noticed Robert was right behind him. This didn't alarm him; he figured they should be low on gas, just like he was. He filled up while Robert put $5 in the SS Nova. Carl told him it had been good rolling with him the last eight hours and he was indeed headed to Detroit.

Robert said he should have smooth sailing here on in; the police did not work traffic along that route. They shook hands and Robert introduced the three guys in the car with him. They understood his skepticism; he was traveling alone, and a car with four White guys rolled up on him. They shook hands once again, and he told Carl to be safe. He had about three hours left on his trip. Carl told him the SS Nova was a sweet car and that was the car he really wanted. Robert asked how he ended up with the Chevelle SS, and he said it was a long story as he got in the car.

He was dog-tired. It was 11:15 p.m., and he still had almost 150 miles to go. He popped the clutch and rolled down the ramp to I-69 north, headed for Detroit. A little over an hour later, at 12:30 a.m., he rolled into Marshall, Michigan, and stopped to stretch his legs. While he was stretching his legs, he called Bradley and said he was in Marshall, Michigan. He had never heard of it, and Carl said it was about an hour and a half away. He heard the loud music in the background and asked what they were doing. Bradley said he and Janie had a few people over and they were hanging out.

Bradley told him to slowly roll and bring it on and said there was somebody there who wanted to speak to him. A few seconds later, Pam came on the phone, saying hello. He told her he was a little over a hundred miles out and would be there in about an hour and a half. He asked if she would hang out and wait for him to get there. Pam said she would wait on him and told him to drive safely. They hung up, and Carl revved the Chevelle up and hit I-94 east. When he got to Bradley's house, the house was dark, and he thought everyone had left.

He pulled into the backyard driveway and let himself in the den. Pam came downstairs wearing a duster and said Bradley and her aunt had taken a couple of people home. He looked at the clock and realized it was 3:30 a.m. He had forgotten Detroit was in the Eastern Time Zone and an hour ahead of Marshall. He was tired; he had been driving a little over twenty hours and logged over 1,100 miles. He picked up the phone and called Rachel to let her know he made it to Detroit safely. She picked up the phone on the first ring and breathed a sigh of relief when she heard his voice.

It was 2:30 a.m. in Texas, but she didn't care; she wanted to talk to him. He told her he was tired and said he would call her tomorrow. Rachel wanted to see if he would lie and asked if Pam was there. He took a deep breath and said she was, and she reminded him to use condoms with these fast-ass gals! Carl said, "Good night, Mama. I'll call you tomorrow." Then hung up. He turned, and Pam was up in his space, hugging him as she kissed his neck. She said she was glad he made it safely, and when he hugged her back, he felt her body under the duster. She was naked.

He said he was tired and he would unpack the car in the morning. Pam snapped her fingers, saying she forgot Bradley wanted him to leave the keys out; he was going to unload the car for him. He reached in his pocket and handed her the keys, saying he was going to shower. Pam put the keys on the bar, as Bradley had instructed, and went upstairs. She dropped the duster on the foot of the bed and slid in the bed. A few minutes later, Carl came out of the shower wrapped in a towel. He dropped the towel on the floor and slid in his bed next to Pam.

He felt her smooth skin and started to kiss her on the neck and mouth. He was tired but rolled over on top of her, and she moaned as they rocked their hips together.

The sun shining through the window woke Pam up the next morning at seven thirty. She pulled on a sundress and went outside to unload the car for him. Mrs. Douglas from next door was in the backyard and asked if Carl had come back from Texas. Pam said he had but was still sleep; he got in off the road about 3:30 a.m. She introduced herself and said to tell him breakfast would be ready at 10:30 a.m.

She saw the look on Pam's face and said Bradley was like her son and Carl was like her grandson. She told Pam she was welcome to come to breakfast if she wanted.

It took an hour, but she got the car unpacked and his stuff in his room. She was shocked she made quite a bit of noise and he did not wake up. She took the sundress off and slid back in bed next to him, feeling sure he was not going to wake up in time to go to breakfast next door. She turned the radio on to WJLB. She wanted to catch the Sunday-morning *Quiet Storm* show.

At 9:30 a.m., Carl started to wake up. He heard the music on the radio. Pam snuggled under him, and he hugged her and dozed off for a few minutes. He woke up again, and his mind started to clear. He realized Pam was in the bed with him and rolled over on top of her. Aretha Franklin's song "Giving Him Something He Can Feel" came on as they kissed and made love to each other. They were in the flow as Millie Jackson's song "It Hurts So Good" came on. Pam heard the lyrics to the song and thought, *Damn, this describes me!*

Carl was lying back when she said the lady next door invited them to breakfast.

He looked at her, asking what time she wanted them there, because he was hungry as hell. When she said ten thirty, he looked at the clock. It was 10:15 a.m. He picked up the phone and called Mrs. Douglas, saying he just woke up, and asked if he could still come to breakfast. She laughed, saying, "I bet you did just wake up. Take a shower because don't nobody want to be smelling you." When he saw his bags were in the room, he assumed Bradley had unloaded the Chevelle. He pulled Pam out of the bed, saying, "Come on, we need to shower."

When he went past Bradley's room, he saw Bradley was not there and wondered where he was. This was unusual. Bradley was not a morning person and was not usually gone this time of morning, especially on a Sunday morning.

They jumped in the shower together and cleaned up, while she thought about the Millie Jackson song she heard while they were having sex. They walked next door and rang the doorbell at 10:45 a.m. Ralph opened the door and let them in, saying his grandmother was in the kitchen. He asked Carl if Pam was his girlfriend, and they looked at each other.

A few seconds later, he said Pam was his girlfriend and she was going to be a junior in college. He wondered how Carl could get all these girls; they seemed to be falling all over him. They ate breakfast and thanked Mrs. Douglas for cooking for them. Before they left, she asked Carl what was going to happen with his court case. Carl said he didn't know; the trial was set to start in a week. He looked at Mrs. Douglas, saying he could not believe it had been almost a year since this happened. She assured him it would be okay; everyone knew this was a chop shop before he started working there.

They left Mrs. Douglas's house, and he asked Pam what she wanted to do today. When she said talk, he was caught off guard. Pam usually liked to ride out, but she wanted to talk today. They went in the house, and he sat on the couch, but she said they should sit at the table. She got the dominoes out of the kitchen and placed them on the table. Carl rolled his eyes when Pam asked what she was to him. She kept eye contact with him as he rolled the thought around in his mind. Before he could say anything, she reminded him she had been having sex with him on and off for almost a year.

She wanted to know how she could be sure he was not going back to Michelle. Carl caught that wave and said she knew Michelle broke up with him. Pam glared at him, saying, "I have a gut feeling, if she called right now, you would run back to her." He assured her that was not the case, but she didn't believe him. Carl flipped the conversation, saying, "You asked what you are to me, stability in a crazy world." He looked her in the eyes, saying, "When we first had sex, you said you not a virgin, but you not a hoe either." He said that was him, and he was totally confused at this moment.

He was very familiar with the song and asked why she felt he took her heart in the palm of his hands and squeezed it. Pam laughed, saying, "That girl Van you boned for a week, she my cousin Derrick's girl." His eyes flew wide open. Felicia said Van was fucking Derrick, but she didn't say Van was his girl. Pam said her family was very angry with her; she had fallen for the guy they thought broke up Derrick and Van. Pam said, "I tried to tell them you did not know Derrick, but they did not believe me." Pam went on to say, "When you went to Mumford and was a star, I was glad I was in Texas."

Pam said her cousin Derrick put up a good front. "But he was oh so happy when the administrative hold was released and you went back to Texas." She said, "He was really happy you had to struggle for playing time in Texas but was a star here. He is really bragging how that most of the big schools are recruiting him and you have one scholarship offer from Wayne State, of all places. This is funny to Derrick because good players don't go to Wayne State." Pam said her heart was crushed because she just knew when they got back to Texas, He would break up with Michelle. "But you broke up with me."

She admitted she liked having sex with him and that was the reason she couldn't break up with him. He kept his eyes locked with hers and asked, "Who I have sex with, Pam?" He didn't wait for an answer and said, "You, baby, nobody else." He went on to say the girls at Marshall High wondered about him because he would not take any of them out. He laughed as he said he did not even go to the prom. He raised his voice slightly, saying, "But I *still* had sex with you, Pam." He added, "I love Michelle, and probably always will." He asked again, "Other than Michelle, who I have sex with, Pam?"

She looked at him and said she didn't know of anyone else.

He smiled at her, saying, "I don't know about throwing your heart against the wall, but this the part where I bounce ya like a rubber ball." He held his hand out and gently pulled her out of the chair.

A few seconds later, they were on the couch and he was on top of her. Pam cried tears of joy. She could not believe she had caught feelings for this guy. She worked as a receptionist and paralegal at Norma Law Firm, answering the phone and doing legal research. She had been barred from his case. Norma knew the relationship between them.

When nobody was looking, she pulled his case file. She was all in and wanted to know if he was about to go to jail. She turned to the summary narrative on the last page and read what another attorney at the firm had written. It started saying there was no credible evidence showing Carl knew he was working at a chop shop. The narrative went on to say, since he lived in Texas, he did not have knowledge of the rumor the station was a chop shop. The summary went on to say the most likely conclusion would be that the state of Michigan would try to "wedge" him for his testimony.

In the pathway to acquittal section, the attorney had written he believed the state would dismiss charges on Carl at the very last minute. Pam was glad to read this; she could see he was about to put this behind him.

Carl showed up at the city/county building in downtown Detroit at 8:15 a.m., just as Norma had instructed. She was waiting for him in an interview room, and the bailiff directed him to the room. He was shocked to see Pam sitting there with her; she didn't say she would be working his case. Norma said Pam was her best assistant and hoped he did not mind her being there.

He said he didn't and took a seat across the table from them. Norma explained she expected the state to open their case with him being an accomplice with full knowledge of everything. He listened as she said she believed their strategy was to "wedge" him as a witness against the other defendants. She explained his advantage was, the surveillance on the station was started in September, and he didn't start work at the station until June of the next year. She further explained that the inability of the state to place him at the scene before that time was a huge advantage.

She then asked Carl if there was anything she needed to know. Was he under indictment in Texas? Did he have charges she did not know about? Carl said he was clean, and she said that was good. At 8:55 a.m., they were called in the courtroom and seated at the defendant's table. Norma was next to him, and Pam was on the end of the table. The bailiff gave the "All rise" command as the judge walked into the courtroom. He seated everybody, and the bailiff read the charge, *State of Michigan v. Carl Allen Hampton*. It seemed surreal when the Bailiff said, "The charge is grand theft auto, aggravated."

The judge called both attorneys to the bench, and they stood before him. He asked if the defendant was a minor when these allegations took place. The assistant district attorney acknowledged that he was seventeen at that time. He reminded the assistant district attorney, "If we call witnesses and present evidence, jeopardy attaches." The state's attorney knew that if jeopardy attached and she had to dismiss against Carl, she could not try him again. Norma told the state attorney the ball was in her court and stood looking at her. A few seconds later, the state attorney said she had a plan.

She asked the court for a seven-day administrative hold while they performed a character workup on Carl. Norma objected vehemently, but the judge said she had a right to do that. The judge said they needed to step back and directed Norma to prepare Carl for the decision about to be handed down. Norma sat down, saying he was not going to be tried at this moment. She explained the state attorney had asked for a seven-day administrative hold and the judge had granted it. Carl said cool; he was on a twenty-three-day administrative hold before.

Norma held his hand and said he would have to do this administrative hold locked down. Carl had a blank stare when he looked at Norma, asking, "What the hell?" She explained this was normal and was actually a good thing. Carl looked at her and said, "I did twenty-four days so I can do these seven." The judge announced the decision, and the bailiff handcuffed Carl and escorted him to the holding cell. On the way to the holding cell, he saw Eric, who greeted him with, "What up, bitch? See ya in the dayroom!" Carl thought, *Not this motherfucker,* as they led him to change his clothes.

When he got dressed and checked in, he thought about Eric and said, "Today is not the day, and I'm not the one." A couple of hours later, the transport van arrived, and they were all off to the lockup to wait for their next court appearance.

CHAPTER 31

All Charges Are Dropped
#MichelleIsPregnant

The next morning at breakfast, he saw Eric and tried to walk past him. He put his leg out, and when Carl tripped, he swung on him. The scuffle started, and Carl pounded on Eric. Two guys got between Carl and Eric, breaking them up, and Eric yelled it wasn't over. The breakfast group calmed down, and everyone started to eat. This situation caused Carl to be concerned. Eric was not going anywhere.

The following Monday, Carl stood in front of the judge and saw Rachel sitting in the gallery. She had flown in to see the proceedings. The courtroom fell silent as the judge read, "In the case of the *State of Michigan v. Carl Allen Hampton*, on the charge of grand theft auto, aggravated." The judge continued, "Charges are dismissed without prejudice." The judge then imposed a deadline for the state to file on Carl within sixty days after the end of the chop shop trial.

Before he dismissed them, he said the state was unable to find probable cause to hold him and he was free to go. Carl looked at Norma and asked if that meant what he thought it meant. She said it did and he was free to go home. Carl hugged her and Pam, then thanked them for helping put this behind him. He walked over to Rachel and hugged her, thanking her for coming. It was a celebratory mood at Bradley's house as they listened to music and talked. Carl was glad he could move forward with his life and thought about the Wayne State scholarship.

As he and Rachel talked, he confided that he hated losing Michelle and asked if she thought he could get her back. Rachel said Michelle did not stop loving him; she was scared of him. She asked if he remembered what Shasta said about the look on Michelle's face when she got the C scar on her leg. Carl said he did remember and asked what that had to do with this. Rachel told him it had everything to do with this and explained the C scar was there. "But she knew you didn't do it on purpose. When you held her, she felt the vibe, and her world was good even though she was bleeding."

Rachel said, "This time and with this pain, Michelle does not have anybody that can hold her and make it go away." He listened as Rachel said, "She lives with the pain each day." Rachel added that Michelle was innocent and did not see the evil and the pain in the world. He was shocked when she said the pain of his betrayal caused her to see all the evil and all the pain of the world. It really sank in when Rachel said the one person who could hold her and settle her down, she was terrified of right now. Rachel said that was why she broke up with him—she was scared of him.

Carl owned up to his mistake, saying when he broke the promise, he broke her heart. Rachel said, "Exactly," and told him that was the reason Michelle asked for the broken heart and a chain to hang it on. Carl was shocked when Rachel said she saw Michelle and she still wore the chain with her ring on it. Carl was shocked when his mother said he was going to get a second chance with Michelle, but it was going to be different.

The next day, he took Rachel to see the Motown building on Grand Boulevard. She was happy to see the studio where the Supremes recorded their hits.

Later that day, he took her to see Leonard and his family. Rachel was impressed and asked how he learned his way around the city. Carl said it felt natural to him and he was seldom lost.

The next morning, Rachel was getting her bags together for her flight home when the doorbell rang. She walked over to Carl's room and woke him up, saying there was somebody at the door. Carl got up and went to the door, and it was Felicia! He let her in and told her to have a seat on the couch, asking when she got drop-by privileges. She laughed, saying she wanted to come by and see how he was doing.

Felicia said she heard he was not going to jail and asked if he was cooking breakfast. He pulled her close to him, saying she needed to behave—his mother was there. She sat down on the couch as he went back upstairs with Rachel. She asked who was at the door, and he said his friend Felicia and she was downstairs. Rachel stopped packing and looked at him, saying, "It's 8:30 a.m. Do you think I'm crazy?" Carl said he didn't know Felicia was coming by, and Rachel's demeanor said she didn't believe him.

Rachel snapped and asked if this was the same Felicia on the three-way call. He confirmed it was the same Felicia, and Rachel was mad as hell. Carl saw his mother's demeanor change and asked if they could all get along. She asked where he managed to find all these fast ass gals in Detroit. Carl didn't say anything to Rachel. He thought about how the girls in Detroit were so much different from the girls in Marshall.

When Bradley came home at 11:00 a.m., Rachel thanked him for allowing her the quiet time with Carl. He pulled Carl to the side, asking what the "lil hooker" was doing there. He explained she "popped up," and Bradley hit the ceiling, asking, what the hell he meant "she popped up!" He asked how long she had been there, and Carl said, "A couple of hours." Bradley heard Rachel coming down the stairs and let it go for the time being.

At 2:00 p.m., they loaded the Chevelle and he took Rachel to the airport. She hugged Bradley and asked him to keep their son safe as best as he could. He said he would and held the door for her to get in. Felicia climbed in the back seat, and he cranked the car. He rolled out the driveway and popped the clutch, turning the tires. Forty-five minutes later, they rolled into Detroit Metro Airport.

Soon after check-in, they found Rachel's flight had been delayed. At 5:00 p.m., Carl and Felicia watched as Rachel's flight taxied down the runway and took off. They walked to the car, and he asked Felicia where she wanted to go. Carl was surprised when she said it was chaotic at her house and she needed a break. They got in the car, and he drove home, pulling into the backyard driveway. He and Felicia sat on the couch in the den, watching TV and talking. He could relate when Felicia said her life had been turned upside down.

She was crying when she said Eric got seven years' penitentiary time the same day he was released. She said her parents decided to get a divorce and both were looking for a place. Felicia said she didn't want to live with her mother; she wanted to live with her dad. He understood when she said Alice was pissed because she didn't want to live with her. Felicia said she could not believe her mother was getting a place with her boyfriend. Felicia said she would be a junior in high school this fall and did not know where she was going to school.

He was happy for her when she said she wanted to do hair when she graduated high school.

A few hours later, the phone rang, and it was Rachel saying she had made it back to Marshall safely. He reported for two-a-day football workouts in mid-August. His legal issues had been worked out to the satisfaction of both the school administration and the coaching staff. He was in decent shape when he reported to camp, and the coaching staff was impressed with his speed. The local media set up interviews with Carl, and the common question was his Detroit stats.

The reporters wanted to know how, with stats like he had in Detroit, he had to fight for playing time in Texas. He said they had a lot of linebackers in Texas that were his size with great speed. When asked if he expected to have games in college like the ones at Mumford, he didn't answer. Carl knew not to make remarks that could be stapled to a bulletin board. He said his main goal for the upcoming season was to earn a spot on the team. One of the reporters asked for an exclusive after the first game, and Carl agreed. He ended the interview and went to the showers.

The coaching staff told him to not believe the hype, and he needed to prove himself on the field. This was a novelty at Wayne State, a player being celebrated as one of the best recruits they had landed in a long time.

He and Pam spent a lot of time together and did a lot of things together that summer. As September drew closer, they realized she was going to have to go back to Wiley for her junior year. When he came downstairs, Carl saw the mail on the floor. He looked through it, surprised to find a letter from Michelle. He held his breath as he opened the letter and read it. She was writing to tell him she was moving into an apartment in Dallas and gave him her address. She signed the letter "Love always" and asked him to stay in touch.

He picked up the phone and called Rachel, saying Michelle wrote him to say she was moving into her apartment in Dallas. Pam was standing at the bottom of the stairs and heard Carl say Michelle was moving on with her life without him. Rachel could hear the frustration in his voice and asked if he had gotten clothes to wear to class. Carl said he planned a trip to the mall to buy clothes later that day. Rachel said she and the girls were school clothes and school supply shopping later that day too. He was shocked when Rachel asked him to hold and Carol came on the phone.

He talked to his younger sister, and she asked what Detroit was like. Carl told her there were lots of places to go and have fun. She said she missed him and asked when he was coming home. Carl said he missed her too and said he would be home at either Thanksgiving or Christmas. She passed the phone back to Rachel, and they talked a couple of minutes before hanging up. Pam heard him hanging up and walked back up the stairs. A few seconds later, she walked back downstairs and noticed he put the letter from Michelle in the nook by the door.

Rachel, Hannah, and Carol loaded in the car and left for downtown Marshall. When they came out one of the clothing stores, they met Michelle and Mrs. Burns going in the store. Rachel's mouth fell open when she saw Michelle sporting a six-month baby bump. She looked at Michelle, who said, "Ms. Rachel, I was going to tell you, but I didn't know how." Rachel started to cry and hugged Michelle, saying, "That's okay, baby, I understand." Michelle was crying and said she wanted to tell Carl the morning he stopped by on the way to Detroit but she didn't have the courage.

A few hours later, Mrs. Burns and Michelle sat talking with Rachel. She assured Mrs. Burns she would help with the baby when it got here. Rachel asked Michelle when she planned to tell Carl, and she said she didn't know how to tell him. She asked for her help, and Rachel said this was something that only she should tell Carl. Michelle was crying when she said, "Ms. Rachel, I broke up with him before I knew I was pregnant." Rachel hugged her, saying she did not have to explain anything to her. She said she would call Carl and tell him to call her and she had to take it from there.

Michelle nodded and thanked her. Rachel hugged her again, saying, "Don't worry, I'm going to help you with this baby." Rachel asked how this was going to affect her scholarship, and Michelle said they were going to redshirt her in basketball. She said the academic scholarship was still good; she could handle the work even though she was pregnant. Michelle and Mrs. Burns left as Rachel said she was going to call Carl tonight. Michelle smiled when she said she would tell Carl she was pregnant when he called.

Rachel asked Michelle to wait a second and said, "Eighteen years ago, I was you with Carl's dad."

Mrs. Burns was happy they ran into Rachel. For the first time in a long time, she saw her baby girl smile.

Carl and Pam hung out at Northland Mall, shopping until the stores closed at 9:00 p.m. They bought a lot of clothes and were headed home. Pam wanted to stop at the Wendy's on the Northland Mall parking lot, but Carl suggested they get dressed and go to Big Boy's and then hang out. She thought that was an even better idea and said she was fine with that.

He rolled out of the Northland parking lot and down the Lodge service drive to Seven Mile. A few minutes later, he was unlocking the door in the den and heard the phone ring. He answered and was shocked to hear Rachel on the other end. She asked if he remembered asking her what he could do to get Michelle back, and he said he did. Rachel said she saw Michelle earlier today and she had a feeling she wanted to talk to him. Carl felt the urgency in Rachel's voice and said he would call her. He hung up the phone with her and dialed Michelle's number in Jefferson.

Pam side-eyed him, saying, "I *know* you *not* calling the girl that broke your heart while the girl you having sex with is standing here!"

Carl said he was going to call; he could feel something in Rachel's voice.

A few seconds later, Mrs. Burns answered the phone, and he asked her to not hang up. She assured him she was not going to hang up and said he needed to talk to Michelle. He was really concerned now; his mother and her mother had said he needed to talk to Michelle. She gave him the number for the house of her eldest daughter, Alicia, in Dallas and said Michelle should be there.

Pam was tripping big-time, but Carl called Michelle with her standing behind him. Alicia answered the phone and said, "Hold the phone. She just walked in." A few seconds later, Michelle came on the phone and said hello. Carl said hello and, after a few awkward seconds, said Rachel said he should call her. She smiled, saying she saw Ms. Rachel, Hannah, and Carol earlier today while she was in Marshall. He asked if everything was okay, and she said, "Kinda, sorta," then asked if he remembered the Valentine's Day weekend they spent together.

Carl said he did remember and asked what that had to do with them now. Michelle said she saw his mother and sisters earlier today and they were shocked because she couldn't see her feet. Pam's mouth fell open when Carl incredulously asked, "What do you mean you *can't* see your feet?" Pam knew Michelle was telling him she was pregnant. At that moment, Michelle remembered who he was and said, "I'm pregnant, Carl." He listened as she said the MD said she was a little over six months and would deliver the baby around Thanksgiving.

He quietly listened on the phone. The girl he loved was pregnant in Dallas, and he was in Detroit.

When they hung up, he could see Pam's demeanor had changed as she asked if he was going to Dallas. Carl said he was not going to Dallas, at least not right then. She followed him as he went up the stairs to his bedroom and lay on the bed. Carl was all up in his feelings. Michelle had broken up with him, and she was pregnant. He got extremely mad at Pam when she asked if he was sure Michelle was pregnant for him. Carl said it was time for her to go, and she immediately said he had taken her wrong.

He asked how he had taken her wrong—he heard what she said. She felt some kind of way because they had been having sex all summer and he was acting funny because his ex-girlfriend called, saying she was pregnant. She got her clothes and followed him to the car. Twenty minutes later, he pulled up to the curb at Pam's house. Her aunt Janie was out in the yard and motioned for Carl to come in the house. When Pam walked by, Janie knew something was up—she looked mad! Carl said he had to go, but she insisted he come in for a minute. He got out and walked in the house, taking a seat on the couch. Janie asked him why her niece was mad at him.

Pam didn't give Carl a chance to answer, saying his ex-girlfriend called to say she was pregnant. Janie laughed when she said, "Well, Bradley about to be a grandfather." She looked at Pam, asking why she was mad. "It *is* an ex-girlfriend." Carl said he really needed to go, and Janie agreed. She knew he had some calls he needed to make. He drove home and called Rachel, asking why she didn't tell him Michelle was pregnant. Rachel laughed, saying she just found out that day, just like he did. She said he was about to be a father so he had to grow up and accept his responsibility.

He asked Rachel if she thought Michelle hated him, and she started crying. She laughed through her tears, saying, "Carl, that girl love you, and she will love you a lot more when this baby is born." Rachel explained that Michelle was young and had made plans for them; she was not going to give up. Rachel stopped crying and said he should be at the hospital when that baby was born, no matter what Michelle said. They hung up, and he dialed Michelle at Alicia's house in Dallas. She answered the phone, and Carl said he wanted to talk to her. Michelle said okay and she was glad he called.

They talked about things getting all blown up, and now she was six months pregnant. She asked if he hated her for getting pregnant, and Carl said he didn't hate her and was not mad at her. Michelle said she found out she was pregnant a week before he went to Detroit. She wanted to tell him that morning but did not want him to worry about it while he had the court case. They agreed he would cut the baby's umbilical cord when the baby was born. Michelle said she had been thinking about names and wanted to name it for him and his dad if it was a boy.

She asked what he thought about Bradley Carl Hampton if it was a boy. He said that was cool and asked, What if it was a girl? Michelle said she wanted to name a girl after his mother and herself. He said Rachel Michelle Hampton sounded good too. They talked a while longer and agreed to stay friends so they could raise this child. Carl told her it was surreal that they were about to be parents. Michelle said, "I guess we have to be friends now." She laughed as they hung up. Carl took a shower and thought about how his life had taken a turn.

The phone was ringing when he came out of the shower, and he answered. It was Pam, saying she *thought* they were going to Big Boy's for dinner. He laughed, saying she demanded he take her home. Pam laughed, too, saying she did but *hoped* he would sit her ass down. He dressed and picked her up, and they went to Big Boy's for dinner. She sat next to him in the booth and held him. She knew he was blown away. Pam said in two weeks she would be heading back to Marshall and wanted to spend as much time with him as she could. She laughed, saying it was okay for him to tell her to sit her ass down.

Carl made the team and got a starting outside linebacker position. When the announcement was made, he called Rachel to tell her. He was excited. The team was flying to Washington, DC, on September 8 to play Howard on the tenth.

The transition to college was smooth. He lived in the city and was a commuter student. He met a lot of people during freshman orientation and found out there were a few parties going on. He was more than surprised to see Van Howard during freshman orientation—she was going to Wayne State!

They talked and Van said she broke up with Derrick because he went to Oklahoma to play football. Carl remembered Ronnie Simmons went to the same college to play football. Van asked what he was doing for the weekend and invited him to a party. Carl said he would let her know since he didn't have plans for the weekend.

The football season flew by, and he had a stellar season, putting up outstanding stats. He followed Ronnie Simmons and Derrick down in Oklahoma, making noise. His classes dismissed on the nineteenth of November, and he rolled out toward Texas the next morning.

Carl checked in at the Effingham, Illinois, stop, and Rachel said he needed to go to Dallas—Michelle had gone into labor. She asked him not to rush, that it would be at least twenty-four hours before she gave birth. Rachel called Michelle to tell her she was on the way, and so was Carl. She asked if she could speak to Hannah, and Rachel said sure. When Hannah came on the phone, Michelle asked her to be bedside when her child was born. She could not believe Michelle asked her, and accepted the invitation; she wanted to be there when the baby was born.

Hannah handed the phone back to Rachel and went to pack a bag for the trip to Dallas. Carol made it clear she did not want to go; she was staying in Marshall with Janice and Riley.

A little over three hours later, Rachel and Hannah rolled into the Parkland Hospital parking lot. They found Michelle's room and sat with her, keeping her company. Michelle told Hannah she asked her to come because they needed to be friends. This got to Hannah emotionally, and all animosity toward Michelle melted away.

Twelve hours later, Carl walked in the room.

Michelle water's broke an hour later, and she delivered Rachel Michelle Hampton at 2:48 a.m. on November 22, 1976. Rachel could not believe the baby had a big red spot in the middle of her forehead. Carl cut the umbilical cord, and the nurse put the baby on Michelle's chest. Shasta and Alicia took their baby sister in the shower and cleaned her up while Rachel and Hannah kept Rachel Michelle. Alicia gave her the plate she had packed, and after she ate, Michelle fell asleep. The baby nursed as Michelle slept and Carl watched the miracle of life right before him.

This was overwhelming. He and Michelle had a baby! Carl could not believe how this made him feel about Michelle, and he kissed her while she was asleep. Shasta looked at Alicia, saying, "These two are about to have serious drama!"

Michelle and the baby were released two days later, and she told Carl she wanted to go home. Carl sensed she was not talking about her apartment in Dallas but her home in Jefferson. She snuggled up to him as he drove east on I-30, headed to East Texas. They pulled up at her mother's house, and he got the baby and the bassinet out of the back seat.

Michelle was overjoyed to see her mother and hugged her tightly when she met her in the yard. She cried, saying, "I wanted to come home for a few days." Mrs. Burns hugged her tighter, saying she never needed a reason to come home. Carl took the baby in the house and sat with Michelle until she fell asleep. He sat and talked with Mrs. Burns, who said Michelle was exhausted. Mrs. Burns said, "My baby love you, and now she has a baby for you." Carl listened as Mrs. Burns said she was always going to let his family see the baby.

He said he would be back the next day; he was going home to rest.

Two days later was Thanksgiving Day, and they agreed it would be best if they spent it with their family. Michelle and Mrs. Burns took the baby and went to Dallas while Carl spent the day with Rachel and his family. The Saturday after Thanksgiving, he was hanging out and watching football with a group of his friends. The alcohol and weed flowed as the guys talked trash about life and people. The game between Oklahoma and Nebraska came on, and Carl saw Ronnie Simmons starting for Oklahoma as a true freshman. The announcers said Ronnie was a magician with the football.

They watched Ronnie pitch to his running back, Derrick Dunlap, who was quietly having a big game. The guys asked why he was playing for Wayne State when his friend Ronnie Simmons was playing for Oklahoma. They were shocked when Carl said he practiced against the running back at Mumford. He told the guys Derrick was a big back with great power and speed.

When the game was over, he had rushed for 217 yard on seventeen carries. Ronnie Simmons had rushed for 177 yards on eleven carries and scored twice. Carl thought how he would hate to be a linebacker trying to stop them.

Carl was at home, watching TV and resting, when Rachel asked him to go to the store for her. He bumped into a classmate who told him where a party was later that night. Carl said he might roll through for a few minutes. He decided to go to the party and left home about 9:30 p.m. When he got to the party, it was dark, and the black light made everything seem like it was glowing. When he looked across the room, he saw a tall slim girl that resembled Jackie Hunt. He could not believe it was Jackie, and walked across the room.

He was blown away when he walked up on her and it *was* Jackie. He hugged her, saying hello, and asked how she was doing. They danced together, and he mentioned that he saw Ronnie Simmons on TV today. She smiled, saying she saw the game and they were on the way home from Lincoln, Nebraska, to Oklahoma City. Jackie asked if he knew Derrick Dunlap, who was from Detroit. Carl said he did know Derrick; they were teammates when he played for Mumford. He asked if they could go to his car and talk. Jackie said she didn't think that was cool. After all, he and Michelle had just had a baby.

Carl asked again, and she agreed to go to the car and talk. He stopped by her friends, saying he was going to take Jackie home. Jackie's cousin protested, but she said she would be okay.

They were outside, and Carl pushed Jackie against the car and kissed her. She looked at him, saying, "I know Michelle broke up with you, but what about the other girls I heard about?"

Carl asked, "What other girls?" Michelle was his girl, and she broke up with him.

Jackie realized what her sister meant when she said she was Ronnie's girl but she was Carl's woman: she wanted to have sex with him.

He stopped kissing her and said, "We can go. I won't press you to do anything." He opened the door, and she slid halfway across the seat. He got under the wheel, and Jackie was right under him.

He drove to Jefferson and parked in the parking lot in front of her house. Carl started kissing and slowly undressing her. Jackie protested, saying she was Ronnie's girl, and he just had a baby with Michelle. She was shocked when he said, "You were my girl before Ronnie or Michelle came along." She moaned as he kissed her neck and kept undressing her.

A minute later, he rolled on top of her, and she grunted as they rocked their hips together. She cried as he kissed her neck and said she had always been his girl.

Later, Jackie put her clothes back on, kissed him sensuously, and said they needed to figure out what they were going to do. Carl said he would call her as he walked her to the door and kissed her again. He stood on the porch watching, as she stepped in the house and closed the door. He got back in the Chevelle, cranked it and popped the clutch, turning the tires as he headed back to Marshall.

ABOUT THE AUTHOR

Victor grew up in Marshall, Texas, and played football with the Mavericks, the local high school team. He later graduated Wiley College with a bachelor of science degree in business administration. His early career was spent in the sale of technology products, mainly PCs. He credits the time spent selling technology solutions with teaching him the finer points of sales and customer service.

Victor has been in the real estate and new home construction business for over twenty years. His goal is to provide every client with a "Wow!" experience, the feeling that the red carpet has been rolled out for them. He does this through a combination of experience, education, and an extreme commitment to excellent customer service.

He wrote *Above the Clouds* because it was a story that needed to be told—a young man growing up poor on the wrong side of the tracks. The story shows how, through education and perseverance, the greatest of obstacles can be overcome. Many who have read excerpts of the book feel it is his life story, but while he drew on the familiarity of people around him, it is not a biography. He recalls one published author telling him to get started, to write about things he knows.

Victor's hobbies include working out (he calls himself the "cardio kid") and playing golf. He resides in the Dallas, Texas, metro area with his wife, daughter, and grandkids. He can be reached by email at vkwhitfield01@gmail.com, or you can send him a tweet @victorwhitfield.